Deadly Thanksgiving

A Senior Sleuth Mystery · Book 2

MAUREEN FISHER

Deadly Thanksgiving
by Maureen Fisher

ISBN 978-1-9995755-3-3

Edited by Stacy Juba
Cover by Streetlight Graphics

Discover more about Maureen Fisher
http://www.booksbymaureen.com

Chapter 1: A Memorable Arrival

I CIRCLED OUR RESORT LOBBY WHILE checking my phone for the fiftieth time. The Lifestyle Manor vehicle containing our final coach-load of guests was two hours and 26.5 minutes late. Worse, one of those guests was our cousin Minnie. The minicoach must be lying in a ravine, a twisted, smoking heap of blackened wreckage. Hey, it happens. The Trans-Canada Highway through the Rockies is one of the most dangerous roads in Canada. This was an ominous kickoff to a week that could make or break Grizzly Gulch Guest Ranch's very existence.

"For goodness' sake, Clara, stop catastrophizing. Worrying won't make them arrive any faster."

My oldest sister's words jolted me back to reality. I bit back a sharp retort. Although I was pushing sixty and a co-owner of Grizzly Gulch, Abby still regarded me as her neurotic, over-emotional and impulsive baby sister. Too bad she'd ignored the glowing guest reviews describing me as the most empathetic, thoughtful, and creative events manager they'd ever encountered.

All buttoned up and crisply pressed in a tailored pants suit, her highlighted bob precisely arranged, Abby looked every inch the successful co-owner, CFO, and general manager of our upscale dude ranch. I, on the other hand, preferred a more feminine approach to my appearance, hence my sparkly sandals with modest two-inch heels and a flirty white-on-black polka dot blouse with lacey sleeves over slim-leg black pants.

Taking a deep breath, I made a conscious effort to relax my shoulders and unclench my teeth. "Don't sneak up on me like that. You know I hate it."

"Sorry, hon." Abby's blue eyes swept my face. "Come with me. Let's go watch for them together."

Something inside me loosened a notch. I let her walk me across our tiled lobby, past the Thanksgiving displays of gourds, pumpkins, and shiny red apples, to our main entrance with its panoramic view of the highway's descent through rolling terrain backed by the distant white heads of the Rockies. Pointing to a purple speck halfway down the hillside and moving fast, she said, "Could that be our missing guests?"

We stepped through the revolving door into the bright October afternoon. I squinted at the purple speck, which morphed into a purple minicoach rocketing down the highway. My knees softened with relief. "It must be our guests. Seems the driver's making up for lost time."

The vehicle disappeared into a valley, re-appearing seconds later on the secondary road fronting our property. Upon hitting a speed bump, all four tires left the ground before crashing down again onto the pavement. Shuddering, I imagined the jarring impact on the elderly passengers' spines.

The speeding vehicle fishtailed as it veered into our long, winding driveway. Regaining control, the driver floored it again.

"Too bad you wasted all that energy worrying," Abby said. "I tried to warn you."

She was not wrong.

My lack of response didn't deter her. "I also warned you not to enter Grizzly Gulch in that ridiculous contest. It could be the most costly mistake you've ever made."

Good to know she still resented me for ignoring her veto. I'd gone rogue and paid an outrageous fee we could ill-afford to *Global Destinations*, a mass media conglomerate, to enter Grizzly Gulch in its *Best Vacations* tourism and hospitality contest—a last ditch effort to prevent the bank's foreclosure of our resort.

I swallowed an angry retort. "I'm about to deliver an eight-day experience that'll bring sixty-eight lonely retirees together for food, fun, and frolic, all culminating in a Canadian Thanksgiving feast our guests will never forget. I guarantee the Boomers' Thanksgiving Fling will earn us first prize in the *Best Vacations* contest."

Abby sighed. "That, or force us into foreclosure."

Ouch. That one hurt. I intended to nail this special event with flying colors, proving to my two big sisters I was worthy of their respect. Truth be told, this Thanksgiving event's success was crucial on so many levels, failure was inconceivable.

Instead of slowing, the purple minicoach hurtled toward us at warp speed. Off-key singing and raucous laughter floated out into the crisp, bright October air.

"What's that driver doing?" Abby asked. "I hope he doesn't take out our hydro post—whoa! He's heading straight for us. Watch out!" She pushed me behind a concrete pillar supporting the loading area portico.

Expecting sudden death, I scrunched my eyes shut. Would I see a white light or what?

The squeal of brakes and the acrid stench of burning rubber signaled the vehicle had halted in front of our entrance.

With great caution, I opened my eyes and blinked. Swimming into my field of vision was a picture adorning the minicoach's purple side panel. It showed a white-haired couple, matured to perfection, both displaying alarmingly white teeth and suspiciously few wrinkles. Ornate pink lettering announced *Lifestyle Manor Retirement Retreat*. The last of our guests had arrived.

Abby examined the picture and snickered. "I bet that couple's about to enjoy some afternoon delight. I hope he remembered his Viagra." Every now and again, my sister proved she owned a sense of humor.

Finally relaxing into the unseasonably warm breeze, I released a shaky laugh. "I can't wait to meet the passengers. They sound like a fun group."

Every window on the minicoach was open. Slurred voices belted out an off-key rendition of *Ding Dong! The Witch is Dead* from *The Wizard of Oz*.

Abby made a face. "More like royally hammered, if you ask me."

A woman thrust her head out the window, hair whipping around her flushed face. I recognized Cousin Minnie, her curls now a striking silver instead of the rich, copper-streaked auburn of her younger years.

Minnie Harris is actually our second cousin once, perhaps twice, removed. During her acting career, she went by the stage name, Minerva. Her theory was that if a single stage name worked for Sting, Cher, and Madonna, it would work for her too. Sadly, our Minnie didn't have the talent to pull off a mononym.

She confirmed her identity by waving wildly and yelling, "Yoo-hoo. Clara. Abby."

I waved back and blew Minnie a kiss. "Welcome to Grizzly Gulch."

Turning away, I must have grimaced, because Abby laid a reassuring hand on my arm. "There, there. Once Minnie sobers up, you'll have a great time together."

I stifled a sigh. Abby meant well, but she often made me feel like a toddler.

Fortunately, her phone rang, saving me from pointing out we owed Minnie a vote of thanks for lining up the entire coachload of Lifestyle Manor guests. Once she'd learned of our discounted seniors' week, she'd convinced her retirement home's management to organize a recreational getaway for interested residents.

My sister's rapid departure, no doubt in response to yet another financial crisis, left me alone with our new guests, who were now belting out *Margaritaville*, accompanied by enthusiastic clapping.

I peeked into the closest window. A party was in full swing. Passengers danced in the narrow aisle. Against all odds, a woman in the front row opposite the door was napping. Envy nipped at me. Some folk could sleep anywhere, any time.

The vehicle's door swung open and the white-faced driver hopped out. Spotting me, he hustled over and wrung my hand, saying, "Good luck with this lot. In all my years, I've never seen the likes, and I hope I never do again."

Unless I missed my mark, the poor man was badly shaken. He must be eager to dump the rowdy travelers. No wonder he'd been speeding. To lighten the moment, I said, "The passengers seem lively."

A tic in his cheek spasmed. "You have no idea."

"I'm looking forward to meeting everyone."

"They're all yours, lady. I feel for you. Once I unload their luggage, I'll be in the bar." He headed for the baggage compartment.

Shaking off a trickle of alarm, I hopped on board and surveyed the three double rows of seats. At my sudden appearance, all singing broke off mid-chorus. Eight of the nine passengers swung slightly glassy-eyed gazes in my direction.

"Want a snort?" Minnie asked, slurring ever so slightly and waving a flask. "You might need one."

"Thanks. Maybe later."

The woman sitting beside Minnie, an attractive blonde, giggled then nudged her seat partner with an elbow. "Good golly, Minnie, I think bringing your brandy was pure genius. It sure helped us deal with the, er, unexpected emergency."

Ignoring the proffered flask, I encompassed everyone in a warm, welcoming smile, taking care to make eye contact with each passenger except the woman enjoying her siesta in the front seat. "Good afternoon and welcome to Grizzly Gulch Guest Ranch. I'm Clara Foster, a co-owner of Grizzly Gulch and your events manager for the week. My job is to make sure you're having the best time of your lives."

Across the aisle from Minnie, a lanky man draped his arm around a woman in a flowery dress and heavy makeup. He jerked his chin at the sleeping woman in front of him. "One of us won't be participating," he pointed out.

"And nobody seems to care except me," a passenger in the back aisle seat wailed before dissolving into soft sobs. Her companion dug out a tissue and applied it to the tears streaming down her friend's rich, brown cheeks.

A bad feeling washed over me. Perhaps the woman who appeared to be asleep in the front seat had experienced a stroke or a heart attack. I studied her in alarm. A bungee cord snugged twice around the torso held her upright in the seat.

"What's wrong with this woman? Why is she bungeed into her seat?" I asked, extending a finger to touch her hand. "She's freezing. Is there a blanket?"

Behind the bungeed passenger, a small, pale woman said. "A blanket won't help Lizzie now. She's gone."

I recoiled in disbelief. "She, she … *passed*?" My legs threatened to buckle.

Her seat partner, an attractive man who could have stepped out of the pages of GQ, said, "I'm afraid so." Ignoring my shocked intake of breath, he followed up on his pronouncement with the chorus of *Another One Bites the Dust* in an off-key tenor.

I was guessing the deceased hadn't been universally popular.

The flowery dress woman proclaimed in an upper-crust British accent,

"I understand there's an open bar inside. I could use a stiff drink right about now."

Her seat mate combined a snort with a chuckle. "A stiff drink, my love? You shouldn't say that when there's a real stiff sitting in the front row."

Although the man's companion decreased the volume, her words were unmistakable. "In that case, I'll request a Witch's Brew to commemorate Lizzie."

I reminded myself that inappropriate laughter and jokes were perfectly normal reactions to a highly stressful and emotionally intense situation. Some people even laughed during funerals to mitigate the discomfort of sadness bubbling up inside.

"How about a Devil's Delight?" someone else suggested.

The hairs on the back of my neck prickled. The upcoming week might prove to be more stressful than I'd anticipated.

Chapter 2: A Reunion of Sorts

A DEEP AND FURIOUS VOICE OUTSIDE the minicoach blasted my eardrums. "What is *wrong* with you people? Show some respect for the deceased."

I fought down a burst of panic. The singing stopped in mid-stanza and the sobbing ceased, leaving behind a throbbing silence.

Wondering how an outsider knew about a passenger's death, I whirled toward the door and squinted. Although the sun slanted straight into my eyes, I discerned a man who was tall, built, and imposing. He'd planted himself, legs apart, at the foot of the open door. Every inch of his body screamed authority. If his face looked half as good as the rest of him, he would be spectacular.

"Please state the full name of the deceased."

Several people shouted, "Lizzie Fournier!"

"None of the passengers may enter or leave this vehicle without official permission. You, there. Step outside. Immediately."

He sounded vaguely familiar, but I couldn't place him. Bristling at his curtness and bossy attitude, I injected frost into my tone. "I assume you're talking to me."

"Correct."

I strode forward. Due to a combination of wobbly legs, high-heeled sandals, and lumpy rubber matting, I stumbled and became airborne. Releasing a terrified howl, I was dimly aware of strong, warm hands gripping my waist, arresting my flight, and swinging me down, all in one effortless move. I landed with a jolt, only to find myself plastered against a rock-solid body.

Instead of barking out another command, my saviour said, "I didn't believe anyone could holler louder than my youngest sister during a spider sighting. I stand corrected."

I stiffened. His conversational tone was horribly familiar. Pushing away, I allowed my gaze to travel northward, up, up, up, over the leather jacket to skim a plaid shirt collar encasing a bronzed, corded neck, and past a clenched jaw, tightened lips, high cheekbones, and aquiline nose. Shuttered, black-as-night eyes halted my scrutiny.

Angel of Death, please take me now!

"*You*," I whispered. I'd dated Hawk MacDougall last spring during a visit to Vancouver. With my daughter out of commission from an accident, and her husband absent on a business trip, I'd stepped up to the plate. For three months I was live-in nurse, house cleaner, shopper, cook, and mother's helper for my four grandchildren. Enter Hawk McDougall, a Mountie with the Royal Canadian Mounted Police. He was the first and only man to attract me in the three decades since my lying, cheating, and abusive scumbag of a husband died a timely death.

And lo and behold, several months later, Hawk was scowling down at me.

He still gripped my waist so I ventured a step backward. He let go with mortifying speed. How did he know a dead passenger had landed at Grizzly Gulch? Why hadn't he phoned to prepare me for the shock? And why, oh why, was my stupid heart cartwheeling in my chest?

"Hello, Clara."

Shame, guilt, and a whole host of other emotions seemed to clot into a big, hairy ball inside me. I stiffened my spine, tilted my head back, and stared defiantly at him. "Hawk. Fancy meeting you here. Long time no see. Sorry, can't talk now, maybe later. Gotta run—"

Firm pressure on my arm stopped both my babble and attempted escape. "Oh, but you must talk to me. You have no choice *this* time. I'm assisting on the Grizzly Gulch case."

"So now we're a case?"

"Take a look around you."

I obeyed and did a double take. During my short time on board, I'd failed to notice the arrival of a police car and an official van from the Office of the Medical Examiner, now encircled within yellow police tape along with the minicoach and police car. And how had I overlooked Hawk's very large, very fit companion, who cut an impressive figure in his RCMP everyday uniform of navy jacket and pants paired with a white shirt?

I stared at Hawk in confusion. "But I didn't hear the vehicles arrive."

"The passengers were making so much racket I'm not surprised. Unless it's an emergency, the RCMP out here avoid using the siren near a hotel."

"How did you find me?"

"I'll explain later."

"A phone call warning me you'd moved to Alberta would have been a nice touch."

He removed his red Calgary Flames baseball cap and ran long fingers through his lovely dark hair threaded with more white strands than I remembered. He jammed his cap back on. "Is that a fact? I didn't take you for a coward. A phone call warning me you'd dumped me by text message and flown home, would also have been a nice touch." His expression spoke of anger and something else, perhaps sadness,.

Shame brought heat to my cheeks. Hawk had every right to be upset, but how could I admit I'd fallen in love with him and done only thing I could think of to save myself from more heartache. I'd abandoned the unsettling thrill of romance in favor of safety, something that had been all too lacking during my traumatic childhood and painful marriage. Worse, like the coward I was, I'd broken the news in a polite text message containing an apology along with an assurance the fault was all mine, not his, because I was too damaged to conduct a normal relationship.

Although Hawk probably didn't realize it, he was fortunate I'd stepped out of his life.

"How did you get assigned to this particular case?" I asked, side-stepping his very valid accusation of cowardice.

"After you left, I retired from the RCMP and moved to Cochrane to be closer to my family. I was visiting some old buddies in the Cochrane detachment when a call came through from someone on board this minicoach. Whoever phoned sounded tipsy, and there was too much background noise to decipher much. All the dispatcher got was that a passenger had died, and they were *en route* to Grizzly Gulch. I recognized the ranch name and asked if I could tag along on the call."

"To mess with me?" As soon as I'd spoken I wanted to cut my tongue out.

His lips thinned. "No. I thought this process might be easier for you if you saw a familiar face." He paused. "Truth? I was also hoping for some sort of closure."

My throat tightened with guilt at his unexpected kindness. "Fine. But I must warn you it's my duty to ensure there's no infringement of our guests' rights. I intend to stay with the passengers until you leave." I wouldn't let Hawk or anyone else dismiss me.

"Are you afraid I'll terrify the passengers just to get revenge?"

Actually, yes. "Of course not," I assured him seconds before spectators swarmed into the loading area, surrounding the police tape.

The Mountie, who appeared to be around Hawk's age, strode toward us, an aggrieved frown creasing his forehead. "Here come the looky-loos. I was wondering when someone would notice the vehicles and raise the alarm. Those onlookers have to leave. I want to conduct an informal group interview."

Hawk stepped in. "Hang on, Callum. Before you intimidate the gawkers, I want you to meet one of Grizzly Gulch's co-owners, a former friend of mine."

"One of the famous Foster sisters, I presume."

"Yes. Clara, this is Sergeant Callum Shaughnessy. We worked together in the detachment serving Vancouver's eastside. I would trust him with my life."

The Mountie removed his navy RCMP tactical baseball cap to reveal a rugged face, definitely appealing, and plenty of wavy brown hair. "Nice to meet you," he said, sticking out his hand. "Call me Callum, please."

Shaking his hand, I murmured an innocuous comment to hide my reactions—wretchedness at Hawk's casual words, *former friend*, and shock that we were a well-known name to the local Mounties.

Interrupting my downward spiral, Callum said, "Would you like us to help clear away your guests? You don't want them gawking at a body being unloaded. It's a sight they'll never be able to unsee."

"I appreciate your thoughtfulness, but I'll handle it," I said hastily, scanning the murmuring crowd of employees and guests. "I know someone who'll have the crowd begging to follow her inside. Give me a moment to find my sister."

Both of them agreed.

Dodie's bright orange turkey costume in honor of Thanksgiving should be easy to spot.

A familiar hoot of laughter attracted my attention. My middle sister, our wild child and Grizzly Gulch's third co-owner, Dodie Foster, was our outspoken, impulsive and fun-loving operations manager, overseeing three programs with surprising ease—Food & Beverages, Customer Services, and Housekeeping.

I beckoned her over. The noisy crowd parted to let her duck under the tape. I glanced at the minicoach. All the passengers had disembarked and stood together in front of the luggage compartment, gawking at my sister.

I totally got it.

In honor of the Thanksgiving festivities, she'd crammed herself into a pumpkin-colored ride-a-turkey costume designed to appear as though the wearer was straddling the bird. Fake person legs in black pants emerged from the outfit at waist-level to flank a spherical turkey-body. A fake turkey-neck with a fake turkey-head sprouted from the costume's chest area. Dodie's own head, arms, and legs emerged from apertures in the appropriate places. Imitation turkey-flesh tights ending in red socks and floppy turkey-feet encased her lower extremities. A huge tail fanned out from the costume's bulbous ass.

She approached with a jaunty strut, her fake turkey-head bobbing up and down in front of her, its red wattle a-quiver. "What's up, buttercup?" Dodie asked.

After I made the introductions, I said, "Explanations can wait. I need you to clear this area."

Hawk's mouth curled with amusement at Dodie's costume while Callum out-and-out gaped at what I imagined was his first encounter with a human turkey.

Instead of arguing, Dodie surprised me by saying, "Baby sister, you owe me many answers, but right now, we need to get these people inside. Leave it to the expert." She pivoted toward the crowd and yelled, "People! Listen up!"

When that didn't work, she bounced up and down several times. Every ounce of flesh she owned, and she owned a fair quantity, gave an alarming wobble. Cupping her hands around her mouth she scrunched her eyes shut.

I hazarded a guess. "You're imitating a constipated bird?"

Dodie gave me the middle-finger salute and returned the hand to her mouth. Sucking in some deep breaths, she pursed her lips. The swift gurgling sounds she produced sounded remarkably like a turkey gobble. She repeated the process twice, increasing the volume each time.

Everyone stopped talking and stared at her.

Between wheezes of laughter, I admitted, "That was amazing."

"Education by YouTube." Dodie focused on the guests milling around outside the police tape, shouting, "Listen up, folks. The authorities want everyone to clear the area."

Over the complaints, Dodie cupped her hands around her mouth and yelled, "Grizzly Gulch staff—and make no mistake, I know exactly who you are—the excitement's over. Bellhops, please help these passengers with their luggage. Everyone else, return to your stations."

With the staff departure underway, she hollered to the diminished crowd, "Guests and assorted spectators. Listen up." Once she'd captured everyone's attention again, she strutted in a tight circle, fake-turkey ass and tail feathers a-quiver. "I know you're eager to meet our most recent arrivals, but first, they have some formalities to deal with. After that—"

"Did someone die?" a man hollered.

"Of course someone did," another answered. "Why else would the fuzz be here?"

More regal than a human turkey had a right to be, Dodie's reply was frosty. "As I was saying, the most recent guests will join you as soon as possible. In the meantime, I'm asking everyone to return to the dining room. The bar is still very much open, and you're missing out on some amazing desserts."

"What's on the dessert menu?" a plump woman asked. I swore she was a neighboring rancher, not a guest.

"Besides two kinds of pie, Banoffee and Southern Pecan, Chef Armand has prepared my personal favorite." Confidentiality laced her next words. "It's called Miraculous Better-Than-Sex Cake."

Amidst the burst of laughter, a woman said, "I'll have a big piece. At my age, cake is an acceptable substitute for the real deal, anyway."

"It's better," another onlooker proclaimed.

"I feel your pain," Dodie replied. "Trust me, this cake is better than Big Bart, my battery-operated bedtime companion, and that's saying a lot. For an extra treat during dessert, I will entertain you with rude jokes, unsuitable anecdotes, and more of my world-famous turkey imitations."

Callum said, "I want to join the luncheon."

"Business first," Hawk reminded him.

Dodie nudged me and murmured. "I can't believe you invited our family drama queen to stay in your apartment with you when you could have given her a cabin. You'll have seven days, count 'em, *seven* whole days of togetherness."

"I gave it plenty of thought. First and foremost, we're full. Second, we owe her for bringing in a coachload of guests. And third, this visit will give us a chance to bond."

"Don't go all Pollyanna on me, little sister. Minnie will drive you nuts."

True, that. Minnie was a drama queen.

Dodie marched into the main lodge without a backward glance. Every guest and several ranchers trotted behind her.

Watching the exodus, Hawk said, "Quite a performance. Is she always like that?"

"Pretty much. Guests love her, especially when she's inappropriate."

Callum said. "I can see why."

Although my insides were churning, I hit both men with a cool stare. "I trust this, er, informal group interview won't take long."

Callum said, "It should be over in no time. We talked to the driver while you were inside the vehicle. Your guests have disembarked, and their luggage is being unloaded as we speak. I've confiscated the deceased's luggage for examination back at the station." He glanced at the minicoach. "The medical examiner and his assistant are removing the deceased."

Sure enough, two men hefted a body board down the stairs. A body bag, clearly occupied, rested on top. While the men transferred the deceased to a metal gurney, the coach's passengers stood near the luggage, singing Belafonte's *Zombie Jamboree*. The merry Caribbean sounds of, "*Back to back, belly to belly ...*" filled the air.

The men wheeled the loaded gurney toward the ME's van and hoisted it on board. The ME stripped off his protective gear including a face mask and disposable gloves and booties before approaching us. Hawk and Callum appeared to know him well.

After introductions, Dr. Atticus Lightheart scratched his head. "This is one for the books. I gotta say I've never seen anything quite like it."

"Any ideas about the cause of death?" Callum asked,

"I didn't see any evidence of foul play, but around this place, you never can tell." Atticus winked at me. "Kidding. But I was out to Grizzly Gulch last spring to check out a corpse. Dead bodies seem to be a recurring theme."

So much for hoping our horse trainer's death would go unmentioned.

"Are you telling me there were previous deaths?" Callum glanced at me, then at Hawk, who shrugged.

"Only one." I switched my attention to Atticus. "Please tell me Lizzie died of natural causes."

"No can do at this point. But I'll perform a preliminary exam right away."

"No rush," Callum said. "The case appears routine, we're short-staffed, and my sister, her husband, and their three children are visiting me through the Thanksgiving weekend. I don't know what I was thinking, letting my wife invite them. My house has only three bedrooms, my sister announced she's turned vegan, our dog has the runs from something he ate, and I'm seriously thinking of leaving town for the duration of their visit. Let me know once you have official results, hopefully after my houseguests leave. In the meantime, I'll get my phone to record the passengers' comments before I dash off."

Hawk waited until Callum had disappeared to murmur to Atticus, "Let me know if you find anything unusual. I'll deal with Callum."

Atticus' face lightened. "Great. If I find anything, I'll get back to you today, tomorrow at the latest. Callum will be back in the saddle long before I receive a full toxicology work-up." Atticus hopped inside the ME's van. It roared away, headed for the Big Sky General Hospital.

I frowned at Hawk. "I hope you and Callum don't plan to interview every passenger immediately."

"That's Callum's call. I imagine he'll want to get to know the passengers and hear their description of what happened."

"But the guests need to—"

At that moment, the driver yelled, "Lady, I'm done with the luggage. There's something else belonging to the deceased inside the vehicle. Don't go anywhere."

He climbed into the minicoach while I folded my arms, tapped a toe, and concentrated on ignoring Hawk. After a couple of muffled curses, the driver returned with a bulky item held cautiously at arms' length.

"Its name is Snuggles, and it's your problem now." He handed me a pet carrier full of hissing, growling, slashing cat. "The kitty litter, litter box, toys, treats, and cat food are all with Lizzie's luggage. Good luck. You'll need it."

Hawk stepped forward. "We may have more questions for you. Where will you be?"

"In the bar. I need a drink." At Hawk's nod, the driver hightailed it away.

Phone in hand, Callum re-appeared in time to watch the driver disappear. He cast an incredulous glance at the snarling orange-and-white beast in the crate. "I must have missed something. Is that animal yours?"

"Not for long." I set the carrier down and examined its occupant through the metal bars. Snuggles released a ferocious hiss accompanied by a slitty-eyed glare that hinted of impending doom.

Behind me, Abby sang out, "You-hoo. Clara. Word is, you've inherited a cute little kitty cat."

"I don't know about cute or little, but it's definitely a cat," I replied. "He's only here until Lizzie's family claims him." A low-pitched growl prompted me to ask, "Aren't orange cats supposed to be friendly?"

Abby materialized at my side. "They are."

"Too bad this one didn't get the memo," Hawk said.

"Want to be his foster-mom until he gets a new permanent home?" I asked Abby.

"Nope. If I wanted a cat, I'd own a cat. You should keep him. Ever since Russell died, you've been alone too much."

I had no wish to discuss my ex-husband in front of Hawk, who appeared way too interested. To change the subject, I said, "If no one claims Snuggles, I'll ask our staff if anyone wants to adopt a cat, maybe place a 'Cat for Sale' ad in *High Country News*. If all else fails, I'll drop him off at a cat shelter."

Abby's withering stare announced her opinion of my solution before she favored Hawk and Callum with a tight smile. "I don't believe we've met."

After introductions, she told me, "I'll ask a bellhop to bring the cat supplies to your place along with Minnie's luggage."

We sisters each had an apartment on our main lodge's second floor.

Mine was the corner unit, and Dodie's was sandwiched between Abby's and mine.

Abby stooped to pick up the pet carrier. "You'll fall in love with him in no time. Check out that sweet little face. Why don't I take this cutie-pie up to your quarters? I'll be back in no time to help with registration."

"Knock yourself out."

"Don't worry so much. I have a way with cats. Even if I don't own one, I love them, and they love me back." She crouched in front of the carrier and cooed, "Who's a good boy?" Ignoring the ferocious growl, she answered her own question. "You are, yes you are."

Hefting the cat carrier, Abby marched the animal toward the main entrance. She'd barely reached the door when she stopped to tickle the cat.

"Don't stick your fingers in the cage," Callum hollered.

Ranchers in the next county must have heard her screech followed by an inventive string of unladylike swearwords.

Though Hawk and Callum didn't utter a word, their eyes shone with mirth.

I must explain to my sister once again why cursing in public is a no-no.

Hawk, Callum, and I were approaching the cluster of passengers when a shout stopped me.

"Clara Jane Foster!" Minnie bellowed. "Don't you dare take one more step."

It wouldn't have surprised me if she'd been taking hog-calling lessons.

Chapter 3: Interviews

Cousin Minnie emerged from the knot of passengers and loped toward me. Her broad grin revealed a chipped front tooth. Although she must be in her mid-sixties by now, she reminded me of an ungainly colt.

Her abrupt approach caused Callum and Hawk to shuffle a few feet backward and tip the brim of their caps to conceal half their faces. Their simultaneous reaction must be a Mountie thing. It was amazing how the two tall and imposing men managed to fade into the background yet stay within earshot. People probably talked more freely when they believed a Mountie wasn't hanging on their every word.

Minnie wrapped a pair of astonishingly strong arms around me, enveloping me in a cloud of patchouli. She finally pushed back and studied me, saying, "I love your new hairdo. You could pass for fifty."

I tried unsuccessfully to wriggle away. "Thanks, I think." Since our last visit, I'd had my hair cut into an asymmetrical bob and let the color grow out. Imagine my surprise when I discovered I liked my own hair color, which turned out to be a mixture of soft, ashy brown streaked with pure white and splashes of gray, a combo you couldn't get if you paid through the nose for it.

"It's fabulous to see you, dah-ling." Her arms tightened around me in a frightening manner. "I can't begin to tell you how delighted I am to have the honor of spending the week with you, both of us together in your enchanting apartment. We'll have loads of special girl time."

Yeah, that's what I'm afraid of.

"Absolutely," I said, struggling to breathe, "but remember, as events manager, I'm on call, night and day."

"Work's highly overrated." She released me and twirled, her arms spread wide. "Screw work, I say. Live large. Embrace life. Play hooky."

"Settle down, Minnie. A passenger is dead."

She faced me and planted her feet. "Truth be told, the world is a better place without Lizzie." Her shrewd gaze swept my face. "You look different. Something's happened since I saw you last." After a moment, she laughed aloud. "Aha. You got laid. You finally got your act together and banged someone." My theatrical cousin sounded like a foghorn when she chose to project from the diaphragm. Like now.

The sound of a shoe scraping asphalt caused me to glance around in time to discover Hawk inching closer. My face burned. Even my sisters didn't know I'd had a fling.

"Don't be silly," I said, slanting a wary glance at Hawk.

I had no idea how Minnie had sniffed out my deepest, darkest secret. Hawk and I had, indeed, done the deed—several times—during our last night together in early June. And a most memorable night it had been, that is until I crept away at dawn.

Callum winked at me and strode toward the passengers. Hawk followed, his reluctance evident from his dragging footsteps. Over his shoulder Callum ordered, "Follow me. Both of you." When we hesitated, staring at the two retreating backs, he spoke louder without turning his head. "I don't hear footsteps. Today would be good."

Minnie flung one arm across her forehead, an impressive diva movement she'd perfected, and wailed, "Do you know how long it's been since I've seen Cousin Clara? Can you comprehend how much we've missed one another?"

Callum and Hawk kept right on walking.

Dodie was right. Minnie's drama would drive me nuts. "Don't worry. We have a whole week to spend together." I patted her arm and followed the men.

Seven. Whole. Days.

We joined the passengers who'd circled up beside the minicoach. Most appeared to have sobered up. The woman who'd been crying sat in a wheelchair.

Hawk parked himself beside me while Callum took a position in the center of the circle. "Good afternoon, everyone," he shouted and waited for the buzz to die away.

Beside me, Hawk reached into a pocket for a notepad and pen. I figured he wasn't into modern technology.

Once there was total silence, Callum said, "You've already met Clara Foster, your events manager for the week. I'm Sergeant Callum Shaughnessy of the Royal Canadian Mounted Police and this," he indicated Hawk, "is Hawk MacDougall, a retired Mountie and my sidekick for the day. I'm leading the investigation into Ms. Fournier's death, and I'm about to use my phone to record this process." His tone and the fact that he extracted his cell phone and clicked it on made it clear he was in no mood to mess around. "One by one, I want each of you to introduce yourself. After that, you'll have an opportunity to describe your recollections of the events surrounding Ms. Fournier's death. Once everyone's finished, you'll all be free to enjoy the rest of your day."

He pinned Minnie with a stare. "You there. You and Ms. Foster seem to be well acquainted. Why don't you start us off?"

Minnie jumped in without hesitation. "I'm pleased—no, *honored*—to introduce myself to such a dashing Mountie." She favored Callum with her most sultry pout, and I knew what to expect next. "My name is Minnie Harris, stage name Minerva. You might recognize the name because I'm an actress. Now retired, I direct and act in stage productions at Lifestyle Manor, and—"

"Minnie, Minnie, Minnie," An attractive woman interrupted Minnie in mid-torrent. "You do all that and so much more. Lifestyle Manor owes you a huge vote of thanks, hon." She released a little giggle. "Goodness, we are indeed fortunate to have a talented actress such as yourself staying with us. You contribute so much to our community."

The woman was petite, early fifties I guessed, but appeared younger, with perfect white teeth, bouncy blonde curls, and pert features. A well-cut navy pantsuit draped her curvy figure. The steely blue-eyed gaze she levelled at Minnie was a shocking contrast to her chirpiness.

"Thanks," Minnie said. "How kind of you to say."

Knowing how long-winded Minnie could be about her acting career, I mentally applauded the woman's ability to phrase a reprimand as a compliment.

"I'll go next," the blonde woman volunteered. "I'm Gabriella Chambers, recreation coordinator at Lifestyle Manor. Everyone calls me Gabby, likely because I love to talk." She released another musical giggle. "Besides enjoying a lovely Thanksgiving getaway with my favorite residents, I hope to learn some tips and techniques about event planning from an expert." She gazed directly at me, her toothy smile widening to the point of revealing every molar in her mouth until she dialed it back. "Lizzie's passing is tragic, but not surprising. The poor woman had heart problems."

"She seemed fit as a fiddle to me," Minnie muttered.

Gabby shook her head. "You and Lizzie weren't exactly what I would call *close*, hon." Her tone brimmed with tolerance. She swung an earnest gaze to Callum. "I assure you, Officer, Lizzie died a natural death."

Hawk's pencil moved rapidly across the paper until he raised his head. "Did Lizzie have any other health conditions you know of?"

His question was met with a unanimous, "No."

Gabby said, "Lizzie was a very private person. I doubt she shared her health issues with many residents."

Callum said, "Good to know. The autopsy will reveal the cause of death." He examined each face. "Who wants to go next?"

Minnie nudged me and whispered, "Uh oh. Incoming at three o'clock. Check it out, but be careful."

I followed her gaze. A handsome passenger with gorgeous salt-and-pepper hair and a charming smile strode toward me from his position across the circle. Ignoring the two men in the center of the circle, he gripped both my hands in his. "You must be Clara. You're much prettier than Minnie led me to believe." He winked at Minnie, who glared back.

At my age, I cherished every compliment that came my way, especially one from an attractive man in a cashmere sweater worth more than my entire wardrobe. Unless I was mistaken, he was the passenger who sang *Another One Bites the Dust*.

"Roland Bradshaw." He gave my hands a gentle squeeze. "Did anyone ever mention you have the most enchanting smile?"

Minnie scowled at him. "Forget it, Roland."

Roland's face reddened.

I opened my mouth to smooth over the awkward moment, but Hawk's low growl followed by, "I suggest you two flirt later," caused me to snap my mouth shut.

Roland took one glance at Hawk standing beside me and dropped my hands in a hurry.

A surge of guilt tinged with regret over how I'd treated Hawk clutched at my throat. I didn't blame him for his anger "I'm sure Roland was simply being friendly," I said.

A muscle in Hawk's left cheek jerked.

Roland jumped right in, his hand outstretched toward Hawk. "Roland Bradshaw, at your service. If there's anything I can do to help—"

Hawk ignored the outstretched hand. "You'll be the first to know.

"Don't trust Roland for a second," Minnie in an undertone, ignoring both Hawk and Callum to lead me some distance from the circle. "I call him Roland the Raunchy," she whispered. "He's a catfish hunting for a victim. First, he hit on Lizzie thinking she had a big inheritance, but she gave him the boot. There were others, Eleanor for one, but he dumped them too when he discovered they weren't wealthy. Who knows how many others he's hit on?"

Before I had a chance to quiz Minnie about why Roland might have singled me out, Callum's words sliced the air. "May we please resume before I grow any older?"

Chastened, we rejoined the circle. "I'm sorry," I said. We—"

"How do you do, Sergeant?" A woman's posh British accent cut off my apology. I might as well have been invisible the way she shot out a hand, first at Callum in the middle of the circle, then at Hawk beside me, all the while batting eyelashes so long they resembled small, furry animals attached to her upper lids. "Eleanor Fitzpatrick. Pleased to make the acquaintance of such impressive protectors."

"My pleasure entirely, Ms. Fitzpatrick," Hawk said.

At the same time, Callum offered her a charming smile, saying, "I promise to make this process as painless as possible."

Why did flattery uttered in an English accent turn men into drooling Neanderthals?

"Please. Call me Eleanor." More eyelash batting. Straightening a pink, floppy sunhat tied with a huge bow under her chin, she moved to Callum's side and laid a hand on his arm. "We've been on the road for hours. I, for one, am simply famished."

In response to her proclamation, a tall man with a full head of white hair stepped forward and rescued her hand, tucking it into the crook of his elbow in a proprietary gesture. "Relax, sweetheart. The Mountie is doing his job."

"Thank you." Callum examined the man as if he were a specimen. "Name?"

"Sure thing. Wayne Baker at your service. I would like to make you aware that this beautiful English rose at my side is getting restless." He spoke with a faint but noticeable slur, no doubt due to alcohol consumed on board the minicoach.

In an undertone, Minnie volunteered, "No wonder the poor man drinks. Wayne has more patience than the pope, tolerating that one the way he does." She jerked her chin at Eleanor.

The English rose simpered and used one finger to twirl the swoopy coal-black tress of hair she'd draped with care over one shoulder.

While Hawk scribbled in his notepad, Callum examined a small woman with pale gray eyes, her mousy brown hair tucked behind her ears. Beige pants, matching beige blouse and lumpy beige cardigan rendered her so nondescript I was astonished anyone noticed her. "Your name, please."

Minnie interjected, "This is Phyllis Jennings, an old high school friend of mine. It's because of her suggestion at last year's reunion that I visited Lifestyle Manor and decided to move in. Phyllis and poor Lizzie were inseparable friends."

Phyllis, small and nondescript, with wisps of mousy brown hair liberally streaked with gray, glanced at Minnie and immediately lowered her gaze. She murmured, "I'm so glad Minnie is here with me. Lizzie's death leaves a huge hole in my life." She shoved her hands into her cardigan pockets and studied her feet.

Callum addressed the top of her head. "I'm sorry to hear that, ma'am."

Eleanor curled her lips in a sarcastic grimace and whispered to Wayne, "If Phyllis is so broken up over Lizzie's death, why was she singing along with us in the coach?"

Hawk glanced at me and raised one eyebrow.

Yeah, the passengers' reaction to Lizzie's death wasn't your usual garden variety grief—if, indeed, they felt any grief at all. "Everyone grieves in different ways," I suggested.

"We have two more passengers," Callum said, moving things along.

A large woman with a café au lait complexion and a tweed trouser suit spoke up. "I'm Lois McKibben, and this is my partner, Flo Madison." She put a possessive arm around the shoulders of a brown woman who clutched a walker. "I'm afraid we won't be much help about Lizzie's death. Due to Flo's recent hip replacement, she avoids rough terrain."

I recognized Flo as the woman who'd been crying upon arrival. She'd recovered nicely.

"That's right," Flo confirmed. "We both waited inside the minicoach until everyone else had left so I could take my time getting out to stretch my legs."

"Are you okay standing, Ms. Madison, or would you prefer to head up to the main lodge now?" Callum's tone was surprisingly gentle.

Flo revealed exceptionally fine teeth that shone against her beautiful, caramel-toned face. "I'm fine, thank you. After sitting so long in the coach, it's a relief to stand."

"Good." He addressed the group. "Thank you for your cooperation. This isn't a formal interrogation since Lizzie likely died a natural death. All I'm interested in is whatever springs to mind about the events surrounding the incident. Don't worry. This won't take long."

Each passenger jumped in at once, creating an uproar.

Callum held up a hand. "One at a time, please. First, I'd like to hear about the events leading up to the death."

No doubt feeling a sense of responsibility for her charges, Gabby led off with, "It all began two hours out of Lifestyle Manor. We were driving through the most rugged section of the Rockies when *someone* needed an unscheduled bio-break." She cast a pointed glance at Minnie. "With no facilities on board and no comfort stop for another hour, I remembered an off-road rest area from my hiking days in the Rockies. It's only a little wooden shack with two stalls, but it comes in handy when emergency strikes."

"Foresight is vital," Flo said, interrupting Gabby's dissertation. "As you may have noticed, I'm not too mobile. In case I needed to pee, I wore one of those disposable underwear thingies they're always advertising during *Criminal Minds*."

"That's Flo for you." A huge white grin split Lois' face. "Foresight and consideration for others are her watchwords. She refuses to go anywhere unless she's wearing one."

This was way too much information for comfort.

"If Minnie had the foresight to wear one, we'd have sailed right through," Lois pointed out in an aggrieved tone. "It might have saved a lot of trouble."

"Are you saying Lizzie's death was *my* fault?" Minnie directed an angry scowl at Lois.

As if sensing bladder issues had displaced the sequence of events leading to Lizzie's unfortunate demise, Hawk stepped in and steered us back on track. "Gabby, you were telling Sergeant Shaughnessy about an unscheduled comfort stop in a back-country rest area."

"Right," Gabby said. "I figured Minnie would be first out the coach, but no. Although Lizzie was already on her feet and pushing past everyone before the vehicle stopped, a little scuffle in the aisle when she tried to slip in front of Minnie caused a bottleneck."

"You mean Lizzie tried to butt in." Minnie's eyes snapped with green fire. "Too bad for me she was a whole lot stronger and heavier. That's how she always got her own way."

"As I was saying," Gabby said, "I moved to the front of the bus to break them apart, but an elbow in my stomach slowed me down. Once I recovered, the door was open. Lizzie and Minnie shot outside with everyone else stampeding behind them. Goodness, it was chaos."

"That's not true, Lois said. "Flo and I took our time. Since I have neither children nor a prostate, I don't experience the same bladder problems."

Flo regarded Lois with affection. "The two of us sat together on a large rock in the parking lot." She slid a sly glance at Hawk. "In case you're interested, the driver slipped behind a Jack pine to do his business. I guess he thought he was alone."

Wayne cut his gaze to Callum. "Gabby is outstanding in the fitness department. She should try out for the Olympics. First, she passed Phyllis and Roland, then us, to reach Minnie and Lizzie during the final sprint for the outhouse."

"I enjoy a daily run," Gabby said, turning beet red. "It's a super-duper stress reducer." She giggled at her own joke.

"I still got there first," Minnie said. "I was opening the nearest door when Lizzie yanked me back. Want to hear what she said?" She gazed expectantly at Callum, then Hawk.

"Desperately," Hawk answered.

Minnie took him at his word. "Lizzie said, and I quote, 'Shove off, bitch. This stall's mine'".

In her elegant English drawl, Eleanor said, "Ah, yes. And if I remember correctly, your reaction was quite over the top." She adjusted her floppy sun hat.

"All I said was, 'In case you didn't notice, dumb-ass, there are two stalls.' "

"There was a little more to it than harsh words, hon," Gabby pointed out, shaking her head until the blonde curls bounced. "Let's not forget the little hair-pulling incident."

"Yes indeed," Eleanor volunteered. "Your attack was absurdly vicious."

Wayne patted Eleanor's arm. "There, there, sweetheart. There's no need to get all worked up. Poor Lizzie's gone."

"Why don't you tell us about the incident?" Callum suggested to Minnie while Hawk scribbled away.

Minnie glared at Gabby, then Eleanor, before heaving a gusty sigh. "I'm not proud of it, but it's true. After I pointed out there were two stalls, Lizzie lost her temper and we had a brief disagreement, during which I relieved her of a handful of hair. Gabby was trying to referee. Everyone was yelling. It was chaos. Then Lizzie elbowed me and I shot a fist into her gut. She doubled over, ass-up, so I zipped around her into the nearest stall and locked the door. That was the last time I saw her alive." Minnie yanked a tissue from her pocket and dabbed her damp eyes.

Being an actress, I was certain she could manufacture tears at will.

Phyllis the Invisible, as I dubbed her, picked up the story. "Poor Lizzie darted into the second stall. She stopped howling shortly after she locked the door, but never came out. We had to call the driver to break the door down. He found her on the floor."

"How did you know she was dead?" Hawk asked.

"Lois used to be a nurse," Flo said, sounding defensive. "She tried to find a pulse. Lizzie was dead."

"Out of curiosity," Hawk said, "Why didn't anyone notify the authorities?"

Gabby said, "Naturally, I tried to notify the Mounties immediately, but there was no reception. It was the same for everyone on board. The mountains were too high."

"That's right," Roland agreed. "And no one wanted the driver to leave us stranded in the middle of nowhere with a corpse while he drove ahead to find better reception. The alternative was to leave Lizzie alone while we all went ahead. We voted to stick together and transport Lizzie to the authorities ourselves."

"It wasn't easy to load her into the vehicle," Phyllis said, her face lighting up for the first time. "She was too heavy to carry, but we found a travel blanket so we could drag her back to the minicoach. We considered stuffing, er, placing her in the luggage compartment, but we'd have had to fold her up like an accordion."

My horror must have been obvious, because Hawk threw me a sympathetic glance.

Eleanor glared at Minnie. "Then Minnie got the bright idea for the men to carry Lizzie to the back seat where she could stretch out. They managed to haul her as far as the first row, where she got stuck."

Minnie's mouth twisted in a sneer. "I didn't hear you offering a better suggestion. Who knew Lizzie was packing so much weight?"

Eleanor sniffed her disapproval. "You could have tried to support her head."

"The space was crowded, and Lizzie was, you know, dead."

Gabby summed up the rest of the saga. "Wayne and Roland loaded Lizzie into the first seat, and we resumed our trip."

Flo added, "It was my idea to use a bungee cord to stop her from toppling into the aisle every time the driver took a curve."

"And I closed her eyelids so we could all pretend she was asleep," Lois said. "She appeared so peaceful sitting there, don't you think?"

"By then, I was so upset I forgot to notify the authorities," Gabby said. "We were past Banff National Park when I remembered to call the RCMP. The reception was still spotty, but I was able to report the death and our destination before my phone died."

Callum clicked his phone off. "I think I've heard enough. You're all free to go, at least, for now."

"Not you, Clara," Hawk said. "I need a few moments with you." For Callum's benefit, he added, "Thanks for letting me tag along. My car's in the parking lot, so I'll get myself home after I finish up here."

Minnie, who slanted a quick glance at Hawk, then at me, gave a sly wink. Clearly, she'd connected some dots. "Don't worry about me," she announced. "I'll have a quick bite, then find my own way to your apartment."

She walked away to join the dispersing group, leaving me alone with Hawk and my churning emotions. He wanted an explanation and an apology, both of which he deserved, both of which I dreaded delivering.

The passengers headed toward the main entrance and disappeared inside. Their attitude toward Lizzie's death mystified me. With the exception of some initial sobbing, the predominant emotions appeared to be callous indifference laced with dislike. Then again, if she'd died a natural death, their attitude was irrelevant.

I was contemplating the best way to make a hasty getaway when Hawk placed one hand on my arm. "We need to clear the air. Where can we go for privacy?"

Like it or not, this was showdown time. Resigned, I muttered, "Follow me."

Chapter 4: Showdown

THE GAZEBO, A NEW ADDITION to Grizzly Gulch, was a golden-brown wooden structure, octagonal in shape, with open sides and a brown-shingled roof. Backed by latticed privacy screens, contoured benches lined the interior. Normally, I loved sitting there to enjoy silence and solitude. Today, not so much. But Hawk wanted privacy, and this was the first place that sprang to mind.

I plunked down on a bench as close to the entrance as possible. He sat on the opposite bench and folded his arms. His gaze drilled into me, a typical cop technique.

Hey, this was his meeting. Let him get the conversational ball rolling.

His presence left me weak-kneed and suffering from an advanced case of dry mouth. What if he wanted to resurrect our romance? I had to convince him we were finished, but was unsure where to start. I hid my discomfort by pretending to check my email on my cell phone.

The silence stretched out until I wanted to tear my hair out. The only sound was a flock of Canada geese honking as they flapped their way south to Mexico.

I gathered he planned to out-wait me. Patience was one of his many gifts. Bittersweet memories I'd suppressed of our time together threatened to swamp me.

It all began last spring in Vancouver. We'd first met at a summer sports camp where I'd dropped off my oldest grandson. I was waving goodbye when a Mountie gripping the arms of two defiant teenaged boys marched past me into the office, kicking the door closed. Always a firm believer in eavesdropping, I lurked outside the window and pretend-texted like crazy.

That's how I learned the head counsellor asked the RCMP to scare some sense into two bullies who delighted in tormenting the younger kids.

I'd pegged the Mountie in his mid-to-late fifties, the perfect age for me—youthful enough to enjoy life, old enough for us to be part of the same generation. The fact that he was tall, ripped, and handsome hadn't hurt either. But the clincher that melted my heart was his calm and kind handling of two troubled youths.

I had lingered, we'd connected, and before I knew it, I'd accepted the first of many dates in a wild and wonderful escape from my endless care-giving activities. Knowing my relationship with Hawk was temporary, I'd lowered my defences and enjoyed our time together, telling myself I deserved a taste of excitement. Too bad I'd blown it. Big time.

With afternoon sunbeams dripping through the gazebo's latticework like liquid gold, I let my fingers fly over my phone's mini-keyboard. Pretend-texting was getting to be a habit. I was about to explode when Hawk broke the silence. "Am I making you nervous?"

"Of course not." I shoved the phone in my pocket and ran my fingers through my hair. My ammolite ring snagged, tangled in my smart new hairdo. Pretending nothing was wrong, I tugged so hard I ripped out a clump of hair before liberating my hand.

Hawk gently removed several loose strands. "I advise you not to treat your hair like a battleground when you're nervous," he said gently. "You could end up bald if you're not careful."

The familiar sensation of his heat, solidity, and sheer size nearly unseated me. "Don't flatter yourself. Corpses make me nervous, not you." Good thing he didn't know the ring was a recent indulgence to soothe my broken heart.

After another prolonged silence, he said, "I hadn't taken you for a coward. Guess I misread you."

"How so?" I stared at him in surprise. Big mistake. Those dark, secretive eyes, which used to soften whenever he saw me, were now filled with a different emotion—disappointment or anger, maybe both.

"We had something good going, he said. "We hit it off. At least, I thought we did. Seemed to me we had lots in common, even karaoke."

My tongue glued itself to the roof of my mouth. I was pretty sure I knew what was coming next. In misery, I studied my clasped hands and willed myself not to squirm. Making small talk, I said, "So you've retired."

"Yep. After you walked out on me I kinda lost my drive." Hawk cleared his throat. "I kept replaying our lovemaking session the night we closed the karaoke place—our last night, as it turned out. You gave no hint, not a single clue it was over. I was actually dumb enough to believe we might have a future together."

Shame washed over me. We'd gone to his place and made love for the first time. Then, while he slept, I snuck away without so much as a goodbye to take the next flight to Calgary and home. "I'm so sorry. You deserved better."

"I particularly enjoyed the text message in which you broke the news you were dumping me. A freaking text message. You were sorry, it was all your fault, blah, blah, blah, you were too damaged to get serious about a man. I never heard from you again because you ghosted me. Only a coward does that."

Everything he said was true. I'd run from him like a terrified adolescent. Although he concealed his feelings behind a wall of icy calm, any fool could see how much I'd hurt him. My actions were heartless, cowardly, and about as far from empathetic as you could get. Truth was, I had my reasons. Excellent reasons. Or so I told myself.

Hawk rose to his feet. One stride took him to my bench, where he sank down way too close. I tried to edge away, but he enfolded my hands in his, holding me so I couldn't escape without making a scene. Sneaky. He knew how much I hated scenes.

"I hadn't intended to burst into your life this way," he said. "In fact, I tried to call and email you several times to let you know my transfer to the Cochrane detachment had come through. You didn't answer."

True. I'd done the only thing I could think of to save myself, and pretended we'd never met. Okay, so the way I'd handled our breakup was clumsy, cowardly, and callous, something inconceivable for a people-pleaser like me. Hey, I'd panicked. To cover my discomfort, I responded, "You might have mentioned your plan to retire and move close to me during one of our dates. I could have ended things before anyone got hurt."

"At that point, I had no idea I wanted to retire, never mind move to Alberta."

"But why here? Are you stalking me?" I blurted.

"Not at all. My daughter and her family have lived near Calgary for years. More recently, my son and his family moved here too. I wanted to be closer to them, especially my grandkids, so I moved to Alberta as soon as I retired. I'm renting a place in Stoney Corner, not far from here."

"How did you find me?"

"You mentioned that you and your sisters were co-owners of a dude ranch in Alberta. I was a cop. There are only so many dude ranches in Alberta. I ran some online searches and learned you were a co-owner of Grizzly Gulch." His gaze, dark and steady, raked me.

Okay, so he was hoping for some sort of closure, so closure he would get. Focusing on the distant mountains, I exhaled a deep breath and said, "You were only supposed to be a fling."

"Something you might have thought to mention during one of our dates. I too could have ended things before anyone got hurt."

He'd thrown my words back at me. I hoped my inward cringe wasn't obvious. "You're right," I admitted. "I should have set boundaries. I guess I was having so much fun, I lost sight of my cardinal rule."

"Which is?"

"No more men. Ever." I took another deep, albeit shaky breath. "I came close to forgetting how effortlessly men destroy a woman's soul. I should never have let my guard down and dated you when all I wanted peace, safety, and tranquility. The only way to get that was to build a wall around my heart."

"A wall? You have *got* to be kidding. It's more like a rampart than a wall. A rampart covered with fish hooks, razor blades, and ninja swords, while guarded by rabid bobcats with Tasers."

"Wow. That's harsh." But true. The last thing I needed was a man, namely Hawk MacDougall, ruining my life. Yet here we were—together again.

"Who hurt you so badly all you want to do is protect yourself?"

Hawk's words sliced through my morose thoughts, and my face burned with humiliation. "I don't want to talk about it."

"For your own sake, I hope someday you might explain why you won't let me into your life and your heart."

"I'm sorry. I wish I could."

But it would never happen. The fling with Hawk was my secret. My sisters believed I still grieved the loss of Russell, my husband. I was too ashamed to tell them the truth—that I'd married a man who was, if possible, more abusive than our daddy.

Hawk dropped my hands and stood. "It's like this, Clara. You can stay safe for the rest of your life and try to avoid all possible heartache. But no one said life would be easy. Unless you take risks, you'll miss out on all the fun, adventure, and sheer excitement of life, especially love. Safety comes with a huge price tag."

I considered walking away, but my legs were too rubbery to rise. Forced to sit there in an agony of conflicting emotions, I had a sinking feeling he was right, but I didn't know how to be any different. My tongue bypassed my brain before I could analyze my reaction. "Will I see you again?"

"I have an appointment, but I'll be in touch about the initial findings as soon as Atticus fills me in. I hope you'll think about what I said." He strode away, leaving me sitting alone and heartsick. I liked him entirely too much but had no intention of placing my heart on the line again.

Hawk's car had barely disappeared, when Minnie called my name. My first instinct was to run and hide in a storage room, but I couldn't ignore her panicky cry for help. She was family and my guest. I waved to catch her attention and hollered, "Over here, hon."

Minnie rushed over to the gazebo. She was breathing heavily when she arrived. "There you are. Thank God I found you. I've been hunting all over. You have to help me. I went to your apartment to freshen up before lunch. Abby let me in, then left in a big hurry to deal with a phone call about an outstanding invoice, and now Snuggles has escaped his carrier."

"How could he escape? The carrier has a child-resistant lock."

"He was yowling his head off, so I let him out. Big mistake. The fluffy monster sprang at me, hoping to eviscerate me, but I threw him off. He climbed the curtains and disappeared. I can't be alone in your apartment with him because he wants to rip my throat out."

Reminding myself I loved her, I stood. "I imagine he's more scared than you, Minnie. Let's go. You can put your feet up, take a nap if you like, while I find Snuggles."

Hey, how much damage could an adorable little kitty do?

Chapter 5: Settling In

Minnie clutched my arm and dragged me through the main lobby, intent on returning to my apartment to collar a cat.

Ignoring her constant complaints about Snuggles' reign of terror, I paused at the kitchen entrance and relayed our lunch order to the chef. Minnie must be hungry and I certainly was. Being a co-owner had its perks.

While waiting for our takeout to arrive, I led her around the lobby, pointing out some of Grizzly Gulch's features, like the Thanksgiving decorations I had spent hours arranging, or the cute little reading areas with their subtle blue and terracotta area rugs, or the moose head hanging above the massive stone fireplace. The lobby's character was lost on my cousin. She was intent on finding a vicious feline and imprisoning him again. Too bad for her I planned to give Snuggles free run of my apartment once he'd settled down

A sous-chef bearing our lunch intercepted us and off-loaded two pasta Alfredos with shrimp, two small Caesars, and Chef Armand's peanut butter cookies. Minnie took a couple of the take-out containers, and we climbed to the second floor in silence.

We entered cautiously. "Here, kitty, kitty, kitty," I sang out.

"Shut the door quickly," Minnie snapped, "or he'll escape."

I kicked the door shut and we plunked the containers onto the hall table. "Relax. Snuggles must be worn out by now from all his apartment-trashing, guest-bashing, and general mayhem. I bet he's sound asleep."

"Not bloody likely." She slipped off her gorgeous leather jacket and handed it to me with a flourish, revealing a fabulous blouse I bet was pure silk.

I couldn't resist stroking her jacket's butter-soft leather.

"Please don't paw the jacket. It stains easily. That's Cordovan leather, and it cost me a pretty penny. Also, make sure to use a wooden—not metal—hanger, and don't let it touch another garment."

Minnie had a lot to learn about being a gracious guest. I was experiencing second, third, even fourth thoughts about having her stay with me instead of a guest cabin until I remembered she'd had a tough day—a woman dying, riding for hours with the corpse—yeah, that qualified as a tough day. My cousin needed pampering.

Thrusting aside my irritation, I pushed my coats to one end of the rod and hung her jacket in solitary splendor. With a hospitable smile, I said, "Make yourself comfortable in the living room, hon. Put your feet up and rest while I set out our lunch."

"No way. That feline monster's around here somewhere. I hope he's not in my bedroom. We're going to need some rules about the cat." She seized the food and marched straight down the hallway and into the kitchen, bypassing the combined living-dining room I'd taken such pains decorating.

My bright and airy combination living and dining room breathed elegance, warmth, and welcome. I'd insisted on adding an extra window on the side wall and installing a custom-built set of sliding doors flanked by two narrower panels and topped with a Palladian window. My need for airy rooms with plenty of daylight was fallout from a thirty-six-hour lockup in a dark basement storage area when I was a six-year-old. I'd pissed off my dad by leaving a book on the floor. Of course, he'd made it all my fault that he tripped and sprained an ankle. Naturally, the dozen beers he'd consumed had nothing to do with the incident. Once he'd passed out, Mom snuck me food, water, and bedding. But she'd been too terrified to release me.

Minnie's shriek would have made Jack the Ripper pause.

Please, God, grant me the patience to not kill Cousin Minnie.

I moved quickly, prepared to utter soothing words for whatever disaster she'd imagined. I halted in the kitchen doorway. A rich, ripe stench hit me in the face. My knees weakened with relief when I recalled leaving several windows open to air the place out in preparation for my house guest. The wranglers must have added fresh stall waste to the manure pile.

Minnie continued howling while clutching our lunch with both hands and circling the floor in an odd, lurching dance, hopping mostly on one foot.

"Doing a new folk dance you learned over the summer?" I inquired, removing the takeout containers from her hands and placing them on the counter for fear they'd go flying. "It's certainly energetic. Reminds me of a highland fling, only without the kilt."

"Not dancing, you idiot." She gasped for air. "Trying to avoid putting my foot down."

I bristled at being called an idiot. "Why? Did you stub your toe?"

"Can't you smell anything?" Her question ended on shrill scream.

"Of course I can. It's the manure pile. I forgot to warn Zeke, our barn manager, to hold off on raking it or adding stall waste because new guests were arriving today."

By then Minnie's breath was coming in rasping puffs. "It's not the manure pile. Snuggles pooped on the floor. I stepped in it."

I glanced around to find the mess and swallowed a giggle. "Yes, you did. He must be terrified, poor little fur baby."

"I thought you were supposed to be empathetic."

"You make empathy difficult. Stop hopping. You're only spreading the mess."

"FYI, I'm trying to protect your floor." She cast a baleful glare at me while hopping. "I need to wash my boots. They're tooled leather, cost a fortune. Hopefully, soap won't ruin them."

Trust Minnie to worry about her boots in the middle of a crisis. Ever mindful of hospitality, I zapped into damage control mode, helping her onto a chair and pouring her a shot of gin before removing and washing the offending boots in sudsy water. While she belted back a restorative slug, I used a disinfectant cleanser to wash the kitchen floor. Twice. After chugging my own shot, Minnie, the floor, and I were as good as new. The stench was gone, but the jury was out on the boots. I would ask housekeeping to clean and polish them thoroughly.

"I feel much better," Minnie announced, setting her shot glass on the table. "You'd better check out the rest of your apartment."

"I'm afraid to," I said truthfully, but tip-toed into the dining room I was so proud of. The breath whooshed out of my lungs at the sight of the shambles.

Snuggles had trashed the place. Knick-knacks from a corner cabinet lay smashed on the floor. I didn't mind losing those. They'd belonged to a great-aunt. But my eyes filled with tears on spotting the photograph of my mom beneath its broken frame and shards of glass. I'd swiped it the night I'd left home for good.

A hiss from near the ceiling drew my attention upwards. Snuggles glared at me from his perch on the curtain rod.

Ignoring him, I smoothed out the photo and placed it carefully in a drawer.

"I'm so sorry," Minnie said, coming up beside me and wrapping an arm around my shoulder. "I was afraid something like this might happen."

I sniffed back the tears. "You tried to warn me. But now that I think about it, poor Snuggles must be traumatized. First a bumpy bus ride in a pet carrier, now a strange place, and Lizzie's not here to soothe him."

"You go deal with Snuggles. I know where your broom is. This won't take long."

While she worked, I tried to tempt Snuggles from his perch near the ceiling with soft words and a bowl of kibble. When that failed, I opened a can of tuna, fetched my hand blender, and whipped up a fish smoothie. I lowered the bowl onto the kitchen floor, where the cat would be sure to smell his dinner. Once I stepped away, he crawled to the far end of the curtain rod, leaped down via the window sill, and scampered into the kitchen to dine in solitary comfort. I slammed the door shut behind him.

"Let's give him space," I said, using the brooks-no-argument tone I'd picked up from my daddy. I smiled to prove I wasn't overbearing. "It's warm enough to eat outside on my deck. I'll set the table and dish out food. You're in charge of the wine."

"Leave the door open to air out the place," Minnie ordered, sniffing the air. "It still stinks in here.

She wasn't wrong. The stench was remarkably penetrating.

Lunch on my deck was a resounding success. Everything was delicious, conversation never lagged, not for a second, and wine washed away any residual irritation. Yeah, Minnie and I were bonding. An hour later, we'd polished off everything, including a bottle of Pinot Grigio and two meltingly good chocolate chip cookies apiece.

"I'm so glad we did this." Minnie patted her tummy. "I feel much better now."

"Me too." I pushed back from the table. "I want you to relax, put your feet up. I'll see to Snuggles and tidy up."

"Later. I want to help."

Bearing dishes and cutlery, we entered the kitchen. As soon as we opened the door, Snuggles zipped past us into the living room. The tuna smoothie had disappeared, and the cat was reclining on his favorite perch—the curtain rod. He too had apparently mellowed out.

While I puttered around the kitchen, Minnie explored my apartment.

"What a breathtaking panorama." Due to projection from the diaphragm and precise enunciation, every word Minnie uttered floated into the kitchen.

I stuck my head into the living room to see what was happening. She was peering out the open windows at the view of rolling foothills backed by white-peaked mountains. I returned to the kitchen.

Sucking in a deep breath and exhaling, she intoned, "That crisp, delicious air caresses and stimulates my skin."

I assumed she was reciting lines from one of her stage plays, but refrained from commenting. Let her bask in those bygone glory days.

She clasped her hands at her breasts. "The emerald of the rolling hills, the mysterious pine forests, the turquoise river." She flung her arms wide, a habit she displayed when working up to a grand finale. "This glorious view is to die for."

"I hope not," I said lightly, concentrating on loading the dishwasher, arranging spoons just so in the cutlery rack, ensuring they all faced in the same direction.

Minnie's shriek would have shattered the windows if they weren't already open.

Dreading what I might find, I dashed into the living room. Flapping her arms and wailing, she circled the room while wearing Snuggles. The cat had attached himself to her upper arm by clinging to her lovely blouse. "Get him off," she yelled.

At this rate, her racket would deafen me long before the week was over. "Poor Snuggles only wanted down," I said. "You were blocking the window sill, so he landed on your shoulder."

Minnie flung her unoccupied arm over her forehead, a dramatic action she used far too often. "I'm not worried about the bloody cat," she howled. "Someone shot me."

I had no idea Minnie was paranoid as well as dramatic.

The wine must have made me brave to the point of foolhardy. I approached warily, taking care to avoid slashing claws, snapping jaws, and flying fists.

"Who's a good boy," I said in silly kitty-talk. "You are, yes, you are."

Snuggles must have sensed I posed no threat. His struggles stopped and he let me wrap a hand around his furry middle. His little heartbeat vibrated against my palm. I used my other hand to remove his front paws, gently unsnagging the fabric and settling him on the floor. He meowed once, as if to thank me, and darted across the room to disappear behind the curtain.

Minnie's howls had, thankfully, dwindled to whimpers. Sure enough, her upper arm was grazed, and blood dappled her blouse. "You poor dear. Snuggles did a number on you. I'd better disinfect those scratches, and then we'll get your blouse into cold water to remove the blood."

"I already told you. Someone shot me through the open window. I felt this burning pain before Snuggles landed on me. Sure there are claw scratches, but it's a bullet wound."

My brain scrambled to find other possibilities. "Anyone could have thrown a rock." I'd often wanted to heave something heavy at Minnie to shut her up.

"It's a bullet furrow."

"There was no gunshot," I pointed out in my most reasonable tone. Yep, Snuggles was the culprit, Minnie was overreacting, end of story.

"What if my attacker used a silencer? We need to call the cops."

A niggle of doubt caused me to examine Minnie's injury more closely. Minor scratches crisscrossed a shallow graze. The wound itself was trivial. But I had to admit, it appeared to be a bullet wound.

"If you really were shot, there should be a bullet somewhere. Let's find it before calling the Mounties. But first, I need to disinfect your arm and wash your blouse."

I tended to her arm then her blouse while she changed. We spent the next ten minutes searching for the bullet, checking the walls, flipping over cushions, and hunting inside cabinets, under pictures, and in dark corners.

From my crouching position, I raised my head. "There's nothing here, only some dust bunnies, a letter opener I'd lost, and an old—"

Footsteps creaked in the hallway, interrupting my search. "Who's there?" I yelled, heaving myself upright. "Is that you, Abby?"

"Nope. It's Phyllis." She poked her head into the living room, her pale eyes alight with curiosity. "Is everything okay in here?"

Minnie said what I was thinking. "I can't believe you walked in without permission."

"Sorry." Phyllis sounded anything but sorry. "I was looking around the main lodge when I heard yelling. It took me a few minutes to figure out where it originated."

I hesitated, wondering if she'd overheard us discussing Minnie's wound. "Everything's fine." I explained about the cat attack, omitting any mention of a possible gunshot. There was no need to freak out a guest.

Laughing, Phyllis said, "There's our Minnie for you. Always dramatic."

I might secretly agree with her assessment, but no one else was allowed to criticize my cousin. "Nonsense," I replied. "Minnie is an ultra-sensitive soul. She feels everything more deeply than the rest of us."

"Oh, yes. Of course. You may find her drama an endearing little quirk, but it drove her classmates nuts during high school."

Minnie rescued me by jumping in with, "Thank you for showing your concern, but as you can see, we don't need help."

Phyllis sniffed. "No problem. You two are busy, so I'll get out of your hair. Don't worry about me. I'll see myself out." She disappeared.

"She's always slinking around," Minnie whispered, "eavesdropping and gathering juicy tidbits of information. She was Lizzie's spy, and a fine, thorough job she made of it. Better go check and make sure Phyllis really leaves."

I raised one eyebrow, but followed Minnie's order. On finding the foyer empty, I made sure to lock the door this time. "I wonder how much she heard," Minnie said when I rejoined her.

"I doubt she heard anything important. When she arrived, we were already searching for the bullet. Neither of us was saying much."

Minnie threw her arms around me in an extravagant bear hug. "Thanks for supporting me. She wanted you to join the deride-Minnie club."

I pushed back and stared at her in surprise. "Aren't you two old friends?"

She shrugged. "More like frenemies. I'm sure Phyllis believes I didn't know about her huge crush on my ex-husband. She drooled over Jimmy all through high school." Minnie extracted her phone and punched in numbers. "I'm calling 9-1-1."

"No, don't." I gripped Minnie's hand to prevent her from completing the call. "There's no point in calling the Mounties. We can't prove a bullet caused the scrape on your arm." More to the point, we would never win the hospitality contest with a Mountie grilling our guests about a shooter.

She scowled at me but cancelled the call and placed the phone in her pocket. "Right. Do you believe someone took a shot at me?"

I hesitated for a beat and nodded. "Your injury does appear to be a bullet wound. But I can't imagine anyone did it on purpose. The shooter was likely a hunter with a bad aim. We'll get to the bottom of it."

"I sincerely hope so. Let me point out to you that in the space of one day, there was one actual death at the comfort stop and another near-death here. That's either a huge coincidence or we've got us a serial killer. Guess what. I don't believe in coincidences."

I had to admit Phyllis had a point. Minnie's drama could drive a person nuts.

Chapter 6: Unsettling News

With difficulty, I managed to coax Minnie into taking an afternoon nap, mainly because I needed a break from her drama. During my free time, I tracked down both my sisters in Abby's office and updated them on recent developments, namely the passenger interviews and Minnie's unverifiable near-murder masked by a totally verifiable cat attack. I avoided their big-sisterly advice by ducking their questions about Hawk, omitting mentioning our torrid affair, and cleverly skipping over our showdown. We agreed to a glass of wine at my place before the kickoff dinner, and I waved a cheery goodbye.

I survived the rest of the day by meeting guests, introducing myself, and delivering an impromptu tour of our facilities including the pool area and spa, racquet courts, and barn.

Finally, after much moisturizing, plucking, and primping, I was more than ready for wine. With a sigh, I wandered into my living room to wait. Lowering myself to the sofa, I gnawed my lower lip, unable to forget our monetary problems, which I suspected were worse than Abby admitted. If I was right, a contest win would generate the increase in business volume we needed to meet our mortgage payments and avoid foreclosure. As a bonus, it would hopefully convince my sisters I'd finally developed business acumen in my old age.

Bottom line? I would go to any lengths to win the contest.

To calm my nerves before Minnie and my sisters' arrival, I decided a brief closed-eye visualization would help. My imaginary forest path, burbling stream, and gentle woodland creatures were so lulling, I fell into a semi-trance until Dodie's voice penetrated my consciousness.

"Move it, Clara. Let's find Minnie and get this show on the road. I need that wine you promised."

Abby was more considerate. "Shhhhh. Can't you see Clara's sleeping? All her worrying about—"

"I'm not sleeping." I popped my eyes open and saw orange. A sea of orange so vivid and so vast, I sprang from my chair. "Pluck a duck, Dodie. What are you wearing?"

"You like?"

"Wow. Your dress is certainly, um, festive."

"I know. I'm all set for Thanksgiving." She pirouetted, all the better to display the full extent of her jaw-dropping glory.

Dodie's elasticized dress was stretched to the max, ending a scant inch below crotch-level. The main event, however, was her boobage. Those puppies bulged and undulated as if alive, straining their way to freedom and creating a cleavage abyss deep enough to stash a phone, lipstick, keys, and wallet.

I said the first thing to pop into my mind. "I had no idea your boobs could point upward."

"I know, right?" Dodie grinned at me. "It was quite a construction job. Abby spent the past hour helping with supports to hold everything in place. She cupped her boobs. "Who knew the girls could be perky again? One minute, they're resting on my tummy, all forlorn and deflated, the next minute, they're winched into place by a miracle garment called *The Ultimate Shaper*."

"Are you sure everything will stay put?" I asked. "Our older guests might freak out if the girls make their escape during dessert."

"There will be no escaping," Abby stated. "Trust me. Those girls are firmly anchored by double-sided tape."

I stared at them doubtfully. "If you say so."

"They'll be fine." Abby's amusement faded and her expression grew somber. "But we may not be. Since we're all here, I have important news. It won't take long. Minnie doesn't need to hear this, so let's go somewhere more private."

As the three of us trooped to my small office, my brain whirled with possibilities, none of them good. Once I closed the door and we got settled, I said, "What's up?"

Abby hesitated. "I phoned the bank manager."

A bolt of alarm shot up my spine. The tornado had destroyed most of our guest cabins as well as damaging the barn and outbuildings. Repairs, re-builds, and renovations had cost a tidy fortune, not to mention losing an entire high season's worth of business. Added to what we already owed for massive renovations, our insurance had covered only a fraction of the debt. We'd had a choice. Refinance or fold. We'd re-amortized Grizzly Gulch.

"What did you and the bank manager discuss?"

Abby fixed her gaze on the view outside the window, where the swimming pool glowed like a turquoise jewel in the setting sun. "I asked for an extension on our next payment."

"That bad? Why didn't you say something sooner?" Our financial situation must be more precarious than I'd thought.

"I didn't want to worry you. You already worry too much."

My shiver had nothing to do with the open window. "And?" I prompted, somehow channeling serenity.

"He said the only way he would offer an extension is if we could show him proof of upcoming business, meaning enough reservations to show him we're fully booked through March. He's given us two months to generate those reservations."

My throat closed up. We now had a deadline.

Dodie asked the next question, the one I was unable to ask. "I thought we had more time. What happens if we can't drum up that kind of business?"

After a prolonged pause, Abby said, "The bank will launch the foreclosure process and we'll lose Grizzly Gulch."

I glanced at Dodie. Her horrified expression echoed mine. Wrestling down my hysteria, I dug deep inside to find a teeny-tiny pocket of inner strength. "Okay then," I said airily. "Lucky for us I entered Grizzly Gulch in the hospitality contest. All we need to do is win first prize."

"We don't stand a chance," Abby said. "It's an international contest. Can you imagine how many competitors we're up against? We have no hope of success."

"Thanks for the vote of confidence, Abs. For your information, in our category, which happens to be *Resorts: Ranches & Farms*, we're currently jockeying for first place along with a dude ranch in Montana and a finca in Argentina. If our Boomers' Thanksgiving Fling generates enough five-star reviews, Grizzly Gulch will shoot to first place. The contest is over after that. We can do it. Given our precarious financial state, losing is not an option."

"But we'll need to be outstanding. Special. Different."

"In that case, let's make sure we are."

Luckily, my doorbell's insistent ringing ended a squabble that showed promise of escalating. "Who can that be?" I muttered. "I'm not expecting anyone else." I rushed to the front door, acutely aware my sisters followed on my heels.

Flinging the door open, I found myself staring at Hawk.

The unexpected arrival caused me to suck in a breath. Hawk threw out testosterone like a force field. A black open-necked shirt, black jeans, and lightweight tan blazer draped his lanky frame. I got a whiff of soap and cologne. Yeah, he smelled as delicious as I remembered.

I stood there blocking the doorway. Wiping sweaty palms on my silky dress and hoping I hadn't stained it, I managed, "What are you doing here? I don't recall inviting you over."

"Clara, where are your manners?" Abby chided.

Dodie took one glance at the visitor and said, "Oh, yeah. I vote we let this one in."

"Relax," he whispered as he squeezed past me and into my foyer. "This isn't about us."

Ignoring the buzzing in my ears, I closed the door behind him and muttered, "Don't be shy. Make yourself at home."

He choked out a low, wry laugh. "Don't mind if I do. Sorry to intrude, ladies, but I'm here about Lizzie's death."

I covered my anxiety by saying, "Let's all take a seat, shall we?" At top speed, I darted ahead, leading the way into the living room.

Dodie and Hawk chose opposite ends of the royal blue Ultrasuede sofa, while Abby and I sank into the floral easy chairs flanking the fireplace. I toed off my lovely high heels, which were killing me. Somehow, they'd shrunk over the summer.

Meowing, Snuggles emerged from behind the curtains.

Abby scowled. "I was hoping someone had taken the beast off your hands by now."

"Aw. And here I thought you loved the cute little kitty-cat."

"Not after he attacked me when I was bringing him inside. All I did was reach into the cat carrier to pet him. I hope he didn't leave a scar." She indicated a bandage on her wrist.

As if to prove his docility, Snuggles leaped onto my lap, circled twice, and curled up, purring. "The poor little guy was traumatized." To keep my hands occupied, I stroked his soft, fuzzy head.

Hawk cleared his throat. "I heard from Atticus."

"The Medical Examiner?" Abby said. "We're old friends. I adore him."

"He conducted a preliminary autopsy, and I wanted to break the news in person."

My pulse kicked into overdrive. "He found something, didn't he?"

"Unfortunately, he did. There was a needle track on Lizzie's right buttock, meaning she was most likely murdered."

A throbbing silence broken only by Snuggles' purring filled the room. Dodie, Abby, and I stared at one another across the coffee table. I could read their minds. *Grizzly Gulch won't survive another murder.* My thin thread of control slipped a notch.

Hawk gave an apologetic shrug. "Toxicology results might tell us more about which drug was used for the injection, but I doubt it. If Lizzie was murdered—and he believes she was—it's unlikely the injected substance will leave a trace, especially if we have a smart killer. All this to say there may never be enough proof to lay charges."

Once I regained the power of speech, I said, "That's not possible. Gabby Chambers told us Lizzie had a heart condition. She died of natural causes."

"Atticus admitted he would have missed the needle track altogether if the jab hadn't snagged Lizzie's jeans, meaning she was fully-dressed when it happened. The puncture wound was so faint he had to use a magnifying glass to see it. The injection likely happened during the scuffle in front of the outhouse."

I scrambled to find a logical reason for the needle mark. "What if Lizzie had diabetes or another medical condition or was mainlining illegal drugs?"

"The first thing Atticus did was contact Lifestyle Manor to request her medical history. It seems she had a faint heart murmur, nothing serious, but there's no indication of a medical condition that would require self-injections. As for mainlining drugs, I have difficulty imagining even the most dedicated junkie would jab herself in the butt through a pair of jeans."

I stroked Snuggles with all my might. "Did you notify Callum?"

"Not yet. He has his hands full. Since there's nothing definitive to tell him, I'm certain he would prefer I wait until the final toxicology report comes in."

"In that case, none of our employees or guests can learn about a suspected murder. If anyone asks, I vote we tell them she likely died of natural causes, and it's too soon for the autopsy results to be released."

He arched his eyebrows but remained silent.

To mitigate our seeming callousness, I described the *Best Vacations* contest that offered us a chance to save Grizzly Gulch from foreclosure.

"Out of curiosity, who's on the suspect list?" Abby asked.

"Everyone on board the Lifestyle Manor minicoach," he said.

I felt the blood drain from my face. "Is Minnie a suspect?"

"If I were in charge of the investigation," he said, "she would head my list."

"In that case, I guess we're lucky you're retired," I muttered under my breath.

Although he was simply stating his opinion of what the official position would be, Dodie pointed her finger at him. "Our Minnie wouldn't hurt a fly."

"Others might argue." He dug into his pocket, dragged out his notepad, and flipped through the pages. "Gabby said, and I quote, 'Let's not forget the little hair-pulling incident'". He flicked the quickest of glances at me. "She was referring to a scuffle between Minnie and Lizzie in front of the outhouse, during which Minnie could have injected Lizzie."

Paralyzed with shock, I stopped stroking Snuggles. "Most of the passengers arrived at the outhouse simultaneously. Minnie was too busy elbowing people out of the way to aim a syringe, and she had no reason to kill Lizzie." Although I had no way of knowing if any of my claims were true, I made sure I radiated confidence.

He referred to his notes again. "Gabby also mentioned how Lizzie and Minnie weren't exactly friends."

"Whoa," Dodie said, scowling at him. "That doesn't make Minnie the killer."

"Exactly," I said. "Here's the thing. Someone shot at Minnie this afternoon." For Hawk's benefit, I recited the shooting-slash-cat-attack story once more, ending with, "We couldn't find the bullet to prove her claim, but the wound sure looks like a bullet furrow. She certainly didn't shoot herself." I cast a silent but desperate glance at my sisters for support.

"Clara's right," Abby interjected, picking up on my cue. "Minnie might be a drama queen, but she's also kind and caring. The latest charity she supports is a shelter for homeless women. She's not the killer."

"Let's assume someone did fire a weapon at Minnie," he said. "The shooter was likely a hunter with a bad aim, in which case, Minnie would still be my number one suspect."

"Since Callum in over-extended," I pointed out, "we have exactly one week to find the real killer before all the suspects head back to Lifestyle Manor."

"There's no 'we' involved," Hawk said, radiating determination. "The killer is dangerous. I want all three of you to stay away from the investigation."

Dodie, Abby, and I exchanged glances. Once again, I knew we were on the same wavelength. *There's no way you can stop us.*

"If you were in charge of the case, who besides Minnie would be the suspects?" I asked casually, hoping to extract as much information from him as possible.

Hawk flipped a page of his notebook. "Let's see. Chirpy recreation coordinator Gabby, lovely English rose Eleanor, her steadfast suitor Wayne, the unassuming Phyllis, and horny man-about-town, Roland." He closed his notebook and shoved it into his pocket. "I wouldn't consider Lois, Flo, or the driver to be suspects, at least not for now. They didn't join the others at the outhouse."

I was secretly pleased to detect a hint of jealousy in his crack about Roland. "How would you go about identifying the killer?"

"The usual way. I imagine Callum sent someone to examine the crime scene for evidence. Since the comfort station is open to the public, I doubt they'll find anything significant. Then I'd run background checks on all the suspects, interview friends and family, colleagues and bosses, and conduct follow-up interviews that focus on their relationships with one another and Lizzie."

Abby jumped in while avoiding looking at me. "I have an idea. Why don't you join us for dinner tonight, Hawk? You might notice something we amateurs would miss."

"I agree," Dodie said.

"That's real kind, ladies. Thank you." His smile was such a force of nature, I sucked in my breath. His whole face lit up, his cheeks creased in the sexiest way, and his eyes flashed with goodwill—or could it be triumph?

I hoped my inward groan wasn't evident.

"Got a problem, Clara?" A crafty smile lit Dodie's face.

A tantrum would feel good right about now. "Actually, yes. Hawk's presence might make the suspects uncomfortable. They all know he's a friend of the Mountie assigned to Lizzie's case. Word will spread. What if everyone thinks he's working undercover?"

"Good point," Dodie said. "We manage their expectations by telling them that it looks like Lizzie died of natural causes, but we'll have to wait for autopsy and toxicology results for the official cause of death. Then if anyone asks about Hawk, we'll say he's an old family friend and we invited him to join us for dinner."

While I racked my brain desperately to think of a good reason to object without revealing my past relationship with Hawk, Dodie leaned across the sofa to place her hand on his arm. "Since Clara has no objection, why don't you attend tomorrow's nature walk as well? The event's a special perk for Minnie and her Lifestyle Manor companions."

"Perfect," he said. "Callum's crazy-busy at home, so I can be his eyes and ears for a day. That way I'll observe the suspects in an informal setting. Anything suspicious, and I'll notify him." He swung a guileless glance at me. "Who knows what could happen?"

"Then it's settled," Abby said.

I took a deep breath then let it out slowly. "Whatever."

Dodie nudged Hawk. "Don't mind Clara. She's always rude when she's nervous, and you seem to make her real jumpy. I'm guessing you're the man she met while she visited her daughter in Vancouver."

Was I so transparent? "Whatever makes you think I met a man?" I demanded. "I never said anything of the sort."

"You've been moping around ever since you got home a couple of months ago, hon. No woman mopes so thoroughly unless there's a man involved."

"Now that you mention it," Abby told Dodie, "she *has* been brooding. I confess I blamed her mood swings on dwindling hormones."

I could have kicked my sisters. "You're imagining things," I mumbled.

"Clara was brooding?" Hawk asked hopefully, swinging his gaze to me. "I'd never have guessed."

Dodie pumped a fist in the air. "Aha. I was right."

"It's getting late," I said, changing the subject. "We need to go down to dinner. I wonder where Minnie is."

Dodie refused to be diverted. "You ran away from a hot Mountie? Are you out of your ever-lovin' mind?"

I sighed with relief at the sound of footsteps clicking down the hall. A moment later, Minnie stepped into the living room.

"*Mew.*" Snuggles leaped from my lap and disappeared behind the curtains.

"Ta-da," Minnie said, twirling to give us the full visual effect.

She'd done something sophisticated with her hair, coaxing the white curls to tumble over one shoulder. The slinky gold dress emphasized the gold flecks in her hazel eyes and transformed her from tall and gangly to regal and sophisticated. I noticed Hawk studying the flesh-colored adhesive strip on her arm.

"You clean up very nicely," I said. "Majestic suits you."

"Thanks. You three are lovely too." She stooped to bestow air kisses on both sides of my face, enveloping me in a cloud of patchouli. She favored my sisters with identical treatment. To me, she offered, "Your dress is perfect, Clara. The color matches your beautiful blue eyes, it flatters your breasts, and the clever drape of the fabric masks those hips." She circled Abby, who was wearing her all-occasion little black dress. "I do declare. Aren't you the living, breathing picture of elegance? I adore what you've done to your hair." After bestowing her full attention on Dodie, a broad smile curled Minnie's lips. "As for the lady in orange, words cannot express my awe at your, uh, sense of adventure. I predict you will be the hit of the evening."

I squeezed into my shoes and stood beside Minnie to avoid walking with Hawk. "We'd better head downstairs right away. We mustn't be late."

Once we were all in my foyer, Abby opened the front door. That was when Snuggles, his tail a-twitch, galloped down the hallway toward us, a furry missile headed straight for Minnie.

She stooped to pluck Snuggles from the floor in one smooth movement. Holding him at arm's length, she hip-checked me aside and tossed the squirming cat at the open doorway.

Releasing an indignant yowl, Snuggles flew past Dodie, Abby, and Hawk, to land in the corridor. Making a swift about-face, he darted back inside, ducked between our feet, and raced to safety.

Minnie pushed everyone out into the corridor and closed the door behind us. "I don't feel safe with that animal anywhere near me," she muttered.

"Hey, at least for now, he's my cat," I yelled, staring at Minnie in shock. "Get used to him."

"I can't believe you did that," Hawk said.

Minnie glanced at Hawk's baffled expression. "That beast hates my guts," she explained.

A smile tugged at the corner of Hawk's lips. "Ah, yes. That explains why you threw a perfectly good cat away. Are we ready?"

During our short walk to the dining hall, Minnie said to me, "Sorry about Snuggles. In my defence, he did attack me."

"He didn't mean to."

"Whatever." Minnie moved closer and whispered, "I'm here for you if you ever want to talk about your relationship with Hawk."

"What do you mean?"

"it's obvious you both have feelings for one another."

I suppressed the urge to throttle my cousin. "You have a great imagination, hon."

"Maybe you can fool yourself but you can't fool me. I see right through you."

I turned away to hide my eye roll. Despite Minnie's reputation for analyzing people, she was off the mark about my love life. Way off. The only reason I'd agreed to tolerate Hawk's presence at dinner was so that he could help us to nail a killer.

Chapter 7: The Great Escape

SINCE OLDER GUESTS TENDED TO eat early, I'd scheduled the evening meal for 7:00 p.m. Although we'd arrived five minutes early, the Hoodoo Dining Room was hopping, with many of our sixty-eight guests already seated. Each table held several bottles of wine, both red and white, to ensure an abundant selection. Based on the brimming glasses and uproarious laughter, festivities were well underway.

Two walls of windows offered a spectacular view of the undulating Alberta foothills enveloped by evening shadows. The setting sun gilded the white peaks of the distant Rockies, casting an alpenglow of soft and subtle pinks, purples, and reds against the darkening blue. Soon, a shimmering spill of stars would spray across the black night sky.

While we waited for the hostess, Dodie and Abby whispered to one another. Unable to eavesdrop, I laughed gaily with Minnie as proof to myself and everyone else how unaffected I was by Hawk's presence. Minnie was in mid-sentence when I spied a table where Lois, Flo, and three other guests had gathered with Zeke, our sexy barn manager who also happened to be Abby's main squeeze. Two vacant seats remained.

Interrupting an endless anecdote about her acting career, I tugged Minnie's arm and pointed. "Let's sit over there."

"Really?" Minnie wrinkled her nose. "Flo wears those disposable underwear thingies. I don't want to eat next to someone who might be … you know … at the table."

"That's okay, hon," Abby assured her. "I'd like to sit next to Zeke." With Dodie hot on her heels, the pair sped away to occupy the last two places.

My glare should have caused their heads to explode. My meddling older sisters always thought they knew what was best for me. My guess was they'd orchestrated the seating arrangements to ensure I would end up at the same table as Hawk.

My suspicions grew when Dodie and Abby put their heads together, giggled, and snagged the Monique, the hostess, who was one of our favorite employees. Always ready for fun, she listened, laughed, and headed toward us at a good clip, her blonde hair fastened in an elaborate twist on top of her head. On reaching my side, she said, "I'm supposed to give you a message from your sisters." She backed away and beckoned for me to follow.

I left Minnie's side to join the hostess. "Why all the cloak and dagger?"

"Dodie warned me you would freak out because you're trying to avoid a certain sexy, retired Mountie. If I wasn't happily married, I wouldn't mind having a go at him myself, but I digress. They told me to tell you, (a) the seating arrangement is their gift to you, (b) to stop being such an idiot, and (c) you're welcome."

I was still absorbing this not-so-cryptic message when Monique spoke up. "Good news, folks. I've found a table with empty seating for all three of you. Follow me, please."

Since I had no choice unless I made a scene—and my sisters knew I would rather poke my eyes out with a blunt stick than cause a scene—I joined Minnie and Hawk to trail along behind Monique. At the other table, my sisters smiled like a pair of Cheshire cats. I slowed down to scowl back and give them the universal two-fingered "I'm watching you" sign. They both replied with finger-waves.

Minnie matched my pace. "What was that little interaction all about?" she asked.

"Nothing. Absolutely nothing." I glowered at my sisters one more time, and we trotted to catch up with the others.

Phyllis, Gabby, Eleanor, and Wayne were already seated at a table for nine, leaving five vacant chairs side-by-side. Noticing a lineup at the entrance, I assured Monique we would seat ourselves, and she should tend to the last stragglers.

She did not protest.

On my assumption that Minnie would enjoy sitting beside her old high school friend, I sat in one of the middle seats, leaving the chair beside Phyllis empty. Minnie, however, was chatting with Wayne while, based on Eleanor's expression, pissing off his lady-love. I'd barely opened my mouth to tell Hawk I was saving the seat beside Phyllis for my cousin, when he lowered himself into the chair in question. There was nothing I could do without making a scene.

Phyllis, unremarkable in a gray dress with a matching gray jacket, twisted her head to check out her neighbor. After acknowledging Hawk with a slight nod, she turned away.

Roland, another latecomer, darted forward to claim the empty seat on my other side, leaving Minnie with no choice but to take the remaining vacant seat. Too bad for her she was wedged between the two Lifestyle Manor residents she detested most—Eleanor-the-English-Rose, draped in a flounced dress with a plunging neckline, who appeared to be skin-grafted to the ever-tolerant Wayne, and Roland-the-Raunchy, who resembled a lounge lizard in an elegant white jacket coupled with black pants and a pink silk shirt, unbuttoned to display tufts of graying chest hair.

To put the diners at ease, I arranged my face in a social smile and said, "Good evening, fun-seekers. You're all looking very festive. I hope everyone's relaxed and ready to party."

"What's with the Mountie's good buddy here?" Roland asked, jabbing a thumb in Hawk's direction. "Is he here to spy on us?"

Oozing testosterone, Hawk bared his teeth at Roland in what might pass for friendliness to, say, a pride of lions. "Since you asked so nicely, no, I'm not here to spy on anyone. I'm here because Clara and her sisters are close friends of mine." Under his breath, he asked me, "Exactly how close are we supposed to be?"

I chose to ignore both Hawk's question and the roaring in my ears, and hastened to rescue the situation. "Hawk was free this evening, so we invited him to join us for dinner."

"But he's a friend of the Mountie in charge of Lizzie's case." Eleanor pointed out. "Isn't that a little odd?"

My muscles tensed. Would Hawk reveal the ME's initial examination results?

Hawk shot Eleanor the same grin he'd used to charm me out of my special panties. "Not at all. I'm an old family friend."

Fortunately, Katie, our young Australian server, pre-empted more evasions by offering to pour wine. She got nine takers.

I was swallowing a bracing gulp when Wayne extricated his arm from Eleanor's grip, stood, and ambled around the table to hover beside me. Bending over, he said in a confidential tone, "I have a question."

"Certainly. How can I help you?"

"When can Eleanor ride the mechanical bull we noticed at the back of the barn? I'd like to schedule a couple of sessions." He glanced at Eleanor before murmuring, "She's always dreamed of riding a mechanical bull. I want to be the one to make it happen."

I struggled to stay calm. "Sorry, Wayne. We decided that Bucking Bully is too dangerous for seniors to ride."

"Eleanor doesn't see herself as a senior. She won't be happy with your answer." He stomped back to his seat.

Thinking that Eleanor would have to deal with this minor frustration in life's great journey, I polished off my wine and stood. On reaching the podium, I welcomed our guests and acknowledged the tragic demise of Elizabeth Fournier, known to all as Lizzie. After a brief speech, during which I scrambled for words to describe a woman who, apparently, was less than popular with many of her travel companions, I toasted Lizzie before introducing Chef Armand to review the Thanksgiving week's dining plan. Wild applause indicated either interest or inebriation, likely both, and allowed me to scurry back to my table.

Our head chef, a man of great girth, talent, and temperament, marched into the dining hall, white hat slightly askew. Of indeterminate age, I guessed him to be in his fifties. A broad smile indicated one of his rare affable moods. Perhaps he'd enjoyed a slug or two of the good stuff he hid on a high kitchen shelf especially for such occasions.

I would bet my bottom dollar no other ranch in the contest had a chef quite like Chef Armand. This might or might not work in our favor.

"*Bon soir, mes amis*, good evening my friends," he shouted into the microphone. His bellow silenced the room.

Some guests had the audacity to continue their conversation, prompting him to yell, "*Silence s'il vous plait*. Please be silent."

A corner table of women, clearly avid happy hour fans, continued chatting and giggling.

He paused, glared, then roared, "*Immédiatement*."

The air pulsated in the resulting silence.

"*Merci, mes amis*. Thank you my friends," he hollered into the mic. "This week will be a Canadiana gustatory experience for Grizzly Gulch's cherished guests. My chefs will prepare much unique Canadian food.

"What sort of unique Canadian food?" Dodie asked, winking at him.

"*Bien*, most lovely lady." He winked back. "I am so happy you inquire. For example, during *les petits déjeuners*, the breakfasts, we will feature much Canadian bacon. At other meals, we will serve many Canadian dishes of, how do you say, *qualité supérieure*." For example, *tourtière* and *cipaille*, with *féves au lard* and *poutine*. For dessert, there will be treats like *chômeur*, *tarte au sucre*, and Nanaimo bars. For the more adventurous gourmet, there will be *langues de morue,* even beaver tails. You can ask me later what those delicacies are."

He whirled and disappeared into the kitchen.

We placed our orders with Katie, during which time I wanted to throttle Eleanor for issuing detailed instructions about her meal, covering the seasoning, cooking methods, and food presentation. Once Katie scuttled away, I said, "I hope you all enjoyed your first afternoon at Grizzly Gulch."

"I had a lovely time," Gabby assured me. "I visited your sweet little goats and their llama. Golly, those goats sure are cute."

I took this as an opportunity to promote an activity. "The goats are used in goat yoga, which is extremely popular."

"What? Your goats practice yoga?" Gabby asked with a giggle.

I shook my head. "Goat yoga is regular yoga, but carried out in tandem with real, live goats we trained to interact with participants in specific poses. I urge you all to try a session. Many of our reviews mention the sheer fun of our goat yoga classes."

"And the llama?" Roland asked.

I sipped my wine and said, "Did you know llamas are fantastic guard animals?"

"How fascinating. I had no idea." Roland's smile bathed me in sunshine.

Paying not the slightest bit of attention to the low rumble in the back of Hawk's throat, I knocked back a huge slug of wine. "It's true. Larry the llama protects our goats from coyotes, dogs, foxes and such. As for larger predators like bears or cougars, he's too smart to attack them, but on occasion, he has warned us danger is near." I encompassed both Roland and Gabby in an expansive gesture. "I hope I can coax you both into signing up for goat yoga."

"I wouldn't dream of missing it," Gabby assured me. "I love yoga and I adore goats."

Aided by wine, the warmth of kinship washed over me. "It seems you and I are in a similar profession. I'm called an events manager, you're a recreation coordinator. I fell into this position when we inherited Grizzly Gulch, mainly because my sisters nominated me. What led you into this career path?" I was blatantly fishing for personal information, anything at all that might illuminate dark motives for murder.

Gabby's eyes sparkled. "I adore working with the elderly. As a teen, I volunteered at a long-term care facility to help with meals, read to the residents, that kind of thing. I always knew I wanted a career working around older people, so I got my Masters of Social Work. A top retirement home in Edmonton hired me."

"What was the home's name?" I asked, sensing the conversation had captured Hawk's attention. Improvising, I explained, "I have friends living near Edmonton. They're hunting for a good retirement home for his parents, one offering staged levels of care to meet their needs as they age."

Before she could answer, our starters arrived—steak 'n' bacon bites with béarnaise sauce for some, country kitchen button biscuits with jam and ham for others.

"What a feast. I'm ravenous. Let's not talk shop right now," Gabby said. "I'm more than happy to discuss retirement homes later." She raised her voice to address Minnie, who sat directly across the table. "Minnie, I want to thank you for mentioning the Boomers' Thanksgiving Fling to me. What a wonderful idea, especially for residents who don't have anyone to spend Thanksgiving with."

Eleanor toyed with a steak bite, sawing it into quarters and using her knife to maneuver a morsel onto her fork before smearing on béarnaise sauce. Success achieved, she said, "I'm certain Minnie only wanted to indulge in more poker games with Wayne since you've banned poker at Lifestyle Manor." Her British accent was less crisp than usual, likely due to free booze consumed during Happy Hour combined with dinner wine.

Gabby said, "Good golly, I banned those games due to the violence."

Phyllis, who'd been silent up until that point, was quick to add, "Those poker games sure did cause a ruckus." Her pale gray eyes were alight with malice.

Minnie flushed a deep and rather alarming shade of scarlet.

"I heard Minnie and Lizzie got into quite a knock-up fight after the last poker game," Eleanor said in a conversational tone. "Players had to pry you two apart."

Minnie plunked her fork down and swiveled in her chair to glare at Eleanor. "Lizzie was a lousy poker player, lost a small fortune to me over several poker nights. She accused me of cheating. I never cheat. I don't have to. One thing led to another. I might have called her a fat cow. Next thing I knew, she attacked me. Players had to pry her off me. The woman was vicious. See this?" Minnie peeled her lips back to reveal her teeth. "She ruined my veneers and chipped my tooth. I'll look like Snaggletooth until my dental appointment next month. Too bad Lizzie's dead because I'd planned to make her reimburse my dental work."

I tried to steer Hawk's attention away from Minnie, venturing, "Eleanor, I love your British accent. What part of England are you from?"

"Oh, a twee little town outside London. I doubt you would know it."

Twee?

"When did you come to Canada?" Hawk asked, switching his laser-focus to Eleanor.

"I came over as a young woman and married a Canadian. The change was a terrible shock for me—the frigid winters, the miserably hot summers, the mosquitoes, and please don't get me started on the sheer boredom due to lack of, er, social and cultural environments."

I was about to ask Eleanor some pointed questions about her background when Phyllis annoyed me by chiming in. "Yadda, yadda, yadda. English rose versus wild frontier. Boring. We've heard the story a million times."

Beside me, Hawk's laser focus remained on Eleanor, who'd made short work of her appetizer. After forking up her last morsel of steak dripping with béarnaise, she positioned knife and fork together on the plate. "Minnie," she said, taking a moment to dab her lips with her napkin, "I hope you aren't too upset about tonight's seating."

Minnie's forehead creased. "What are you jabbering about? Why would I be upset?"

Eleanor groped for Wayne's hand and entwined her fingers with his. "You can't flirt with Wayne over dinner."

Minnie's nostrils flared. "I don't flirt with Wayne."

My tension mounted.

Wayne gave Minnie an apologetic shrug before raising Eleanor's hand and kissing her palm. "You have nothing to worry about, sweetheart. You're the only woman for me. Besides, we all know Minnie is interested in someone else."

That was a newsflash. Minnie had made no mention of a new man in her life. I intended to quiz her later.

Eleanor pouted at Wayne. "But you're always sneaking off to be with her."

"Minnie's teaching me how to play poker so I can sit in on your poker games. It was going to be a surprise."

After a beat, Eleanor said, "You're learning to play poker because of me? Brilliant." She half-stood, flung her arms around his neck, and planted a huge kiss on Wayne's cheek, branding him with a bright pink lipstick smear.

Roland closed in and whispered to me, "Eleanor's a mean-spirited, cold-blooded shark. Tell Minnie not to let the woman get to her."

Surprised at his consideration of Minnie's feelings, I said, "Thanks. I will."

An abrupt movement attracted my attention. Hawk had propped his arms on the table and was shamelessly eavesdropping on every word of my conversation with Roland.

Roland ignored Hawk and said in a sexy rumble, "After dinner, I'm taking a taxi to the casino up the road. Why don't you join me? A little roulette will take your mind off work."

He was handsome, attentive, and charming. Strangely, I didn't feel the teeniest spark of interest. Bearing in mind Minnie's warning that Roland was a con artist and gigolo, I said, "Much as I'd love to, tonight's not good for me."

"Aw, come on. It'll be fun."

Hawk said, "You heard the lady. Don't pressure her into a date she doesn't want." Anger pulsed off him in waves.

Minnie, who was working on her second glass of wine, said, "It seems we have a little macho competition happening over Clara. If you ask me, Hawk's a vast improvement over Roland."

Roland swung toward Minnie. "I don't recall anyone asking for your opinion." His furious scowl contradicted his calm words.

Luckily, our server arrived, interrupting what was shaping up to be an acrimonious exchange. Katie lowered the loaded tray onto a serving table and doled out the poached salmon entrées. Once finished, she said, "I'll be back in a jiffy with the pork tenderloin orders."

"Yoo-hoo. Don't forget my apple sauce," Eleanor yelled at the server's retreating back. "And don't forget I want my meat pink, gravy on the side, no potato, and lightly cooked broccoli instead of those yukky green beans."

"I hear you have a new suitor, Minnie," Gabby said. "It's a shame he couldn't join you."

With a tight little smirk, Phyllis said, "Don't tell me one of your boyfriends has dumped the queen of Lifestyle Manor already."

Minnie shrugged. "Of course not. He hated to miss this trip, but he got a last-minute invitation to join his son's family during the holiday weekend."

I wanted to know more about the man in Minnie's life. Then again, there had been no time for a heart-to-heart exchange.

The pork dishes arrived. Everyone, even Eleanor, appeared to put hard feelings aside and demolished their meals with gusto. Chef Armand had outdone himself again.

I couldn't wait for the evening to end.

Everyone had gobbled down dessert and was working on coffee and after-dinner drinks when the calls of, "Tur-kee! Tur-kee!" rang out.

I glared across the room at Dodie.

She smiled back and waggled her fingers.

I shook my head in silent warning.

If anything, her smile broadened, no doubt at the prospect of creating a scene. Unlike me, Dodie loved a scene.

I drew a finger across my throat in a slashing motion.

She winked back.

"What's going on between you and your sister?" Hawk asked.

"They want Dodie to do her turkey-gobble imitation. I'd hoped we could get through our kickoff dinner without any of her, ah, weirdness. Also, I'm not a hundred percent certain her dress can withstand more chest expansion."

The calls of "Tur-kee! Tur-kee!" grew louder, more insistent.

Dodie popped up and blew kisses to the room. Her orange dress clung to her ample curves like a second skin. The applause dwindled slowly, replaced by an expectant hush.

With much fanfare, Dodie sucked in a deep breath. In response, her rib cage expanded and her exposed bosom quivered most alarmingly. Through pursed lips, she produced a wavering turkey gobble, admittedly not her best effort.

The crowd didn't care. They went wild. Servers stood still. Kitchen staff emerged, with Chef Armand leading the way. Demands for more rang out.

The clincher occurred when someone shouted, "Louder!" Someone else took up the cry and soon the dining hall echoed with shouts of, "Louder! Louder!"

Dodie raised both arms and waited. Once a hush descended, she cupped her hands around her mouth. With her eyes squeezed shut, she took one deep breath followed by several more. Each breath caused more chest expansion. Her boobage undulated, threatening to spring free from the supporting Lycra.

I silently willed *The Ultimate Shaper* to continue its Herculean support task.

Although I sat two tables away, the twang of double-sided tape snapping as it released its payload was unmistakable.

In an epic wardrobe malfunction, those quadruple-Ds sprang wild and free. For several seconds, nipples seemed to be everywhere. Eventually, the girls settled down, swinging in glorious and somewhat pendulous abandon.

But quitting wasn't in Dodie's vocabulary. Clapping her hands over the unruly twins, she demanded help.

Ever the gentleman, Zeke emptied two bread baskets and handed them to Abby, who in turn applied them to the appropriate areas for containment. After much fumbling by Dodie and some assistance from Abby, they managed to wrestle the girls into submission. With Abby clamping the bread baskets to her chest, Dodie cupped her hands around her mouth again and produced the day's loudest and longest series of gobbles yet, until she dissolved into helpless cackles of laughter along with the audience.

One of Dodie's most endearing character traits was her ability to laugh at herself.

While the audience exploded with calls of, "Encore," cheers, and wolf-whistles, Dodie, Abby, and the bread baskets rushed from the dining hall, presumably for wardrobe adjustments.

I whispered to Minnie, "That went well, don't you think? I'm going to sneak out."

"Coward. You're only leaving so you can avoid Hawk."

I ignored her comment. "Feel free to stay and enjoy the evening."

"Hawk's a keeper," Minnie whispered. "If you let him go, you deserve to be a lonely and bitter old maid with only your horrid cat to keep you company. A man like Hawk deserves happiness, and if you won't make him happy, rest assured there are plenty who will try."

All I could focus on was that Hawk and I would be thrown together again on tomorrow's nature walk. I fled the dining hall.

I limped to my apartment with Minnie's words lodged in my brain.

Chapter 8: Nature Walk Begins

I'd left the dining hall after dinner in a foul temper. My sleepless night didn't improve my mood any the following morning. I'd preplanned today's nature walk specifically for Minnie and her Lifestyle Manor companions. Who knew they would turn out to be suspects in a passenger's death? And if that wasn't stressful enough, Dodie had gone and invited Hawk—the very man I wanted to avoid—to join us. With Abby's able assistance, the pair thrown us together for an entire morning.

Too bad my big sisters would be bitterly disappointed to learn their matchmaking efforts had failed. There would be no romance in my future. Not today, not tomorrow, not ever. My mission today was threefold—provide an informative and enjoyable experience to guests in the hopes of scoring some five-star reviews, ensure that no one killed Minnie, and, most important of all, maintain a sensible distance from Hawk.

No surprise, I was first to arrive on the lodge's side porch at 8:55 a.m. Throughout my childhood, the sight of my father smacking my older sisters around for being late had taught me promptness was a virtue. My late husband's fists had reinforced the message. Unlike my father, Russ had no qualms about inflicting physical punishment on the baby of the family.

I lowered myself into a red Adirondack chair to savor the crisp October morning while admiring the mile upon mile of grasses upholstering the Alberta foothills. A light breeze scented with autumn leaves and underscored with pine ruffled my hair and went a long way to improving my mood.

Footsteps alerted me to another early arrival. When Hawk rounded the corner, a lightning bolt of awareness shot through me, and I swallowed hard to avoid drooling. He wore chinos and an unzipped lightweight hoodie over a plain, white tee-shirt, which lovingly molded his chest. With a wary head-tilt, he sank into the chair beside me. A whiff of soap and sexy man made my pulse scramble. I could swear my bones went squishy.

To hide my reaction, I injected my voice with ice. "Good morning, Hawk."

"Think we could call a truce?" he suggested.

Heat rose in my face. He was right, of course. "Sure."

He studied me. "You feeling all right?"

"Never better."

"You're a bit flushed."

My face grew hotter. He probably assumed I was having a hot flash, instead of feeling frisky. "It's unseasonably warm out today, don't you think?"

"Not at all. I was wishing I'd worn a heavier jacket."

I gazed longingly at the path leading around back and far away from Hawk's scrutiny. Since flight was unthinkable, I stayed put.

Roland's approach was a welcome interruption. He was impeccably dressed in a baby blue turtleneck under a matching pullover, navy slacks with knife-edge creases, and well-shined boots. He zeroed in on me like a homing pigeon. A dazzling smile showcased excellent veneers. "Good morning, foxy lady," he said by way of greeting. "My, my. Don't you look delectable today?" He leaned against the porch railing.

I shoved clenched fists into the pockets of my purple fleece. His overt attention was making me uncomfortable. To end it, I said, "You're a silver-tongued devil, but flattery will get you nowhere."

The clatter of more footsteps interrupted a potentially awkward situation. Wayne, encumbered by Eleanor clinging to his arm, approached us. I wasn't sure if she was staking her claim or needed support to stand. From his harried expression, I was guessing both. The man was a saint.

"Good morning, everyone," Wayne greeted us. "What a glorious day for a hike."

"That's debatable," Eleanor mumbled, her face hidden within the shade cast by her floppy sun hat.

"Someone might have consumed a wee bit too much wine last night," Wayne said, his tone indulgent.

"Rubbish. I'm in top-notch condition."

While Eleanor protested, Minnie, in full tourist chic of cargo jacket, turtleneck, and pants, a slouchy safari hat, hiking boots, and a small backpack, burst onto the scene in time to hear Eleanor's denial. Removing her sunglasses, my cousin scrutinized Eleanor's face and winced. "Ouch. Definitely not top-notch. Your greenish tinge tells me you have—what do you Brits say?—a hum-dinger of a hangover." She released a bray of laughter.

Eleanor scowled back. "And you, my dear, are dressed like a big game hunter from one of your second-rate plays. All you need is a gun."

"What do you think's in my backpack?" Minnie's tone had all the delicacy of battery acid.

"Tell me you're not bringing a gun," I whispered to Minnie in alarm.

Minnie leaned over and murmured in my ear, "Of course not. I hate guns. But Eleanor doesn't know that."

An uneasy silence settled over us as the newcomers found chairs. I wondered if Hawk was toting a gun. Luckily, Gabby's arrival with Phyllis, who was decked out in matching mud-brown everything, broke the tension.

"Good morning, all," Gabby said, adjusting her Toronto Blue Jays baseball cap as she bounced onto the porch. "I can't wait to see what Mother Nature has in store for us today." She giggled as if she'd said something amusing.

"Nothing good, so far," Eleanor muttered. "Is anyone else joining us?"

"No," I replied, standing. "This is it. Lois declined because of her bad hip. Flo volunteered to keep her company." To forestall more discussion, I kicked into action by delivering my rehearsed spiel about elk avoidance. Although the elk rutting season was ending, the bull elk were still aggressive and would happily attack anyone in the vicinity. Too many unwary tourists ignored advice to stay a safe distance away from the elk. Some were lucky enough to survive.

"What about bears?" Eleanor asked.

"Bears are busy fattening up for hibernation. They won't attack unless you surprise them, so I advise you to make noise. Whistle, laugh, talk to one another. But in case we meet one, I brought two canisters of bear spray."

"And cougars?" With an exaggerated shudder, Eleanor removed her gigantic sunhat and handed it to Wayne for safekeeping. Like something that size could get lost.

Ignoring Eleanor's disapproving frown, Wayne crumpled the hat and stuffed it into his pocket. "Don't you go worrying about anything, honey-lamb. I'll protect you from critters."

"There's nothing to worry about," I said. "We haven't had a cougar sighting for several years, but they don't like bear spray any more than the bears do. I'll take one canister and lead the way." I gestured at Hawk. "I'm hoping Hawk will volunteer to take the other bear spray and follow behind to make sure no one straggles off."

Hawk took the canister without comment, no doubt recognizing my ploy to keep him at arm's length.

After distributing walking sticks, I said, "We'll hike as far as the waterfall."

Phyllis tapped my arm. "I read something about an abandoned silver mine in the vicinity. It's near a waterfall. Will we be able to see the mine?"

"Oooh, how exciting," Gabby said, clapping her hands. "I do hope so."

"The mine is called Rushing Waters. Sorry to disappoint, but it's off-limits to the public."

My announcement met with such a chorus of disappointment, I felt compelled to elaborate. "It was abandoned during the late 1800s when the silver ran out. After an earthquake hit the area, a massive crevice opened up inside the mine's entrance. Locals boarded up the entrance. Then back in the '60s, two hikers disappeared near here. It's said the pair pried off some boards and snuck inside the mine hoping to find nuggets. Their bodies were never found. Most believe they fell into the abyss. A few years ago, Parks Canada strengthened the barricade. Entry is strictly prohibited."

"Too bad. I've always wanted to see an abandoned mine," Phyllis said wistfully.

We set off with me leading and everyone else strung out behind. Although Hawk trailed the pack, I was hyper-aware of his presence, a strangely comforting feeling. Glancing over my shoulder, I noted Phyllis had attached herself to Minnie, closely followed by Roland, Gabby, and finally, the inseparable duo of Eleanor and Wayne. Given Eleanor's hangover and Wayne's tendency to stop for a smooch, Hawk had his work cut out for him to ensure the pair kept up with everyone else.

As we walked, I let my troubles fall away. Even the weather seemed happy. The sun shone warm in a sky shimmering with pure, clear blue. I filled my lungs with sweet mountain air flowing down from the Rockies.

The forest closed in on us, and the air grew chilly. Avoiding embedded rocks and tree roots, I led the way along a dirt path, which paralleled the river but avoided the rim. Crumbling edges posed a threat to the careless hiker, who might tumble all too easily into the treacherous waters below.

I stumbled and recovered my footing, aware of the bear spray's comforting weight in my pocket. I gave a running commentary, pointing out how overhead, wind sang through the pines and gray jays clicked and chattered warnings to one another. There was great excitement when a flock of white-tailed ptarmigan burst into flight with a series of guttural clucks. I explained how their twig-brown feathers would turn snow white, making them virtually invisible during the winter.

I twisted my head to verify everyone was keeping up. To my dismay, Roland was way too close behind me. To hide my uneasiness, I continued my spiel on the vegetation, animals, and birds. I doubted anyone paid attention, but it saved me from having to fend him off.

After we'd walked for another fifteen minutes, the sound of surging water increased, and a faint track leading to the viewpoint opened up. Continuing my chatter, I strode onto the track, halting at a granite outcrop with a view of the churning river. The water was a remarkable shade of milky turquoise from dissolved minerals in the glacier melt.

Once everyone came together, we marveled in silence at the hypnotic power of the river as it squeezed between narrowed banks before widening into an ever-changing surge of froth-laced water.

White-faced and immobile, Minnie stared into the rushing water. "I never learned to swim." She gave a dramatic shudder.

Phyllis chuckled. "It's true. Minnie always wears a life jacket if she's anywhere near Lifestyle Manor's pool."

Minnie shrugged. "I don't take chances around the water."

Gabby pointed downstream. "Why is there a rope with red flags tied to it stretched across the river?"

"Glacier Falls is around the next curve," I explained. "The rope is a rescue line to prevent boaters or anyone who falls in from being swept over the falls. Several people drowned before Parks Canada installed the rope and life rings."

Minnie gestured downstream. "I saw an eagle, or maybe it was osprey. Let's find it." She whirled around and darted past me, heading back to the main pathway.

I hurried to overtake her, saying, "Let me go ahead of you. I have the bear spray."

Minnie let me pass and waited for Phyllis. Behind me, they chatted about their high school days.

Happy to walk alone, I knew with certainty I could rely on Hawk to ensure the remaining guests' safety.

Once I arrived at the main path, Minnie and Phyllis were close behind. There was still no sign of the others. They must be well back. Bushes forced us to walk single file. Although hidden by underbrush, the river roared toward Glacier Falls and its freefall into Dead Man's Gorge.

"It's definitely an osprey," Minnie shouted. "I saw it fly toward the river. See? There's its nest."

Sure enough, a dead tree's bare bones towered black against the cloudless sky. The messy pile of sticks and twigs balanced precariously on the highest branch must be the nest. Swinging my gaze around, I let out a low growl. Minnie and Phyllis had disappeared. Sighing, I backtracked along the main path until I saw the faintest of animal trails approaching the river. Someone, likely Minnie, had tossed the barricade aside.

"Minnie!" I yelled. "Turn back. The river bank is unstable here. You do not, I repeat, do *not*, want to end up in the river."

Minnie's words floated on the breeze. "We're fine."

I peered down the trail toward the dead tree in time to catch Phyllis disappearing around a curve.

I checked the main trail behind me, but the rest were still out of sight. If I followed Minnie and Phyllis, no one would know our whereabouts. Surely the pair could keep one another safe for a few more minutes. In an agony of uncertainty, I waited for everyone else.

Once the group reached me, I explained what had happened.

Hawk's brows slammed together. "If necessary, I will hog-tie them and drag them back. I want everyone to wait here." He swung his gaze to me, adding under his breath, "This bunch here needs you here to keep them calm. Don't worry. If either of them falls in, I'm a strong swimmer."

Hawk disappeared down the animal trail toward the osprey tree, leaving me to entertain a group of disgruntled guests and ensure their safety. Once he was out of sight, Gabby squeezed past me by executing a couple of bounces, saying, "I had to vouch for everyone's safety before Lifestyle Manor would give us permission for this outing. I must find Minnie and Phyllis."

Short of tackling Gabby to the ground, I had no way of stopping her.

"I've never seen an osprey's nest," Wayne said. "Let's go, Eleanor."

Apparently Roland felt the same way.

They all loped toward the river, leaving me to hurry after them. So much for my authority. Muttering under my breath, I squeezed through the underbrush after them.

The rescue line spanning the torrent was tied around the osprey tree's trunk. The other end was lost in a stand of lodgepole pines on the far side. Locals called this spot the point of no return.

Parks Canada employees had hung two pre-packaged white life preserver rings, each with its coiled rope, on the trunk. The roar of thundering water filled the air. Glacier Falls, a mere 200 feet downriver, crashed into Dead Man's Gorge.

My nerves rode the surface of my skin. Where was everyone? Surely Hawk had prevented them from heading downriver toward the waterfall.

I hollered his name and held my breath.

A moment later, his answering shout floated from upriver.

I blew out a relieved sigh and picked my way along the path. A short distance upriver, two pre-packaged orange life jacket vests, each with a coiled rope, hung on the cliff rising from the path. Dense underbrush clawed at my fleece, snagging the fabric. I should have worn a windbreaker.

Bursting into an open area, I found Hawk standing alone and pacing, his features tight with worry. Everyone else milled around upstream, jockeying for position along the river bank, stopping occasionally to stare into the water and point. Minnie, the farthest away, stood on a granite shelf hemmed in by bushes.

"Get down from there, Minnie!" I shouted. "You don't want to fall in."

"This is the best spot," Minnie hollered back. "I can see dozens of fish from here."

Hawk must have been watching for me. Keeping his gaze fixed on the guests, he edged sideways until we stood shoulder to shoulder. "Thank God you're here. I don't know how you keep track of everyone. They won't stay together."

"Welcome to my world."

"We didn't see an osprey, but then an eagle flew upstream. They all followed the bird. Then Phyllis saw a huge fish in the water. Apparently the river is teeming with them. Now, they're planning a return visit to do some fishing."

"Yeah. Sometimes it's like herding cats." I glanced upstream, searching for Minnie.

The splash was barely audible over the roar of Glacier Falls.

After I did a quick head count, a feeling of doom gripped me. Every guest except Minnie was present and accounted for. Fearing the worst, I swung my gaze to the churning river.

Chapter 9: Disaster & Heroism

My heart lodged in my windpipe. Minnie, sweeping along in the foaming water, flailed her arms in a wild attempt to keep her head above the surface. Her safari hat bobbed behind her, still attached by its drawstring tie.

"Minnie!" I shouted, running along the bank beside her, leaping over rocks and branches, trying to match her rapid pace while the current swept her downriver. "Kick your feet. If you drown I'll never forgive you."

Truth be told, I would never forgive myself for letting her out of my sight.

Putting on a burst of speed I had no idea was possible, I sped away from the others. Hawk crashed past me through the underbrush, snatching a life vest, and scrambling to the water's edge. By the time I reached him, he'd already donned the life vest and kicked off his boots. Without the slightest hesitation, he dove into the icy water.

"She went under," I shouted, glancing at the water while I continued racing downriver toward the osprey tree and the rescue line.

Upstream, Minnie's head popped out of the water. Hawk plowed through the heaving current, angling toward her. He'd gauged his trajectory well. The current thrust her toward him. "Grab hold of me," he yelled to Minnie.

No fool, she wrapped her arms around his neck. Together, they bobbed toward the falls. The rescue line was their last hope before Dead Man's Gorge swallowed them.

The pair was nearing the rescue line when the current eddied around a rock, sweeping them closer to shore. Life jacket or not, it was clear Hawk was having trouble keeping two people afloat. Frigid water slapped their faces, trying to suck them under.

They swept toward the rescue line. At the exact moment they reached it Hawk shot both hands in the air and latched on, halting their swift rush to certain death. Waves crashed over their heads in an attempt to suck them under.

With my heart leaping in my chest, I slid down the embankment to the strip of rocky shore below the osprey tree. Wayne and Roland appeared at the top and surveyed the situation before they slithered down beside me.

Hawk still gripped the rescue rope while Minnie clung to his back like a monkey. The current clawed at their legs in a quest to drag them toward the falls. If he let go, they'd be swept away in an instant.

Struggling to be heard over the waterfall's thunder, I shouted to Wayne and Roland. "Hawk can't do it alone. He needs help."

Wayne's face was a mask of worry. "I had a triple bypass last year. The doctors told me to avoid undue exertion."

Roland shook his head. "No way. I can't swim."

I wasn't too big on it myself. "Never mind. I'll do it," I said.

"Don't lose your balance or you're a goner, life ring or no life ring," Wayne said.

I unfastened both life preservers from their hooks on the tree. Only after I'd uncoiled the ropes, did the fear hit me. If my idea didn't work, I was in big trouble.

I arranged everything the way I'd visualized it. First, I stepped into one life ring, unwound its rope, and tied it around the osprey tree. Next, I unwound the second life ring's rope, fastened it around my waist, and gripped the ring, ready to toss it to Minnie. That way, if I lost my footing, neither of us would go over the falls—provided Minnie held onto the life ring.

Cupping my hands, I shouted, "Hey, Minnie. Catch the life ring, hang on and let go of Hawk. I'll haul you to shore."

"Okay." Minnie's answer was barely audible above the water's roar.

"Hawk, can you get yourself to shore without Minnie on your back?"

He shouted something undecipherable. I hoped he'd agreed.

I braced myself and used both hands to toss the life preserver to Minnie. And repeated it several times. Each time, my throw fell woefully short.

In desperation, I kicked off my boots, stripped off my fleece jacket, and stepped into the icy water. My legs went numb and my knees buckled. Discomfort was irrelevant. I gritted my teeth, waded out, and flung with all my might. This time, Minnie managed to snag one arm around the life preserver.

"Okay, release Hawk," I yelled, bracing for the drag of a person, swinging at the end of a rope like a pendulum. There was a blessed moment of slack during which the rope played out and the current swept Minnie downriver until the rope ran its course. All 165-plus pounds of Minnie stopped short in the water, nearly slicing me in half. Ignoring the pain, I planted my feet and reeled her in like a huge tuna. After what felt like hours, but was, in reality, only a few minutes, she was flopping around in the shallow water where I stood.

"Well done." Hawk shouted.

My sense of accomplishment blindsided me. I, who seldom went into water over my head, never mind glacier-fed water rushing toward a waterfall, had helped save two lives. To verify, I glanced back. Without Minnie hugging his neck, Hawk was close to shore.

That was when Wayne finally stepped into action. No doubt feeling guilty, he splashed into the water toward us with hand extended. He hauled Minnie out first, then helped me to scramble onto dry land.

Panting and shivering, I collapsed on the ground beside Minnie and glanced at her face. If I was freezing, Minnie must be verging on hypothermic. Her tremors were so violent, she was in danger of chipping another tooth. Noticing my purple fleece, which had landed on the rock beside her head, I crawled over to retrieve it. After removing her sodden cargo jacket, I helped her into my warm, fuzzy hoodie. She released an audible sigh once I'd zipped it up.

While we recovered our breath, Wayne cast a surreptitious glance at Eleanor. She waited beside Gabby and Phyllis at the top of the incline, her expression dialed to furious. For some reason, Wayne was most definitely in the doghouse. Surely she couldn't be jealous he'd hauled Minnie to safety.

Hawk made it to shore under his own steam and collapsed, his legs immersed in the water. To my astonishment, Roland jogged to the edge, one hand extended. Hawk latched on and let Roland hoist him onto dry land, where he dropped to the ground, chest heaving. His face was bone-white, his lips blue, and he shivered uncontrollably.

Wayne, to his credit, noticed the problem. He dashed over while shrugging out of his down-filled jacket and handed it to Hawk, who stripped to the skin and shrugged into the coat. Due to Hawk's shaking hands, Wayne zipped it up, then unfastened the hood and flipped it over his head.

Meanwhile, I held Minnie's hair back and murmured soothing words while she vomited up what seemed like half the river, but was likely only several gallons.

Once she'd finished, I found my boots and shoved my feet into them. Thanks were offered and accepted all around. Wayne and Roland gathered up wet clothing. The rest of us heaved ourselves to our feet, resigned to a steep climb. At least it would get the blood flowing.

Somehow, we all made it to the top in one piece.

Eleanor pounced on Wayne and much to my disappointment, dragged him far enough away to prevent eavesdropping. Whatever they were talking about must have been acrimonious, because once they were done, Eleanor flounced away leaving Wayne, who appeared agitated and, yes, angry.

Forcing them from my mind, I retrieved the phone from my purple fleece covering Minnie and called Zeke. After describing the situation, I joined everyone else. "Zeke's on his way with all the help we'll need. They'll meet us on the main trail."

"G-good," Hawk said through blue lips. "I'm b-b-butt-ass cold."

Watching him shiver, I experienced a flash of clarity that left me breathless. How had I not recognized Hawk's goodness earlier? This was a man who cared only about doing the right thing. His own comfort or safety wasn't on his radar. And if that wasn't the flat-out sexiest thing about him.

He was a rock. A solid rock. Someone I could rely on. And I'd been a coward. A lily-livered, yellow-bellied coward. "We need to talk in private," I whispered, tugging his sleeve to coax him behind a thicket of dense underbrush.

"What's up?"

"Without you, Minnie would be dead. I don't know how to thank you,"

I whispered, wrapping my arms around him, encountering a wall of muscle Wayne's puffer jacket couldn't diminish.

He cut off my spate of words by tipping my chin up with one finger. "I can think of a couple of ways." He pressed his chilly lips to mine, crushing my mouth under his as if he'd been thirsting for me, as if he wanted me more than his next breath. My knees weakened. I snaked my arms around his neck, telling myself I needed support. The kiss we shared with sensual abandon left my head reeling. Based on the luscious, liquid heat pooling in my lower belly, I was not over Hawk. Not by a long shot. I'd only been kidding myself.

Through a fog of lust, I registered a crashing in the underbrush.

Coming to my senses, I drew away and clamped my mouth shut in case anything really, *really* stupid popped out—for example, "*Why, yes. I believe I would like to jump your bones.*"

A second later, Minnie burst from the bushes. "There you are. I wondered where you two had disappeared to," she said through chattering teeth, letting her gaze bounce from Hawk to me and back to Hawk. She gave me a conspiratorial nudge. "I'm happy to see you've come to your senses."

Subtle. Real subtle. My face heated up, as did the urge to throttle her.

Any opinion Hawk might have on the matter was hijacked when Phyllis emerged from the bushes carrying the boots Hawk had discarded before his leap into the river. "I thought you might need these."

"That's real thoughtful. Thanks." He accepted the boots.

"No, thank *you* for rescuing my friend," Phyllis replied. "I nearly lost my breakfast when Minnie fell into the river. I don't know what I'd do if I lost another friend in the space of two days."

"It was nothing. I'm a strong swimmer," he said, struggling to yank on his boots.

"Don't be modest. You risked your life to save a woman you only met yesterday. Not many men would do that."

Hawk smiled at me. "I couldn't have saved Minnie without Clara's help. She saved two lives all by herself today."

Heat crawled up my neck and lodged my cheeks. "Don't exaggerate. Even with Minnie clinging to you, you would have made it to shore under your own steam."

Next, Phyllis gripped Minnie's hands and rubbed them. "You poor,

poor dear. Your hands are chunks of ice, and no wonder. You fell into a glacier-fed river. What were you thinking, going so close to the edge?"

With a scowl, Minnie extricated her hands and shoved them into the hoodie's pockets. "It wasn't like I did it on purpose."

"Are you sure about that, hon?" Phyllis asked. "It sure was an attention-getter."

Steam was practically puffing from Minnie's ears, so I hastened to say, "We should return to the main trail right away. Zeke and his wranglers will be waiting for us with ATVs."

While the guests made sure they had everything, Minnie took me aside. "I d-didn't fall in," she said in an urgent whisper. "Someone p-p-pushed me. I didn't want to say anything in front of Phyllis. If she knew, it would soon be public knowledge."

After the shock subsided, I murmured, "We'll get to the bottom of who pushed you, I promise. But not now, not here. We need to get you and Hawk back to Grizzly Gulch and into dry clothes. I want you to walk with him so I don't need to worry about anything else happening to you."

Could Phyllis be right? Or maybe Minnie was reluctant to admit she'd gone too close to the edge and tumbled into the river.

Hawk and I traded places for the short hike to the main trail. This time, Hawk led the way with Minnie close to his side. Behind them, Roland walked alone, then Gabby bounced along beside Eleanor, who was giving Wayne the cold shoulder. Next, Wayne stomped along in silence beside Phyllis, thwarting her attempts to engage him in conversation, and I trailed along behind the pack, glad to be alone.

I was on autopilot until Phyllis' whisper caught my attention. If I have one superpower, it's an exceptional sense of hearing. Mom used to tell me a bat would envy my hearing. While tiptoeing behind them, I held my breath and strained to eavesdrop.

Phyllis was taunting him. "Your girlfriend's ignoring you. I doubt Eleanor appreciated it when you went out of your way to help Minnie."

"You think Eleanor's jealous?" Wayne gave an unconvincing laugh. "That's ridiculous. It's nothing but a harmless little tiff. It'll blow over in no time."

"Good luck with that. I predict you'll regret helping Minnie."

"Why would I regret it? Minnie's my friend."

Phyllis released a tinkling laugh, the first I'd heard her utter. "You helped the woman Eleanor views as her arch-rival. But I was referring to something else, something bigger."

"What, then?"

"Minnie knows too much about your past. Just like Lizzie did."

"I have no idea what you're talking about."

"You know exactly what I'm talking about."

I took longer strides, hoping to close the gap so I'd hear every word.

"Why are you telling me this?" Wayne asked. "You trying to stir up trouble?"

"Of course not. I'm curious, though. See, two weeks ago, I accidentally overheard you in the common room, spilling your guts to Minnie, and—" Phyllis broke off in mid-sentence. When she started up again she was whispering.

I didn't dare get too close or I would tread on their heels. Although I strained to listen, all I heard was, "… your affair … Lizzie's obsession with you … blackmail ..." Phyllis spoke normally again. "It was fascinating to hear."

"And your point is?" Wayne sounded uneasy.

I held my breath and trod quietly, avoiding twigs that might crack and remind them I was within earshot.

When Phyllis spoke again, her words were clearly audible. "My point? Lizzie is conveniently dead, and a day later, Minnie tumbles into a raging torrent and nearly drowns. Coincidence? You tell me."

I'd missed the details, but I'd heard enough to deduce Phyllis had overheard Minnie and Wayne discussing events that might incriminate Wayne for two crimes—Lizzie's death and the attempt to drown Minnie. But why would Phyllis mention this to him? If she really thought he was a killer, I doubted she would tip him off thus placing herself in danger. No, there had to be another reason. Perhaps to sow seeds of suspicion elsewhere?

After a lengthy silence, Wayne said, "Phyllis, you're a malicious she-devil. Are you accusing me of doing something bad?"

"I'm sure the timing is all coincidental."

A snorting noise indicated Wayne's disgust. "I've heard enough. I'm going ahead to find someone else to walk with."

I slowed down to distance myself from Phyllis. I refused to walk with anyone, even Minnie's friend, who appeared to be deliberately stirring up trouble.

Five minutes later, we were surrounded by Grizzly Gulch wranglers, who'd arrived with three four-seater ATVs, blankets, and hot beverages for all. While most opted for hot toddies, I asked for cocoa before pulling Hawk aside and whispering, "I just overheard a weird conversation between Wayne and Phyllis. Minnie might be able to provide clarification, so I want to meet with you both once we get back."

"I was about to say the same thing," he said. "Minnie insists someone pushed her in, and I want to find out who might have hated or feared her enough to kill her."

"Did you notice where people were standing when she went in?"

"No. They were all milling around. Did you see anything suspicious?"

A pang of guilt struck me. I'd been so focused on Hawk's presence at the time, I hadn't paid any attention to the others. "No. Everyone was excited about the fish. I remember seeing Minnie standing upriver on a granite shelf overlooking the river. I don't think anyone else was near her."

After downing our drinks, we all piled on board the ATVs and roared away. The racket made it impossible for me to talk to Hawk. Upon arriving at Grizzly Gulch, Roland hopped down from the ATV he'd shared with Wayne, dashed over, and extended his hand to me. Seeing no alternative, I allowed him to help me down from the vehicle. Without letting go, he murmured, "I believe this evening's entertainment is line dancing. Would you consider joining me as my date?"

Hawk disembarked on the other side and sauntered around the vehicle to stand beside me. Without touching me, without saying a word, he conveyed the impression of being simultaneously macho and possessive, quite a feat. "Sorry to disappoint you Roland, but I believe Clara agreed to join me for drinks this evening." Roland dropped my hand with unflattering haste. Hawk winked at me to let me know he was giving me an easy out.

Happiness bloomed inside me. Perhaps I hadn't burned all my bridges. "Yes I did. We have so much to discuss."

"But my special surprise will make you a real happy woman, babe," Roland said. "A whole lot happier than playing catch-up with a retired cop."

"Mountie," Hawk interjected.

My, this was awkward. "Your persistence is impressive, Roland, but Hawk is right. I made a commitment to spend the evening with him."

"Once you see the surprise I have in store for you, you'll forget all about Mr. Retired Mountie." Roland glanced in Hawk's direction. "No offence."

"None taken." Hawk's smile was feral.

Remembering our need for good reviews, I infused my voice with regret. "I'm sorry, Roland, but my sisters and I have a rule. We don't date guests."

"Babe, I'll take that as a maybe." Roland winked and swaggered away.

Chapter 10: Proof of Innocence

While Minnie and Hawk changed into warm, dry clothes, I prepared a pot of coffee for our talk. It was warm enough to sit outside, and a good opportunity to use my deck, which faced the pool. A faint odor of chlorine tickled my nostrils. I'd barely set everything down, when Hawk arrived right on the dot of 11:30 a.m. A soft, seductive warmth stirred inside me. His baggy UBC sweatshirt, jeans that were faded in all the right places, and black running shoes were ridiculously attractive.

Any thoughts of romance receded when Minnie flounced onto the deck, announcing her presence, first with pathetic sniffles, and followed by a flood of tears and sobs. Flinging her arms around Hawk's neck, she clung like a burr. "You're the first man ever to risk his life for me. I don't know how to thank you enough." She shot me a meaningful glance, which I interpreted as, *Don't be dumb enough to let this one escape.*

Over Minnie's shoulder, Hawk's eyes pleaded silently for my help while he awkwardly placed his hands on her arms, a move I suspected was a stealthy attempt to pry her loose. Raising his voice, he said, "I'm glad you suffered no ill effects."

"Let's all sit and have coffee," I said, arranging mugs and pouring a steaming brew I'd scented with cinnamon.

After hugging him again, Minnie let me steer her to the loveseat facing the pool enclosure. She wore jeans, sandals, and a gold-tone turtleneck under a black down-filled vest. Still-damp white hair curled around her face, and she was makeup-free. Hawk chose the blue Adirondack chair next to my red one, so we both ended up facing Minnie across the coffee table.

Snuggles scampered onto the deck and hunkered down in a sunny corner.

"Does he have to follow me everywhere?" Minnie wanted to know.

"I think he likes you." Ignoring her shudder, I pushed a brimming mug toward each of them and placed a plate of peanut butter cookies within reach.

Skipping the pleasantries, Hawk fixed Minnie with a penetrating gaze and jumped right to the point. "Tell us how you ended up in the river."

Minnie sipped her coffee, then put her mug down. When she raised her gaze, her pretty hazel eyes were haunted. "I told you earlier, and I'll say it again. I did not, repeat, *not* fall into the river. Someone pushed me."

As sincere as she sounded, I still had a hard time believing her. "But I remember seeing you standing alone on the cliff top. There didn't seem to be anyone nearby. I yelled at you to be careful."

"Are you sure you didn't slip?" Hawk asked.

"Of course I'm sure." Minnie selected a cookie and waved it for emphasis. "There were thick bushes surrounding me, thick enough to conceal my attacker. Someone crawled close enough to shove me with something pointed, I'm guessing a walking stick, to make me lose my balance."

Hawk regarded her, unblinking. "Did you see or hear the person?"

"No," Minnie said. "My back was turned. There are no clues and no proof. I don't know if my attacker was a man or woman." After examining each of us in turn, she placed the cookie down before covering her face with her hands. "You don't believe me." Tears streamed through her fingers and a pitiful sob escaped.

Hawk stared at me in panic and whispered, "She's leaking. Did I break her?"

The sobs coalesced into a constant wail, increasing in volume.

"No," I assured him, matching his whisper. "Keep in mind Minnie is an actress. She does this regularly. Her crying jag will pass." I moved to sit beside her on the loveseat. Snuggles leaped beside me and curled up on the cushion. I gave him a quick kitty-tickle behind the ears.

Thankfully, Minnie was too wrapped up in her distress to notice Snuggles. She threw her arms around me and sobbed against my clean navy sweater. "Neither of you believes me," she said between sniffles. "You both think I was careless, fell in, and must now be so embarrassed, I invented a story about being pushed. That, or I did it on purpose, seeking attention."

That about sums it up.

"That's not true, hon," I said, stroking her hair and biting my tongue to avoid mentioning prior dramatic outbursts, some of which were the stuff of family lore. "It must have been terrifying. Talk us through what happened."

The sobbing dwindled into deep, shuddery breaths interspersed with moist snuffles. I handed her a napkin and took one myself.

After I helped Minnie conduct a thorough mop-up, she slumped against me. "There's not much to tell. After you warned me to be careful, I heard rustling in the bushes behind me and something poked me in the back. Hard. I had a split second to decide. Get pushed onto the rocks below, or jump into the river. I jumped."

"When you knew you couldn't swim?" Hoping she hadn't detected my skepticism, I stroked her hair awkwardly. She leaned into me so hard, I had to use my other hand to grip the loveseat's back or crush poor Snuggles. My fingers encountered a hole in the all-weather covering.

Minnie's protests continued. "Believe it or not, it's the gospel truth. I knew the rescue line was nearby. I planned to grip it, assuming I managed to stay afloat."

"Seriously?" I drew back to stare at my cousin. "That's incredibly brave."

"Now do you believe me?"

I didn't know what to tell her. I wanted to believe her, but drama was Minnie's middle name. While I wrestled with my answer, I dug a finger into the hole I'd found.

Snuggles protested vocally at being squashed between the loveseat arm and my butt. After scrambling free, he bounded across Minnie before jumping down.

"Ouch. Claws. That's one rotten feline with abysmal manners." Minnie scowled. "You don't believe me."

In quiet desperation, I curled my finger deeper into the hole and encountered a foreign object. It was hard and cold. Fishing out the object, I examined it with a combination of shock and satisfaction and raised my gaze to Minnie's anxious face. "I do believe you, hon. I also believe someone shot at you yesterday. Here's the proof." I held my palm outstretched to display a bullet caked with what appeared to be dried blood.

Hawk leaped to his feet and spread a napkin on the table. "Place the object here."

I dropped the bullet onto the napkin and used another to scrub my fingers.

He scrutinized the object without touching it, then folded the napkin neatly around it and placed the package in his pocket. Holding another napkin, he studied the sliding door, then examined my apartment's outside wall. Striding into the living room, he disappeared for several minutes. When he returned, he selected a cookie and chewed reflectively while we waited impatiently for his pronouncement.

After finishing the cookie, he said, "It's a bullet."

"Of course it is."

He ignored my interruption. "It's from a small caliber handgun, not a rifle, which hunters generally use. Was the patio door open during the shooting?"

"Yes," Minnie and I said simultaneously. "Windows too," I added.

"I found several bullet holes in the outside wall and one in the window frame, so I used a knife to pry the bullets into a napkin." He patted his pocket. "There's a small grove of poplars across the way where someone would stand for an ideal shot into your apartment. I'll check the area for casings. If I find any, the shooter may have left fingerprints."

"Multiple shots?" Minnie asked faintly. "Someone must really hate me."

"You're lucky whoever did this had a lousy aim. The shooter must have used a silencer and got a lucky shot at Minnie through the side window, grazing her arm. The slight contact changed the bullet's trajectory, causing it to fly through the open patio door to embed itself in the loveseat, where the metal frame stopped it." He folded the napkin around the bullet and placed the package in his pocket, saying, "I'll take this one along with the others and any shell casings I might find into the Cochrane detachment right away. It's evidence for Callum that someone tried to kill Minnie. Forensics will test the casings for fingerprints and the bullet itself for Minnie's blood." He leveled his gaze at Minnie. "I'll need a blood sample. The bandage on your arm will be fine."

She peeled off the bandage, revealing the graze, which was healing nicely, and dropped it onto another napkin, which he rolled up and shoved in a different pocket, explaining, "To keep blood from the bandage from contaminating the bullet. By the way, may I be the first to offer my congratulations. You're no longer a suspect in Lizzie's murder."

Minnie's stunned stare morphed into a glare. She leaped to her feet and flung her hands in the air. "Lizzie was murdered?" Her voice jumped an octave. "I was a *suspect*, but you didn't see fit to mention *that* teeny-tiny detail to me?" she yelled.

Filled with remorse, I described what we knew about Lizzie's death, which was likely a pre-meditated murder based on a needle track on her butt, and how her blood would probably not provide concrete proof. Most killers worth their salt would use a fast-acting, fast-disappearing poison.

Minnie paced the deck while muttering to herself about the injustice of being considered a suspect. Once she fell silent, she presented her back to us while white-knuckling the railing, her head averted. At last, she asked quietly, "Might I ask why you failed to mention I was a suspect?"

I recognized the signs. She was going to blow. Most men vacated the area when Minnie pitched a fit, and rightly so.

But not Hawk. He stepped closer to her and gently lowered a hand to her shoulder. "I asked Clara not to mention my suspicions to you. I'm so sorry, Minnie, but everyone knows you had a fight with Lizzie and she chipped your tooth. Not only that, you had a dust-up in front of the outhouse at the comfort stop. I had to be certain of your innocence. You have every right to be angry, and I'm guessing you're also sad and scared. Sad we didn't trust you enough to tell you everything, terrified your attacker might try again."

Minnie didn't speak, but her knuckles had turned pink again and her shoulders dropped into a more natural position—both good signs.

Hawk maintained light contact with her shoulder and kept talking, all calm and friendly. "Other than Lois, Flo, and the driver, who all stayed near the coach, everyone on board the Lifestyle Manor minicoach was a suspect. It's my fault, not Clara's. She and both her sisters tried to convince me you were innocent, but I couldn't make an exception until I was certain." He patted his pocket. "For the record, I believe someone pushed you into the river. Although we can't identify your attacker, at least not yet, this bullet is enough confirm that someone wants you dead."

"Thanks." With her anger defused, Minnie faced us. "I have a hard time believing someone from Lifestyle Manor killed Lizzie, then tried to kill me twice. I might not like them all, but murder? And why kill us both?" She shuddered. "Now I don't know who I can trust."

"Don't trust anyone until we learn the truth," Hawk warned her, "and don't go anywhere alone. Someone must accompany you at all times."

"Okay. Now what?" Minnie said.

"Tell us why somebody might want you and Lizzie dead."

"I'm happy to talk, but not here. It's too easy for someone to sneak under your deck to eavesdrop. Let's go somewhere else."

She made a good point. I went so far as to peer over the railing and check, but found no one crouching beneath my deck. "You're right," I said. "But it's nearly lunch time. We should eat first. Missing lunch might raise a red flag with the killer."

Hawk, who'd listened to our discussion in silence, said, "You're right. Let's all go down to lunch together. We'll keep our conversation lighthearted, normal.

"Okay," I said, "but first, we need to bring Dodie and Abby up to speed about everything that happened this morning. We all need to be on the same page."

"Invite them up here," Hawk said. "There's no time to go anywhere else before lunch."

A worried frown wrinkled Minnie's forehead. "Duh, eavesdroppers?"

"We'll go inside with the windows closed. No one will hear us," he assured her.

"Sounds like a plan," I agreed. "I'll call my sisters and invite them up so we can bring them up-to-date."

"Before you do, I have an important request," Hawk said. "There is no doubt in my mind someone's trying to kill Minnie. I want to move in."

I must have heard wrong. "Move in?"

"Yes. Into Grizzly Gulch. On a temporary basis, of course. The place needn't be fancy, but it should be close enough that I can ensure Minnie's safety and continue to mingle with the suspects. If anyone asks, you can tell them no one should be alone over Thanksgiving, especially retired Mounties whose family is busy."

Minnie clapped her hands. "I love it. I've always wanted to be part of an undercover operation."

My brain darted around hunting for an escape hatch, not unlike a ferret in a cage. Hawk would be way too close for comfort. But try as I might, his idea made sense and his presence would comfort Minnie. "Okay. I'll ask Abby if she'll lend you her apartment. It's been sitting vacant since she moved into Zeke's quarters."

"Perfect," Minnie said. "And after lunch, we'll find somewhere private, and I'll tell you all I know about the suspects." She chortled. "I'll be your inside informant. We need a code word. Let's call our afternoon session the memory dump."

In response to my urgent calls, Abby and Dodie arrived at my place to be debriefed on our morning activities.

"This had better be important," Abby muttered, flinging herself onto my sofa. "Chef Armand is almost ready to serve lunch, and you know I like to attend as many meals as possible with our guests, especially during the start of an event."

"What's the scoop?" Dodie asked as she perched on a chair. "I've heard some disturbing rumors about your nature walk."

Hawk and I did much of the talking, with Minnie adding her fair share, and my sisters interjecting questions. Twenty minutes later, we'd covered the nature walk with Minnie's tumble into the river, followed by the subsequent discovery of a bullet, which exonerated Minnie as a suspect in Lizzie's death, but confirmed she was, indeed, a target. After I broached the topic of Hawk moving in, Abby offered her apartment for as long as he needed.

With Hawk's move to Grizzly Gulch confirmed, he said, "Now that my relocation is happening, I realize it might not be as easy or as fast as I'd first imagined. I have a lot to do—errands to run, clothes to pack, and activities to re-shuffle."

Dates to cancel? I glanced around, praying I hadn't blurted the words aloud. Apparently I hadn't.

Minnie's wide smile broadcast her relief. "I feel so much safer knowing you'll be nearby. Don't forget to pack enough stuff for a week's stay. It might turn cold, so be sure to bring sweaters."

"I shouldn't be gone more than a couple of hours," he assured us. "I'll be back for Minnie's memory dump by mid-afternoon."

"That's an optimistic estimate if ever I heard one," I pointed out. "You also need to deliver the bullet, casings and Minnie's blood sample into the

Cochrane detachment for testing. I'm sure the visit will take longer than you think. The drive there and back alone will take over an hour and a half, and there will be paperwork, camaraderie, and coffee."

Abby chimed in to remind him, "You also wanted to track down Lizzie's relatives and ask if anyone was willing to take Snuggles. And don't forget to call Callum and fill him in on what happened this morning."

He groaned. "Now that you spell it out, I can see I'll have a busy afternoon. Perhaps I'll hold off on asking if anyone will take Snuggles until I'm sure Lizzie's family has been notified about her death. As for Atticus, I'll phone him later."

"Even so, you'll be lucky if you're back in time for dinner. I propose that we women proceed with the memory dump and fill you in later."

Dodie interjected, "I've got a staff meeting I can't wriggle out of."

"Okay, we three women," Abby said. "Clara and I are perfectly capable of getting Minnie to spill her guts."

That was true. The trick would be to stop her.

Recognizing the stubborn jut of Hawk's jaw, I hastened to add, "One of us will take detailed notes." I intended that person to be Abby, while I did the questioning, though she didn't know that. We could iron out the details later, hopefully with my idea prevailing.

"I don't like it. There must be a better way."

Yeah, Hawk would say that. It seemed he hated relinquishing control, even for a few hours. The intimidating scowl on his face made me question our suggestion, but I refused to back down. "I don't blame you for wanting to join us," I said before playing my trump card. "But let me remind you that this is a life and death matter. We need to know everything about the suspects, and sooner rather than later."

After a long silence, he surprised me by saying, "Okay. But I hate leaving while things are so uncertain. I want you to promise at least one of you will be with Minnie every moment until I return."

Abby and I promised.

Minnie shattered the tension by saying, "Hey, let's keep this within reason. I do *not* want company when I'm in the bathroom or if I get lucky with one of those cute wranglers."

After we finished laughing, we went down to lunch together, and managed to enjoy ourselves, mainly because Minnie was an entertaining story-teller with dozens of anecdotes about her acting career. If anyone wondered if we were worried about Minnie's safety, I was certain our laughter dispelled any suspicions.

As soon as we finished eating, Dodie hurried off to her meeting while Abby, Minnie, and I gathered in front of the main entrance to wait for Hawk to maneuver his Grand Cherokee out of the parking lot. Ostensibly, we were there to see him off and get any last minute instructions. In reality, I wanted to make sure he'd left before we nailed down a location for Minnie's memory dump.

He stopped in front of us and stuck his head out the window, no doubt to deliver last minute instructions. Confirming my suspicions, he said, "Don't you go prying or investigating on your own. It's too dangerous. Remember, there's a killer on the loose."

"We're not likely to forget," I said, wondering if he would ever leave. "Abby and I will stick to Minnie like Velcro until you return."

"One more thing, Clara. A moment, please?" I stepped closer to the open window. "I'm requesting your time this evening."

I stared at him. His gaze was dark, steady, and inscrutable. I must have hesitated too long, because Minnie's elbow-jab caused me to release a gasp of pain. "Ouch," I yelped, rubbing my throbbing arm. "You're supposed to give us privacy. Why did you do that?"

"To let you know only a fool would turn him down," she said, winking at Hawk.

Heat crept up my chest to my neck and into my cheeks. Ignoring our audience, I whispered to him, "You mean like a ... a date?"

"Yes."

Excitement made my head spin. He was offering me a second chance. This man was honorable, clever, honest, and oh, so sexy. In spite of my misgivings, and there were many, in spite of the fear clogging my heart, every cell of my body begged me to agree.

"Yes. I believe I can carve out some time."

The austere planes of his face relaxed, and something deep inside me ... warmed. My cold, dead heart, I realized with surprise. I resisted the insane urge to jump into the passenger seat and throw my arms around him, and rest my head on his chest.

He surprised me by saying, "Let's have dinner in Canmore. I know a place with a whole lot more privacy than Grizzly Gulch's dining hall. It has decent food and better karaoke. It occurred to me we needed practice."

"At eating or karaoke?"

Although he maintained a straight face, the dimple I adored appeared in one cheek. "Karaoke. We were great. Let's show them how it's done."

"Okay." On the outside I maintained my cool, but inside, I buzzed with excitement.

"Good decision," Minnie said while Abby nodded her approval.

Hawk reached out the window to high-five me before roaring off.

Once he'd departed, Minnie clutched our arms. "Guys, I'm going stir-crazy. I didn't want to say anything in front of Hawk, but is there somewhere else we can go for this memory dump? I need to know the suspects are far away, at least for the afternoon. Mountains and open space would be good."

Abby and I looked at one another. Abby spoke first, "I know the perfect spot. It's not too far, it's deserted this time of year, and the scenery is spectacular."

"Sounds perfect. Where is it?" Minnie wanted to know.

"Quarry Lake. It's an incredible mountain lake with plenty of open space and lovely views. If anyone asks, we'll say we spent the afternoon sightseeing."

"I'll bring bear spray, just in case," I said, thinking that perhaps this small act of caution might settle Hawk down once he learned we'd gone off on a mini-road trip.

Chapter 11: The Memory Dump

A half an hour later, Abby backed the Grizzly Gulch truck into a perfect parking spot at Quarry Lake, where I intended to pick Minnie's brain about each of the suspects. I exited the passenger side and opened the back door to help Minnie out. Mountain breezes and sunshine made it a picture-perfect day. The small lake's glassy surface reflected a deep blue sky above the mountain panorama of Ha Ling Peak, The Three Sisters, and the most eastern hump of Mount Rundle, affectionately known by locals as Eeyore. In the surrounding grassy meadows, fluorescent gold poplars shimmered, their leaves a brilliant contrast to the evergreens.

After Hawk's departure, Abby and I had managed to steal a quick moment of privacy to discuss the interview approach. I'd suggested I be the primary questioner because I understood Minnie's eccentricities and trusted her gut instincts about people, trained as she was to analyze the stage characters she played. Because Abby's logical brain allowed her to see parallels and draw conclusions that went unnoticed by others she should apply that talent to documenting the interview as well as digging deeper with follow-up questions.

Abby didn't fight me on my proposed division of labor, an excellent sign of mutual respect.

The three of us walked in silence until we found a remote picnic table. A dense pine thicket concealed us from onlookers. The sweet, clean scent of grass, evergreens, and that undefinable, distinctive smell of autumn wafted toward us on a light breeze. Adding to the heady mix was the scent of wood smoke and grilling meat wafting from a fire pit on the opposite side of the lake.

Once seated, I took soft drink cans from the cooler and set them on the table next to the chocolate fudge brownies I'd cadged from the kitchen.

Minnie closed her eyes and took a deep breath followed by several more.

While waiting for Minnie to finish her ritual, Abby tapped her fingers and shifted impatiently on the bench. I gave her a warning nudge. Just when I sensed my sister was ready to erupt with frustration, Minnie opened her eyes, blinked twice, and said, "I feel at one with Mother Earth. I'm ready to talk now."

I restrained myself from intoning, "Amen."

Abby demonstrated self-control too, saying, "This must be upsetting for you, Minnie, but we need to figure out who might want both you and Lizzie dead. Let's examine all possibilities, no matter how remote." She extracted a notepad and pen from her purse.

I, on the other hand, reached for a brownie. "Let's start with Wayne," I suggested.

"Wayne? Why? He's the last person who'd attack me."

"I'm not so sure." I hated to upset her, but we needed to know the truth. "During our hike home this morning, I was behind Phyllis and Wayne. I got the impression Phyllis accused Wayne of killing Lizzie and pushing you into the river."

"Good grief," Abby said. "Did you tell Hawk?"

"No. I wanted to hear Minnie's explanation first."

Minnie wrinkled her forehead. "It's ridiculous, that's what it is. I can't imagine why Phyllis would say such a thing. She must be mistaken. Wayne wouldn't hurt anyone, especially me. We're friends. I'm giving him poker lessons so he can join Eleanor's poker games. What motive could he have for killing me or, for that matter, Lizzie?"

I took a deep breath, dreading her reaction. "Phyllis implied both you and Lizzie knew too much about Wayne's romantic history for comfort. Now Lizzie is dead, and he might be worried you'll blab." Craving sweet, chocolatey goodness as an antidote to the indignant blast I sensed was imminent, I took a huge bite of fudgy brownie.

"Excuse me?" Minnie's voice could have sliced steel. "*Blab*?"

After some fast chewing, I swallowed with difficulty. Coughing to dislodge crumbs from my throat, I washed the remains down with a swig of cola. Minnie thumped my back—maybe a little too enthusiastically.

Recovering, I said with some difficulty due to the burning in my chest, "Sorry. Bad word choice." I cleared my throat again and launched into a description of every word I'd overheard—which, admittedly wasn't much—how Phyllis had accidentally overheard Minnie and Wayne discussing secrets, an affair, and blackmail, all pointing to Wayne as a killer.

Minnie's shocked gaze slammed into me. "I hope you don't believe Wayne killed or attacked anyone based on Phyllis' say-so. She may be my friend, but the woman has issues."

"Perhaps. But there's no denying Lizzie is dead and someone did try to kill you."

Minnie went silent. I took another bite of brownie, smaller this time. A quick glance told me Minnie was practically snorting fire.

"Wayne's the one who told me his story in the first place, so why would he want to kill me now, huh?" she asked.

I held up both hands. "Calm down. We're only trying to sort things out."

Her gaze softened marginally. "Fine. Are you interested in hearing the *real* story instead of the overblown fiction Phyllis imagined?"

"Of course."

Minnie blew out a long breath. "Phyllis was Lizzie's sidekick and informant, always sneaking around, searching for information to help Lizzie intimidate and blackmail the residents. There was no way Phyllis *accidentally* heard my conversation with Wayne. She deliberately eavesdropped. It makes her feel important, poor woman." Minnie snapped her mouth shut.

I wanted to shake her. She had an annoying habit of forcing her audience beg for more information. "You were telling me the real story," I reminded her.

"Right. Two weeks ago, Wayne approached me with a problem about Lizzie. Seems he and his wife used to socialize with Lizzie and her husband back in the 80s. After one drunken dinner party, Lizzie came on to Wayne and dragged him into the broom closet. They had a stand-up quickie, followed by a brief affair. Wayne ended things with Lizzie because he loved his wife and was consumed with guilt. Lizzie, on the other hand, divorced her husband and wouldn't leave Wayne alone. She pestered him for decades, like she'd phone, or he'd glimpse her in a shopping mall or outside a restaurant, always waiting, always watching. Two years ago, after his wife died, Wayne sold his ranch and moved into Lifestyle Manor. You'll never guess who moved in three months later."

I struggled to hide my impatience. "I'm guessing Lizzie." I gave Minnie a gentle prompt. "You were getting to the part about why Wayne needed to talk to you about her."

"Humph." Minnie resumed her story. "Fine. So Lizzie followed him around, begging for a date, insisting to everyone who would listen that she intended to make him husband number two. To make matters worse, Eleanor knew about it and was freaking out. Wayne wanted my advice. Believe it or not, he trusted me not to *blab*." She fixed me with a steady stare, expecting a response.

"Again, I apologize."

Minnie nodded and continued talking. "Wayne and I went into an empty common room for privacy. It was late. No one else was around, but we closed the door anyway. Too bad we didn't think to lock it, because when we finished, the door was open a crack. I bet Phyllis opened it and listened in." She set her jaw and glared at the lake, no doubt contemplating vengeance.

"And what did Wayne tell you?" I glanced across the table at Abby to assess her reaction. She was frowning while scribbling notes and munching on a brownie.

Minnie's eyes gleamed. "Lizzie's infatuation was raging out of control. After his fourth or maybe it was fifth rejection, she threatened to broadcast news of their affair to Eleanor and his daughters who, according to Wayne, had placed their mom on a pedestal after she died. To them, their deceased mom had no flaws."

Abby raised her head. "That's not a motive for murder."

"Exactly. But Wayne was worried that if his daughters learned he'd cheated during the marriage, he'd never see his grandchildren again."

"Ah. *There's* the motive." Abby resumed writing.

"Wayne was equally frantic that Eleanor might dump him. I didn't have the heart to tell him she'd never dump him because she wanted his money."

Abby stopped writing. "Maybe, maybe not. But Eleanor's jealousy strengthens his motive to get rid of Lizzie. Why didn't you mention this earlier?"

Minnie glugged down a mouthful of cola, likely to buy herself time.

After taking a brownie, she said, "Because I promised Wayne I wouldn't tell anyone." She crammed a chunk of brownie into her mouth.

"I see. Did you give Wayne any advice?" I asked. Minnie lived to offer advice.

After much chewing, she swallowed and said, "I told him to tell his daughters and Eleanor about his affair before Lizzie did. Plead for forgiveness. Throw himself on their mercy."

I was impressed. That was great advice, though I doubted Phyllis had stuck around that night to hear Minnie's wise counsel.

Abby glanced up at Minnie. "Did Wayne follow through on your advice?"

Minnie shrugged. "No idea. We'll need to ask Eleanor, Wayne, or his daughters."

I thought it over and issued my verdict. "It sounds like Wayne's off the hook for going after you, Minnie. But unless he followed through on your advice, he's still a candidate for Lizzie's murder. It's a loose end we'll need to follow up on."

At that point, Abby rendered her proclamation. "Not exactly true, Clara. Arguably, Wayne might have a reason to kill Minnie, but only if he ignored her advice and decided to kill Lizzie anyway. If he was the killer, he'd be afraid Minnie would remember the discussion where he confided in her, and realize he had a motive for murder."

And there was Abby's analytic mind in a nutshell. She noticed holes in the logic.

"Hey, you're barking up the wrong tree." Minnie protested. "You don't know Wayne the way I do. I strongly urge you to consider Eleanor, both for Lizzie's murder and for going after me. I swear the wilted English rose would kill me in a heartbeat."

"Why?" I reached for another brownie, then changed my mind.

"Jealousy over Wayne, of course. Eleanor is convinced he's getting it on with me during our poker lessons."

"What can you tell us about Eleanor?" I asked.

Minnie responded with a snort. "She's an aging seductress whose beauty was her main lure for attracting men, preferably wealthy men like Wayne. She's had extensive work done to her face and body, but time's running out. Nature has a way of reasserting herself. I admit Eleanor plays an upper-crust, wealthy Brit skillfully, but she's neither upper-crust nor wealthy. The woman is a low-class con-artist."

Abby glanced up from her notepad. "Why do you say she's not upper-crust?"

"I'm an actress, darling. I have a trained ear. I learned to imitate British accents for various plays. For example, whenever Eleanor gets angry," Minnie switched to a broad Cockney accent, "she goes right bonkers, luvvie."

I wanted to applaud, but restrained myself.

Abby clapped her hands in appreciation. "That was amazing. But how do you know she needs money?"

"She borrowed cash from Wayne to cover huge gambling losses, plus, she's a leech. She never picks up a restaurant tab or contributes to a birthday gift."

"But why hit on Wayne?" I asked. "He doesn't strike me as wealthy."

"Don't let his down-to-earth attitude deceive you. Wayne sold his ranch for a small fortune to a developer. He's also old-fashioned about his women. Since he prefers them ladylike and helpless, ladylike and helpless is what Eleanor delivers." Minnie bared her teeth in a vindictive grimace. "She's as helpless as a tarantula."

"What do you know about her background?" I asked.

"Well … she's pretty tight-lipped about herself. She emigrated to Canada from England, is cagy about her origins, used to be married, is now divorced. Nothing else."

"Why would Eleanor want to kill Lizzie?"

"Jealousy. The same reason she wants to get rid of me. Lizzie made no bones about wanting to marry Wayne. There's speculation she joined this getaway hoping to coax him into giving her riding lessons, not necessarily on a horse, if you get my drift."

I couldn't help chuckling.

Abby glanced up. "We're drifting off-topic, Minnie. Let's get back to discussing Eleanor's motive for killing Lizzie."

"Sure thing. Last month, Lizzie and Eleanor had a showdown over Wayne. Threats were uttered on both sides. Lizzie pasted Eleanor. The shiner lasted for weeks. Everyone commented on it." Minnie paused. "Goodness, there's something else I'd completely forgotten. Eleanor may have had more than one motive to kill Lizzie." She regarded us expectantly.

Abby's jaw was getting a little bunched. "Don't make me beg," she said through clenched teeth. "Go on."

Yeah, I wasn't the only one who found Minnie's mannerisms frustrating.

"After punching Eleanor, who dropped like a stone, I might add, Lizzie whispered something to her. I was close enough to hear every word."

Abby's deep scowl indicated she was at the end of her rope, so I fixed Minnie with a penetrating stare. "What did Lizzie whisper to Eleanor? Tell us before Abby explodes."

"She warned Eleanor to back off Wayne unless she wanted her whole sordid past to become public knowledge."

Abby's expression must have convinced Minnie to elaborate because she hurried on. "All I know is Lizzie occasionally hired a private investigator to dig up blackmail material. I'm sure Phyllis can tell you more."

Abby scribbled more notes. Once finished, she laid her pen down and flexed her fingers. "Well done. That's an excellent starting point."

Minnie flushed with pleasure. "Thanks."

"That's two down, three to go," I said. "Let's discuss Phyllis next."

Abby picked up her pen and waited.

Minnie shrugged. "She's harmless, poor thing. We go all the way back to high school. In her mind we're friends. She used to follow me around like a puppy, gave me free tutoring in math and physics. Without her help, I would have flunked out. I felt sorry for her then, still do. I try not to hurt her feelings, and avoid her whenever possible."

"So during high school, Phyllis was a dark planet orbiting around your dazzling sun-star," I said.

"Perhaps," Minnie admitted. "I never viewed our friendship that way, but I was popular, whereas people barely noticed her."

"What happened between you two after high school?"

Minnie hesitated, but once she got rolling, the words spewed out. "We went our separate ways. As you know, I studied theater arts in Vancouver, married my high school sweetheart, then divorced him, followed by two more husbands. After number three, I gave up on marriage and concentrated on my acting career. Poor Phyllis stayed home to live in Revelstoke with her dysfunctional mother, never married, and ended up a Bylaw Compliance Officer, you know, someone who enforces city bylaws and regulations and responds to complaints from the public. After my third marriage tanked,

Phyllis and I re-connected. Last year we met up at a high school reunion, she invited me to visit her at Lifestyle Manor, I liked the place and moved in three months ago."

"You said Lizzie and Phyllis were friends," I pointed out.

"Yes. Aside from me, Lizzie was Phyllis' *only* friend. Lizzie had no one except Phyllis." Minnie nibbled her lower lip. "Phyllis often did Lizzie's dirty work, snooping, eavesdropping, and digging up people's dirty little secrets."

"But why would Phyllis want to kill Lizzie?" I asked.

"Who knows? They had a huge falling out last week, but that happened so often, no one paid attention. Lizzie's treatment of Phyllis verged on abuse. She bossed her around, belittled her a lot. She was forever mocking her for being an old maid."

"In other words, Phyllis may have snapped."

"I guess it's possible," Minnie said, sounding dubious, "but I doubt she has a violent bone in her body."

"Anything's possible with this group," Abby muttered. Speaking normally, she said, "Let's close the book on Phyllis for now."

"Sure thing." Minnie took another slug of her cola.

"Let's talk about Gabby Chambers," I suggested.

"Not a huge fan," Minnie said, "but I can't imagine why she would want to kill either of us. Gabby's too perky, way too friendly and enthusiastic for my liking, but everyone else seems to like her."

"How long has she been working at Lifestyle Manor?" I asked.

"Let's see. Someone told me she arrived mid-April, so six months."

"And before Lifestyle Manor?"

"I'm guessing Vancouver, but only because her brother lives there. Come to think of it, I've never heard her talk about her past."

I shook my head. "I have a hard time picturing Gabby as a killer."

Abby said, "Hawk mentioned doing background checks on every suspect."

"Roland Bradshaw is the only other suspect," I said. "He may be a gigolo and a con-artist, but I'm hard-pressed to imagine him killing anyone."

"Not so fast," Minnie exclaimed. "We can't rule out Roland. He's on the hunt for a wealthy wife. I spoiled his moves on you by telling you he's a catfish."

"Seriously?" I asked. "Why would he think I was wealthy?"

Minnie's cheeks went bright pink. "Um … I might have mentioned you were co-owner of a highly successful dude ranch."

I huffed out a long-suffering sigh and consoled myself with another brownie. I intended to compensate with a salad, no dressing, for dinner.

While I chewed, Abby said to Minnie, "So Roland had a motive to get rid of you for spoiling his seduction attempts. Is there anything else we should know about him?"

"He didn't get along with Lizzie. I'm pretty sure she had some sort of information on him she used as blackmail material."

"How did you find out?" I asked.

"I overheard something."

"Tell us what it was, hon." Abby urged. A muscle in her jaw flickered.

"One evening a few weeks ago, I saw Lizzie and Phyllis sitting in the garden, heads together. This was right after my tiff with Lizzie, so I thought they might be discussing me. I snuck up behind them and crouched in the bushes behind their bench to listen."

"What did you overhear?"

Minnie spread her arms in a dramatic gesture. "Lizzie was telling Phyllis she'd learned Roland was a widower several times over."

"And how is his marital state relevant?" Abby asked.

"Lizzie told Phyllis she planned to have her PI follow up on their deaths. Funny thing is he never mentions a wife, never mind wives. I always figured he was single or divorced."

I tilted my head at her. "Could Roland have killed his wives?"

Minnie shrugged. "Who knows? Even if he didn't kill them, several dead wives might be a red flag for prospective marriage material. And if he did have a hand in hastening their deaths, then Lizzie had discovered the mother lode of blackmail material, in which case, Roland had a powerful motive to kill her."

I took a thoughtful swig of cola, hoping the caffeine would kick-start my brain. "Even if Phyllis doesn't know how Roland's wives died, she'd surely know if Lizzie was blackmailing him. But how do we find out? I doubt she will tell either of us."

Minnie pointed out. "She might spill her guts if Hawk asks. I'm pretty sure she prefers men to women."

Abby shrugged. "I guess it's worth a try."

"To summarize," I said, hoping to bring the meeting to a close, "Wayne had motive to kill Lizzie and a weaker motive to attack Minnie, one which can be ruled out by talking to Eleanor and his daughters. Eleanor and Roland had motive to kill both women. Phyllis, although perhaps lonely and a tad unhinged, appears to have no motive to kill either Lizzie or Minnie. And finally, there's Gabby, who also appears clean. I'm certain Hawk will do some digging into all the suspects' backgrounds and I'll suggest he ask Phyllis about Lizzie's blackmail attempts."

Abby stood and stretched. "In the meantime, the killer may try again, so we've got to remain on high alert."

Thinking of how a killer on the loose would destroy any chance we had to win the contest, I added, "And we must do everything in our power to prevent the guests from learning someone murdered Lizzie, and is now trying to kill Minnie."

A thoughtful expression crossed Minnie's face. "Besides us, Dodie, and Hawk, only the killer knows someone tried to kill me. Twice."

"That's not exactly true, I said. "Phyllis heard you say someone pushed you."

"Oh, don't worry about her," Minnie said airily. "She believes I was talking nonsense while in a state of shock. I'll say I was embarrassed about tripping over my walking stick and tumbling into the river. She'll believe that."

"Sounds good. Let's make sure someone accompanies Minnie at all times," I said, pretending her scowl indicated compliance.

"And since we're supposed to act normally," I continued, "I suggest you both attend the goat yoga class tomorrow. Dodie too."

At Minnie's groan, I patted her hand. "Not to worry, hon. I'll round up all the suspects and coax them into joining us. A yoga session will give us an opportunity to assess everyone in a relaxed setting."

"Sorry, I can't attend, but what about Hawk? Will you invite him to goat yoga?" Abby asked

"Maybe. But I'm sure he'll have better things to do with his time."

"Speaking of Hawk, once we return, I'm going to type up my notes and give them to him." She waved her notepad. "That'll bring him up to speed on our findings about our suspects."

"Great idea, Abs. You compile the best notes." I stood and tossed the remnants of our picnic supplies into the empty cooler.

She peered at me with concern while prying the cooler's handle from my grip. In a whisper intended only for me, she said, "You sure you're good with tonight's date?"

She was too perceptive by far. How could she know my brain warned me to keep him at arms-length, but the rest of me wanted to grab hold and hang on for dear life?

"I will be," I said, willing it to be true.

I intended to conquer my fear, and tonight would be the perfect start.

Chapter 12: Date Night

THE TABLES IN THE BIG Sky Bar and Grill were packed with an assortment of tourists and locals. Country and western music filled the air, and the place was hopping. Hawk had reserved a back corner table where it was somewhat quieter, and as soon as we were seated, he ordered a rich, red Cabernet Sauvignon. I sipped my wine, savoring its complexity, hoping a healthy gulp or two would lighten his mood. Pretending to study the menu, I slanted him a glance. His scowl told me something had gone amiss during the afternoon.

"Problem deciding what to order?" I asked.

"Nope."

Okay, so something was bugging him, and I had a feeling the something might be me. "You've been unusually quiet since we left Grizzly Gulch. What's wrong?"

He continued to study the menu. "I read Abby's notes."

"And?"

"They're truly amazing—detailed and complete. You managed to cover a lot of investigative territory in a short time."

"But?" Surely, he wasn't in a huff because we'd done such a fine, thorough job of analyzing each suspect without his input.

He raised his head and drilled me with a stony, dark-as-night gaze. "What were you thinking?" His outrage was so potent, I might as well have advocated a cull of the Canadian beaver.

I had an unwelcome flashback to my father towering over me while glowering in a similar manner, and gave a mental head-shake. This wasn't my father, Hawk had never exhibited a mean streak, and I suspected I was missing something important. Gathering my courage, I stiffened my spine and said, "Could you please elaborate?"

Shania Twain belted out *Man! I feel Like a Woman* at top volume.

Forcing me to lean in for his answer, he murmured, "What were you thinking, driving to Quarry Lake? There's a killer with a gun taking pot shots at Minnie. Did it not occur to any of you that you might be followed and gunned down?"

Actually, no.

I leaned back. Refusing to let him intimidate me, I followed my therapist's advice and took two deep, soothing breaths. Rational thinking returned. This was Hawk. Fear was unnecessary, and defensiveness was the wrong approach. A normal response would be unruffled, friendly.

"You sound worried, but there's no need," I said, pleased to achieve a cool, untroubled delivery. "Abby, Minnie, and I talked it through and decided it would be safer to discuss our suspects in a spot where no one could find us. We decided on Quarry Lake because the parkland around it is fairly open and no one could sneak up to eavesdrop or take us by surprise. We notified Dodie of our decision so no one would worry. During the drive, we kept a close watch for a pursuer. Although no one followed us, we took nothing for granted. On our arrival at Quarry Lake, we parked and waited at least five minutes to case new arrivals. Or bears. There were none of either variety. Abby and I made sure to pack bear spray. And before you ask, we stuck to Minnie like Velcro all afternoon, as promised."

With my heart thundering in my chest as if I'd run a marathon, I knocked back a healthy slug of wine.

The blonde server, likely in her mid-forties and oozing sex appeal in a micro mini and low-cut top, chose that moment interrupt our conversation. I couldn't help but notice that while she took our order—steak and kidney pie for Hawk and a bison burger and fries for me—she bent over a little more than necessary, offering him a tantalizing glimpse of the Promised Land.

After she disappeared Hawk remained silent for so long, my lingering anxiety ratcheted up a notch. He must be furious with me. But I was determined to outwait him instead of indulging in my normal nervous babbling.

At long last, he rubbed the bridge of his nose as if in pain, and said, "I apologize. I was unfair to you. In my defence, I was and still am worried sick you'll do something foolish to win that contest, and get yourself killed in the process." He drained his wine and refilled both glasses.

And there was the missing puzzle piece. He'd been worried and angry because he cared for me. My heart kicked hard. I replied, "If anything, I'm the one who owes you an apology—and an explanation."

"For what?"

"For how I treated you last spring."

"Not necessary. Let's put the past behind us and focus on the present." He regarded me with his customary ease. But his tapping fingers and tight lips revealed tension.

His vulnerability clutched at my heart the way nothing else could. "I want to explain why I bailed on you without a word."

"Only if you're ready."

Oh, I was so, so ready. I cleared my throat, uncertain where to start. I settled on

"I've missed you. More than you can possibly know. I can't begin to tell you how many times I've wished I'd done things differently. You were right. I was a coward. And here's why ..." I hesitated, wondering where to start.

"It's okay, you don't need to tell me anything that makes you uncomfortable."

"I want to. Really. It's only—"

Our server sashayed over to place our plates in front of us. "Here you go. Enjoy."

"It looks delicious," I said.

She stared at Hawk while moistening her upper lip with the tip of her tongue. "If you need anything else," she paused, "and I mean *anything*, please let me know."

"We're good, thanks," he said, never looking away from me.

Once the server flounced away, he reached for his knife and fork.

I generally have a healthy appetite, but the butterflies invading my stomach had killed my appetite.

"Are you not eating?" he asked, cutting into his flaky pie crust and releasing the fragrant steam.

I shifted in my seat. "Guess I ate one many brownies at Quarry Lake." True enough, but it wasn't the brownies affecting my appetite. I pushed my plate toward him. "Help me with the fries."

"Don't mind if I do." He forked some fries onto his plate and followed up with a squirt of ketchup before raising his gaze to my face. "You were about to explain why you're a coward."

I plunged in before I chickened out. "You already know I'm the youngest of three girls. What you don't know is I was a mistake. Mom had more than enough on her hands trying to shield two girls from our father without adding another. See, Daddy was an ugly drunk and wife-batterer, not to mention a serial womanizer."

A low, raw sound ripped from Hawk's throat. "I can guess the rest. You don't need to spell it out." His mouth tightened into a thin line, white against tanned skin.

"No, I want to tell you everything." While he demolished his meal, I popped a fry into my mouth to mask my hesitation. Everything I was about to reveal would surely turn him off. But at least he would know the truth.

I took a deep breath. "Daddy claimed he loved us, but he used to beat Mom over the tiniest infraction—like his soup wasn't hot enough, or it was too hot, or the tablecloth was stained, or she'd left shoes in the hallway—you get the drift. After a while, hitting Mom wasn't enough to get him off. By the time I was three, he was hitting my sisters too, always carefully. Visible bruises would land him in big trouble. Abby tried to avoid his beatings by being perfect. Sometimes it worked, mostly not. Dodie was the mouthy one. You can guess how she fared. But he never, ever, hit me. I was Daddy's pet. His little girl. I was the only person who could make him stop hitting my mom and sisters by using cute and ultra-perky antics to distract him. My strategy usually worked, except for the time he locked me in the basement for a day and a half."

I glanced at him to assess his reaction and got lost in the heat and raw power of his eyes. They flashed with fury. Fury on my behalf.

I intercepted an outburst. "It's okay. My parents died in a car crash years ago. He insisted on driving drunk and ..." I stopped speaking because there was a big, huge ball of emotion clogging my throat.

He put down his cutlery to clasp my hand. "I'm so sorry you had to suffer through such traumatic events."

"There's more." I extracted my hand to save him the embarrassment of dropping it himself once he found out the truth.

I was working up the nerve to reveal more when our server sashayed over. She directed a flirty smile at Hawk. "I hope you're enjoying your meals."

"They're great," I said, shoving fries around on my plate.

"Best in town," he said, never breaking eye contact with me. "You were saying?"

The server took the hint and departed.

"Where was I? Right. Immediately after high school graduation, I got myself a position at the Banff Springs Hotel and left home, mainly to escape Daddy. I loved everything about living in the Rockies—especially the freedom. While working at the hotel, I met a travelling salesman attending a conference there. He swept me off my feet in one of the most romantic places in the world—Banff. In one short week, I fell in love, quit my job, and married Russell. I was barely twenty to his early thirties."

"You were still a baby."

"Yeah, but I didn't think so. On the contrary, I felt grown up, certainly grown up enough to fall in love, or lust, as the case may be. I had no clue Russ would be worse than my daddy. Besides being a drinker who delighted in using fists and anything else that was handy to discipline me, he eroded my self-esteem until it shriveled and died. It all started slowly, first by pointing out my mistakes or correcting me, but it soon escalated to mocking, belittling, and generally acting as if my elevator didn't go near the top floor. I realize now he wasn't clever at all, far from it. He boosted his ego at my expense."

Hawk banged his cutlery down. "The worm belongs behind bars. It's not too late to press charges. Let me help." His voice was gritty with emotion.

I melted. He truly cared. "Russ died in a boating accident a month before our daughter's birth. He'd rented a boat on Lake Huron during one of his many business trips to Ontario and was out sailing with another woman. Neither Russ nor his girlfriend knew how dangerous submerged rocks were in the area. Their boat hit a rock and capsized. They weren't wearing lifejackets. I got the phone call the next day. He was forty, I was twenty-eight." Realizing I was hungry after all, I took a savage bite out of my bison burger.

He stopped eating. "I can't believe he cheated on you. The man was a cretin."

A tenderness I didn't know what to do with seeped over me. I clamped my lips together. How could I admit to Hawk I'd felt no sorrow on learning about his death, only relief? I must be a heartless bitch.

He stared at me, unblinking. "His death meant you had your life back. Now you could enjoy your baby, discover your intelligence, and build your self-esteem without a sadistic husband to terrify you."

His response gave me the courage to admit, "Truth be told, my sisters and I did a happy dance. And recently, after much therapy and many tears, I've reached a point where I feel grateful to Russell. After all, he gave me Wendy, my gorgeous daughter, and now four adorable grandchildren."

"You never told me how you managed to raise Wendy on your own. It couldn't have been easy."

Funny, I hadn't minded at all. "I lucked into a position as a live-in caregiver for my next-door neighbor, who suffered from a heart condition, had no family, and adored babies. She was a lovely woman, gentle and funny, who treated us as if we were her own family. On her death, she left me the house and a nice nest egg, enough for Wendy's university tuition and to support us comfortably, provided I was careful. Then two years ago, my sisters and I inherited Grizzly Gulch from our Uncle Benny, a confirmed bachelor who died doing what he loved—riding fences on his ATV."

"I'm not surprised you're reluctant to allow another man into your life."

"I may have been a tad hasty on that decision. I'd convinced myself that taking care of my child and anyone else who needed my help would be reward enough. Turns out I might have been wrong."

"Wrong, how?

"Um … you seem to have turned my world upside down."

"I feel the same way."

"I have something else to tell you."

"You can tell me anything."

The server interrupted our conversation again, removing our plates and handing us dessert menus. "Can I bring you another beverage?" she asked Hawk. The way she batted her eyes at him must surely create a brisk breeze. "A little dessert, perhaps? I recommend the English trifle."

"Perhaps later."

Taking the hint, the server sighed, and departed with a final eyelash flutter, reluctance written in her posture.

"Now where were we? Oh, yeah. Besides the fact that I've turned your world upside down, there was something else."

My hand was so damp with sweat, I put my glass down in case it slipped away from me. "I'm terrified to let go and trust you. It didn't work so well for me in the past."

Hawk encased my hand in his. "Your hands are freezing. And a little damp. Take a deep breath. You're safe now."

The warmth of his hands enclosing mine gave me the courage to say, "You never wanted to talk much about yourself. In fact, you were amazingly nimble at ducking personal questions. What deep, dark secrets are you hiding?"

He hesitated.

"That bad, are they?" I asked in a joking tone.

"Bad enough. Many women won't get involved with someone of mixed blood. I didn't mention it because I didn't want to scare you away."

I scrutinized his features, took in the high cheekbones, aquiline nose, dark eyes. "I'm guessing you're half First Nation."

"Yeah. That's why I always appear tanned no matter the time of year. I'm Nakoda Nation on my mother's side. She belonged to the Bearspaw band. But I'm Scottish on my father's side, which explains my love of British food, including porridge, deep-fried Mars bars, and organ meat, particularly in haggis or steak and kidney pie. I hope that's not a deal breaker."

"I can work with it. You never mentioned your childhood. Was it difficult for you growing up?" I continued eating, enjoying my burger for the first time tonight.

He shrugged. "I survived. Kids at school bullied me. They called me a half-breed and shoved me around. Luckily I was an early developer. I grew tall, strong, and agile. It helped that I learned how to use my fists. Once I fought back, the bullying stopped. Truth be told, I beat the crap out of the ringleader. It felt great."

"You fought back. Good for you. He deserved it."

"Here's the thing, Clara. Many bullied or abused kids are unable to fight back. I vowed I would do everything in my power to protect other helpless children and even the bullies themselves."

"When we first met, you were dealing with a couple of potential delinquents. The way you handled those two boys who'd tried to skip class is what first attracted me to you." That, plus he was smokin' hot, though I didn't reveal that observation.

"Since we're sharing, what else can I tell you about myself?"

"I already know you're a widower but you've never talked about your wife."

Hawk's expression told me I'd struck a nerve.

"I wasn't ready to reveal the full story," he admitted. "I'm still not, but I want you to know that Anne was an amazing woman, a social worker with the kindest heart. We had one son and one daughter, both now living near Calgary. Anne's death nine years ago devastated me." He stopped talking, as if too tormented to continue.

I refrained from pushing. He would reveal the entire story if and when the time was right. "I'm so sorry."

"Thanks. I never believed I could care as much for another woman until you came along. After our second date, I knew you were perfect for me."

Guilt made me hide my face in my hands. "And I skipped out on you."

Gently easing my hands away from my face, he murmured, "Let's put the past where it belongs—behind us. I would like a do-over."

I raised my head. "So would I. I'll do my best, but I must warn you I'm not sure I'll be able to let another man all the way into my heart." But right now, oh, how I wanted to.

"I get it. You suffered a lot of pain, both emotional and physical. What can I do to make you trust me?" he asked.

I lowered my gaze to study my plate. Perhaps I sensed he would try to prevent me from taking a few calculated risks to save Grizzly Gulch from foreclosure. And I'd seen signs that he might be overprotective, hyper-vigilant, and a tad controlling. I didn't want to second-guess my every move in the hopes of gaining his approval. I took a deep breath. "I don't know what to say. Be a good listener. Respect my opinions, especially if mine differ from yours. Don't boss me around or try to control me. Forgive me if I make mistakes—and I will." I thought hard, "And above all else, be kind and gentle."

"I can do all of that. We'll take it slow."

Right about now, I was far from sure I wanted slow. But slow was safe, and safe was inside my comfort zone, a place I was reluctant to leave. I nodded my agreement, but fair was fair. "What do you want from me?" I asked.

He appeared to give my question serious thought because he stopped eating. At last, he said, "Be yourself. I adore you exactly the way you are. And most important of all, tell me the truth. I can handle pretty much anything if you're straight with me. What I can't abide are lies, evasions, and errors of omission."

I hesitated. Would my goal to win the hospitality contest, regardless of whatever pesky risks I might encounter, be a show-stopper? Ever the people-pleaser, I delivered the answer I knew he wanted, no, *needed* to hear. "Sounds perfect."

Appalled that I'd kicked off a new start for our relationship with an evasion, I welcomed the guitar riff signaling the karaoke portion of the evening was about to begin. Rescued from the need to elaborate on my answer, I held out my hand. "Listen. The music's starting. Let's race everyone to the microphone."

Chapter 13:
Roland Ups His Game

OUR DINNER AND KARAOKE DATE at Big Sky Bar and Grill was the most enjoyable time I'd spent with a man since, well, my previous dates with Hawk. It was well after midnight when I finally rolled into my king-sized bed, too keyed up to fall asleep. The room, with its Wedgewood blue walls, white California shutters, and blue-and-white bed linens, seemed too big and lonely. My silky sheets might be a sensual pleasure, but they could never come close to the presence of one Hawk MacDougall sprawled beside me, all warm and rumpled and sexy.

Like a fool, I'd chickened out on arriving home. He hadn't argued, but simply pressed a gentle kiss on my lips and disappeared into his temporary quarters down the corridor, leaving me heartsick and yearning. Patience was highly overrated.

Pounding my pillow into submission, I told myself I'd dodged a bullet. Better to stay safe inside my lonely cocoon than take another chance on love. That's the thing about love. Pain and joy are all wrapped up together in a big tangled ball. I preferred to think my caution was a pre-emptive strike against heartbreak.

Fortunately, no one witnessed my solo return. Minnie, in a rare gesture of discretion, stayed at the opposite end of my apartment with her bedroom door closed.

A slight mattress shift indicated Snuggles had graced me with his presence. Arranging himself on my spare pillow, he yawned once, cocked one leg over his head in a highly undignified manner, and licked his kibble and bits area, such as it was, then curled into a tight, furry ball. I was certain his presence had little to do with friendliness and everything to do with the cat treats I'd stowed in my bedside drawer.

After I'd re-read the same page of my cozy mystery several times, the doorbell rang. Assuming Hawk missed me as much as I missed him and had come to sweet-talk his way inside, I unlocked the door to let him in.

I was so, so wrong.

"Surpri-i-ise," Roland greeted me, his eyes glazed. In spite of my protests, he darted past me into my foyer, kicking the door shut behind him. His burgundy bathrobe, gleaming with a satiny sheen, sported black lapels, black detailing, and a black satin sash. The implement he carried resembled a whip with an elegant ebony handle and long, black leather fringes tipped with burgundy rosebuds. Alcohol fumes filled the air, jump-starting unwelcome memories.

Taking advantage of the fact that shock had slowed my reflexes, he kept on going, weaving his way down my hallway, forcing me to scamper along behind. My bedroom door stood open. He took it as an invitation and entered, positioning himself at the foot of my bed.

I stepped inside and faced him. "You. Out," I said in a brooks-no-nonsense tone.

Snuggles hissed and leaped off the pillow to disappear behind the curtains.

"Aw, don't play hard-to-get, babe. We both know you want this."

He'd misconstrued my earlier politeness as a come-on. I reminded myself there was nothing to fear. Minnie was in the bedroom down the hall, and both Hawk and Dodie were one loud holler away. Not that I wanted or needed help. Nope. I was perfectly capable of facing down an unwanted intruder myself. Thankfully, I'd thrown on my un-sexiest flannel nightie.

Prepared to unleash my temper, something I seldom did, I remembered Roland was a Grizzly Gulch guest—a guest who would undoubtedly influence others to leave a one-star review if I freaked out on him. I needed a new tactic so I switched on the charm. "Roland. What a surprise. You must be lost."

"Nope. I'm exactly where I want to be," he said, slurring his words.

My heart gave an unpleasant little lurch. I had to find a way to make him leave without calling for help, if only to prove that I could. To buy myself time, I pointed to the strange whip he carried. "What's that thing called?"

"It's a flogger. Women love it." He whacked it against his thigh, exactly the way Russell had always whacked his belt when preparing to teach me a lesson for, say, leaving my shoes at the front door or overcooking his steak.

I reminded myself I was no longer a young wife under her brutal husband's thumb. I channeled all the inner strength I possessed and fisted my hands on my hips. "You're making one gigantic mistake."

"Stop playing hard to get. Admit it, babe. You're hot for me." In a shockingly abrupt move, he darted toward me, his hand outstretched.

I side-stepped his grope and scrambled onto the bed. "I'm not your babe, and I'm most definitely not hot for you." After crawling to the opposite side, I swung to my feet and glared at him. "You're drunk."

"Smart as well as beautiful. I'm also ready, willing, and able. I took a little blue pill, so I can last all night." The bedside lamp highlighted the erection tenting his satiny robe.

"Fudge nuggets," I whispered.

As if on the same wavelength, Snuggles growled while clawing his way up the curtain to the safety of the curtain rod.

"Get. Out. Now," I ordered.

"Bossy women turn me on. I'm gonna to rock your world, babe." Using one hand, he untied his sash and jutted his hips. "Ta-da."

With a swish of satin, the fabric swung open revealing a sight I could never un-see. Under the robe, Roland wore nothing but a glistening coating of oil. Expensive clothes had concealed a multitude of sins, including sagging man-boobs, a paunch, and a network of varicose veins.

I clapped a hand over my mouth to suppress my gag reflex.

"Let me introduce you to Lord Hardwick," he announced, his twig bouncing up and down while the berries swayed. "Every rock-hard inch wants you to play with him."

A surge of clean, cold anger washed over me. After Russell's death, I'd vowed I would never, *ever* take crap from another man, and that included a horny guest. "Put that thing away, Roland, and I don't mean the flogger."

He ignored my command. "I took Viagra and got myself manscaped, which is no picnic I might add, and all for you. It's time to par-tay." He dropped onto the rumpled sheets and attempted to crawl closer on all fours. Fighting the drag of my Suite Dreams memory foam mattress, Roland said, "How can you sleep on this thing? It sucks you down like quicksand."

A glance confirmed Lord Hardwick was in danger of digging a trench in my bed covers. I shuddered and backed away. "Get off my bed. You'll leave an oil slick."

"It's Candu Body Oil for men, very expensive, lovely and slippery." On reaching the edge, he hopped to the floor and took a step toward me.

A red haze clouded my vision. "I can't believe you think oil's a selling point."

"Don't worry. You'll appreciate it once we get going." The flogger thwacked again, this time followed by an agonized squeal.

Some leather strands had wrapped themselves around Lord Hardwick, tangling together in a bouquet of leather rosebuds.

I stifled a snicker.

"Freakin' frick frack. I've gotta be more careful," Roland muttered with a whimper, fumbling with both hands to untangle the strands and free his joystick. Due to constriction, Lord Hardwick matched the hue of the burgundy robe.

While I edged toward the door, Snuggles leaped to the floor and dropped into a crouch, hind legs coiled beneath him, every muscle quivering, his unblinking yellow gaze riveted on His Lordship.

Step by stealthy step, the cat crept forward. His belly brushed the plush carpet, his orange tail tip a-twitch.

I halted my retreat to watch the unfolding drama.

The leather strands parted and Lord Hardwick sprang free, miraculously erect, sprightly, and prepared for action. Roland, clueless of the peril awaiting him, uttered a triumphant, "Ta-da," at the same moment that Snuggles, a hunter at heart, launched himself at his prey. Front claws gripped the bouncing Lordship, while flailing back claws dug into manscaped thighs.

A blood-curdling shriek filled the air. Roland dropped the flogger and thundered around the room, bouncing off furniture while trying to dislodge his hissing assailant.

As they rocketed past, I could have sworn Snuggles winked at me.

They'd circled the room twice when the bedroom door burst open and Minnie charged in with flaring nostrils and an anxious expression. "What's happening? Is someone being murdered?" She skidded to a halt and stared. "Pluck a duck. *That's* a sight you don't see every day."

Roland's shriek jumped another octave.

"Is that your mating cry?" Minnie asked. "It's surprisingly resonant."

His response drowned out the cat's yowling with a string of f-bombs ending in a wail as the pair careened toward the door.

By then, the windows were rattling, Lord Hardwick was deflating, and Snuggles was hanging on for dear life.

"Don't let him leave," I yelled to Minnie. "Guests mustn't learn of this incident." I reached for my phone on the bedside table.

"Whoa. I'm not going near that dude," Minnie said. "He's buck naked and slicker than a slice of pork belly."

With the snarling Snuggles still firmly attached, Roland headed for the door. I tried to block his way, but a little fancy footwork helped him evade capture. An elbow to the gut slowed him down some, but he kept going.

There was no way I was letting him escape in his current state. I stooped and picked up the flogger. Snapping it in the air near his feet, I had the satisfaction of watching the leather strands twine around his ankles to bring him down like a felled ox. He lay on the floor, writhing, while Snuggles clung to his shrinking prey.

I was a natural with the flogger.

I'd barely recovered my wits when a bare-chested figure loomed in the doorway. Hawk's expression was thunderous. Leaking testosterone from every pore, he sauntered inside and glared.

A tsunami of desire swept through my body, blindsiding me. Exactly the right amount of lovely chest hair narrowed before disappearing into jeans riding precariously low on his bare hips.

"What's going on here?" Hawk's cold, gravelly utterance caused all activity to cease. All except Snuggles, who continued to knead Mr. Hardwick with his front paws.

"If I'm not mistaken, Snuggles is scent-marking Roland's pride and joy with the glands on his paws." Minnie smirked at Roland. "I guess that makes you his bitch."

I didn't take my gaze off Roland. "It's okay. I have this under control."

Hawk's lips curved in a badass grin. "So I see."

Roland stopped writhing and propped himself on one elbow with his other hand extended to Hawk in a pathetic gesture for help. "Thank God you're here."

"Don't count on me for help." Hawk ignored the outstretched hand. "You do realize there's a cat attached to your privates, don't you?"

"Duh! Of course I do. You've gotta help me. I'm afraid to pull him off." Roland reduced the volume to a hoarse whisper. "These women are psychotic." He struggled into a sitting position.

"We can hear you," I informed him.

Roland released an unsettling wail. "Please make her remove the cat."

Hawk propped himself against my dressing table and folded his arms. "I doubt that's within my power."

Overcome by a pang of conscience, I ran to my bedside table and dug into the drawer. A shake of cat treats persuaded Snuggles to release Mr. Hardwick and dart toward a food source.

Roland scrambled to his feet while snatching up his robe from the floor. He shoved his arms into the sleeves and drew the heavy satin fabric together, mercifully concealing his family jewels.

Hawk's expression softened as he regarded me. "I see you and Snuggles have reached an understanding."

"He promised not to hurt me so long as I fed him tuna and treats."

While Snuggles crunched on a chicken-flavored nugget, Roland turned his back on us and bent down to disentangle himself. The leather strands had wrapped themselves around his ankles good and tight. At last, the final strand released its grip. He shoved the flogger's handle into his robe's deep pocket, leaving a handful of limp strands dangling outside.

Hawk's scowl returned when he addressed Roland. "What on earth were you thinking?" He flicked a sheepish glance in my direction. "Sorry. This is your party."

His empathy gave me a full body buzz. I pinned Roland with a full-on glare. "I reiterate Hawk's question. What on earth were you thinking?"

Roland glance darted from me to Hawk, then back to me. "It's complicated."

"We have all the time in the world." Hawk crossed his long legs at the ankle, all relaxed and leaning against my dresser. "Why are you're sniffing around Clara like a besotted horndog?" He stopped and shrugged at me. "Sorry, force of habit. Continue."

"You'd better make it good, Roland," I said.

After a long silence, he said, "I … I couldn't help myself." He bestowed a wide-eyed gaze of sincerity at me. "You're the woman of my dreams, Clara. You're beautiful, kind, cultured—"

I interrupted Roland in mid-gush. "Don't try to hand me a load of horse pucky. Why are you really here?" I sauntered closer and in a surprise move, yanked on the trailing strands dangling out of his pocket, liberating the flogger into my waiting hands. "You thought I was rich. Admit it." I slapped the handle into my palm a couple of times, enjoying smacking sound it made.

"Ridiculous."

I skewered Roland with a glare. "I may be Grizzly Gulch's co-owner, but I'm neither rich nor the least bit interested in you. And FYI, your seduction approach needs a major overhaul."

"This washed-up actress," Roland jerked a thumb at Minnie, "must have filled your head with lies about me."

"I'm not washed-up, you slime ball. I'm semi-retired."

Sensing an impending explosion, I adopted a soothing tone. "Minnie has my back. She's very protective, doesn't want to see me get hurt."

"I've never hurt a woman in my life, at least not physically," he paused and flashed his perfect teeth, "although I may have broken a few hearts in my day."

"Maybe I should break your head instead," Hawk interjected in a tone would have shamed a KGB interrogator. His menacing posture and silky delivery would have made a stronger man than Roland soil his tighty-whities.

Roland must possess extraordinarily tight sphincters. "I didn't mean anything by tonight's visit. Comes from having one too many beers and a couple of joints. Speaking of joints, I feel kinda dizzy." He collapsed onto the bed and tugged his robe together.

Minnie voiced my thoughts. "For a man who was prancing around naked a few minutes ago, you're demonstrating surprising modesty."

I was grateful Hawk had my back, but for once, this was my show. "We seem to have veered off-topic." I closed in on Roland and snapped the flogger, pleased with his squeal. "We were having a little discussion about you hurting people."

Roland cringed away. "There's n-nothing to tell. Really."

My euphoria disappeared in a flash when I realized my daddy and Russ must have felt the same way when they terrified me. The thought sobered me up in a big hurry and I lowered the flogger.

Minnie chimed in with, "That's not what Lizzie told me. She said you'd hurt plenty of women."

I released a gusty sigh. "This is taking too long. Perhaps I should call our barn manager to help Hawk cart you away," I mused. "I should warn you, though. Zeke's meaner than a badger on steroids when dragged out of bed after midnight."

Zeke would undoubtedly be amused to hear my description of him.

Roland's gaze brimmed with wariness. "Much as I hate to speak ill of the dead, Lizzie lied, or at least twisted the truth. Sure, I may have hurt some women, but only emotionally, never physically, or at least only with their permission." He gave an 'aw, shucks' shrug. "It's not my fault if they fell for me. I've never been a one-woman man." He refused to meet my gaze.

"What are you not telling us?" I asked.

A bead of sweat trickled down Roland's neck to disappear under the black satin collar. "Truth is, I'm into BDSM."

Minnie whispered to me, "BDSM means Bondage and Discipline, Dominance and Submission, Sadism and Masochism."

"I know what BDSM means, hon," I whispered back.

Ignoring our exchange, Roland eyeballed the flogger in my hand. "That's my flogger. Her name is Fanny."

I swore Hawk suppressed a snicker.

Roland leaped off the bed, yelling, "She's mine. You can't have her." With the speed of a darting cobra, he yanked Fanny from my grip.

As I backed out of Fanny's range, Roland said, "You'd be surprised how many women, some men too, enjoy a little discipline behind closed doors, always consensual, mind you, never violent. I call these sessions *Fun with Fanny*. Some Lifestyle Manor residents tell me it's on their bucket list." He perched on the edge of the bed and tenderly placed Fanny on his lap.

I muttered, "Let the record show BDSM isn't anywhere near my bucket list."

Minnie, who'd remained surprisingly quiet, spoke up. "Here's the thing, Roland. I've been listening to you and studying your body language. So now I'm going to let you in on a little secret. See, I have a special gift."

"Congratulations."

"Bite me," she said. "As an actress, I need to understand my characters, both inside and out, get into their skin, their heads, their thoughts. That's how I grew to be a superior judge of character. Matter of fact, it's a lot like being a con artist."

Roland's grin wobbled, but only for a second. "I'm happy for you, babe."

Minnie released a derisive snort. "You might not be so happy to learn I'm on to you. There's more you're not telling us. Lizzie thought having all your wives die on you was suspicious. She bragged about blackmailing you."

Roland bathed us in an innocent gaze. "Well, she tried, but didn't get far with her blackmail." He spread his arms. "I'm innocent of any wrongdoing."

"Tell us about your wives," I said. "How many did you have?"

"Four. I'm a widower four times over."

"How did they die?"

"Natural causes. Vera had a massive heart attack. Lucinda died in a car accident." At Minnie's eye roll, he said, "She was a terrible driver, had her license revoked, but needed an ice cream fix. She took the car while I was napping, end of story. Hazel died of Alzheimer's, and a stroke took Nell in the middle of one of our *Fun with Fanny* sessions. I didn't kill any of them, and I have death certificates to prove it."

"Better keep them handy in case you need them," I advised him.

Hawk unfolded from the wall. "I've heard enough." He checked the time. "It's late, Roland. Unless Clara wants to press charges about tonight's little visit, I see no reason to call the Mounties."

I shook my head. "I won't press charges. Let's write this episode off as an unfortunate misunderstanding. I'll call a wrangler to walk Roland to his cabin, but first, I'll dig out my first-aid kit. It contains antibiotic cream and those new Gorilla Power Adhesive Strips."

"Planning to play doctor and patient with me, are you?" Roland asked hopefully.

"Not in this lifetime. You'll tend to yourself."

Minnie snickered. "It's a good job he's manscaped down there."

While Roland discreetly doctored himself, I phoned a wrangler and gave him instructions to escort an inebriated guest from my quarters to his cabin. Six minutes, much cursing, and several whimpers later, Roland, Fanny, and his escort departed.

Once they disappeared, Minnie announced, "I'm too jittery to sleep. Anyone else?"

"Yeah. I'm wide awake too," I admitted. "I need alcohol."

Hawk said, "I'm on board."

"I'll pour the drinks." I slid a glance at his chest hoping he'd forget about the shirt. Blood rushed to my face when he noticed I was staring.

"I need a shirt," he said. "I'll be right back."

By the time Hawk returned, fully clothed, Minnie and I had migrated to the kitchen. I'd fixed us stiff drinks. She'd already downed two shots of Canadian whiskey and was working on her third.

As we crowded around my kitchen table, I slid an unobtrusive glance at Hawk, and breathed deeply. Oh, yeah. He smelled of soap and something citrusy and piney, all combined with his own distinctive scent. His knowing assessment of my face indicated he suspected my thoughts, which, truth be told, were triple-X-rated.

He smiled at me, a slow, melting one I was certain had set more than a few hearts pounding. "Well done, Clara. You're a born interrogator."

Flustered, I shifted in my chair and said, "I must admit it felt pretty good." It was the first time I hadn't felt at a disadvantage during a dispute with a man.

I faked a yawn, hoping Minnie took the hint. It would be lovely to have some alone time with Hawk. "Let's make this quick. We have goat yoga tomorrow."

"I assume I'm invited," Hawk said, "and I'll be there."

"That's not necessary," I assured him.

"Nothing could keep me away."

A tingle trickled down to places I was starting to believe time had forgotten.

"Fine by me," Minnie said through a yawn. "The booze has kicked in. I'm sleepy."

"Do either of you want my opinion on whether or not we continue investigating Roland?" Hawk asked.

We both assured him we did.

"Right, then. Let's discuss the attacks on you, Minnie. Does Roland have a motive to kill you?"

Minnie examined him as if he'd sprouted had two heads. "Absolutely. I bragged about Clara, making Roland think she's rich. Then he heard me warn her he's a gigolo. He was afraid I would influence his next meal ticket to reject him."

"To keep this quick, let me be the voice of reason," Hawk said. "It might be a motive, but only if the attacks on you took place after tonight's rejection. Clara was friendly to Roland all along, friendly enough to raise his hopes for romantic success. I doubt he'd mess up his chances with her by killing you."

"I agree," I said. "Roland is sleazy, but I don't believe he attacked Minnie. Until tonight, I'd made a point of being nice to him." At Minnie's appalled expression, I said, "Hey, we need every good review we can get to win the contest."

"Bummer," Minnie said. "I forgot the contest. But what about Lizzie? Okay, so Roland's wives may have died natural deaths, but knowing Lizzie, she likely threatened to spread the word he'd murdered them, and wouldn't that really put a crick in his dick with the next lucky lady?" She threw back her head and cackled with laughter.

"Roland seems to have no reason to kill Lizzie other than to stop her from spreading rumors about him," I said. "It's pretty weak as motives go."

"I agree with Clara," Hawk said. "I think we should rule out Roland, at least for now."

Minnie's eyes gleamed. "In that case, my money's on Eleanor. She's totally jealous of me."

"Go to bed, Minnie. We're all tired." I rose to my feet, hoping she would take the hint.

She did, giving me a sly wink I pretended to ignore. My heart galloped in my chest at the idea of being alone with Hawk. I was more than ready to take it to the next level.

Once Minnie was gone, Hawk rose too. I couldn't suppress a wicked little shiver of anticipation. Wrapping his arms around me, he lowered his lips to mine, which opened obediently. His gentle kiss zapped through me from head to toe and lingered in all the fun spots in between, sending a cascade of delicious shivers through my entire body. He backed away first and gripped my arms, gazing down at me tenderly.

"Um … " I managed. Blindsided by the tsunami of desire sweeping through me, I had apparently lost the power of speech.

Hawk, on the other hand, did not appear similarly afflicted. "Not tonight, sweetheart. I want you to be sure."

He called me sweetheart. "I am."

"You've been traumatized and must be exhausted. When we do make love, I need you to be one hundred percent certain." He kissed the tip of my nose and headed for the front door. "Don't worry about walking me to the front door. I'll see myself out." Over his shoulder, he said, "If we don't see one another at breakfast, I'll see you at goat yoga tomorrow."

After he'd left, I locked up and lay wide awake, quivering with lust, for a long, long time. If he'd wanted me to beg, he couldn't have picked a better strategy.

Chapter 14: Yogis and Yoginis Gather

Snuggles made a great alarm clock. If not for the hungry feline's insistence on breakfast, I would have done the unthinkable and snoozed through our most popular activity at Grizzly Gulch—goat yoga. Our Pygmy goats were so adorable in all their bleating glory that even the grumpiest guest couldn't help smiling when one climbed on board for a cuddle.

Happy guests leave five-star reviews. Better still, relaxed guests let their guard down, often over-sharing personal information. Today, I had high hopes for both outcomes.

I shouted for Minnie. The only response was a feline yowl. Dragging myself out of bed, I went about placating a hungry cat. Trying to ignore the pathetic meows, I prepared Snuggles' breakfast according to Abby's instructions—tuna with two leftover shrimp chopped into it, all sprinkled with dry kibble topping. He twined around my feet with chirpy happy-purrs. I'd poured the day's first double espresso and loaded it with cream and sweetener when I noticed Minnie's note on the kitchen table.

"*Gone to breakfast, see you at yoga. XOX Minnie.*"

I'd been abandoned for the dining hall's gourmet delights. No problem. I welcomed the peace and quiet before facing our suspects during the morning goat yoga session.

Breakfast—raisin bran, one multi-vitamin for women over fifty, and another fully loaded double espresso—perked me up. Unfortunately, the caffeine also jangled my nerves, raising my anxiety level. If our guests learned the truth of Lizzie's murder and two attacks on Minnie, we could kiss our contest win goodbye. It didn't help that I'd either outgrown my cute floral yoga outfit or it had shrunk. Sighing, I threw on my relaxed-fit leopard-spotted tunic top over black leggings.

After tidying the kitchen and scratching Snuggles' soft, furry head, I pocketed the key and set off, determined to greet our yoga participants with serenity.

The paved pathway from the main lodge wound between fragrant stands of lodgepole pine, spruce, and fir. Horses whinnied in a distant pasture. During my walk, I raised my face toward the sun, brilliant in a sky shimmering with pure, clear blue. Sweet mountain air flowing eastward from the Rockies smelled of autumn and sunshine, but carried a promise of winter.

At times like this, troubles seemed far away. What could possibly go wrong?

The path forked, one arm leading to the barns and outbuildings, the other to the recreation hall, which doubled as a yoga studio. Newly renovated after the tornado, our rec hall echoed our main barn's structure with its gabled roof and overhanging eaves. The building was bright, airy and restful, the perfect location for yoga, especially since we'd added a fenced goat paddock along one side.

I absorbed the pastoral view of eight tiny goats leaping and playing with one another in the paddock while Larry, our guard llama, reclined regally in a sunny corner.

I was well on my way to feeling grounded when I noticed a woman standing inside the yoga studio's back door. My blood pressure spiked. Her face was in shadow so I couldn't make out her features. We always kept the door to the goat paddock locked. She shouldn't be there. I raced toward the fence.

The woman squealed with excitement as she entered the paddock and bounced toward the bleating goats. The bouncy stride and eager squeals were a dead giveaway. Only Gabby bounced everywhere, accompanied by enthusiastic chirps and giggles.

Larry lumbered to his feet and sauntered closer to his charges. Stomping one two-toed foot he fixed an unblinking gaze on Gabby. His long eyelashes and cute, fuzzy topknot often fooled guests into believing he was sweet and harmless. And generally, he was. But squealers, especially bouncy, squeaky squealers, riled him up, and a riled-up Larry tended to eject streams of green, stinky gastric juices at those who upset him. His aim was deadly accurate.

I moved quickly to head off a confrontation. Leaning over the fence, I shouted across the paddock, "Good morning, Gabby. Please slow down. We don't want to frighten the goats."

Nor do we want Larry to feel threatened.

Blithely unaware of the danger she courted, Gabby adjusted her trajectory. Blonde curls a-bouncing she headed toward me. "Good golly, Clara. Those little goats are so cute, I could cuddle them all." She released a high-pitched giggle.

I checked out her midriff-baring tie-dyed yoga outfit. Motivated, I sucked in my tummy. "You'll get your chance in a few minutes. How did you get inside the yoga studio? I must remind the wranglers to keep the doors locked."

"Oh, please don't do that. It's my fault. I asked one of those cute cowboys to let me in." Her grin was sheepish. "When I put my mind to it, I'm hard to resist."

She wasn't wrong. "Why don't you join me on the front porch?" I suggested. "The instructor likes to be alone in the yoga studio while she arranges everything and gets herself grounded in preparation for leading the session."

"Of course." Gabby retraced her steps. Larry swiveled his head to track her progress. She disappeared inside and I marched along the side fence toward the porch.

Approaching voices caused me to swing around. The sight of Hawk striding toward me in jogging shorts and a black tee-shirt lovingly molded to his torso gave me a full-body buzz. Several paces behind him, Minnie, who carried a brown paper bag, chatted with Phyllis while they approached at a more leisurely pace. Phyllis' baggy gray sweatpants and stretched-out tee-shirt were a stark contrast to Minnie's stylish black leotard outfit.

Hawk reached my side. Pretending to be unaffected by his presence, I waved at the two women and yelled, "What's in the brown paper bag? Yoga snack?"

"Chef Armand's bran muffins. He insisted I take them. I'm planning to offer them around after yoga," Minnie said as she and Phyllis caught up with us.

Hawk flashed me a quick, easy grin. "Hi beautiful." Draping a proprietary arm around my shoulder, he kissed my cheek. "You're looking mighty fine."

My insides transformed into goo—the horny, I-want-to-jump-your-bones kind of goo. If I didn't know better, I could believe my body was still producing hormones. "Thanks. You do too," I replied, wondering if his sexy one-day scruff felt soft or scratchy. Heat pooled in my belly. Hoo boy, I was in danger of falling deeper.

Minnie's gaze sharpened as if she could read my mind. "Is there something you two want to tell me?"

"Nope," I said.

Wayne joined the group. Miracle of miracles, he was alone. This was the first time I'd seen him without Eleanor as a permanent attachment.

As if reading my mind, Wayne said, "I doubt Eleanor will join us. She wanted to, but she's exhausted." He told Minnie in a stage whisper, "It's all your fault."

"Really? How so?"

I held my breath and waited for his explanation.

Wayne winked at Minnie. "I took your advice."

"Bad move," Phyllis interjected. "Minnie's advice sucks. After graduation, she advised me to accept a position as Bylaw Compliance Officer with Revelstoke City Hall. The job was a dead end. I never got a promotion, never had a chance to spread my wings. Worse still, I got stuck at home for four decades to deal with my mother. She had a new ailment every day."

I couldn't believe Phyllis blamed Minnie for her own inertia and incompetence.

Minnie ignored Phyllis and stared at Wayne. "What advice of mine did you take?"

He shrugged. "I'd already told my daughters about my affair with Lizzie, and last night I came clean with Eleanor."

"Way to go," Minnie said. "No more secrets."

"The affair wasn't exactly a secret," Phyllis said. "Lizzie told me."

They both ignored Phyllis. "How did Eleanor react?" Minnie wanted to know.

"At first, she freaked out," Wayne said.

"Well, duh. It's not the kind of thing a girlfriend likes to hear."

Wayne laughed. "Turns out she was upset because I'd confided in you about the affair. We were up late drinking and fighting until I managed to convince her you and I weren't a thing, never would be, and she was the only woman for me. Afterwards, we stayed awake for another reason, if you get my drift."

Minnie grinned. "Huh. So you got lucky. Instead of blaming me, you should thank me. Groveling would be acceptable."

My brain whirled. Wayne's revelations changed everything. "I need to talk to you about, uh, your apartment," I told Hawk, tugging him out of earshot.

"What's wrong with my apartment?"

"Nothing." Distracted by how good he smelled, I shook my head to clear out the lust. "It was an excuse to discuss our suspect list without Phyllis listening in."

"Sure thing. If that's how you want to play it."

I ignored his knowing expression. "Wayne eliminated half his motive for murdering Lizzie by confessing to his daughters before she died. Last night's similar confession to Eleanor happened too late to exonerate him, but I view that bygone affair as a weak murder motive."

"I agree. But couldn't Eleanor be disguising her anger with sexual gymnastics?"

"She and Wayne seem besotted with one another."

"I thought women found it easy to fake sexual satisfaction." Hawk's grin faded. "Please tell me you didn't fake anything with me."

Heat crept into my face. "Absolutely not. But God knows I faked it often enough with Russ to avoid a beating or worse."

It was his turn to turn brick red. "The bastard. If he wasn't already dead, I—"

I cut him off in mid-rant. "Here's the thing. Minnie told us Eleanor was a con artist. I wonder if she's convincing enough—or desperate enough—to use a sex marathon to persuade Wayne she believes Minnie is his poker buddy instead of a girlfriend." I forced myself to stop talking.

He let a prolonged silence stretch out, then spoke slowly. "If you're correct, Eleanor appears guiltier than ever." His face creased in a broad grin. "No wonder I'm attracted to you. With that kind of reasoning power, you make an amazing investigator."

He appeared about to kiss me when an approaching jogger encased in fuchsia Spandex distracted us both. Squinting into the sun, I discerned a body shape that screamed *Dodie*, but that was impossible. My sister loathed jogging. Furthermore, she had duties back at the lodge.

We rejoined the group while Dodie simultaneously lurched to a halt beside me. Her bosom heaving and dripping face an alarming shade of scarlet, she bent over at the waist to suck in great gulps of air.

I stepped forward in alarm. "Are you okay? Why are you here? Aren't you needed back in the kitchen or at the front desk?"

After a lengthy pause, she straightened and ignored my question. "Whoever said jogging . . . *puff* . . . is addictive . . . *puff, wheeze* . . . is a lobotomized liar."

"You don't look so good," Minnie told Dodie. "I hate to tell you, hon, but your face matches your hot pink outfit."

"She's right," I said. "Why are you jogging? You hate jogging."

Dodie straightened slowly. "Maybe I need to lose a pound or twenty. We don't want a repeat of the first night's dinner incident."

"Everyone found your boobage's break for freedom hilarious," Phyllis offered. "It's now officially known as The Great Escape."

We all wisely kept our mouths shut, but I noted Hawk's eyes twinkled.

"You sure you're okay?" I asked Dodie.

"I'm dandy." Tugging at the crotch of her crop pants, she said, "These yoga bottoms, on the other hand, are not. Isn't Spandex supposed to be forgiving? This thing gives me a wedgie."

"Maybe if you bought the right size?" Phyllis suggested.

Dodie shot Phyllis a lethal scowl. "It'll stretch."

"Hope springs eternal," Phyllis replied.

Dodie switched her attention back to me. "I'm here because our yoga instructor called in sick this morning. I'll have to lead the class. There's no one else."

"No way," I said. "I'm going to re-schedule the class. The last time you led a yoga class, you let the goats escape. It took five wranglers all afternoon to round them up. Larry spat on one of the poor guys. He was so grossed out he handed in his resignation. Zeke had to offer him a bonus to stay."

"Not to worry." Minnie laid a hand on my arm. "This is, indeed, your lucky day. Dodie won't have to lead the class after all. You may not know this, but I used to be a yoga instructor before I became an actress."

"Of course you were," Phyllis muttered.

Minnie ignored the comment. "I watched some videos about goat yoga last night. I consider myself more than qualified to lead the class."

"There's typical Minnie for you, always the center of attention," Phyllis said.

"That's because of my leadership skills."

"Others call it being a show-off and know-it-all."

There was some truth to what Phyllis said. I hoped Minnie hadn't exaggerated her ability to lead the class. Her tendency to overestimate her talents had tripped her up on more than one occasion.

"Aren't you two supposed to be friends," I asked Phyllis.

"Oh, we are," Phyllis assured me. "But someone needs to keep her in line. I like to remind this one about how she ignored me all through high school, stole the boy I loved, married him, then kicked him to the curb." She held out her hands with a what-can-you-do shrug and patted Minnie's arm. "Don't worry. All the girls had a crush on Jimmy. I was no exception. It's no big deal."

"I'm sorry if I hurt you," Minnie said. "I never wanted to offend anyone."

"I was teasing, silly. I got over Jimmy eons ago."

"So we're good?" Minnie asked Phyllis.

"Better than good."

Meanwhile, Pete, a cute wrangler in well-worn jeans and boots, a neckerchief, and checkered shirt, had shooed the goats inside. Minnie nudged me. "Do you or do you not want me to lead the class?"

I'd been so distracted by the squabbling, our need for a yoga instructor had slipped my mind. "Most definitely. I couldn't be more grateful. Thank you."

"Smart answer," Dodie agreed. "Since I'm here, I'll stay for the class. Right now, we need to prepare the hall for guests. I'll help Minnie put booties on the goats and lay out the mats. Yoga setup's harder than you think. Follow me."

Minnie and Dodie bustled past us and entered the building.

A flurry of new arrivals included several guests I hadn't met earlier. We exchanged introductions while congregating on the porch. Knee pain, hip replacements, blockages of various types, and other assorted health issues, each more cringe-worthy than the last, were the main conversational topics.

Frantic bleating interrupted a woman's sprightly tale involving diverticulitis. Dodie and Minnie must be rounding up goats to attach soft leather booties onto their tiny hooves. I hoped Pete had stayed to help.

The storyteller shrugged and continued her anecdote as if nothing unusual was happening, "So I doubled over in agony—"

"Oh, no you don't, you little devil," Dodie yelled, drowning out the anecdote. "Son of a *peach*!" This was followed by a loud thud.

I cringed, but at least she'd refrained from swearing.

"Baaa-a-a-a," a goat cried, at least I assumed it was a goat.

Undeterred, the woman continued her story at top volume, hollering, "I ended up in hospital with two real cute doctors—"

I closed the main door, hoping to muffle the sounds of conflict. It didn't work.

By then, the woman was bellowing to be heard over the ruckus. Her punch line was lost in the continuous bleats, squeaks, shouts, and Dodie's occasional *fudge nuggets*.

At long last, the yelling, thundering, and bleating died away. A few minutes later, Dodie materialized and stood beside me. She swiped at the sweat streaming down her face and onto the brown paper bag she was holding for Minnie. "Mission accomplished. No fatalities," she announced to the group, evoking laughter.

A booming gong tone reverberated into the golden morning air, signaling the start of yoga. I sucked in a deep breath. *Happy guests, relaxed guests,* I repeated inwardly as I threw the door open.

Chapter 15: The Zen of Goat Yoga

Dodie and I flanked the yoga studio's door while the participants streamed past us. I peeked inside, compelled to double-check that all was well—not necessarily a given with Minnie and Dodie doing the setup.

I blew out a relieved sigh. Everything was immaculate, from the whitewashed walls to the easy-clean laminate flooring, which fooled most into thinking it was genuine white oak planks. Five rows of yoga mats in front of a raised platform met my uniformity standards. Occasional bleats emerged from an enclosed pen at the far end of the room.

Minnie was in her element. Standing front and center on a raised platform, she held a microphone in one hand and a soft-headed mallet in the other. Behind her, a brass gong—gleaming, exotic, and massive—hung suspended from an intricately carved wooden stand.

Minnie shouted into the mic, "Yogis and yoginis. Welcome to goat yoga at Grizzly Gulch. Please remove your shoes, take a mat, and make yourselves comfy. You'll find pillows near the door."

Everyone seized a pillow. Some took two.

While Dodie and I waited until all participants had entered, I entertained myself by admiring Hawk as he ushered Phyllis into the back row. He remained standing until, with distressingly little effort, she'd arranged herself on a pillow. Only then did he adopt the lotus position on the adjoining mat.

He smiled at me. I melted.

Gabby and Wayne slipped into the row in front of Hawk, while others filed past and occupied mats at the front of the room.

Dodie tapped my back and whispered, "Let's go. Move."

Before she could elbow me aside and commandeer the empty mat beside Hawk, I kicked off my shoes, collected two pillows, and hustled inside. I tossed my pillows onto the mat beside him and plopped down gracelessly, taking care not to let a geezer-grunt escape.

A moment later, Dodie squeezed past me to the last empty mat. First, she placed a brown paper bag on the floor behind the mat, explaining that Minnie had asked her to safeguard her bran muffins while she led the class. Next, she clambered onto three stacked pillows with loud grunts.

"I don't see Roland," Hawk commented. "Can't say I'm surprised. He must have the king of hangovers."

I replied softly, "Just as well he's not here. Minnie might flip out."

In front of us, Wayne swiveled around and said, "I'm saving an extra mat for Eleanor in case she changes her mind and joins us."

"How lovely," I lied, thinking he'd do well to dump the gold digger. Wayne was a lovely man, kind, enthusiastic, and obliging. He deserved better.

I was chastising myself for my mean thoughts when a shrill, "Yoo-hoo!" pierced my eardrums.

Every head in the room swiveled to watch Eleanor sashay inside and sway toward Wayne. Her mauve yoga top with purple chevrons and matching tights must have set him back a pretty penny.

"Brilliant. Here's the naughty boy I'm searching for." She executed a series of complex stretches and bends as a prelude to squatting in a perfect lotus position on the empty mat beside him. At close range, the greenish tint to her skin and dark circles beneath her eyes were visible under a thick layer of foundation makeup. Booze and wild monkey sex were taxing for women over a certain age.

Gabby's disapproving expression revealed her opinion of Eleanor.

"So who's here today?" Eleanor scanned the crowd in front and glowered at Minnie before twisting her head and looking down her long English nose to assess our row. She faced forward again. Nudging Wayne, she said in an undertone, "Oh, dear. Did you check out poor Phyllis?"

Proving she had excellent hearing, Phyllis used her pointer finger to jab Eleanor between the shoulder blades. "What exactly does 'poor Phyllis' mean?"

"Ouch." Eleanor swiveled her head to scowl at Phyllis. "Watch who you're poking, dearie. You might regret it," she drawled. "To answer your question, it's time you invested in a new yoga outfit. The one you're wearing reminds me of a bag lady." She faced forward again, missing or ignoring Phyllis' murderous expression.

Perhaps Eleanor should worry about her own safety.

I was deciding how to break this newsflash to Hawk when Minnie's voice boomed through the microphone. She introduced herself, finishing with, "If you've ever dreamed of having a Zen experience, this is your lucky day. Our goats will transport you to a magical place."

Phyllis killed the buzz of excitement in a big hurry by saying, "I'm not sure how letting a goat herd trample on us can possibly transport anyone to a magical place."

Minnie released a disapproving sniff, but she did an admirable job of hanging on to her temper. "Goats are loving creatures, attentive, and interested in people—a lot like dogs. They are adorable, expressive, and fun animals with personality to spare." She pinned Phyllis with a steely gaze. "With a big old attitude shift, perhaps you'll enjoy the experience."

"Don't hold your breath," Phyllis muttered. She shouted, "Let's get this show on the road. The sooner we start, the sooner we're out of here."

Minnie's complexion pinkened. "If you're wondering why the goats come to us—"

"I wasn't," Phyllis said.

Undeterred, Minnie continued her spiel. "It's because for baby goats, also known as kids, jumping and climbing are their way of playing. Mother goats let their babies jump and climb all over them. So if a goat climbs on you, that means it likes you enough to consider you family, therefore safe. Goats know instinctively who to trust. They can sense the energy you project. Positive attracts, negative repels.

Someone else yelled out, "Enough talking, already. Where are the goats?"

"Yeah. If they're not here in a minute, I can still make the trail ride."

Displaying exemplary self-control, Minnie said through clenched teeth, "I wasn't quite finished, but I'll give the remaining explanations and instructions during the session. Have fun, people. You too, Phyllis. Be one with the herd."

She placed her hands to her heart center in prayer pose. "Trust the goats, and please repeat after me, "Baaaah-mastay."

Everyone but Phyllis adopted the prayer position and intoned, "Baaaah-mastay."

Minnie whacked the gong, triggering a chorus of plaintive bleats. I swore the sound waves loosened several fillings.

"I hope she lays off the gong," Hawk muttered. "Listen to those poor animals."

"I'm sure she knows better," I replied, infusing my words with a certainty I did not feel.

"Don't count on it," Phyllis said.

Luckily, Pete flung open the door to the goats' pen, diverting me from making a reply I would regret. The appearance of eight tiny goats in red leather booties springing into the room triggered the desired response. Coos of delight and squeals of laughter from our guests filled the air. The goats snuffled our feet, head-butted one another, and leaped onto laps for snuggles and kisses.

The most adorable tan and white goat named Rosebud landed in Hawk's lap and nuzzled a fuzzy head into his face for a kiss. How cute was that?

My first goat was a sweet little white one named Creampuff. She walked daintily onto my lap and curled up for a quick cuddle and stole my heart before she capered away.

On noticing Phyllis was goatless, I leaned across Hawk to console her. "Remember what Minnie told us," I whispered. "It's all in the energy we project, so think happy thoughts."

Phyllis pretended she hadn't heard me.

Amidst bleats, giggles, and chatter, the sound of rustling paper distracted me, but I tried to ignore it. The scrunching and crackling increased in intensity. I twisted my neck to find a fuzzy black-and-white goat named Fluffer standing behind Dodie, his nose thrust into the paper bag. He came up for air, munching enthusiastically, his cute little face coated in crumbs.

Beside me, Dodie had also clued in to what was happening. "Stop," she hissed at Fluffer, reaching for him. "Spit out that muffin."

Being a goat, Fluffer ignored her command and whirled away from her grasping fingers, swallowing a mouthful so large, he made tiny gagging sounds. Ribbons of brown paper dangled from his mouth. With a loose, sideways chewing motion, Fluffer made quick work of the paper. Swallowing, he leaped onto my lap and nuzzled me. I fell in love.

Dodie moaned in dismay. "Lord love a duck. That goat ate all Minnie's bran muffins. She won't be happy."

"Neither will the goat," Phyllis said.

I stroked Fluffer's head. The culprit gazed at me and blinked a pair of dark and disconcertingly intelligent eyes, snuggling his head under my chin.

Phyllis, who'd been listening avidly to every word, waved to attract Minnie's attention. "Yo, Minnie," she yelled over the racket. "A goat ate your bran muffins."

Minnie scowled. "And you're telling me this, why?"

"Constipation must be an ongoing problem for you." Phyllis' grin was pure spite. "I'll never forget those things you brought to class. You called them Powerful Bran Muffins. No one wanted to eat them, but you convinced me to give them a try."

"I remember all too well." Minnie giggled. "I didn't mean you should eat four."

The unfolding drama held everyone captive.

"You ate four bran muffins?" someone asked. "That was brave."

Laughter rippled through the crowd.

My stomach did several flip-flops. This most definitely was not the Zen experience I'd hoped to create for our guests.

"You kept insisting," Phyllis shouted. "I thought it meant you liked me."

"Hey, I offered them to everyone. I'd baked them myself and they were delicious." Minnie fisted her hands on her hips. "I didn't shove them into your mouth. You pigged out voluntarily. Who knew you'd have to run home for a change of underwear?"

"That was the most humiliating moment of my life," Phyllis wailed while Fluffer slipped off my lap and danced away behind us.

Hawk's whisper tickled my ear. "Phyllis' hostility begins to make a lot of sense."

"Eeeeeck!" Phyllis levitated a good six inches off her pillow.

Behind her, Fluffer's jaws moved rhythmically. A scrap of what appeared to be gray tee-shirt fabric hung from the corner of his mouth.

No fool, the goat scampered off.

Phyllis snarled at me. "I hate goats. They're smelly and have nasty, sharp little hooves. You owe me for a new tee-shirt. I can't imagine what idiot thought goat yoga would be a good idea in the first place."

I knew I should feel sorry for her. Somehow, empathy eluded me.

Happily, Minnie interrupted my lame apology by picking up the microphone and hollering, "It's time for me to lead you through some yoga positions, which will allow the goats to take advantage of you."

"Are you implying something inappropriate?" Phyllis asked, smirking.

"She should be so lucky," Dodie whispered in my ear, causing me to stifle a snort of laughter.

Minnie kept her cool, replying, "Certainly not. I was simply saying some positions—and by positions I mean *yoga* positions—make it easier and more tempting for the goats to jump and climb on you."

Phyllis said, "Besides jumping on us, do goats also poop on us?"

I had to hand it to her. She was no quitter.

"We call it leaving a blessing." Minnie directed a high-voltage smile at Phyllis. "Goats sometimes leave blessings on your mat. Not often, but it does happen. They say it's good luck."

"You have *got* to be kidding." Phyllis pursed her lips in disapproval.

"You probably meant to say, 'You have *goat* to be kidding'," Minnie said her smile noticeably strained. "If so, my answer to you is a resounding, 'I kid you not'".

With one notable exception, everyone in the audience laughed. There might be hope for some favorable reviews yet.

Hawk murmured in my ear, "Got any ideas why Phyllis hates Minnie?"

I shrugged and shook my head. "Other than the Powerful Bran Muffin incident? Not really. Phyllis told us they were friends."

As goats cavorted around us, Minnie continued her spiel. "We don't feed the goats before a session to discourage them from leaving, um, blessings."

Dodie whispered to me, "Too bad the food ship has already sailed."

I snickered as Minnie wrapped up with, "Goat Grandpa told me these goats are vegetarians, so their blessings are small pellets, like coffee beans. They're not messy, they don't smell bad, and all you have to do is shake off your mat."

Phyllis shouted out, "That's disgusting. And who is this Goat Grandpa anyway?"

From the way Minnie scowled at the heckler, I could tell she was ready to blow. "Goat Grandpa will sweep up the blessings," she said icily, bellowing. "Pete. Come on out and say hello."

A moment later, Pete sauntered out from somewhere behind the goat pen. To a blast of applause, he brandished a broom and dustpan before retreating into the shadows.

With one goat on her lap and another sniffing her hair, Minnie said, "Our session kicks off with forty-five minutes of Hatha flow yoga, followed by fifteen minutes of savasna. While we move through gentle poses, our goats will explore and play on and around us, cuddling up to you, sometimes falling asleep. The yoga session will be followed by extra time for goat cuddles, photos, and relaxation."

"Hopefully without the benefit of goat blessings," Phyllis said.

My palm itched to smack her.

"Will this session start today or tomorrow?" some smart aleck asked.

"Immediately," I called out, mainly for Minnie's benefit. "And if you enjoy the experience, I remind you to please mention it in the review you post at the end of your Grizzly Gulch getaway."

To my vast relief, Minnie got going. With occasional whispered assistance from Dodie, she led us through various positions, demonstrating remarkable flexibility with each move. Some poses, like Cat-Cow, encouraged the tiny animals to leap onto our backs for a goat massage. Thankfully, their booties softened the sharp little hooves. Others, like Kiss-of-Goat, had goats cavorting through our legs and for an upside-down kiss. My cheeks ached from laughing.

The goats might help us win the contest and save Grizzly Gulch from foreclosure.

The forty-five minutes passed in a flash, with Minnie calling out instructions while goats pranced on our chests and tummies, nuzzled our faces, and raced around the room. To end the session, we stretched out on our mats for Goat Savasna.

After fifteen minutes of welcome silence, marred only by loud snoring from one participant, Minnie said with surprising gentleness, "Bring the energy back into your bodies by wiggling your fingers and toes. Return to your bodies slowly and gently. When you feel ready, stay with that feeling of relaxation and slowly come to a sitting position." Once everyone was seated once more, she said, "The goats await you. Stay as long as you like. Ask questions, take photos, enjoy more goat cuddles, and have fun."

"You call this fun?" Phyllis asked.

"Uh-oh," Dodie muttered. "Is that smoke I see puffing from Minnie's ears?"

I swore the microphone picked up the sound of grinding teeth as Minnie rose to her feet. She hoisted the mallet, made several practice swings, possibly imagining Phyllis' head as her target, then walloped the gigantic gong with every ounce of strength she possessed.

The penetrating gong tone was unlike the gentle sound our regular yoga instructor produced. Instead of the melodic, resonating tone I anticipated, painful waves of deep and sonorous vibrations reverberated inside my skull like a pinball machine, filling the room with a raw, booming groan reminiscent of an underwater humpback whale.

Goats immediately launched into flight, springing, bouncing, and galloping around the room while uttering shrill bleats of terror. Fluffer passed us on his second circuit and made a sudden U-turn. His dark eyes gleaming with purpose, he headed for our row and executed a flying leap onto Phyllis' lap.

She tried to dislodge the little creature, but goats were built for climbing. The harder she pushed, the deeper he dug. Instead of tumbling off her lap, Fluffer balanced on her thighs and hunkered down. In front of the entire yoga class, he emptied his bowels onto her lap.

We all gasped. Everyone, that is, except Dodie. She snickered before whispering to me, "I think Fluffer got a real accurate read on Phyllis' negative energy."

This was no coffee bean blessing. Nope. This was a most impressive and un-goat-like bowel movement—massive, loose, and smelly, triggered undoubtedly by Minnie's over-zealous gong action, and aided by her six bran muffins.

A gag-worthy stench filled the air.

Phyllis howled. In response, Fluffer released residual spurtage. Recovering, she dumped him off her lap. Being a goat, he landed on his feet and danced away.

Silent now, Phyllis sprang upright. I watched in horror while Fluffer's colossal blessing slithered slowly down her pants, splatted onto her bare feet with a soft plop, and spread out onto the mat.

Hawk's breath tickled my ear as he whispered, "Did I or did I not warn you about Minnie, the gong, and the goats?"

I laughed. "You most certainly did."

"This is all your fault, Minnie," Phyllis cried, extricating her feet from the blessing and pointing. "Your bran muffins went through that … that …" She paused to take a deep, shuddery breath. "That fluffy little sewage-generator faster than beans through a cowboy. Congratulations. You and your horrible gong managed to scare the crap out of a goat."

"And an impressive heap of crap it was," Dodie whispered.

A strained silence descended on the room during Phyllis' exit. She stomped to the door, picked up her shoes, and shoved them into her pockets. Before making a bare-footed disappearance, she shouted, "Be afraid, Minnie Harris. Be very, very afraid."

Feeling remorseful, more than a little shaken, and worried, not only about bad reviews, but also Phyllis and Fluffer too, I stood to address the crowd. "It's okay folks," I said, managing to sound reassuring. "A goat blessing never hurt anyone. Phyllis needs time, but she'll be fine." I signaled for Pete to remove Phyllis' yoga mat and clean up the mess. I must tell Abby to give him a healthy bonus.

The remaining guests burst into spontaneous applause. Soon everyone was laughing and talking at once.

"Best yoga class ever," someone shouted.

The odor of antibacterial disinfectant gradually replaced the stench.

Seeing everyone chatting, laughing, or taking selfies with goats, I took a stab at projecting a calm demeanor, telling Hawk, "I'm guessing bad reviews won't be a problem, but I'd better go make sure Phyllis is okay."

Concern flashed across his face. "It wasn't your fault. You couldn't have prevented what happened. If I were you, I'd let her cool down some."

"I have to make things right."

"Give her a little time to clean up. Then I'll join you. She likes me."

Warmth rippled through my body, but I said, "No way," in an automatic rejection. "Yes. Wait." I pressed my forefinger and thumb to the bridge of my nose. "No, but thank you. I appreciate the offer, and as a co-owner of Grizzly Gulch, Phyllis is my problem, not yours." I placed my hand on Hawk's shoulder. "See you later."

"Check that. But remember. My offer of assistance is open-ended, no strings attached."

I acknowledged him with a weak nod and fled the building.

Chapter 16: Solitude Interruption

There was no sign of Phyllis outside the yoga studio. For her sake, I hoped she was standing under a scalding shower. I felt nothing but relief over my unexpected reprieve from my most pressing obligation—groveling to Phyllis. Hawk was right. I would make amends after she'd cooled off, not to mention hosed herself down.

I needed solitude. Hawk's offer to help me deal with Phyllis required clear thinking, and I did my best thinking outside. I zipped across the path in front of the yoga studio and lowered myself onto a bench tucked into a pine grove. With luck, no one would notice me lurking in the shadows.

I let my eyes close and breathed in the pine-fragrant air. I'd day-dreamed often enough about a faceless partner—though truthfully, he hadn't been faceless since I'd met Hawk—someone willing to share life's heavy lifting with me. Now that the offer was on the table, the reality was far more difficult than I'd imagined. It would be too easy to rely on him, whereas my real problem lay in the fact that I was reluctant to trust myself. I mentally shelved the issue to deal with later.

Uncrossing my legs, I prepared to spend the next ten minutes achieving clarity through deep breathing and visualization. Hopefully, I could clear my head and make a decision.

"Mind if I join you?"

My eyes popped open and I straightened on the bench. How had Gabby found me? I was in no mood for company, especially her chirpy, cheery company. Ever the people-pleaser though, I shifted a few inches and patted the bench. "Be my guest."

"Actually, I *am* your guest." With a giggle, Gabby sank down beside me, her blonde curls tumbling around her face. "When you raced out the yoga hall, you seemed upset, so I followed you to offer moral support."

Resigned to a polite conversation, I swallowed my sigh. "Thanks. Some people are more challenging to deal with than others."

"Agreed." Gabby removed a yellow-and-red bag of mini Coffee Crisps from her jacket pocket and ripped it open. "You need chocolate." The way she shook the bag at me reminded me of the way I shake the bag of cat treats at Snuggles.

"You have no idea," I said, snatching one. While I recognized my response mirrored that of Snuggles, I didn't care.

"Take more."

"Thanks." Grateful for this unexpected gesture of kindness, I took a handful and ripped one open.

We munched in companionable silence for a few minutes while yoga participants exited the studio.

Gabby spoke first. "You're worried about Phyllis."

"Yeah." I let out a heartfelt sigh. "I have to make things right with her. It won't be easy."

She faced me, her blue eyes earnest. "I get it. There's one like Phyllis in every group. We events managers must remain calm and pleasant at all times, especially while dealing with our guests' issues, both real and imaginary, as well as any fallout they might cause."

At last. Someone who understood. "My sisters can't relate to my stress," I said. "They think my job's all fun and games. But we on the front line have to keep our guests happy. We solve their problems, keep them entertained, and listen to their troubles, every hour of every day, no matter how crappy we feel."

"Would it help if I told you many of us find Phyllis, er, difficult? She has no friends other than Minnie, who mostly ignores her, and then there was Lizzie."

"What was that relationship like?" I asked around a mouthful of chocolate.

"It was one-sided. Phyllis followed Lizzie around like a puppy. Lizzie, on the other hand, took shameless advantage of Phyllis, manipulating her into doing her dirty work."

"Dirty work? In a retirement home?"

"Golly, yes. In my humble opinion, as people age, they tend to drop their masks and reveal their true selves, which are often mean-spirited. Many retirement residences are packed with rivalry, back-stabbing, and gossip." Gabby moved closer and whispered, "For example, Lizzie's hobby was blackmail, and blackmailers need to know their victims' secrets. Phyllis was her stool pigeon."

I pretended I hadn't heard this already. "That's quite an accusation."

"But true. I overheard Lizzie sweet-talking Phyllis into spying on residents."

This news flash fit with Minnie's suspicions. "That actually makes sense. Phyllis seems to slip through life like a ghost, then pops up in the most unexpected places."

Gabby's little giggle was contagious. "Exactly. She's so inconspicuous, residents don't notice her. She's the perfect spy. I believe the most recent dirt she dug up involved Eleanor." She deposited the candy bag between us. "Help yourself."

I grabbed another handful. "What did she learn?"

Gabby shrugged. "No idea. If you play your cards right, perhaps you can coax Phyllis to fill you in during your chat."

Right. When pigs grow fluffy pink wings and swoop over Grizzly Gulch.

"Perhaps," I said. "My main objective right now is to apologize for today's fiasco. I need to make amends." But I doubted anything would change Phyllis' low opinion of me. She would never open up to me about secrets she'd accumulated through spying.

Gabby laid a hand on my arm. "I think we could be friends. Please let me help." She squeezed my arm.

"How?"

"Phyllis likes me. She thinks I'm a good listener. I calm her down and empathize while she complains. It's amazing how revealing those complaints tend to be."

I couldn't imagine why a guest would want to embroil herself in this mess. I shook my head. "You're a guest, Gabby. Relax. Enjoy our activities or kick back and read a good book." Hawk's offer of support was growing more appealing by the second.

"But I love solving mysteries." With a pout, she extended the candy bag in wordless invitation.

Like one of Pavlov's dogs, I extracted another handful while kicking myself about how, although I was pushing six decades, I still found it impossible to refuse a request. My father and Russ had me well-trained. The penalty for a refusal had always been unpleasant.

Floundering to conjure up a good excuse, I popped a Coffee Crisp into my mouth and chewed. Not only was I being ridiculous, but I was also stringing her along. It was high time I learned how to say no. Russ could never backhand me again. I counted to ten, then said, "I'm terribly sorry, Gabby. I need to talk to Phyllis privately and apologize. You go on ahead. There are some things I must finish up in the yoga studio."

"Party pooper." Gabby's grin assured me she was kidding. "No problem. We'll see one another later."

"Thank you for the support and the chocolate. I feel much better."

"Of course. And don't worry. I understand." She jumped to her feet and went motionless. "Oh my goodness. I don't believe who's on the front porch." She pointed.

I squinted. "Who is it? Their backs are turned."

Gabby ignored my question. "Good golly, I never thought I'd see those two together without violence involved. I had to separate them more than once. I'll never forget Eleanor telling me, and I quote, 'I jolly well refuse to let a frightful drama queen like Minnie ruin my chances with Wayne'".

My pulse accelerated when I recognized their yoga outfits. Minnie and Eleanor were chatting while descending the steps, side-by-side. "Shhhh," I hissed, tugging Gabby onto the bench again. "That's too weird."

We both slid lower.

"Why are we hiding?" she asked.

"Curiosity." Something strange was afoot, and I intended to surprise Minnie and pry the truth from her. "I don't want them to see us. They sure are cozy for two women who were at one another's throats not long ago. I can't imagine what they're discussing."

"I know, right? I thought they hated one another."

"Me too. Seems we were both wrong. They must have kissed and made up."

Minnie and Eleanor had meandered onto the path to the main barn. They stopped for a few seconds to chat with a wrangler, then continued their stroll, disappearing inside the barn.

"You really think so?"

"Anything's possible." But I wasn't convinced. Something was up with them. "Ready to leave now? There's barely enough time to change before lunch."

"Sure thing. I'm starving." Gabby bounced to her feet.

Remaining seated, I said, "On second thought, I need a little more alone time to reflect. You go ahead."

"Okey-dokey. See you later, girlfriend." She whirled around and bounded away, veering off onto the path leading to the guest cabins.

Once Gabby was out of sight, I stopped trying to figure out why she'd befriended me and sat in stillness for several minutes. My next moves grew clear. I needed to find Minnie and determine why she and Eleanor were suddenly so chummy and what they were doing in the barn. Next, I would find Hawk and reject his offer of assistance. Although his presence would no doubt go a long way toward smoothing things over with Phyllis, this was something I needed to do alone.

Pleased with myself, I heaved to my feet and headed off to find Minnie to quiz her about Eleanor.

Chapter 17: Solo Conflict Resolution

MINNIE WAS NOWHERE TO BE found in the apartment. Most likely she was laying low in case I insisted she accompany me to Phyllis' cabin to apologize for the Fluffer disaster. Little did she know I intended to confront her about her sudden friendship with Eleanor.

I switched gears and focused on another goal I'd set for myself—to tell Hawk that much as I appreciated his offer of assistance, I intended to deal with Phyllis myself. To bolster my self-confidence, I showered and got dressed in my butt-minimizing jeans, boob-maximizing bra, and a lovely burgundy cowl-neck sweater. I also primped a little. Okay, a whole lot. I was adding a final swipe of lash-lengthening mascara when Hawk's text arrived: *I'm meeting my son for lunch, will return in time to help with apology to Phyllis if you want my help. XOX*

Based on my sighting of Minnie and Eleanor sauntering together and chatting like old friends, my upcoming meeting with Phyllis had taken on greater significance than a mere apology. It was crucial to our investigation that I coax her to share everything she knew about Minnie's new best friend, Eleanor.

Churning with nervous energy, I postponed the apology by devouring a quick sandwich in my kitchen. A girl had to eat didn't she? I also had certain event management responsibilities as well, so I after I'd eaten, I participated in the preparations for both the afternoon pickleball tournament and tonight's entertainment, which was a dance evening with Willie and the Big Sky Mountaineers.

By mid-afternoon, I was immersed in a discussion of tournament logistics when Hawk returned. His quick and easy grin caused my stomach to flip-flop. Striding forward, he cut me away from the herd. I went willingly.

"I'm all yours," he informed me, causing my pulse to accelerate. "I'm ready, willing, and able to help you with the apology." My pulse returned to normal.

Admitting I was refusing his offer to help with Phyllis was harder than I'd anticipated. Although he'd given me an opening, I chickened out. Instead of a direct answer, I pulled a slick politician trick, intended to distract and divert, and yakked at great length about my post-yoga chat with Gabby over Coffee Crisp, emphasizing how Lizzie's blackmail may well have provoked her murder, and wrapped up with the grand finale—Minnie and Eleanor's budding friendship. He stood there the entire time, all quiet and calm, his expression impassive.

When I finally stumbled to a halt, he said, "Good work. You uncovered major implications for the case." He gazed at me with an expression midway between mild pain and resignation. "Are you finally ready to talk to me? *Really* talk?"

I squirmed under his steady gaze, "I've been talking for the last ten minutes."

"You've been babbling to avoid saying something you're afraid I won't like."

"Um ..."

"I know. You're speechless, right?"

He knew me so well in such a short time, and that touched me in ways I didn't know I could be touched. "Okay," I whispered around the lump in my throat. "As much as I appreciate your offer to help with Phyllis, I need to do it alone."

"In that case, you have my whole-hearted admiration and support." His gaze drifted to my lips. "All things considered, it seems to me a small display of gratitude is called for."

Placing my hands on his shoulders I stood on tiptoe, intending to plant a big, smacking smooch on his chin, which was the closest part I could reach.

Faster than a ninja, he lowered his head until our lips connected. Slow and sweet at first, the kiss quickly intensified until heat consumed me. It was the kind of kiss that melted the hard, cold knot that had occupied my chest for so long I'd taken its presence for granted.

Once he'd fried several thousand of my brain cells, he lifted his head and gave me a steady gaze. We were both breathing hard. I blinked, came back to earth. To conceal my strong and somewhat terrifying reaction, I said, "I hope my gratitude came across."

His lips curved in a badass smile. "Loud and clear. Now, tell me the truth. I know you must be dreading this confrontation. Why go it alone when there's no need?"

This might well be my last chance to get real with Hawk, to quit pretending everything was a-okay when truthfully, it wasn't. I looked away because it was easier. "I believe I'm broken. I need to learn to trust myself before I can trust anyone else, and the only way I can think of is to jump into situations that scare me."

"I get it. You're facing your fear and you need to do it alone." He cupped my face, his hands gentle, as if cupping a baby bird. "You're not broken, Clara. Maybe a little dented, but who isn't?"

I extricated myself and turned my head away to hide my distress. After a moment to collect myself, I said, "Whenever I feel like a phony, which, incidentally, is far too often since I'm a people-pleaser in a people-pleasing job, I beat myself up. Bad idea, right? As long as I feel obligated to make everyone else happy, I'll never be whole or happy myself." I walked away.

He caught up with me. "There's no need to hide your insecurities from me. I would never use them against you."

I sensed that, but I was reassured to hear him say it. I stopped walking long enough to say, "Thanks. I believe you. Will I see you later?"

"Try to stop me." He gripped my shoulders with both hands. "You'll be great. There is no doubt in my mind you'll win Phyllis over."

Only after he'd walked away, did I remember I hadn't discussed or even mentioned I intended to coax Phyllis to spill her guts about Eleanor but had no idea how to tackle it. All I could do was trust I would succeed without raising suspicions that Lizzie's death was a murder and, more to the point, she was one of the suspects.

Hawk would be far from pleased if he knew my sleuthing plans.

Ten minutes later, I came to a standstill in front of Cabin 66. The scent of evergreens sharpened the air. Jays squabbled in the overhead branches, emphasizing the silence. Feeling horribly vulnerable, I climbed onto Phyllis' wraparound porch and pressed the doorbell. This would be easy-peasy, I assured myself. I could do this without Hawk's assistance.

After a longish wait, the door opened a smidgen. One pale gray eye peered out. "Oh, it's *you*," the eye's owner said.

Sensing venom behind her words, I waggled my fingers. "Truce."

"Is Minnie with you?"

"Nope. Just me."

"Figures. Some things never change. She never acknowledges, never mind apologizes, for any damage she caused or feelings she hurt."

I did not point out it was hardly Minnie's fault that Fluffer had chosen Phyllis' lap as his personal toilet. "I'm here to apologize," I said. "What happened to you was … unthinkable. I want to make it right."

A one-eyed glare was my reward. "Get lost. Thanks to *your* goat and *your* idiot cousin, my yoga outfit and favorite sandals are ruined. I had to call maintenance to remove them and sanitize the cabin. You might want to give them a bonus for their efforts." The words sizzled with the force of her anger.

Phyllis was not in a forgiving mood. Truth be told, I couldn't help but empathize. Sensing an imminent door-slam, I had the presence of mind to use my shoulder to hold the door open. For a scrawny woman, she was remarkably strong.

"Wait," I said, addressing her eyeball. "I don't blame you in the slightest for being upset. Given the same circumstances, I assure you I would be furious, embarrassed, and plotting my revenge."

Silence. I figured I'd struck a nerve.

"Please? Let me in. You won't regret it. I promise."

"Fine." Phyllis opened the door and stepped aside. "I'm still airing out the cabin."

On entering, I stifled a gag. The cabin smelled of floral air freshener with a suggestion of *le parfum de poop*. Thankfully, a side window stood open.

No wonder she felt hostile. In her shoes, I would too.

She plunked down on a loveseat and huddled into the corner, small and vulnerable with her arms folded across her cardigan, a gray one today. "I've never felt so humiliated in my entire life," she whispered.

I had several choices, flight being my personal favorite. Since cowardice, though tempting, was unacceptable, I could either stand there like a misbehaving schoolgirl or find my own seating. I selected the armchair opposite Phyllis and sank into it.

"Let's get this over with," she said, her devoid of discernable emotion.

Studying her carefully, I imagined the humiliating and unpleasant situation she'd endured in the yoga class, a situation she hadn't asked for, and one she most definitely hadn't deserved. In spite of the fact I disliked her, a wave of compassion swept over me. Once I visualized her lack of meaningful friendships and a loving relationship, I had no trouble imagining how lonely and sad her life must be.

My apology came effortlessly and from the heart. I spoke for five minutes and finished by saying, "I blame myself for Fluffer's accident, and am so, so sorry. There ought to be a 'No Food Allowed' rule in the yoga studio, and that ridiculous gong should be banned. As soon as I return to my office, I intend to create a sign for the yoga hall and have the gong removed." By then, we were both sniffling a little.

"And Minnie should be barred from ever giving yoga lessons again."

"Agreed," I said, thinking it was highly unlikely Minnie would ever extend that offer again anyway. "To demonstrate how sorry we all are about the incident, we intend to replace your ruined yoga outfit and mat with two new ones. Choose designer labels, whatever you want. The sky's the limit. We'll work out the details later."

"For real?"

"Absolutely. And that's not all. We're also extending an invitation to you and any guest of your choice to enjoy another week at Grizzly Gulch. The invitation is open-ended and, of course, at no charge to you."

"You mean free? All expenses paid? Two people? Any time?"

"Exactly."

"I know exactly the person I'd like to bring."

"That's wonderful. Do you mind telling me who it is?

Phyllis proved she could laugh. "All I'm willing to say is that it's most definitely not Minnie."

"I thought you were friends."

She shook her head. "I used to think so too. I even invited her for a guest visit at Lifestyle Manor, hoping she would come to live there and I'd have another friend to hang with besides Lizzie."

"What happened?"

"You need to know Minnie to understand."

"She's my cousin, we're sharing my apartment. I know her as well as anyone possibly could."

Phyllis cocked her head and stared at me, as if assessing how I might react to her news. At last she said. "Okay. She did move into Lifestyle Manor. I was so excited I could hardly breathe, figuring we would spend plenty of quality time together. That didn't happen."

"Why not?"

"Oh, you know Minnie. She's charming, striking, and so full of life everyone is attracted to her. She makes friends easily, whereas I'm shy, awkward, and frumpy. Once Minnie moved in, it felt like history was repeating itself. Within a month, she'd made tons of friends, whereas I might as well have been invisible—exactly like in high school."

"No one deserves that, especially an old friend."

"I'm not as bad as people like to paint me, you know."

This was my opening. I took a deep breath and inspiration struck. I paused, gathered my thoughts, and cut to the chase. "I have a hard time believing Minnie would choose to spend time with someone like Eleanor instead of a loyal friend like you."

"Minnie and Eleanor? You must be mistaken." She stared at me as if I'd grown another head. "They can't stand one another. You've seen how territorial Eleanor is. She's afraid Minnie's got the hots for Wayne, but I have my doubts. Wayne is crazy about Eleanor, and I've seen the way Minnie flirts with a certain slightly older man. Romance is in the air at Lifestyle Manor, take my word for it."

As tempting as it was to quiz Phyllis about Minnie's mystery man, I focused on learning more about Eleanor by dropping my bombshell. "When I saw Minnie and Eleanor together this afternoon, they appeared pretty cozy, all smiles and giggles while heading for the barn."

Phyllis snorted, but resumed talking. "I can't imagine what they have in common. Minnie may have plenty of flaws, insensitive and selfish being two of them, but at least she's genuine. Eleanor's a fake through and through." She repeated what Minnie had already told us about how Eleanor had embellished her appearance with plastic surgery in order to attract a wealthy man like Wayne, and now he worships her.

The wistful tone of Phyllis' words triggered a tiny pang of sympathy in me. The poor woman had likely never experienced romance, never mind love. "I gather you disapprove of their liaison."

Seconds ticked by. At first Phyllis hesitated, but finally said, "Eleanor's a con artist, inside and out. Even Roland, our resident catfish, backed away from her. Word is he recognized they were birds of a feather. One con-artist recognizes another."

"You're amazing. How do you know this?"

"Lizzie asked me to unearth everything there was to know about Eleanor. It's easier than people think, you know? I searched the Internet, talked to guests, examined public records. She has a history of love 'em, empty their wallets, then leave 'em."

It seemed Minnie and Gabby were right. Phyllis had been Lizzie's spy. Her brain must be stuffed with secrets. I let it go for now, saying, "You are truly an incredible woman. Observant and brilliant as well as discrete."

Phyllis flushed with pleasure. "Oh, I don't know about that."

"No, really. I've seldom been more impressed."

"Really? Well here's something else. Fitzpatrick is Eleanor's married name. She grew up in England, Exeter to be exact, came to Canada in 1980, ostensibly to visit Alberta. Instead of returning to England, she stopped off in Edmonton, where she met and married a Canadian. I'm afraid that's all I know, but it was a starting point for Lizzie. She got more dirt on Eleanor from a private investigator she hired because of his contacts in England. Lizzie never did fill me in on what she learned, but I suspect she'd started blackmailing Eleanor before she died. I'm guessing Eleanor may have a criminal record back in Exeter. She might be running a con on Minnie."

"I can't thank you enough for your caring. I'll have to have a straight talk with Minnie." I stood and prepared to leave. "I hope we'll see you at the dance tonight."

"It's too soon after ..." Phyllis hesitated, "after, you know. People will laugh."

"I wouldn't let them, but I understand if you don't want to join us this evening. By tomorrow, it'll be old news and people will be talking about something else." I stood.

Phyllis walked me to the door and tolerated a hug.

I was walking away, when I turned my head in time to discover her gaze was riveted on my departing figure. She waved and closed the door. The lock clicked.

While assessing my level of success, I retraced my steps from Phyllis' cabin along the meandering pathway. I had succeeded in calming her down as well as learning more about Eleanor, so I gave myself a gold star. Better still, I now viewed Phyllis as a woman with redeeming qualities, someone I could sympathize with. On rounding a bend, I halted in surprise at the sight of Hawk sitting on a bench beside the pathway, and reading a paperback. I tiptoed across the pine needles and halted behind him, intending to surprise him.

His hearing must rival my own, because he twisted his neck to study me. Closing his book, he patted the seat beside him. "Sit. Relax. Talk to me."

I wasn't about to argue. "I assume you were waiting for me."

"I was. How did it go with Phyllis?"

"Excellent." I described how my apology had gone down and followed up with everything she'd told me about Eleanor including her suspicions about blackmail, and finishing with. "Seems Phyllis was happy to throw Eleanor under the bus."

"Way to go. I knew you could do it. I'm certain you extracted more information from Phyllis than if I'd tried. People tend to be suspicious of former cops." His gaze was so heated, it was a wonder I didn't spontaneously combust.

"How do you want to handle the next step of the investigation?" he asked.

The simple question curbed my self-congratulation. I frowned, unhappy to be caught off guard. "I'm not sure. We know Eleanor most likely got married in or near Edmonton. Ideally, I would drive up to Edmonton and stay overnight. That way, I could learn her maiden name by searching the marriage registry, maybe interview some people in person, possibly her ex-husband."

"I gather you can't drop everything and take off to Edmonton for a day."

"Sadly, no. And neither can my sisters, especially with the hospitality contest looming over us."

"I would be happy to do it."

"I don't know." I gnawed my lower lip. "Let's walk back to the main lodge. I want to tell my sisters and Minnie the news."

Once we resumed walking, he said, "What's the worst that can happen if you relinquish control and rely on someone else for a change?"

"The worst thing?" I mulled over his question for a moment, matching him pace for pace. "I would re-live a nightmare. The last time I tried it, I married a monster."

"In case you hadn't noticed, I'm not Russ," Hawk said, "And this isn't a marriage proposal. I'm simply offering to help you with a difficult situation. I would do the same for any friend who needed assistance."

I reined in the insane urge to throw my arms around him and rest my head on his chest. "Thank you. I accept your offer." He couldn't know how much I valued kindness and compassion in a man. Throw in patience, integrity, and an abundance of dependability not to mention so much sex appeal it weakened my knees, and you have an electrifying combination. Having reached a decision, I mumbled, "Would you please follow up on Eleanor?"

"I thought you would never ask. I have friends in Edmonton who will put me up for the night. If I start right away, I'll get there in time for dinner. Tomorrow, I'll hit the marriage registry, conduct a few interviews, then contact my friend in the Devon and Cornwall police force and give him Eleanor's maiden name. He owes me a favor. If Eleanor has a criminal record, he may remember her. Otherwise, he'll search the old files for the information."

It wouldn't surprise me in the slightest if Eleanor had a lengthy criminal record in England, but I had enough to worry about, not the least of which was to ensure Willie and the Big Sky Mountaineers had everything they needed to make tonight's big dance a success.

I didn't dare relax in case something went wrong.

Chapter 18: Bucking Bully

THE EVENING DANCE FEATURING WILLY and the Big Sky Mountaineers was a success. Even Phyllis relented and showed her face, occasionally appearing to enjoy herself. It didn't hurt that Abby had begged Zeke to send his wranglers over to ask the guests to dance, and to pay special attention to Phyllis.

The next day, what with lining up participants for an impromptu talent show that evening, coaxing Chef Armand to give a cooking demonstration, and acting as tour leader on an afternoon trip into the town of Banff, there was scarcely a moment to breathe, let alone wonder how Hawk's trip to Edmonton was working out.

When I crawled home after the talent show, which turned out to be a hilarious event, Hawk still hadn't returned. As if to compensate, as soon as I released Snuggles from the bathroom, the joyful cat flung his body at me, purring and twisting so hard, he caused me to stagger. I rewarded him with a cat treat and loved on him for the compulsory amount of time. That accomplished, I barely managed to brush my teeth and remove my makeup before falling into bed. Within seconds, I was zonked.

Much later, a muffled meow roused me. Something—or someone—had disturbed Snuggles. On high alert, I sat bolt upright in bed and fumbled for the clock. 12:28 a.m.

Outside my door, Minnie whispered, "Shut up if you know what's good for you." I assumed she was speaking to the cat.

A moment later, the click of my front door closing had me thoroughly awake and bouncing out of bed. Minnie had snuck out like a horny teenager. How could she forget there was a killer on the loose?

Something odd was going down, something Minnie knew I would disapprove of. Otherwise why avoid me? I was certain Eleanor was either her target or her partner-in-crime. Either way, Hawk relied on me to make sure Minnie stayed safe.

Frost was forecast for tonight, so I stuffed my feet into thick socks and the first pair of boots I found, which happened to be my work boots. After throwing on a wooly toque and down-filled puffer coat, I locked up behind me. Tiptoeing downstairs, I crept silently through the lobby, evading the night staff who hung out in the back office, and slipped outside.

A flash of movement on the path leading past the yoga hall to the barn attracted my attention. Muttering a couple of words no true lady would utter, I sped toward the barn, berating myself over forgetting to lock Snuggles up again. Worse, I'd left my phone and mini-flashlight in my bedside drawer. Fortunately, I'd insisted on solar lighting along all our pathways.

I was panting when the dark shadow crossed the barnyard and slipped around the side of the barn, likely headed for the back door to avoid the stable area. Horses got testy when an intruder interrupted their nighttime slumber.

I increased my pace until I was practically jogging, something I preferred to avoid. Making a mental note to join a gym, I sprinted along the far side of the building where Zeke's apartment, the one Abby now shared, was located. Their lights were out, and all was quiet inside. By the time I reached the barn's back entrance, I was gasping for breath.

The door, normally double-locked, stood ajar.

The back of my neck prickled. This was so, so wrong. Due to a crisis last spring, we double-locked all barns and all outbuildings at night. Bad things happened when guests wandered around at night without supervision.

Unwilling to barge in, I propped myself against the outside wall to think. Okay, so I also needed to catch my breath. Once I was breathing normally again, I and ran a hand around the doorframe, hunting for the padlock. The open padlock dangled from its hoop.

Either Zeke had forgotten to do his regular nighttime walkaround—a highly unlikely omission—or a wrangler had opened the door for some unknown reason, a reason I was certain involved Minnie and Eleanor.

With my heart thumping heavily in my chest, I stuck my head inside.

The only sound was a sleepy nicker from the stable area. Everything seemed peaceful enough until I heard the echo of rapid footsteps on wooden floors.

Once I slipped inside, there was enough light for me to pick my way through the tack room at the rear of the barn. I emerged without incident into the stable area where Bucking Bully, our new mechanical bull, resided. Zeke had parked him in the open area across from the four stalls we reserved for sick, injured, or pregnant trail horses.

Minnie paced the floor in front of Bucking Bully.

I ducked into the shadows. Surely, she wasn't here for the mechanical bull. I'd explained to her how bull-riding was strictly forbidden until we had a lawyer prepare a special waiver. Also, Bully needed a key and an operator.

I was about to call out when a figure emerged from the stable area and joined Minnie. "You're here at last. Brilliant. Pete was all set to leave and take the key for the control console with him. I had to beg him to stay. He's in the stable area right now." The words, spoken in an unmistakable British accent, revealed Eleanor's identity.

"Sorry about that," Minnie said, not sounding sorry at all, "but I fell asleep."

"I should have known a woman your age wouldn't be able to stay awake after 10:00 p.m."

"Hey. You're my age if not older, and I'm sixty-three."

"I've been told I look a good fifteen years younger than you."

Minnie's laugh rang out. "Enjoy your fantasy, Grandma. A face lift or two won't stop a withered old crone like you from losing the bet we made. I hope you're ready to endorse my friendship with Wayne."

By then, they were both cackling with laughter the way old friends do. This was getting weirder and weirder.

"Don't be a plonker, you old cow. Oi've never lost a bet in my life." Eleanor had dropped her posh British accent. "Don't break any of those brittle old bones taking a header off Bucking Bully. When you go arse-over-teakettle, be prepared to kiss your time with your good poker buddy, Wayne, goodbye."

Fudge, Fudging McFudgster! They had a bet on who could stay on Bully the longest—with Wayne as the prize.

"I should go first," Minnie said.

Eleanor released an unladylike snort. "You must be barmy. Who says?"

"I'm doing you a favor. I should have the first ride, which I intend to nail. You'll get your turn after that while I videotape you. Anyway, you owe me."

"Do tell."

"Without me, this wouldn't be possible. Pete's only helping us because I told him we had Clara's blessing to ride the bull provided none of the other guests found out. Then I begged him to operate the controls for us tonight." In the face of Eleanor's silence, Minnie added, "You're welcome."

Nice. My own cousin had lied. *About me.* There would be consequences, but right now, I needed to know if either of them had spun more lies.

At Eleanor's lack of response, Minnie continued. "Pete told me Bucking Bully has a variable Buck-and-Spin speed control box. He warned me he'd only activate the gentlest motion—the one that accommodates seniors, kids, and chickens."

"Well done," Eleanor said, reverting to her usual upper-crust accent, "especially since you meet two of those three criteria."

And here I'd hoped the two women had buried the hatchet. Silly me.

"Better watch your step, Grandma, or I'll tell him to give you a higher setting."

"At least there's an emergency 'Stop' button, and a thick foam landing pad to cushion your bony arse."

My brain was struggling to make sense out of what I was hearing when someone emerged from the stable area. "Good. You're both here," Pete said, striding into the control area beside Bully. "Let's get started before Zeke hears you two ladies, and tears a strip off my hide." He paused a beat. "Are you certain Clara said this would be okay?"

"Dead certain," Minnie said.

I'd barely stepped forward to stop this nonsense when a vicious blow to the back of my head clouded my vision. Uttering a groan, I stomped my heel down hard onto something soft and yielding. A faint crunching sound and my assailant's sharp breath intake told me my heel had struck its mark before my knees gave out and I sank to the floor.

Next thing I knew, a rough hand was slapping duct tape around my head several times, covering my mouth. My wrists and ankles received the same treatment as I lay inert. Hands gripped my ankles and dragged me into a corner. Thankfully my attacker had taped my hands in front of me.

My assailant wore gloves, black clothing, and a ski mask. I got the impression of a slim, wiry form, but I couldn't tell if the person was a man or woman, young or old.

Pete must be unaware of any problem because Bully's motor started up and idled.

As I watched helplessly, the sinister shape limped along the wall while keeping to the shadows before ducking inside Bully's control area. Unable to remove the duct tape across my mouth, I couldn't yell a warning.

With an excited laugh, Minnie climbed on board. "Okay, Pete." She patted the foam head with jutting horns. "Let 'er rip."

Desperation drove me to worm my way up the wall and into a sitting position. The exertion increased the pain in my poor, throbbing head and brought tears to my eyes. Once I blinked the moisture away, my eyesight was clear with no double vision. My woolly toque, now missing, had likely saved my life. Using both taped hands, I focused on my ankles and struggled to peel away the duct tape.

As sweat trickled down my face, I had no choice but to listen to the mechanical bull start slowly, then speed up and whirl in a series of killer spins.

"Hey! That's fast enough," Minnie yelled. "Pete? What the …? You trying to kill me?"

Pete didn't answer. Bully was leaping and plunging and whirling at the fastest speed possible, one designated, "Smoke Snorting Action."

While struggling to remove the tape around my ankles, I glanced at Minnie. She clung to the rawhide neck yelling, "Stop this thing."

"Hit the emergency stop button on Bully's neck," Eleanor yelled to Minnie.

"If I let go to press the button," Minnie hollered, "I'll go airborne."

"There's an inflatable safety cushion."

"At this speed, I'll fly across the corridor and into a horse stall."

"I'll go back there and stop it," Eleanor yelled, dashing inside the control area. I hadn't fully recovered when a screech of rage filled the barn. Two people appeared to be wrestling for the controls.

Neighing and kicking warned me the ruckus had woken the horses.

I gave up on the duct tape and had resorted to worming my way toward the control area when a thump warned me someone was on the move. Certain it wasn't Eleanor, I managed to roll into the figure's path. In total silence, the person stumbled over my prone body, aimed a kick at me, and hobbled to the door, leaving my ribs aching.

I had to stop Bucking Bully. With great difficulty, I did a combination butt-walk and floor-roll, aiming for the control area. I by-passed the bucking machine with Minnie bouncing and hollering on its back, inched past Eleanor, who was spread-eagled on the floor, gasping for air, and rolled myself into the control area. Despite my taped hands, I managed to grip the control panel's frame, hoist myself onto my knees, and aim a double-fisted punch at the Stop button.

Bully's gyrations stopped instantly.

I slithered to the floor, landing on the cushiony mat, and lay there, panting while Minnie slid off Bully's back to kneel beside me.

"Mmmmmpfh," I said, hoping she recognized me.

She scrutinized my duct-taped face. "Clara? Is that you? What happened?"

"Mmmmmpfh," I repeated, holding out my hands.

Her hands shook as she attempted and failed to remove the tape.

"Oh, Minnie." The wail emerged from the gloom behind me.

"Down here," Minnie replied.

Tears streaming down her face, Eleanor staggered toward Minnie. "Thank God, luv. I thought you were dead," she said, collapsing beside us on the mat and shoving Minnie's hands aside. "You're in no shape for the job, old woman. I'll take care of the tape." Without warning, she ripped the duct tape off my wrists, removing two, maybe three layers of skin.

Swallowing an agonized shout, I flexed my hands to restore circulation, then undid my ankles. Finally, I tackled the tape wound around my mouth and head. I took it slow and gentle, mainly to avoid ripping off my lips and every hair on my scalp. Even so, the duct tape had clumps of hair attached to it when I was finished.

Minnie examined me in horror. "What happened to you?"

While the three of us sat on the mat beside Bully, I described the little I knew about my attack. I was summing up when Pete staggered out from Bully's control area, one hand clamped to his head.

I flinched at the sight of blood trickling down his face. Rising to my feet with some difficulty, I stepped forward. "I gather the intruder attacked you too."

"Yep." Pete removed his bandana and mopped his face with it. "Good job it was only my head."

You've gotta love a stoic man. "Did you see or hear anything?" I asked.

Pete shrugged. "I didn't think anyone else was here until I regained consciousness and heard the ruckus. If you'll excuse me, I'm going to find the first aid kit in the tack room." He stumbled away into the darkness.

Eleanor clambered to her feet and hauled Minnie upright.

"What happened back here?" I asked.

While supporting Minnie, Eleanor said, "The mystery intruder must have attacked Pete before taking over Bucking Bully's controls and cranking them up to the highest speed. I tried to get inside to stop the action, but the creep must have seen me. Anyway, I caught an elbow in the solar plexus. I swear someone was trying to kill Minnie."

"I'm okay, hon," Minnie assured Eleanor. "I'll never forget the way you tried to stop my attacker. Why, if it hadn't been for Clara and you ..." Her tear-choked words trailed away.

I recognized the signs. Minnie wasn't finished with her display of gratitude, not by a long shot. The nurturer in me wanted to comfort her, but right now, I needed facts, not prolonged drama. "I want you both to explain what you were doing." I tackled Minnie first. "I'm disappointed in you. How could you lie to poor Pete about how I gave you permission to do something so dumb?"

"I'm interested to hear this as well," Zeke said, emerging from the tack room looking cute, all rumpled and irritated. "I thought I heard some goings-on out here."

More footsteps rang out from behind us in the stable area. On recognizing Hawk's determined stride, I squinted into the gloom. It was getting to be like Grand Central around here. Moments later, he draped a warm, strong arm around my shoulders. "What's going on?" His gaze assessed each of us in turn, his frown growing deeper by the second. "I took a walk to stretch my legs after my long drive. Next thing you know, it sounded like someone was being slaughtered. Why didn't you phone me?"

"I was asleep when I heard Minnie sneak out my apartment. In my rush to follow her, I forgot my phone. We're all fine, at least, we are now."

Zeke stepped into the control area and pocketed the key. "I'm placing the keys to Bucking Bully in my office safe. Tomorrow, I'll conduct a briefing with all our wranglers. No one, employee or guest, is allowed to ride the mechanical bull until all the safety protocols are in place. I'll also warn everyone about an intruder lurking around the barn."

"Let's find us a seat while we sort out what happened," Hawk said.

"I'll go first," I volunteered, once we sat on the benches lining the tack room. "Turns out, Minnie and Eleanor intended to take a midnight bull ride. I didn't get far inside the barn because someone attacked me, as well as Eleanor and Pete, who'd agreed to acting as Bully's control operator." For Zeke's benefit, I said, "That's was because Minnie lied and said I was okay with it. I believe the attacker was determined to get at Bully's control panel, hoping to injure or kill the rider. Everyone else was likely collateral damage. Minnie was almost killed ..." In the nick of time I stopped myself from adding the word, "again," wrapping up my explanation with, "The attacker wore a ski mask, black clothes, and could have been a man or a woman."

Eleanor was next, saying, "This is my fault. I was jealous of Minnie's friendship with Wayne, so I challenged her to a riding contest. If she won, I'd stop hassling her over the private poker lessons she's giving Wayne. If I won, she'd quit those lessons, no argument."

"I had no intention of losing," Minnie interjected, "Imagine my surprise when we bonded over our trash talk. Believe it or not, this old British broad has a sense of humor."

"A better one than this old Canadian slut, Eleanor said, grinning at Minnie."

"Beg to differ," Minnie said. "Anyway, after we talked for ages and actually got to know one another, I convinced Eleanor I had no romantic interest in Wayne. We decided it would be fun to go ahead with the challenge anyway."

Eleanor placed an arm around Minnie's shoulders. "By then, I trusted this one enough to share my heartache with her." She paused a beat. "Oh dear, I feel so foolish. I learned Wayne respects athletic women, so I wanted to impress him by riding Bucking Bully. He said a mechanical bull was too dangerous for a woman my age. *My age.* Can you believe it?"

Silence.

Seeing we were all too wise to answer, Eleanor continued, "I asked Minnie to take a video of my winning ride on her cell phone and send it to Wayne. I thought my athletic ability and courage would impress him so much, he'd pop the question."

"I told her she would never win," Minnie continued, "but so long as she didn't mind looking like an idiot, I would be more than happy to record her losing ride and send it to him."

Eleanor cast a beseeching gaze at all of us. "I feel so foolish. Please don't tell Wayne about the bet." Gripping Minnie's arm, she said, "I never thought I would say this to you, of all people, but I owe you an apology for overreacting to your friendship with Wayne. My only excuse is that I'm in love for the first time in my life."

"Good, because Wayne can't stop drooling over you. Frankly, he's not my type. In fact, I'm seeing someone else, another Lifestyle Manor resident."

"Brilliant. Who is it?" Eleanor asked.

"Can't say."

"Why not?"

Minnie shrugged. "I promised to wait until he's ready to go public. It's not serious, though, at least not at my end. Marriage isn't for me. Been there, done that. Three times, to be precise." She threw back her head and laughed. "I'm too old to break in a new husband. But it doesn't mean I don't enjoy some hanky-panky with an attractive and wealthy man. Anyway, I sense there's something important he isn't telling me, and that's a huge red flag."

It was time to leave before word of the attacks leaked out. "We don't dare sit around chatting any longer. We're lucky no one besides Hawk and Zeke heard the yelling. I suggest we keep this entire incident to ourselves, otherwise the guests might panic."

Or complain about rampaging mechanical bulls in online reviews.

With Pete's return, Zeke shone a flashlight at the wrangler's pupils, testing for concussion. "Everything seems normal. You okay to get yourself to the staff quarters? I'll check in on you once we're finished here."

Pete laughed. "I'm fine. There's no need to babysit me."

Earning my undying gratitude, Zeke went all macho on us. "Let's go folks. The attacker is still out there." He told Hawk, "I assume you'll accompany Clara and Minnie to the main lodge."

"Yep. I'll get them home safely."

Zeke slapped Hawk on the back. "Good man. Once I set the alarm and lock up here, I'll walk Eleanor to her cabin."

Hawk, Minnie, and I set off for my apartment.

Fifteen minutes later, Minnie patrolled my dining room's perimeter for a cat on the loose, while Hawk and I sat at the table drinking cocoa laced with Kahlua.

"Someone tried to kill me again tonight," Minnie announced, checking behind the curtains. "Murder by mechanical bull must be a new one for the books."

"Why don't you join us at the table?" I suggested. "I poured you a special cocoa."

"I'm fine here. Snuggles hates me."

"I already checked. He's asleep on my pillow. I forgot to lock him up when I went out."

Hawk paid no attention to the drama over Snuggles' whereabouts. "Let's review our suspects one by one to see who might have had motive and opportunity."

"Agreed," I said. "My attacker was slim, wiry, and my height or an inch or two taller. Wayne's tall and brawny, and Roland is flabby, soft, and taller, so neither man was the intruder."

"Those are important details," Hawk said. "That leaves only the women."

My ankles throbbed painfully, reminding me of the ease with which my attacker had dragged me across the floor. "For what it's worth, she's strong enough to pull me into a corner." I took a contemplative sip of hot chocolate.

"We haven't found any motive for Gabby to attack me," Minnie said. "Is she off the hook?"

"Not yet," he replied, dashing my hopes of her innocence. "What about Phyllis?"

"Oh, Phyllis is in the running," I said, wishing it wasn't so. "From all accounts, Lizzie was horrible to her, and I suspect she's not as close a friend of Minnie's as we were led to believe. "

Minnie seated herself at the table, apparently trusting the place was Snuggles-free. While stirring her cocoa, she added her two cent's worth. "Clara's right. Based on the hissy fit Phyllis threw in yoga class, she's been harboring a grudge against me since school days." She took a dainty sip. "Except for the high school bran muffin incident—caused mostly by her own greed I might add—I can't imagine anything else I might have done to make her hate me."

I rolled my eyes at Minnie's lack of empathy. "Other than her huge crush on your ex-husband in high school and the fact that you ignored her altogether once you moved into Lifestyle Manor? Phyllis told me she'd thought you were her friend, but you made her feel invisible, exactly like in high school. She felt as if history was repeating itself," I said bluntly, mentally comparing Phyllis' build to tonight's attacker. "It's hard to tell, but Phyllis might well be slim and wiry under those baggy clothes she wears, and I sense she's strong for her size. She's definitely the right height for my attacker."

"One thing's for sure," Minnie said, "Eleanor wasn't tonight's attacker. We were face-to-face the entire time."

"True," I said. "But the jury is still out on whether or not she was Lizzie's killer."

"Have you forgotten?" Minnie said. "Eleanor had no motive to kill Lizzie."

"Actually, it's quite possible Eleanor did have a motive," Hawk said. "I was able to track down her background, so anyone else could have done the same thing. There's plenty of blackmail fodder."

Struck by pangs of guilt, I exclaimed, "You tracked down Eleanor's background? You should have said something sooner. In the heat of tonight's attack, it slipped my mind."

"It was nothing. All I did was search the Marriage Registry for Eleanor Fitzpatrick's maiden name. She was born Eleanor Daisy Brown in the city of Exeter, in Devon, England. You won't believe what else I learned from phone calls to friends who served on the Devon and Cornwall police force."

"Don't mess with me. What else did you learn?"

"Eleanor Brown and one Patricia Evans were partners in a series of insurance scams in Exeter back in the '70s."

"Are you sure?" Minnie asked.

"One of my pals on the police force used to live in Exeter. He's retired to Cornwall now, but the name Eleanor Brown rang a bell with him. He'd worked her case, but it was never solved."

"What happened?" I asked.

He glanced at me. "For a couple of years, Eleanor and a girlfriend staged car accidents, then submitted claims for fake injuries and vehicular damage. The police were able to nail Patricia, but by then Eleanor had emigrated to Canada, where she married a Liam Joseph Fitzpatrick and became an honest Canadian citizen. After her divorce, she retained her married name, likely to make it difficult for British police to track her down."

"Or because 'Fitzgerald' sounds classier than 'Brown'," Minnie pointed out. "So if you were able to find Eleanor Brown, then so could Lizzie's private investigator."

"No question about it."

"In that case, Lizzie could have been blackmailing Eleanor about her past insurance fraud activities," I pointed out. "Even if all danger of prosecution has passed, Eleanor wouldn't want Wayne to learn about her former life of crime. Love is a powerful motive for murder."

"Noooooooo," Minnie wailed. "Eleanor's my friend."

"Let me see if I've wrapped my head around this correctly," Hawk said. "We can rule out Roland and Wayne for both crimes, leaving only the women. All three women fit the physical profile. First of all, we can't ignore Gabby simply because we haven't uncovered a motive. Phyllis clearly has pent-up hostility against Minnie, but enough to attack her? We have no idea. There's a chance she killed Lizzie, namely because Lizzie was often nasty and ungrateful to her faithful spy. And finally, there's Eleanor. Blackmail could well have been Eleanor's motive to silence Lizzie. So the question is, can we rule any of the three suspects out on the attacks on Minnie?"

We considered our options in silence.

"I wonder why the killer is so determined to kill Minnie on this trip and not when everyone gets back home."

"Good point," Hawk said. "We may never know if we don't find the killer."

"I want to rule Eleanor out as my attacker," Minnie said. "She tried to save my life by attacking the intruder, and got elbowed in the solar plexus for her trouble."

"I'm actually the one who pressed the stop button," I pointed out gently.

"Only because Eleanor was rolling on the floor, doubled up in agony."

Hawk ran his fingers through his hair. "Are we a hundred percent certain Eleanor wasn't involved in any way? What if she hired someone else to take out Pete and mess with the controls?"

"No way," Minnie said. "We only started planning it after the goat yoga class. That would be short notice to find a trustworthy hit man."

I didn't comment on the oxymoron. "Wait," I said. "When I watched you and Eleanor head for the barn after yoga, you both stopped to chat with a wrangler. What was that all about?"

Minnie's expression told me she thought I'd lost my mind. "Eleanor wanted to talk to him about a riding lesson, that's all. Zeke called him away, so he gave her his phone number, end of story." She studied me in dismay. "You don't think—"

I cut her off. "I'm sure the contact was perfectly innocent and didn't involve Bucking Bully." I placed a hand on Hawk's arm to capture his attention. "Could you please talk to Zeke and find out more? Hopefully, we can rule out Eleanor as Minnie's attacker, either directly or indirectly."

"Will do, Hawk said. "But let me point out that if Eleanor did kill Lizzie but wasn't Minnie's attacker, we've got two criminals to deal with, not one. He checked the time. "It's late. We'd better pack it in and grab enough sleep to function tomorrow."

"What do you have planned?" I asked.

"I want to do a thorough background check on Gabby."

"Good idea." I paused, groaned, shook my head. "I'm an idiot. I can't believe I almost forgot the most important point of all. Whoever my attacker was, I broke a bone or two in her foot, so she'll be limping."

Chapter 19: Powerless

I was enjoying a happy dream involving Hawk when something, perhaps a tiny vibration or my sixth sense, jolted me awake. I ripped off my sleep mask. My bedroom was pitch dark, not time to get up yet. My bladder disagreed.

Staggering into the bathroom, I obeyed nature's call, which grew more urgent with every passing year, and groped my way back to bed, wide awake by then. Several clicks of the light switch assured me my bedside light wasn't working. Neither was the ceiling light. A walkaround revealed the power was off throughout my apartment.

I had the wits to remember I'd plugged my phone into the charger, so I made my way into the kitchen and checked the time. 4:02 a.m.

Hopefully, the power outage affected only my apartment. If all of Grizzly Gulch was left without power, we were in deep trouble. Peering out the window, I detected a sprinkling of lights on the distant hill and concluded the power outage was localized.

That did not bode well. What if someone knew about our urgent need to win the hospitality contest and had sabotaged our electrical system?

My pulse skyrocketed. Stripping off my nightie, I threw on jeans and a sweatshirt. Lacing up my work boots, which I'd kicked off in the foyer after the Bucking Bully incident, I headed out to investigate. The tiny portion of my frontal lobe that still functioned properly registered our stairs were backlit by emergency lighting. That meant the power outage affected all areas of the main lodge.

Yeah. This was deliberate.

Stepping into the lobby I rounded the corner at a run, okay, a fast walk, and smacked into a warm, hard body standing in the shadows.

"Oof," the warm, hard body's owner said. Recognizing Hawk, I relaxed into the strong hands gripping my shoulders to stop my headlong gallop. Red emergency lighting highlighted his worried frown, casting vertical shadows between his brows. "Slow down, Clara. It's only a power outage," he said.

"I know. Something woke me up."

"Me too. Then I saw flashlights down the laneway, so I figured I might as well get up and investigate. It's been a busy night."

"Did you check the main dining room and kitchen?" I asked, dreading his answer.

"I did. The main lodge has no electricity."

"This is bad. Really, really bad, especially the kitchen. How can Chef Armand prepare breakfast?" Picturing our guests waking up in frigid cabins left me lightheaded. "We have to do something."

"I was about to head outside to do a walkabout."

"I'm coming with you," I said.

He held the door open, and I preceded him into the frosty, star-studded night. Halfway down the darkened laneway, a flashlight beam sliced the night. A muffled conversation broke the silence.

"That sounds like Zeke and Abby," I muttered. "Let's go."

Hawk shone a pencil flashlight on the pathway ahead of us. I found myself all but trotting along beside him. It felt good to take action.

We arrived at the scene to find Zeke and Abby shining flashlights on a mini backhoe loader positioned across the laneway with a hydro pole collapsed on top of it.

Abby ran forward to hug me, while Zeke greeted us with, "Glad you're both here. Now we don't need to wake you up."

Drawing on a scrap of internal fortitude I had no idea existed, I pulled myself together. Surprising myself with my calmness, I said, "I assume this is why the main lodge has no power. What happened?"

"Someone stole our mini backhoe and knocked down one of our power distribution posts. This was no accident. See these gouges in the wood?" Zeke gestured at the downed pole. "The driver took several runs at the power pole before managing to topple it and bring down the wires. It's lucky no one was electrocuted. I had to shut off the power at the main panel."

"Who would do something like this?" Abby asked.

Hawk replied, "Someone with a grudge."

"How could anyone steal the backhoe?" I asked. "There's a protocol for storing the keys somewhere safe."

Abby, who'd been pacing around the backhoe, jumped in. "If you'll recall, the barn was open for an hour or two because two lunatic guests, one of them our cousin Minnie, wanted to ride Bucking Bully. It would have been easy for someone to snatch the keys from their hook in the tack room."

Zeke had obviously discussed the Bucking Bully incident with Abby. "How bad is the damage?" I asked.

"Well ..." He examined my face and hesitated. "It could be worse. This post carries power to the main lodge only. If the driver had gone after the master post near the main road, the entire ranch would be blacked out."

"What about the guest cabins?"

"That's the good news. The guest cabins, barn, and outbuildings are on a different circuit altogether. The power outage doesn't affect them, and the guests won't be inconvenienced."

"So it's unlikely whoever did this was an employee," Hawk said slowly, his forehead wrinkling as he thought his way through the puzzle. "I assume the staff are aware of the distribution post setup. A staff member out to inflict maximum damage would go after the main pole."

Zeke scratched his head. "You're telling us it was likely an outsider, a guest or a neighbor. We're on good terms with our neighboring ranches. Somehow, I can't imagine a neighbor trotting over in the middle of the night to find keys and take out a hydro pole."

With growing excitement, I said, "Meaning the saboteur was a guest."

Hawk's eyes gleamed. "Exactly. And we can be more specific than that." At my impatient gesture, he said, "I suggest the person who took out the hydro pole is the same person who tried to kill Minnie with the mechanical bull."

"That makes sense," I said, getting excited by the idea. "And if so, we identified three suspects. After ruling out Wayne and Roland, we're left with the women—Phyllis, Gabby, and Eleanor, and Eleanor. Since Zeke was walking Eleanor to the cabin, that narrows down the suspects to Phyllis and Gabby."

"The timing's right," Hawk said. It fits with when the intruder escaped. The keys were available for seizing during a race to the back door. The backhoe was parked behind the barn, nice and convenient, next to the back door."

For the first time, I sensed we might be nearing a breakthrough in the case. "Because the attacker plowed right over Eleanor to escape, I'm guessing she was furious she'd failed to kill Minnie. She likely went straight from barn to backhoe, planning to damage Grizzly Gulch as much as possible."

"Good thinking," Hawk said.

"Perhaps we can turn on a generator or two until power is restored," I suggested, feeling ridiculously proud of my problem-solving abilities.

Zeke's silence was prolonged and ominous.

"What's wrong? We do have a generator, don't we?" I gazed at Abby, then Zeke, then shifted my gaze back to Abby. "Please tell me we have a backup generator."

She avoided my imploring gaze. "I'm afraid not," she admitted. "We couldn't afford the generator system we'd ordered. I had to reschedule it. Don't you remember? All three of us approved the change. It's due for installation next week. We thought it best to wait until after Thanksgiving to avoid disruption."

Air left my lungs in an audible whoosh. "You have *got* to be kidding," I managed.

She gazed at me with an older sister's special brand of pity. "Sadly, no."

"Here's an idea," I said, hearing my desperation. "Abby, you have vendor contacts. Perhaps you can use your influence and get a generator installed a few days early."

"I'll try, but I doubt anyone can lay their hands on a generator, never mind a hotel-sized one. Last week's blackout north of Calgary caused a run on generators."

I groaned aloud. I'd forgotten. We hadn't been affected, and at the time, I'd had a few other things on my mind—like preparing for the Thanksgiving week getaway and, oh, yeah, winning a contest that would put us on the map.

Zeke said, "If it's any consolation, the water supply is fine. Power to the well pump is on the same circuit as the barn, and it's working."

"That's great. Thanks." I cleared my throat and rewarded him with a weak thumbs up. "I'll announce the power outage to our guests over breakfast. Right now, I need to find Chef Armand and try to calm him down or he'll freak out. Once we've finished, I'll come right over and fill you in on his reaction and strategize."

Hawk said, "There's no need for you to face Chef Armand alone. If you don't mind, I'll join you."

As usual, Hawk had my back. I flashed him a grateful smile. Turning to Abby, I said, "I need you to invite Dodie and Minnie to our chat. Minnie's more than familiar with the attack in the barn, but Dodie isn't. And they both need to know about the power outage, so would you mind filling them in? We should be back around 5:30, assuming all goes well."

"That's a big if," Abby said.

"Thanks for the encouragement, Sis. You're number one in my book too." I addressed Zeke. "You're part of our management team, Zeke. Can you join us?"

He shook his head. "Thanks, but not this time. I want to get this mess cleared away before a guest stumbles on it. Abby can brief me later."

"Good luck with Chef Armand," Abby said, adding, "You'll need it."

I scowled at her. "Your sympathy, compassion, and sensitivity are unbounded."

Hawk threw an arm around my waist and gave me a squeeze. "Between the two of us, your temperamental chef won't stand a chance. Wait and see."

"Spoken like a man who's never tangled with our head chef. When Chef Armand gets upset—and make no mistake, he'll be upset upon hearing about the power outage—he tends to be nastier than Gordon Ramsay on a bad day."

During the short walk back to the main lodge, my apprehension over Chef Armand's response gained more traction. There was a strong probability he would resign when he heard of the power outage and recognized the challenges ahead. On reaching the kitchen's side entrance, I told Hawk, "Chef Armand always arrives in the kitchen at 5:00 a.m. sharp for the breakfast prep work. We have to settle him down before the rest of the kitchen staff arrive or there will be mass resignations."

He surprised me by saying, "Want my opinion?"

Not really, but I slipped into people-pleaser mode. "Of course," I said brightly.

"We men tend to relate well to an approach that appeals to our sense of pride. Show your appreciation for his skill as a master chef before hitting him with news of the power outage. You could say something like how grateful you are for his talent and loyalty because you're facing a difficult situation, one a lesser chef couldn't handle. Tell him you'll support him in every way possible, then ask for his advice. Men live for those times when women ask for their advice."

"That's not an opinion. It's advice disguised as an opinion, but I love it all the same. Want to help me ambush him before he learns for himself about the power outage?"

"The pleasure is all mine." At the sound of a car door closing, Hawk continued, "And if I'm not mistaken, we're just in time."

A large man wearing a white chef's uniform and carrying a chef's *toque blanche* emerged from the parking lot's shadows, headed for the side door and muttering under his breath as he approached. I made out the word, "*Merde*," repeated several times.

Hawk gave me a thumbs-up, and I called out a cheery, "Good morning. Chef Armand?"

"*Oui*? Who is there?"

"It's Clara and Hawk," I said.

He drew closer and stopped in front of us, hands on his well-padded hips, and gave a curt nod. "You must talk to the night staff about leaving on some lights. How can I be expected to find the kitchen when everything is dark?"

"Come around with us to the front door. It will be easier," I said, thinking of the large fireplace and comfy chairs.

Grumbling, he followed us. Hawk held the door open. I walked inside with Chef Armand on my heels.

Peering into the lobby, he said, "*Mon Dieu*! Why is it so dark in here?"

"I'll fix that." I groped my way to the fireplace, where we stored a fire igniter in the hearth log container. After I'd succeeded in lighting several pumpkin-shaped candles on the mantelpiece, I ignited the newspaper under a pile of kindling.

"Let's sit here while the fire catches. We'll be warm in no time." I cleared my throat. "I need your advice, Chef Armand. You're the only person I can turn to." I indicated an armchair flanking the fireplace. "I want explain what has happened before the rest of the staff arrives."

Hawk winked at the frowning chef. "I hope you can settle her down. I tried, but haven't had much luck."

The kindling made a warm, crackling sound.

Once we were seated I took a deep breath and said, "We have a small electrical issue."

"Small electrical issue?" Chef Armand yelled, leaping out of the chair. "How small is small? You cannot expect me to feed guests without the electricity."

Hawk jumped up to snag the volatile chef's elbow and maneuver him back into the chair. "For a man with your talents, this is nothing, a mere annoyance. Let's hear what Clara has to say, then decide the best way to tackle the situation."

I held out my hands to warm them while fastening my most earnest gaze on Chef Armand's face. After moistening my lips, I explained about the power outage, trying to put a positive spin on what was basically a disaster.

Nobody spoke. I let the silence stretch out while burning wood filled the room with a merry crackle.

At last, Chef Armand asked, "But how will I prepare meals without electricity?" Anguish filled his voice. "We won't even be able to use the toaster, never mind produce a Thanksgiving dinner with the roasted turkey and the silky gravy and all the fixings. *Merde alors.* You expect me to … to pull *le lapin*—the rabbit—out of a hat?" He flung his arms into the air.

If ever there was a time for me to project self-assurance, this was it. Looking him in the eyes with unflinching directness, I said, "Chef Armand, I have the utmost confidence in you. I can't think of anyone better qualified than you to guide and lead the kitchen staff under these trying conditions. Only someone with your culinary genius and people skills can salvage the situation. There's no one else on the planet I would choose to face this issue." Although I meant every word, I hoped I hadn't gone too far.

Hawk backed me up. "I know Clara's asking a lot from you. But you strike me as a man with imagination, skill, and great courage, a man who rises to a challenge."

Chef Armand's expression lightened. "This is so. I am a man who embraces the most difficult of tasks with gusto."

I released a long, slow exhale. "You won't be alone," I assured him. "We're all on your side. We will do everything humanly possible to help."

"And I'll get all the extra help I need? I must have runners to carry food to and from the kitchen."

"Zeke will assign wranglers to kitchen duty. I promise. Better still, when we win the *Best Vacations on the Planet* contest, I will contact the organizers to suggest a full article about how our head chef saved the day when the power went out at Grizzly Gulch."

"With photos of me?"

"Yes."

"*Très bon.* You must inform the guests this will be—how do you say?—a rustic Canadiana experience … with the emphasis on rustic. My cooks will put to good use the old wood stove in the kitchen plus there are many barbecues."

"We have extra-long extension cords, so you'll be able to use the electric frypans, slow cookers, and a turkey fryer you ordered especially for Thanksgiving. All you'll need to do is plug the appliances into the outdoor electrical outlets in the parking lot." Another thought struck me. "The power outage doesn't affect Zeke and Abby's quarters off the barn. I'm sure they'll be happy to offer their stove and fridge, and there are two freezers out there too."

"Have you ever been to a Hawaiian luau?" Hawk asked. "You know, when they cook an entire pig on hot stones, seal in all the juices with leaves, and cover everything with sand?"

Chef Armand jumped to his feet. "*Oui.* We can do something similar, only with the turkeys. The wranglers will dig food pits. Turkeys will be placed on top of hot rocks and covered with the leaves of cabbage or lettuce. Everything will be buried under a layer of earth and baked all day until the meat is tender and succulent. *Mon Dieu.* Those birds will be *délicieux.*" He brought the fingers and thumb of his right hand together, kissed them lightly, and joyfully raised them into the air.

This was turning out to be fun.

"Our freezers are full of the home-made pies and pasta dishes, dozens of appetizers, and gallons of soups and stocks of various kinds. We'll offload the delicacies that must not be permitted thaw to Zeke's freezers, perhaps those of neighboring ranchers, too. Even without the electricity, everything else will stay frozen, at least until the Thanksgiving celebration."

"What do you think you'll serve for tonight's dinner?" I asked, genuinely curious to hear his answer.

He gave my question ample consideration. "Barbecued steak and chicken, I think, accompanied by the roasted potatoes and root vegetables, coleslaw as the *salade*." The chef's list of possibilities increased in volume. "As for bread, one of my cooks is an Aussie, always bragging about how he makes delicious Australian damper in the live coals. Tonight, he will—how do you say?—put the money where the mouth is and make his damper in a fire pit. For dessert, guests can make their own s'mores. I will offer the ice cream, which must be eaten before it melts, with maple syrup or chocolate sauce."

"Count me in," Hawk said.

"*Mais oui*. Then on Sunday, our guests will dine on the Christmas Eve tourtières I made last week and froze. We will tell the guests they are called Wild West Meat Pies. I will use barbecues instead of ovens to bake them, and serve them with my home-made chili sauce, potato salad, and barbecue beans. Dessert will be Death by Chocolate and Luscious Lemon Bars."

"Leaving only Monday's Thanksgiving dinner," Hawk said.

Chef Armand said, "We must be ingenious. Inventive. We will cook the turkeys in a fire pit, also the deep fryer, with bacon and maple syrup Brussels sprouts, cornbread stuffing, smashed truffled potatoes smothered in *sauce à la dinde*—how you say 'turkey gravy'—and my world-famous pies for dessert."

"It all sounds delicious," I said, my mouth watering.

While feeding several more logs into the fireplace, Hawk said, "The fireplace in the dining hall will provide plenty of heat during meals, especially if you ask guests to dress warmly."

"At least the weather forecast is unseasonably warm right through Thanksgiving," Chef Armand said, rising and placing his *toque blanche* on his head. Taking a pumpkin candle in each hand, he said, "*Maintenant*, I have much to do. I go now and phone Zeke. Next, I will explain to my staff what is required of them and get them started on breakfast while I re-work the menus." With a wave, he disappeared into the gloom, shouting, "Do not worry, *mes amis*. We will rise to the challenge. This will be fun."

I slumped down in the chair as it sank in that a potentially explosive situation might turn out to be a blessing if handled properly. It was my job to get everyone on the same page, and to do that I had to convince Abby, Dodie, and Minnie everything would work out fine—at least food-wise.

Chef Armand was right. This would be fun, provided the killer didn't view the power outage as a golden opportunity to target Minnie again.

Chapter 20: A Surprise Break in the Case

Bearing a thermos of high-test coffee and a jumbo box of Chef Armand's maple-pecan Danish pastries, Hawk followed me into my apartment at 5:30 a.m. Chef Armand was onside for a rustic Canadiana Thanksgiving. It was now time to sell my sisters on our brilliant strategy for extracting success from a power crisis. With their backing, or even without, I was certain I could win the guests over.

I was relieved to find Dodie, Abby, and Minnie in my dining area, semi-awake and up to speed on last night's events. Snuggles, who'd bunked down on my bed, hadn't condescended to join us. While Hawk sat, I closed the curtains against snoopers, poured steaming mugs of coffee, and distributed them before seating myself between Hawk and Minnie. Mid-table, napkins and the box of flaky Danish pastries rested within easy reach.

Dodie bit into a Danish. Her face took on an orgasmic expression.

As hostess, I took charge of our meeting. Over Hawk's finger drumming, I said, "Welcome, everyone. By now, I assume we're all on the same page for our most recent crisis. If we all cooperate, I believe we can turn this power outage into one of Grizzly Gulch's biggest success stories."

After stifling a yawn, Abby said, "Great, because Zeke called the emergency hotline, even phoned around to call in favors. No one's available to restore our power lines until after Thanksgiving. Private property issues are low priority during a national holiday."

Hawk stopped drumming his fingers on the table. "Let's discuss our next steps."

This was a man accustomed to being in charge. Although I empathized with his impatience, I placed a hand on his arm. "We will, but first, back to the power outage and how it affects the guests. I want everyone here to know I intend to present the electrical malfunction to our guests as a positive enhancement to their Thanksgiving week. Let's all reinforce the message. We can't let a little power outage impede our contest win."

"And how do you propose to explain it?" Minnie asked.

"Here's the thing. Guests don't know we suspect sabotage. We'll tell them we're experiencing a power outage in the main lodge due to a tipsy wrangler having a little accident with our backhoe. Our switchboard is down temporarily, but cell phone coverage is not affected. If anyone needs to borrow a cell phone, we will make one available. The guest cabins are not affected in any way. And finally, for a special treat, we're providing a genuine, rustic Canadiana Thanksgiving weekend experience, a fabulous four-day event that begins today."

"Yeah, like that'll fly with Chef Armand," Abby said, lifting her mug to her lips.

In my peripheral vision, I caught Hawk squirm in his seat and gulp his coffee before heaving an exasperated sigh. Ignoring him, I stated calmly, "Matter of fact, Chef Armand is on board and enthusiastic." I proceeded to summarize our meeting with him, including the gala Thanksgiving dinner, finishing with, "Hopefully guests will view the power outage as a perk and leave us good reviews."

Predictably, my sisters' reaction was lukewarm. Perhaps they needed specifics. I'd barely opened my mouth to elaborate on the brilliance of our plan when Hawk interjected with, "Good. Now, let's discuss our next steps to find Lizzie's killer and Minnie's attacker." He radiated impatience.

Minnie's phone rang before anyone else could express an opinion. She glanced at her phone, leaped to her feet, and said, "Sorry. I have to take this. You go ahead." She rushed from the room.

"I wonder what that's about," I said, reaching for a pastry and chomping down. "Good grief, these are sinfully good," I mumbled.

"I'm sure we'll find out," Dodie replied. "Minnie's not one to keep secrets."

"Now, about our next steps," Hawk said, stepping into take-charge mode. "I intend to interrogate our two suspects for both the runaway mechanical bull incident and the power outage."

Thinking of all the feathers Hawk might ruffle with his Mountie-style interrogations, I shot Dodie a silent *please help me* message.

"Let us do the questioning," Dodie said, correctly interpreting my panicked gaze. "Chef Armand needs your services more. There's no need for you to waste your time when you're one of the few people he can get along with. Phyllis and I had a nice chat at the dance. She seems to tolerate me, so I'll tackle her while Abby has a girl-to-girl chat with Gabby about her whereabouts last night."

"Fine." Hawk subsided in a cloud of frustration and popped half a maple-pecan pastry into his mouth.

I was preparing to launch into the details of our strategy for producing a gala Thanksgiving dinner in the absence of electricity when Minnie charged into the room

"I have big news," she announced.

"Who phoned?" I asked.

"Charles Dubois, the guy I've been seeing. He's another Lifestyle Manor resident. Actually, we're more friends than lovers, though lately, he's been pushing for more commitment than I'm willing to give."

"He felt compelled to call at five thirty in the morning?"

Hawk stiffened. "Did you say Dubois?"

"I did. Is there a problem?" Minnie asked.

Hawk's lips tightened. "Gabby is now officially a serious suspect."

"No way," I said. "Why?"

"While I was searching the Marriage Registry for Eleanor's maiden name, I also investigated Gabby Chambers. I didn't mention it earlier because the name I found didn't mean anything to me at the time. You'll never guess her maiden name."

"Dubois?" I ventured.

"Bingo."

White-faced, Minnie collapsed into her chair as if her legs no longer supported her. "Shut the front door! No wonder I always had an uneasy feeling Charles was hiding something from me. Now his phone call makes sense."

"What exactly did he say to you?" Hawk asked.

"He was slurring his words, so at first I thought he was drunk, but it turned out he was in the hospital and hooked up to a morphine drip. He slipped in the shower yesterday morning and underwent hip replacement surgery late afternoon. You'd think they would operate right away, but no—"

I glanced at Hawk. Sensing his utter frustration, I said gently, "Please, Minnie, get to the point."

"Sorry." She flashed me a remorseful glance. "Charles then tells me his hospital bed was uncomfortable and someone down the hall moaned throughout the night, so he couldn't sleep. He'd tried calling Gabby around midnight. When she didn't answer, he'd tried me next, still no answer. He asked if we were out on the town together." Minnie released a forced chuckle.

"No, you were not out on the town," Abby said. "I understand you and Eleanor were sneaking into the barn to ride Bucking Bully."

Minnie had the grace to blush.

"Gabby was the first person Charles called," Hawk pointed out. "They're definitely connected, likely father and daughter." He turned to Minnie. "What did he say next?"

"The morphine must have fogged his brain because he asked me to give Gabby an important message. He wants her to visit her nice nurse friend, Raquel Mendoza, at the Big Sky General Hospital in Calgary."

"Why would he want her to do that?" Hawk asked.

"He said he was real worried about Gabby. He'd always liked Raquel, said something about how she'd always been a good influence and perhaps she could straighten Gabby out. Then a nurse came into his room and he had to end the call."

A throbbing silence filled the room. After a few seconds, I said, "Why did Charles and Gabby keep their relationship a secret?"

In a tiny voice, Minnie said, "I guess because the employees at Lifestyle Manor are forbidden to have any relatives living there. Favoritism and all that."

"And can we assume Charles Dubois is wealthy?" I asked.

Minnie shrugged. "Probably. We never discussed money, but he used to be a successful investment dealer."

"So with him dating you, Gabby's likely worried about her inheritance."

"She has nothing to worry about. He's not really my type."

"But Gabby doesn't know that," Hawk pointed out patiently. "It gives her a motive to kill you. And if Lizzie knew about their relationship and threatened to reveal it to Lifestyle Manor's senior management, Gabby would be fired due to staffing policy."

"Giving Gabby a motive to kill Lizzie as well," I pointed out.

Abby frowned. "I hate to say, but that's a pretty weak motive if you ask me."

"But not to sabotage our electrical grid," Dodie interjected, "unless there's more we don't know." She cast a suspicious glance at me. "Does Gabby have any special reason to harm Grizzly Gulch?"

"Um … Maybe," I said. "I smashed the metal-reinforced heel of my work boots onto the attacker's foot and heard something crunch. If Gabby's walking with a limp today, she's guilty, and strongly motivated to do as much harm to Grizzly Gulch as possible—and, by extension, to me. Revenge is a compelling motive."

A broad grin spread across Hawk's face. "Remind me not to rile you up."

A wicked little shiver of anticipation skittered down my spine.

"Focus, you two," Abby said, shaking her head. "That may not be enough to prove she attacked anyone or tried to kill Minnie using Bucking Bully, but it's a good motive for sabotage, don't you think?"

"Definitely," Hawk said, "The next steps of the investigation are clear. A visit with Raquel Mendoza is in order for the afternoon. At this rate, I might nail a killer sooner rather than later."

I frowned at Hawk's use of the word, "I." It was clear he assumed he'd be leading the interview due to his advanced interrogation skills.

A frantic pounding at the door interrupted our meeting. I dashed to the door to find Chef Armand in a state of high anxiety. "We have a kitchen rebellion on our hands. They do not listen to me. I have much need of *Monsieur* Hawk in the kitchen."

Hawk strode toward us. "I heard that. I'll be right down," he said with resignation.

"Come. *Immédiatement*." The frantic chef snagged Hawk's arm and tugged. I got the impression that if necessary, he would hoist Hawk over his shoulder and bear him away.

Resisting Chef Armand's attempt to drag him into the corridor, Hawk said, "*Oui*, I'm coming." To me, he said, "I'll contact Callum, explain about Gabby, and try to convince him to find a judge willing to issue a search warrant for her cabin."

"Sounds good. I'll phone Raquel Mendoza to set up a meeting."

"Okay." His stern gaze encompassed all of us. "Do not, under any circumstance, go anywhere alone. I want each of you to take someone with you at all times."

"Count on it," I assured Hawk as Chef Armand hustled him away, with Abby and Dodie hot on their heels.

That left me alone with Minnie, who said, "I don't care what Hawk thinks. I'm coming with you to interview Raquel this afternoon."

To buy myself some time to formulate a tactful rejection of Minnie's assertion, I popped a chunk of maple pecan pastry into my mouth, only to have it enter the wrong passage. With a flurry of napkins, Minnie took my minor food malfunction as an opportunity to hammer a fist into my back. I wasn't sure if she intended to help or punish, but her treatment dislodged the blockage.

After I finished coughing and spraying crumbs, I wiped my streaming eyes and said, "You may *not* come with us to interview Raquel. Hawk expects you to stay here."

Minnie's determined gaze was steady. "Too bad. I'm coming."

"No way. I'm accompanying him. If you came too, the poor woman might feel intimidated and clam up altogether."

"Be that as it may, it's *my* life that's at risk. I'm terrified to stay here alone with Gabby running loose, and I refuse to follow Abby or Dodie around like a puppy." She jutted her chin. "I'm coming, and you can't stop me."

"Hawk will refuse."

She fisted her hands on her hips. "So what? Tell him he doesn't need to come because I'm coming with you."

I got a rush at the thought. Panic followed, and then guilt. "I can't do that."

"Yes you can. You're not a helpless little girl, and Hawk's not the boss of you."

I let Minnie's words sink in. She was right. Hawk wasn't my boss. More to the point, he was neither my brutal father nor abusive husband. I was free to make my own decisions. Hey, perhaps I would crack the case and, as a bonus, impress both my sisters.

"You're right," I told Minnie. "We're both intelligent women, more than capable of asking questions. I'll explain to Hawk that you'll be safer accompanying me to the hospital than sticking around Grizzly Gulch waiting for Gabby to pick you off. Besides, he should be here to give Chef Armand the moral support he needs, and to collar Gabby if and when she returns."

Minnie's eyes danced with glee. "I was a cop in one of my plays. I have the role down pat, so I'll take the lead during the grilling."

"No way." Apprehension trickled down my spine as I imagined the dramatics she would unleash. "You're much too close to the situation. Tell you what. Let me handle Raquel, and you can step in if I forget anything."

"We'll see," she replied with an enigmatic little smile. "Let's go, or we'll be late for breakfast. If memory serves, you have a speech to deliver to your guests. Something about a power outage?"

Chapter 21: Some Answers at Last

MINNIE AND I MIGRATED TO the main dining hall, where we sat together and placed our order for breakfast—a tower of pancakes, maple syrup, and sausage for her, fresh fruit, an egg-white omelet, and dry toast for me to offset those outrageously rich maple pastries. While we waited for our meal, I scanned the guests' faces, but didn't see Gabby. Icing her foot, perhaps?

After knocking back a slug of coffee Minnie nudged me. "Isn't it time for your speech?"

I nodded, collected my thoughts, and marched to the microphone, hoping I projected confidence. For the next few minutes, I described the power outage caused by the downed hydro pole, omitting any hint of sabotage or criminal activity, while assuring our guests that the rest of their week would be a special treat—a genuine rustic Canadiana experience they would never forget.

In response, everyone was good-natured about the inconvenience—everyone, that is, except Phyllis, who looked as if she might be sucking on a lemon.

True to form, she kicked off with a multitude of complaints, asking difficult questions about meals. I answered by trotting into the kitchen and asking Chef Armand to say a few words to our guests. Never one to shy away from the spotlight, he explained the meal situation with fervor, punctuating his description of our rustic Canadiana Thanksgiving with much arm-waving and a smattering of French expressions, many of which our guests wouldn't understand—I hoped.

Once Chef Armand disappeared back into the kitchen, I apologized again for any inconvenience the guests might experience, thanked everyone for their understanding, and assured them that we would go out of our way to ensure their enjoyment. I almost begged them not to let the power outage influence their reviews, but changed my mind. There would be time enough to ask later. We had three days left to prove Grizzly Gulch was the best in the business.

Unobtrusively wiping my sweaty palms on my jeans, I returned to my seat while the dining hall buzzed with conversation and speculation. On the whole, our guests accepted the inconvenience with good-natured comments.

During the meal, Minnie and I didn't talk much. On my part, I was obsessing about the best way to tell Hawk that Minnie and I would conduct this afternoon's interview. Minnie, on the other hand, was no doubt mentally rehearsing lines from her role as a cop. With luck, our meeting with Raquel Mendoza this afternoon would shed light on Gabby's role, if any, in Lizzie's death and the attacks on Minnie.

Once breakfast ended, we stayed seated to finish our coffee and, in Minnie's case, scarf down her daily bran muffin. "Have you seen Gabby this morning?" I whispered.

"As a matter of fact, no," she whispered back. "Maybe she has a broken foot."

We both cracked up and were making our way to the exit when the receptionist entered the dining hall and spotted us. "Oh, Clara," she said, waving at us as she minced toward us, her high heels clacking on the tiled floor. "Just the person I'd hoped to find. There's something I thought I should mention."

"Sure thing, Lexi."

"Gabby Chambers stopped by the desk real early this morning, like around 6:30. She said if anyone came asking for her, I should, like, tell them she'd taken a taxi into Canmore to meet a friend and would be back in time for dinner. She also said no one else needed to know she'd left the property unless there was, like, an emergency or something." Lexie paused, eying Minnie in dismay. "Oh, dear. I wasn't supposed to tell anyone. You won't mention this, will you?"

"My lips are sealed," Minnie assured her.

"Did you notice if Gabby was limping?" I asked.

"Sorry, no. Another guest arrived with a complaint about her cabin phone not working and asking to borrow a cell phone."

After I thanked Lexi and she disappeared, I said to Minnie, "Too bad she didn't notice a limp."

"Yeah. If Gabby was my attacker, she'd have plenty of time to get her butt to the Canmore hospital for an x-ray. If you broke her foot as you suspect—and I hope you crushed every one of those twenty-six bones—the least they'll do is prescribe painkillers. But unless we can prove she committed a crime, we may never know for sure if hers was the face behind the ski mask."

"I sense we're on the brink of a breakthrough," I said, refusing to contemplate the alternative. "Raquel will fill in the missing puzzle pieces."

"I hope so. Otherwise you'll be stuck with me until Hawk and Callum solve the case."

Minnie shadowed me all morning to the point where it became a major irritant. She'd stuck like Gorilla Glue during a bathroom break, hovering outside the stall until I was finished. The setup activities for a morning pickleball round robin provided her with many opportunities to offer opinions on the subject. I'd also made the strategic mistake of letting her sit in on a video chat with the local business association, where she'd thrown in her two cents' worth about having a destination wedding in our barn. How had I forgotten how pushy she was?

Loaded with box lunches, we were headed to my apartment to prepare for our jaunt to the hospital to interview Gabby's friend when we spied Phyllis sitting the porch swing, reading a book. A fast about-face took Minnie to the porch, where she plopped down on the swing, cornering Phyllis for a cozy chat. When I reached them, Minnie was in full-blown inquiry mode, all friendly chatter and good fellowship, asking Phyllis if she'd managed to sleep through the excitement of the hydro pole take-down. According to Phyllis she'd retired early and slept soundly until morning, leaving her without an alibi for either the mechanical bull incident or the power pole takeout.

Filled with envy about Phyllis' ability to sleep throughout the night without requiring two pee breaks, I succeeded in pulling Minnie away.

"That was a waste of time," I whispered as we entered the main lodge. "We couldn't tell if Phyllis was limping."

"Huh," Minnie said, climbing the stairs to my apartment. "Her foot didn't appear swollen. Anyway, a little goodwill goes a long way."

When we arrived, I'd barely closed the door when she informed me, "I'm off to freshen up my makeup and gather necessities for an interrogation," leaving me to imagine a tool kit packed with pliers, a lighter, and perhaps a Taser.

By the time I opened the door to Hawk, his marathon emotional support session with Chef Armand had left him looking frazzled and drained. His hair was all cute and rumpled, as if he'd run his fingers through it in fits of frustration. His unbuttoned flannel shirt hung untucked over a black tee-shirt and well-worn jeans.

I invited him into my living room for an update on morning activities. Once I was seated beside him on the loveseat, I sucked in a deep breath and filled him in on what Lexi had told me about Gabby and her trip into Canmore for the day, postponing the moment where I would break the news that Minnie and I would be conducting the interview with Rachel Mendoza. When I finally got around to it, with several false starts and an apology, I pointed out that since he wouldn't be joining us, he'd be free to do whatever he wanted for the rest of his day.

To my astonishment, he'd listened to my garbled explanation without interruption, without any sign of irritation, never mind the fury I'd anticipated. Once I wound down, I held my breath, waiting for the explosion.

"Okay," he said, taking my hand and playing with my fingers. "I want you to phone me as soon as your interview is over."

"That's it? Okay?" I tried to extract my hand, but he tightened his grip.

"Do you realize you're cute when you're nervous?"

The way he studied my face made my heart do a little skip and a jump. I chose to ignore his crack about nervous. "So you're not angry?"

"Of course I'm not. I don't blame Minnie for being afraid of another attack. She'll be safer away from here. Between the pair of you, I'm certain you'll succeed in prying every scrap of relevant information from Raquel. In fact, this change in plan may work out for the best."

I moistened my lips. "How so?"

"Now that I'm free to do other things, I may not return until late this evening."

"Where will you go?"

He smiled at me, a slow, melting one I was certain had set more than a few hearts pounding. "Worried?" He raised my hand, turned it over, and traced a circle on my palm using his tongue.

Fiery sparks exploded in every nerve ending. "Devastated," I said, finding myself short of breath. "What are you planning to do with so much free time?"

After depositing a kiss on my palm, he released my hand and stood to pace the room. "I didn't have any luck reaching Callum about obtaining a search warrant for Gabby's cabin. I suspect he's ducking my calls, so I'll corner him at home around dinnertime. With a little luck, he'll invite me to join them for the meal. But first, I'll pop into his RCMP detachment. They all know me there, and I have several phone calls I need to make."

"Why not use your own phone?" I asked turning my head to track his progress around the living room.

"Calls originating from police headquarters are more likely to be answered than ones from a random cell phone. My first call will be to Lifestyle Manor's H/R Manager to ask for a faxed copy of Gabby's resume and a list of her references. From there, I intend to call every reference, also Lifestyle Manor's CEO, get him to admit that Gabby slept with him in return for the event management position. Then I need to document everything—the attacks on Minnie, Lizzie's blackmail habit, and our suspicions about Gabby, all the evidence Callum will need to convince a judge to sign a search warrant for the cabin."

"That's a lot of ground to cover.

"It's not as bad as it sounds. I've made a good start on compiling our case." He stopped in front of me and took a thumb drive from his pocket and waved it under my nose. "Once you fill me in on the results of your interview today, Callum should have enough information to convince a judge to issue a search warrant. Luckily, he lives next door to Judge Brightheart. She's married to his best friend, Joseph."

"But what if she's away for the long weekend?"

"Let's deal with that if and when the time comes." He shoved the thumb drive back in his pocket and studied my face. "If what we suspect is true,

Gabby is dangerous, and she may return to Grizzly Gulch before I do. I want you and Minnie to stick together, no matter what."

"We will. I promise."

"And I don't want either of you to take any unnecessary risks."

"We won't." If we took any risks at all, which of course we wouldn't, they would be highly necessary.

"Promise me."

"Promise." I stood and wrapped my arms around him. What started as a hug turned into a passionate kiss, verging on desperation. I forced myself to let go.

He gripped my arms. "I'm not sure what I would do if something happened to you."

Those words left me with conflicting emotions—a ton of guilt overlaid by a soft, squishy feeling. He really did care.

Late morning found me behind the wheel of a Grizzly Gulch pickup with Minnie riding shotgun as we headed for the Big Sky General Hospital to interview the nurse who hopefully would shed more light on Gabby's background. A lot was riding on this meeting. Without new information, Lizzie's killer and Minnie's attacker might well avoid detection and strike again.

Once we arrived at the hospital, I parked the truck and squeezed Minnie's hand. "Don't worry. I won't rest until we collar the person who killed Lizzie and attacked you."

Minnie responded with a brief nod, squared her shoulders, and we entered the hospital. On approaching the cafeteria, a hum of conversation and clatter of dishes greeted us. Minnie would have rushed inside, but I snagged her arm to halt her. I needed to set some ground rules.

"What's wrong?" she asked.

"Nothing, at least, I hope not," I replied, my stomach twisting with apprehension. I hadn't insisted that Minnie tone down her dramatic tendencies. Big omission. "Perhaps we should have discussed this sooner," I ventured, "but I managed to establish a connection with Raquel when I talked to her this morning, so I'll set the tone."

Minnie saluted and barked out a snappy, "Yes, Sir."

I restrained myself from uttering an automatic snarl.

Squeezing between tables, we had no trouble finding Raquel. Wearing pale blue scrubs, her brown, curly hair corralled in a ponytail, she sat alone reading a paperback. A mug of coffee rested at her elbow next to a plate containing a pile of fries and the remains of a burger, a feat of self-control I could never bring myself to emulate. Daddy had always made sure we cleared our plates.

As if sensing our arrival, Raquel lifted her head. She snapped the book shut and examined us. I made the necessary introductions, avoiding mentioning that we weren't here in an official capacity. Assuming a stern expression, Minnie hip-butted me aside to step in front of me and pump Raquel's hand.

I glared at Minnie. She was playing the role of lead investigator to the hilt.

Once we'd seated ourselves, Minnie jumped right in, all businesslike cop attitude. "I know you must be busy, Ms. Mendoza. Thanks so much for agreeing to meet with us on such short notice. We're trying to clarify a few things."

"Please. Call me Raquel," she said, a glint of respect in her eyes, "and you're most welcome. Your assistant said you wanted to talk to me about Gabby."

Assistant?

I needed to gain control of the meeting. "I'm the one you talked to this morning, Raquel. Minnie's my cousin, my houseguest, and a retired actress who kindly agreed to accompany me as a courtesy."

Raquel swung her gaze in my direction. "What has Gabby gone and done now?"

In my peripheral vision, I noticed Minnie's brow wrinkle. Sensing she was on the verge of blurting out Gabby was trying to kill her, I adopted my most authoritative tone. "Why do you ask that, Raquel? Was Gabby a rule-breaker during her time here? Maybe worse?"

Raquel stared at me in surprise, rather as if a cockapoo had risen up on its hind legs and recited an excerpt from Shakespeare. She said, "Gabby believed rules were for others, not herself."

That didn't sound like something a friend would say. I'd opened my mouth to grill her some more, but Minnie was faster. She flashed a quick, easy grin at Raquel, saying, "I'm dating Gabby's father. Charles mentioned you two were good friends."

Raquel's expression lightened. "Gabby and I used to be best friends in high school. After graduation, we went our separate ways. I went into the nursing program at the University of Alberta, and Gabby got married. Her husband was a wealthy lawyer, so she skipped higher education. But we kept in touch, saw one another several times a year, more often when she moved to Calgary after her divorce." She paused and huffed out a sigh. "I was newly divorced as well—actually I never re-married—so we hung out a lot."

"I totally understand, hon," Minnie said. "I've been married and divorced three times. I should have quit after one."

I jumped in again to steer the conversation back on track. "Did Gabby get a job after her divorce?"

"Oh, yes." Raquel swung her gaze to me. "She'd signed a prenup. The divorce left her practically penniless. The only job she could find was clerical work, which barely covered the rent."

"Isn't her father wealthy," I said.

"Yes, but he's a firm believer in the tough love approach. He was always telling her she needed to stand on her own two feet."

"So then what happened?"

Raquel gazed at me with an expression mid-way between irritation and resigned respect. "After three years of minimum wage jobs, a clerical assistant position opened up here at Big Sky General. The salary was a notch higher, so I told Gabby about the opportunity. She applied, I gave her a glowing recommendation, and she got the job." Under her breath, she muttered, "Big mistake."

I shot Minnie a quelling glance, saying, "But then she quit her job at the hospital in June to work at Lifestyle Manor."

"It was a big step up from clerical assistant." Raquel moistened her mouth with a sip of cold, scummy coffee.

Gabby's change in career also came on the heels of Minnie's move into Lifestyle Manor. There was something strange going on here, and I was determined to learn more. "Lifestyle Manor is picky about its staff. Surely Gabby didn't have any events management experience."

Raquel squirmed—actually *squirmed*—in her seat. "Maybe … uh … I'm not sure."

I pressed harder. "Exactly how did she score a job in a retirement residence?"

After a long pause, Raquel said, "Gabby was desperate to work at Lifestyle Manor. Seems her father had moved in there as a resident. You know what it's like in those retirement homes. Ten women for every man."

"Yeah, I've noticed," Minnie said.

"He told me he'd found himself a new girlfriend."

"That would be me," Minnie interjected.

"Right. So Gabby was frantic, worried the woman—you—might be taking advantage of her daddy and her inheritance. She wanted to be close enough to prevent the romance from heating up, and … " As if realizing she'd said too much, Raquel snapped her mouth shut.

"And?" I prompted

Raquel released a resigned sigh. "And I helped her embellish her résumé with false event management experience."

I sensed Raquel knew more. A whole lot more. "How enterprising. What else?"

"To seal the deal, she also slept with the head of the Lifestyle Manor chain."

I hit her with a surprise jab. "What did Gabby do to upset you?"

"I don't know what you mean."

"I think you do. A few minutes ago you let it slip that helping her get a job here at the hospital was a big mistake. You assumed we didn't hear, but this senior citizen has better hearing than a German shepherd. So let me re-phrase my question. Why do you regret helping Gabby get the job here at the hospital?"

Raquel didn't answer directly. "I'm not sure what to say. Gabby and I haven't seen or talked to one another since mid-September when she dropped by the hospital during a weekend visit."

September fifth was when I'd informed Minnie about the Boomers' Thanksgiving Fling at Grizzly Gulch, after which she'd convinced Gabby to organize a trip for Lifestyle Manor residents who wanted to attend. Yet Charles hadn't accompanied Minnie to Grizzly Gulch. There must be a good reason.

I steepled my hands on the table and fixed Raquel with a steady gaze. "You're holding back something important."

I watched with interest while Raquel's face morphed from bright pink to sickly pale. Taking pity on her, I softened my voice. "No one's blaming you for anything, hon. We're trying to get to the bottom of something that happened this week."

Raquel took a deep, shaky breath. "As I mentioned, Gabby's last visit was mid-September. Later, I discovered something."

"This is taking too long." Minnie hip-checked me to one side, slamming her hands down on the table in front of Raquel and going nose-to-nose. "What did you discover?"

Several heads turned. Luckily no one was close enough to hear the exchange.

Raquel's cheeks drained of color. "W-when we did inventory at the end of September, two vials of potassium chloride were missing from a locked supply room cabinet. The drugs in the supply room were my responsibility." A fat tear rolled down her cheek.

"Would an injection of potassium chloride kill someone?"

"Oh, yes. It would all be over in a few minutes. It's an agonizing death, and virtually untraceable. Since potassium is always present in the human body, elevated levels of potassium in the blood are not conclusive proof of anything."

"Then what happened?"

"I phoned Gabby right away. She laughed and denied stealing anything. Then she warned me I should be more careful with my keys. She must have taken an imprint of my keys on a previous visit and had copies made. There's no way I would ever have left the drug cabinet open. I could tell she'd stolen the vials and was mocking me."

Minnie moved closer and drew her lips back in a snarl. "Why didn't you report the theft right away to your superior?"

"I was afraid of being fired," she blurted, the tears flowing freely down her cheeks. "Please don't say anything."

Minnie straightened up and patted her hand. "Don't worry, hon. If necessary, we'll put in a good word with your superior."

After Raquel calmed down, we resisted her efforts to find out what Gabby had done, thanked her, and took our leave.

Once we got outside, the first thing I did was phone Hawk and tell him the results of our interview. His appreciation warmed me up all over. Unfortunately, tracking down Gabby's boss at Lifestyle Manor and her references had taken longer than he'd anticipated. He was still at the RCMP detachment making phone calls, and would fill me in once he returned. He figured he'd be leaving for Callum's house late afternoon, so would be late returning to Grizzly Gulch.

Traffic leaving the city was heavy, so I was grateful Minnie didn't distract me with conversation. Once we got onto the Trans-Canada Highway she said, "We did an awesome job of getting Raquel to open up."

I wasn't going to let her off the hook so easily. "You came down on the poor woman like a battering ram. That was uncalled for."

"I was afraid you would let her wriggle off the hook."

"So you used the sledgehammer approach."

"It worked, didn't it? We make a good team. You opened her up, I closed the deal."

I couldn't deny that Minnie's technique had worked with amazing speed and effectiveness. "Let's recap what we know. Gabby stole two vials of potassium chloride. That gave her the ability—let's call it the means—to murder Lizzie."

"But there's no proof that will stand up in court," Minnie wailed. "A decent lawyer will point out anyone could have stolen the vials, Raquel included."

Undeterred, I continued, "The rush for the outhouse also gave Gabby the opportunity. And if Lizzie had learned Charles Dubois and Gabby Chambers' father were one and the same, that provides motive as well. A fatal accident would be the best way to remove a blackmailer. Permanently."

"So Gabby had means, motive, and opportunity to kill Lizzie. But why would she attack me?"

I pulled into the passing lane. "There's one other possibility." I spoke slowly, gathering my thoughts. "You told us there was a scrimmage in front of the outhouse where you jabbed a fist into Lizzie's gut, causing her to double over. You managed to duck around her to score a first seating in the outhouse. What if Gabby was going for your butt and jabbed Lizzie's by mistake? A fatal accident would be an excellent way to remove a rival for Daddy's lovely money. Permanently."

I sensed Minnie was regarding me with something akin to awe. "No one knew Charles was Gabby's father." After a long pause, she said, "Even I didn't know about their relationship until Hawk pieced it together last night. Charles must have told Gabby something about us that set her off." She gnawed her lip. "In fact, now that I think about it, Gabby seemed to be needling me about Charles at the beginning of this getaway. Remember she said it was too bad my new suitor hadn't joined us and asked where Charles was? Now that I think about it, I believe she was fishing for information."

We drove in silence. I passed a logging truck, a tour bus, and two camper vans. "Everything we know is supposition."

"Someone has to search Gabby's cabin. I bet it's full of incriminating evidence, like a gun and a syringe full of potassium chloride."

I risked another glance at Minnie. "Hawk's hunting for Callum to push him to get a warrant to search Gabby's cabin."

"On Thanksgiving weekend? With no concrete evidence? I seriously doubt a search warrant will materialize before Thanksgiving."

If that happened, Callum would either delay the Lifestyle Manor group's departure, or the residents would return to the retirement home with Gabby still gunning for Minnie. Neither prospect was acceptable.

"We need to find Abby and Dodie," Minnie said. "Between us, surely we can figure out a way to stop Gabby."

A few miles later, inspiration struck me. It was so simple, yet so brilliant, I almost swerved onto the soft shoulder. Straightening the vehicle, I applied serious thinking to my idea, filling some gaps. Yeah, it was doable, provided it received my sisters' buy-in and their help. The more I turned my idea over in my mind, the more I liked it.

I pressed down on the accelerator.

Chapter 22: A Plot is Hatched

It was late afternoon when Minnie and I wheeled into Grizzly Gulch's parking lot. Time was running out, and a sense of urgency gripped me. If Gabby launched another attack, odds were she would succeed in killing Minnie. It was time to share my plan for stopping Gabby. My proposed solution must come across as a no-brainer without a single weak spot or potential glitch. Otherwise, Abby and Dodie would veto my idea.

Wine being a sure-fire way to ease the process, I pulled out my cell, texted my sisters, and dangled the bait: *Major break in case. Will reveal all over fine Beaujolais. My place. Five minutes.*

Dodie and Abby materialized in record time. Sipping wine, we sat in my living room while Minnie and I recounted the bombshells Raquel had dropped during the afternoon. With a few detours—mostly Minnie's—we started with Gabby's background, moving on to the complications of Minnie's friendship with Gabby's father, and ending with Gabby's theft of the potassium chloride.

I concluded by saying, "Although there's no way to prove it, at least not yet, Gabby killed Lizzie and is responsible for Minnie's attacks." I gentled my voice. "Bottom line?" We must find enough proof to stop Gabby. If we don't, she will remain at large to kill Minnie. It may not happen right away, but she'll succeed eventually."

Total silence greeted my dramatic announcement. Even Minnie, who always had a reaction, remained mute.

Snuggles let out a loud, "Mew," simply to remind us of his presence. Having announced himself, he glared, daring anyone to come near. I doubted Minnie noticed him. Satisfied we would give him the space he needed, he closed his yellow eyes while basking in a patch of late afternoon sun. His purring rumbled through my living room.

Since my words appeared to have immobilized everyone, I topped up the wine. Minnie regained motion in her arm and drained her glass. I filled it again. Her uncharacteristic stillness meant she was either speechless at my eloquence or frozen in terror over the imminent danger she was in. I suspected the latter.

"Meditating, are we?" I asked.

Abby's face mirrored distress as she broke the silence. "Let me see if I've got this straight. Based on a chat with this Raquel friend of Gabby's, you believe Minnie was, and still is, Gabby's intended victim because she's dating Gabby's wealthy father, thereby stealing her meal ticket."

The shrill note in Abby's voice caused Snuggles to abandon his patch of sunshine and scoot behind the drapes.

"Yes."

"And you believe Gabby used the potassium chloride she stole from Raquel to kill Lizzie by accident. Minnie was the true target. In other words, Gabby jabbed the wrong ass because with all the pushing and shoving going on, Lizzie presented her butt as a target."

Abby was edgy, that was clear. "Yes again. But in the interests of full disclosure, there's a remote possibility Lizzie's death might have been premeditated murder if—and it's a big if—she was blackmailing Gabby about being a resident's daughter and would face firing for violating policy. I consider that a weak motive for murder and have ruled it out."

Dodie chimed in with, "It does make weird sense."

Minnie's forehead was so deeply wrinkled it resembled corrugated cardboard. "This is horrible. It's the first time I've heard it all put together. If you're right, Gabby tried to kill me four times. *Four times*! She held up a hand to count on her fingers. First by an injection of fast-acting poison, second by shooting at me, third by pushing me into the river, and fourth by mechanical bull."

"I'm afraid so."

Abby and Dodie exchanged a worried gaze. Spelled out in such blunt terms, I could see why everyone, especially Minnie, who hadn't joined all the dots until now, appeared stunned.

"Nice going," Dodie whispered to me. "See what you've done? Minnie's terrified."

"So Gabby will continue trying to kill me until she succeeds," Minnie whispered.

"I'm so sorry," I said.

Minnie's uncharacteristic calm was unnerving. Where was the drama queen? The hand wringing? The explosion? It occurred to me that perhaps I'd come on a tad too strong, but facts were facts. I was trying to grab their attention so we could solve a problem.

As if on cue, Minnie bounced to her feet. Striding my living room carpet, she made sweeping gestures, as if on the stage. Her agitation flushed Snuggles from his hiding spot.

That was better.

"I have a target painted on my back." she wailed, side-stepping an agitated cat. She whirled to stomp in the opposite direction. "I can't stay here and I don't dare go home. I'll need to find another retirement home." She raked her fingers into her hair. "But Gabby would find me again." Up and down, up and down she paced, until she dropped to her hands and knees. Crawling to the curtains, she peeked out.

Dodie raced over and yanked the curtains closed. "What are you doing?"

Remaining crouched, Minnie glared at Dodie. "Making sure Gabby isn't outside waiting to take another shot at me."

Dodie fisted her hands on her hips. "I suppose you think presenting yourself as bait is the best way to find out."

"Fine. Bad idea. Now can someone help me up?" Minnie asked.

I rushed over to help Dodie haul Minnie to her feet, an awkward process seeing as how my cousin was tall, gangly, and mildly arthritic.

Dodie and I resumed our seats while Minnie paced some more. She stopped in front of me. "Should I go into police protection? You know, like a safe house?"

My heart squeezed with pity at her plight. "No proof, no safe house."

"Maybe I could change my identity and move to, say, Inuvik or even Tuktoyaktuk. I hear residents up there are hospitable." Her breath hitched and tears trickled down her cheeks. "But the Arctic is so remote. And cold. And there are hungry *polar bears*." A squeak escaped. Pretty soon the caterwauling would begin in earnest. Not that a good cry wasn't warranted.

Abby took a huge hit of wine. "And exactly how do you propose the proof will appear?"

"Well, in an ideal world, a Mountie would get a search warrant for Gabby's cabin and find the evidence I'm certain is hidden in there—the gun, hypodermic, and a vial of poison. Problem is, Callum seems to be unavailable, and it's doubtful a search warrant for the cabin will come through before Thanksgiving, if at all."

Abby folded her arms across her chest. "Thank you. Very helpful."

Time to cut to the chase. "I have an idea."

"It'd better be good."

I sucked in a deep breath and crossed my fingers, then my toes. "It occurred to me that RCMP protocol regarding illegal searches acts as a constraint for a Mountie like Callum, perhaps even a retired Mountie like Hawk. Happily, as a private citizen, I'm not constrained by the same rules. Also, as a co-owner of Grizzly Gulch, I have valid reasons for entering cabins." I paused to gather my thoughts. "There's one teeny-tiny time constraint. The search must be done after dark and before Hawk returns. He mustn't know. If he catches wind of it he'll freak out."

After a prolonged beat of silence, Dodie said, "You intend to toss Gabby's cabin."

"That's the idea," I said.

"Are you insane?" Abby said. "Gabby might kill you too."

Like magic, Minnie's tears had dried up. "I, for one, think it's a brilliant idea. I'm coming with you. We'll find enough proof to put Gabby away for a long, long time, and I'll be able to breathe freely again."

"Minnie's right," I said. "We'll have the advantage of surprise, and let's not forget Gabby has a broken foot."

"Brilliant," Abby said, the word dripping with sarcasm. "Why didn't I think of this?"

Even Dodie, my adventurous sister, said, "Seriously? What if Gabby catches you, huh?"

"She won't. Not if we coordinate our efforts."

"No way," Dodie replied. "If Gabby finds you in her cabin, she's likely to haul out her gun and shoot to kill."

"I agree. Convince us," Abby said, "or I call veto."

I concentrated on projecting confidence. "I suggest we do it while

Gabby's at the after-dinner entertainment. That's where you two come in and run interference," I said, pausing for effect. "You'll need to stop Gabby from going anywhere near her cabin until we're finished."

Dodie's forehead puckered with worry. "We're not as spry as we used to be. What if we can't stop her?"

My solution was, in my humble opinion, nothing short of brilliant. "If you can't stop her, you text me the word 'Gone.' On the off-chance we don't escape in time, I'll simply explain to Gabby how we gave the housekeeping staff time off to be with their families for the Thanksgiving weekend, and Minnie volunteered to help with the bed turndowns and pillow chocolates."

Dodie said, "Good idea. Believe me, Gabby's accustomed to the housekeeping staff dancing attendance on her all week, bringing her softer pillows or extra pillow chocolates. My staff draws straws for her cabin. Short straw loses."

Abby aimed a cynical gaze at me. "I still don't like it. Gabby is a desperate woman. What if something goes wrong?"

"How can it? But if worst comes to the worst, I have some martial art training."

Dodie snickered. "If you count three sessions at my Karate Crones lessons, you're in deep trouble already."

I gave her the middle finger salute.

Minnie drained her glass and stood, her hands fisted on her hips. "I'm in all the way. This is life or death for me. If we wait for a warrant, I'm toast."

Rising, Abby said, "Fine. We'll keep watch and text a warning if Gabby leaves."

Dodie, having finished her wine long ago, stood. "Okay. Let's hope your karate skills aren't required. I'll give our housekeeping staff the evening off although that means I'll have to do all the remaining turn-downs and pillow chocolates myself." She gave a hard-done-by sigh.

Ignoring Dodie's attempted guilt trip, I said, "Then it's settled." I flung my arms around the three women I loved most in the world. "Together, we can pull this off."

"You guys are the best," Minnie said. "I love you all."

Abby and Dodie departed, while Minnie went down the hall to freshen up for dinner. leaving me alone in my living room, which now seemed too quiet.

I was cautiously optimistic. With vigilant coordination, we would pull it off, and my promises to Hawk would be fulfilled. I would take no unnecessary risk and neither Minnie nor I would be alone at any time.

I could only hope Hawk would see it that way too.

Chapter 23: A Killer's Takedown

When Minnie and I arrived at the campfire, Gabby was already seated. We joined the group toasting marshmallows, making s'mores, and belting out campfire songs to the accompaniment of a couple of guitars. Once we'd made certain Gabby had noticed us, we hunkered down for a few songs before slipping away as unobtrusively as possible. The tang of wood smoke and an enthusiastic rendition of *Four Strong Winds* accompanied our departure. Both grew faint as we hurried through the grove toward Gabby's cabin.

"Got the keys and your phone?" Minnie asked as she led the way.

I patted my jacket pockets. "Yep. Chocolates too." I displayed the bag Dodie had handed me as we slipped past her in the dark.

Once we closed in on Gabby's cabin, I slowed down, my chest heaving from the unaccustomed exercise. Minnie's powerful shove caused me to stumble. I windmilled my arms to prevent myself from sprawling onto the pathway. "Hey," I said, scowling over my shoulder at her. "I won't be any help tossing Gabby's cabin if I sprain an ankle."

She nudged me toward the stairs. "Don't be such a slowpoke, Clara. We gotta hurry." She vibrated with anxiety.

I understood Minnie's urgency. If we didn't find evidence tying Gabby to the crimes, she would repeat her attempts to kill Minnie. "Take it easy," I whispered, climbing onto the porch. "We're trying to be unobtrusive." My master key rotated smoothly in the lock. Minnie shoved me inside, slammed the door behind us, and slumped against it, panting hard.

"I should have known you would panic," I muttered while catching my breath in the foyer. "I ought to have left you at the campfire and brought Dodie instead."

"Hawk ordered us to stick together, right?"

"Not exactly," I replied. "He said neither of us should go anywhere alone."

"Picky, picky, picky." Minnie paused inside the threshold, sweeping her gaze around the place. "I love it. Classy, yet comfortable."

I thought so too. The foyer with its mirrored closet opened into a spacious living area. A table lamp threw its warm glow into the room. Two armchairs, each upholstered in easy-clean crimson Ultrasuede, flanked a gas fireplace. The matching sofa offered an enticing spot to curl up with a book. Throw pillows, a picture window, and framed photos of nearby Banff National Park added to the charm. Two stools stood beside a quartz counter separating the living room from the compact yet well-appointed kitchenette.

On the off-chance Gabby would return, I adjusted the blinds to conceal our presence without blocking the lamplight.

"Why all the caution?" Minnie regarded me with suspicion. "Your sisters agreed to text a warning if Gabby left early."

"I'm being cautious. Gabby might give them the slip. Or there might be a guest emergency."

"Good point. Or they might forget to warn us."

That would never happen, not when our lives were at stake. "Let's split up to save time. You search the living area and kitchenette. I'll do the bedroom and ensuite."

"Nah. I want the bedroom and ensuite. Nothing reveals more about a woman than her bedside drawer." Minnie ducked past me and marched toward the bedroom. "What exactly are we hunting for?"

"A hypodermic needle and vial of potassium chloride would be good," I told her back. "Also a gun and silencer."

"Hmmph," Minnie replied. "Just testing. I knew that."

"Let's keep our voices down."

After searching for ten minutes, nothing interesting turned up other than a baggie of weed in the mini-fridge.

On her return from the bedroom, Minnie asked, "Any luck?"

"Nope. You?"

Her shoulders slumped. "Two filmy négligées, a pink vibrator, and some sleeping pills. Seems Gabby hoped to get lucky, but came prepared in case she struck out."

I shook my head in frustration. "Gabby stole two vials of potassium chloride from the hospital. She used one on Lizzie, so the other must be around here somewhere. Did you check inside the toilet tank?"

"I did."

In desperation, I cast my gaze at the foyer. My pulse picked up speed, and I darted into the entry area to stare at the ceiling.

"Anything up there?"

"These cabins are winterized. There's insulation in the crawl space above the ceiling, and the entrance hatch is in the foyer. I need something to stand on."

Minnie dragged a kitchen stool over. "I'm taller. Help me get up on this thing."

After much boosting and steadying, she muscled the hatch cover aside and ran her hands along the inside. "There's something in here."

"Is it a gun?"

"No."

That was not good news. It likely meant Gabby was armed. I endured several more nerve-racking seconds during which Minnie balanced on tiptoe while I gripped her thighs, pretending I could prevent a nasty fall. At last, she grunted with satisfaction and brandished a small leather pouch.

"Catch," she said, tossing the pouch to me.

I snatched the object in mid-flight.

After replacing the hatch cover, Minnie sprang to the floor, landing with a thud beside me. "Open the pouch," she urged. "Hurry."

I unsnapped the fastener. A vial of clear liquid and two hypodermic syringes, both with plastic safety shields, lay nestled inside. We stared at one another. I wasn't sure if I should feel satisfaction or dismay.

After a prolonged pause, Minnie drew in a shaky breath. "So it's true. Gabby murdered Lizzie, and I'm next in line for a lethal injection."

I placed a consoling hand on her arm. "Let's put the stool back and get out of here in case she—"

The lock clicked and the door flew open, letting in a gust of cool night air. I whipped my head around and found myself staring down a gun muzzle. I raised my gaze to stare into Gabby's implacable blue eyes.

"Hi there," I chirped. "Surpri-ise! We're the pillow chocolate fairies. We thought we heard something in the crawl space. Raccoons like to migrate indoors for the winter, so we decided to investigate." I slipped a carefree giggle past the constriction in my throat. "I hope that's okay."

"It's not. And what you're doing is called an illegal search. Nothing you've found will be allowable in a court of law."

I gave up the pretense. "Got tired of singing *Kumbaya*, did you?"

"Move," Gabby ordered, waving the gun, complete with an attached silencer. She limped inside and closed the door gently, turning the lock. "Hand over the pouch and empty your pockets."

I stepped in front of Minnie, placing the pouch in Gabby's hand with fingers made clumsy with terror. "I notice you have one foot immobilized in a walking boot. Did you break it?" I asked, pleased I sounded as if nothing out-of-the-ordinary was happening. As if I wasn't facing certain death.

Gabby slipped the pouch into her pocket. "It's nothing. A little mishap."

"I'm glad it's not serious," I said, going for a conversational tone. "You're back early."

"Yeah. I got suspicious when I hadn't seen either of you for some time."

Minnie whispered to me, "I wonder where your sisters are."

Gabby aimed a blinding white smile at us. "Oh, one had to leave the campfire to help a guest, and the other, the idiot who likes playing dress-up in a turkey suit, tried to tail me. I took care of that one." Her pert delivery was at odds with her sinister words.

A knock at the door caused all three of us to freeze. Gabby motioned her gun at us, demanding silence. "Who's there?" she called out, all breathy and sultry.

"Gabby?" I recognized Hawk's voice. "You in there? I need to talk to you and get your advice about Minnie. It's important."

She glanced at the door. "I'm busy."

I took advantage of Gabby's momentary distraction to plant my feet. Drawing on my sketchy karate training, I focused every ounce of my energy on achieving power and speed. Tightening my slack core muscles to gain stability, I uttered a fearsome battle cry while whirling on one foot and kicking out with the other.

I got lucky. The gun flew from her hand.

She squealed in rage and dove for the gun, but Minnie was faster. "Oh, no you don't, bitch." She stomped the heel of one cowboy boot onto the outstretched wrist.

Something cracked, and it wasn't a twig.

Gabby's features twisted in agony. "You broke my wrist," she cried.

"Nice," Minnie said. "That's what I was going for."

Proving she had excellent core muscles, Gabby heaved herself upright while using her good arm to cradle the other.

Next thing I knew, the wooden doorframe splintered. The door crashed open. Hawk barged into the cabin and halted, scanning the area. "Where did she go?"

I scanned the room and caught Gabby limping silently out the back door and into the night.

The whole place shook when Hawk roared, "What were you two thinking?" Instead of waiting for an answer, he raced for the back door, his face a mask of anger. Over his shoulder, he said, "Never mind, we'll talk later." His penlight clicked on and he sprinted away in the direction Gabby had taken.

Minnie followed Hawk, her long legs covering the distance with ease. Groaning inwardly, I jogged after her, trying to pace myself. I hadn't realized Minnie had stopped running until I crashed into her. We both ended up beside Hawk, who was leaning against the fence surrounding the goat paddock.

"What are we waiting for?" Minnie whispered. "She'll get away."

"No she won't," Hawk said. "This paddock is full of goats and one overprotective llama."

I peered into the darkened area, but couldn't see anything.

"How did you learn that fancy kick," Minnie whispered while Hawk ignored us.

"A Jackie Chan movie provided the inspiration," I whispered back, "and I already mentioned my martial arts skills. A few lessons with Dodie's Karate Crones class taught me the moves. Everything will most likely hurt for a week."

It didn't take long for the pulsating, high-pitched call of an enraged llama to pierce the still night air. Gabby's screams drowned out the bleating goats. To call an aggressive llama intimidating was the understatement of the year. I did not envy Gabby.

Hawk switched on his flashlight and aimed it at a flurry of activity in the corner. Gabby, her good arm extended to ward off a furious llama, backed slowly away from a large, white animal. Larry the llama stalked toward her, his neck outstretched. Dwarf goats added to the chaos, uttering bleats and screams, sounding surprisingly like women in distress.

Hawk cupped both hands to his mouth and hollered, "You might as well come quietly, Gabby. You don't want to provoke Larry."

Gabby spewed a string of curse words strong enough to singe eyebrows.

"You'd best settle down," Hawk shouted. "Larry's working up a good wad of spit, so you don't want to irk him."

From where I stood, Larry appeared plenty irked already, with his ears flat against his neck, tail aloft. His emphatic snort confirmed my suspicions.

"Here's one last warning," Hawk shouted. "His spit consists of saliva mixed with partially-digested stomach contents."

Gabby tried to sidestep, but 400 pounds of irate llama blocked her escape.

"I can't wait to see this," Minnie whispered to me.

Truth be told, neither could I.

Larry blew out some saliva along with air, making a little "pfffffpth" noise. He thrust his head up and down a couple times, then angled it upward one last time before lowering it until the llama and Gabby were nose-to-nose.

I held my breath.

She tried to back away, but the fence was unyielding. Larry stretched his neck as far as possible without dislocating any vertebrae and let fly. The jet of spit splatted her square in the face. Thick goo dribbled down her nose and dripped off her chin. Her scream intensified to a piercing and continuous wail.

Although it was too dark to tell, I knew the noxious substance was green, frothy, and foul-smelling. Gabby's legs gave out, and she slid down the fence post and onto the ground, sobbing while cradling her arm. I didn't blame her.

Hawk opened the gate, strode over to Gabby, and yanked her upright. "It's over."

"At least let me get cleaned up," she said.

"Not until you confess everything."

"Geez. That could take all night," Minnie said. "FYI, she's got a pouch containing a hypodermic and vial of potassium chloride in her pocket. It's the same stuff she used to kill Lizzie. If I were you, I'd confiscate it."

Hawk patted her down and extracted the pouch.

"You don't want to haul me into your fancy SUV stinking like a manure pile."

With his focus on Gabby, Hawk spoke to me. "Clara, would you please contact the Cochrane detachment and ask them to send a car?"

He sounded clipped and formal as he barked out the phone number, but at least we were still talking. "Sure thing," I said, finding my phone and getting busy.

"In the meantime," he said to Gabby, "Tell me everything. And I must warn you. I already know the truth, so lying won't help."

"You have got to be joking." A sneer twisted her face.

"I never joke with someone in custody. Let's get this over with. I'll use my phone to record your confession. Until then, you can stay filthy." Hawk's eyes, when he glanced at me, were dark, dead, and expressionless. He turned away, as if the sight of me revolted him. "You two might as well go to bed. This will take some time, so don't wait up."

I swallowed the lump of apprehension lodged in my throat. "But Dodie and Abby—"

"They're fine. I sent them to bed. We need to talk, but not now," Hawk interrupted.

That meant he was going to dump me. I'd found a man I could love and respect, and I'd blown it in the space of a few hours. The lines of distress furrowing his face mirrored my feelings, but I refused to show I was hurting too. I took a deep breath and clasped my hands together so tightly I feared I was cutting off the circulation to my fingers. "When?" I asked.

"After breakfast."

Great. I had all night to torment myself. I forced back my tears. "Okay. It's a date."

As we walked away, Minnie threw an arm around my shoulders. "Don't worry. This will all blow over. Go to bed, I'll deal with Dodie and Abby."

I had serious doubts anything would blow over. I'd broken Hawk's trust. I feared redemption would be impossible, no matter how hard I tried. Dreading what the morning would bring, I headed straight to bed to lick my wounds.

Chapter 24: Black Moment

Consumed by white-hot pain, I crawled into bed and sobbed my grief into my pillow. At some point during the night, I reached a decision. Hawk meant too much to me to let him dump me without putting up a fight. To convince him I was too trustworthy to be tossed aside, I must retain my cool. By controlling my emotions and using cold, hard logic, I would prove I'd acted in a highly responsible manner while adhering to the promises I'd made. Hey, I might have taken risks, but they were calculated risks, even *necessary* risks, and neither Minnie nor I were ever alone, not for a moment. Most of all, I would not cry, at least, not in front of Hawk.

That's when I fell asleep.

In the morning, I avoided Abby, Dodie, and Minnie by waiting until they'd gone down to breakfast. Once I was sure they were gone, I downed a solitary cup of coffee in my kitchen. Okay, three. I also paced the floor. After an hour had passed, I went downstairs in search of Hawk. He was still in the dining hall, presumably waiting for me in order to dump me.

With my heart thundering in my ears, I strode over and chirped, "Good morning, sunshine." Hopefully, some of Minnie's acting skills had rubbed off on me. "I'm glad I found you. Let's stake our claim on the gazebo for the private talk you suggested."

The private talk I'd been dreading all night long.

His response was a non-committal grunt. We marched through the lobby together, with me greeting guests and employees alike, while he maintained a hostile silence. His cheek muscle flickered as he clenched his teeth. Fighting the pain ripping through my chest, I persevered, waving at an elderly couple, chatting briefly with the receptionist, and generally making nice with everyone I encountered. Once outside, I sucked in a deep breath of crisp, clean air and gushed about the beautiful day lying ahead, and was still prattling on about the unseasonably warm weather, which would surely break any day now, while we seated ourselves in the gazebo.

"We're alone now. You can stop babbling," he said.

"Okay, let's get down to business, but before we do, I've been meaning to ask if you were able to convince Callum to get a search warrant."

The muscle in his cheek twitched again. "Nope. The judge was gone for the weekend, and Callum wasn't home. He'd taken his kids out for the evening to give his wife a break. She invited me to join her and her sister's family for dinner. I accepted."

I drew in a sustaining breath. "I gather I've done something to upset you."

After an extended silence, he said, "I'm not upset. More like devastated. I trusted you. Why, exactly, did you think it was okay to break the promises you made to me as soon as my back was turned?"

Not good. Not good at all. I forced myself to make eye contact with him. "I have four points I want to make. Point number one, Gabby proved she willing to commit premeditated murder by stealing the potassium chloride long before the Thanksgiving getaway was planned. Two, I didn't break a single promise. If you'll recall, I promised I wouldn't leave Minnie alone and I wouldn't take any unnecessary risks. Well, Minnie and I stuck together, and I don't know about you, but I think finding proof that Gabby was willing to commit premeditated murder and kill Minnie—multiple times, I might add—qualifies as a very necessary risk. Three, Minnie was petrified of returning to Lifestyle Manor, and was planning to move to Tuktoyaktuk. I had to do something. And last, but far from least, point number four is so compelling, it's worth mentioning again. If we hadn't searched Gabby's cabin, you wouldn't have the evidence you needed to turn her over to the Mounties and put an end to her attempted killing spree." I paused, assessing whether or not I'd put a dent in his resistance, but his stony expression revealed nothing.

"You're welcome," I chirped, uncaring if those two words sealed my fate.

The vertical grooves between his eyebrows deepened into furrows. "How can you say you didn't break your promise? You risked your life. Gabby tried to kill you."

"And yet, she didn't. I disarmed her. And don't tell me the gun was empty, because I didn't know that. Let me point out once more that I kept both my promises."

"You have a strange notion of what keeping a promise means."

It wasn't easy, but I stopped myself from scowling. "We'd thought it through carefully. Minnie and I had a believable cover story of staff reduction, pillow chocolates, and raccoons. Hey, the evidence was in plain view. Abby and Dodie were supposed to watch our backs and text us if Gabby left for her cabin early. Who knew Abby would get called away, and Dodie would get herself mugged?"

"Seems to me things didn't go exactly the way you planned. By the way, Dodie had forgotten to charge her cell phone. That's why she was heading to Gabby's cabin to warn you, thereby placing her life in danger, too."

I averted my gaze. "Maybe there was a tiny glitch," I admitted. "How did your interviews go with Lifestyle Manor's HR manager and CEO?"

He shrugged. "They confirmed everything Raquel told you. Gabby had fictional event management experience on her résumé. The CEO was a little more difficult. I had to threaten him with an official investigation before he admitted she'd slept with him to get the job."

In case Hawk was waiting for an opportunity to dump me, I rushed in with, "How did you know where to find me last night?"

"I couldn't find you, Gabby, or the rest of you. I got worried and set off for Gabby's cabin. That's when I found Dodie sitting beside the path. Lucky for her, the blow to her head was glancing, and Gabby was too anxious to reach her cabin to stop and finish the job."

"Did Gabby confess?"

"She was so desperate to get cleaned up after Larry spat on her, she admitted she'd killed Lizzie in error. Seems in the stampede for the outhouse, Minnie managed to dodge the needle by ducking away after plowing Lizzie in the stomach. The blow caused Lizzie to double over, placing her ass in the needle's path."

"Ironic, isn't it? Gabby had nothing to worry about. Minnie isn't interested in a committed relationship with Charles."

Hawk sighed, but replied, "Yes, ironic. Gabby also admitted to stealing a loaded gun and silencer from her boss and shooting at Minnie through the open window. she wasn't at all pleased she'd missed. And before you ask,

Gabby tried to kill Minnie again, this time on Bucking Bully after she'd clobbered both Pete and you in order to operate the controls."

"Why go to all that trouble? Why not use her gun?"

"She'd used up all the bullets in the gun trying to hit Minnie the day she arrived. All her shots except one went wild, and even that one didn't do much damage. I was able to pick up one of the casings and send it off for fingerprint testing, but that may come back with her boss' fingerprints. It's lucky she confessed.

"She wore a ski mask and gloves—not the usual items a woman would pack for a fun-filled week at a dude ranch."

"We asked about them. Gabby bragged about how she was proud she'd had the foresight to pack them in case her first try at killing Minnie went wrong. She told me she likes to be prepared."

"Another premeditated attempt at murder. But how did Gabby know Minnie would be in the barn last night? I doubt it was a coincidence," I said, genuinely curious.

"When pressed, Gabby admitted to being suspicious of Minnie and Eleanor's sudden friendship, especially since they were usually at one another's throats. Later that same afternoon, she'd followed Minnie to the barn and overheard her talking to a wrangler named Pete about some sort of arrangement. All she learned was that something big was going down around midnight, and it involved Minnie and Eleanor. That's why Gabby sat behind Minnie during the evening entertainment—so she could keep tabs on her."

"Very proactive."

"She did not, however, expect you to turn up in the barn."

"A dangerous miscalculation on her part."

"Gabby was so angry she was unable to get rid of Minnie via mechanical bull, and also that you broke a bone in her foot, that she stole the keys to the mini backhoe loader on her way out the barn. One way or another, she was determined to bring you down."

"She nearly succeeded," I said. "It would have worked if she'd taken down the main power pole."

"Gabby also claimed she had nothing to do with pushing Minnie into the river."

"I bet she said that because no one can prove she did it. Even Minnie has no idea who shoved her off the cliff."

"Possibly."

"I'm curious. How did you manage to get Gabby cleaned up without someone stepping into the shower with her?"

"One of the Mounties hosed her down and wrapped her in a tarp."

"Nicely done. Well, I guess there's nothing more to discuss. I'd better go find Minnie." I arose, eager to make my escape.

"Not so fast." His voice, although calm, had taken on an edge of steel, warning me to stay put.

I lowered my butt and beamed at him to hide my trepidation. "Yes?"

"First, you disappear from my life without a word. Then I find you again, and you lead me to believe we may have a future together. And now, you ignore my advice and deliberately go behind my back, placing your life at risk. To top it off, if that wasn't reckless enough, you invite Minnie, Abby, and Dodie along for the fun."

My pulse scrambled, and not in a good way. "I didn't break any promises."

He leveled a flat gaze in my direction and lowered his voice to an ominous growl. "You broke the spirit of the promises. Same thing."

Stung by his words and his tone, I felt my thin thread of control slipping. "That's not fair. Those pesky legal constraints, the ones that prevented you from searching Gabby's cabin, didn't apply to us as private citizens, especially to me as the resort owner, and you know it. Our idea was brilliant, and so was our cover story. Minnie deserves a normal, everyday life, one without constant fear of being murdered. She insisted on being part of the cabin search, and I don't blame her. I'd have done the same." I was breathing hard when I ran out of steam.

Annoyance crossed his face. "I'm ending this thing with you, whatever it was, before it goes any farther."

Tears blurred my vision and threatened to ruin my mascara. I blinked them away. "But … no … please let's talk it through. You're the first man I've truly cared for since my husband died."

"Perhaps you should have considered my reaction before you searched Gabby's cabin while dragging Minnie and your sisters into danger at the same time. I have a thing about promises. I can't be with someone who breaks her promises to me—including the spirit of those promises." His tone was one of clipped finality.

An agonizing shudder ripped through me, but I refused to let him see my devastation. "I'm sorry you feel that way."

"I am too. I'll stick around Grizzly Gulch until the Lifestyle Manor group leaves." He stood abruptly and strode away.

I sat unmoving, waiting until his footsteps faded away. Feeling as though someone had punched a hole in my chest and ripped out my heart, I tried to convince myself our breakup was for the best, that it was better we part now rather than later.

Although I hadn't broken down in front of him, he'd left me sitting in the gazebo with my heart aching beyond anything I could ever have imagined. Once you cared, you could get hurt. Oblivious to the tears rolling down my cheeks, all I wanted to do was drag myself to my apartment and hibernate for a year, maybe ten. Reaching deep within myself, I found the strength to stand. Once confident my legs would support me, I took a half-hearted swipe at my tears and used a side door to creep into the main lodge. With any luck, I could avoid—well, everyone—for the duration of the Boomers' Thanksgiving Fling.

Chapter 25: Rescue Mission

As soon as I slunk away, I had second and possibly third thoughts about disappearing altogether. I had contests to win, duties to perform, and sisters to convince. On the other hand, I needed some recovery time before facing my family. I was approaching the back staircase when the distinctive clip-clop of Minnie's shoes warned me of her rapid approach.

I tried to duck into a storage closet but she pounced on me like a duck on a June bug, clutching my arm and swinging me around to face her. "You've been crying, haven't you?"

I sniffled and blew my nose. "What was your first clue?"

"The snot running out your nose. What happened? It's Hawk, isn't it?"

"It's too fresh. I can't talk about it yet, and I don't want anyone else to see me in this state. Let's take a stroll to our pond."

During the walk, I filled her in on Gabby's fate, nimbly sidestepping any mention of Hawk's breakup with me. I needed to lick that wound in private before admitting we were finished. Since the best defence was a good offense, I said, "You don't seem very happy over Gabby's arrest. She's behind bars for the foreseeable future. Why so glum?" I resumed walking, keeping my gaze fixed on the water-lilies floating on the still water of our pond.

Over the squawk of a gray jay, Minnie said, "She told Hawk she didn't push me in the river. Someone did, so if it wasn't Gabby, who was it?"

"I imagine she denied pushing you because there's no proof. You didn't see who did it, so why would she admit it?"

"I won't feel normal until I know for sure."

By then, we'd circled the pond. We continued walking until the path opened up into the barnyard in front of the barn. Soft whickers filled the air. Glad for a distraction, I said, "Oh, good. We're in time to watch Zeke and his wranglers saddle the horses for the morning trail ride. Those big, gentle creatures never fail to soothe me."

"Me, too. Those cute cowboys do it for me every time."

I nudged her arm. "I meant the horses, silly. Let's go inside." A change of scene might divert Minnie's attention from obsessing about her attacker.

She shrugged and followed me into the stables. Immediately, the scent of hay, horses, and a hint of manure filled our nostrils. Oddly enough, there were no wranglers in sight. Some of them must be on Thanksgiving leave, and the rest working outside.

We'd walked the length of the stable area when Minnie's phone buzzed. She studied the screen for a moment. "It's a text from Eleanor. I thought she and Wayne were booked for a day trip to Kananaskis on a canyon and cave painting tour. It must have been cancelled or they had a fight, because she's asking me for help."

"Why?"

"Stupid idiot's up at the abandoned mine, hurt."

"Ask her what happened."

Minnie tapped out the question. Moments later, her phone buzzed with an incoming text. "She says, *Tour cancelled. Today last chance to visit abandoned mine. Sprained ankle. Agonizing. Am alone. Need help.*"

I ignored some distant shouting at the back of the stables. "Are you kidding me?"

"I wish.

"Why you?"

She shrugged. "I don't know. I guess because I'm her only friend other than Wayne."

"But why text instead of calling?"

"Again, I don't know. Some people have plans offering free texting service but outrageously expensive voice plans.

"Tell her help is on the way."

Minnie tapped in the message.

Eleanor's response was instantaneous. *Brilliant.*

I tugged Minnie's arm. "Let's see if I can rustle up a couple of wranglers to go help her instead of us. There's an old road the miners used to remove ore, so it shouldn't take long to get there."

We hightailed it outside. We soon discovered someone had left a gate unlatched, letting Larry the llama and his goats escape. Anyone who wasn't on active duty—and that list included Dodie, Abby, Zeke, and all his wranglers—was out hunting for the animals, last seen, galloping across a neighbor's pasture with a llama leading the herd.

I tried calling Abby, then Dodie and Zeke. It seemed no one was checking their phones. I wasn't about to call Hawk. We were Eleanor's only hope, and I couldn't ignore a guest's call for help. I left Abby a message outlining the situation with Eleanor, and explaining that Minnie and I were embarking on a rescue operation at the abandoned silver mine.

If I didn't hear from her by the time we arrived at the mine, I would try again.

Frantic yowling emanated from the bathroom where I'd locked Snuggles. A wave of guilt washed over me. The poor animal hated his prison of cold, slippery tiles. I would too. The meowing increased in volume until I couldn't take it any longer. Ignoring Minnie's warning, I released the cat from his incarceration. He shot past me with a baleful glare and galloped down the hallway to disappear into the living room.

I wasn't worried. He always came when I offered him a treat.

Minnie and I had placed everything we needed for a rescue mission into my foyer. After ten minutes, we'd almost finished packing. I added two water bottles to my backpack and tossed Minnie a third, while Snuggles did a couple of laps around the apartment hunting for an escape.

Besides water, my backpack contained a hatchet, a first aid kit, tensor bandages, two flashlights, and an ice pack fresh from the freezer. After placing a canister of bear spray in my cargo pants' pocket I slipped my Swiss army knife into another.

Minnie offered, "I have a knife stashed in my sock."

"Here's hoping you won't need it."

A loud meow reminded me that my cat was on the prowl. "I've got to nab Snuggles and return him to the bathroom. I don't want to get home and find he's trashed the place again."

"Just put him outside," Minnie advised.

"No way. What if he attacked a guest?" I lunged for the cat. He darted away. I followed.

"This could take all day," Minnie shouted to my back. "Can't you corner him in the kitchen?"

"I'm trying," I yelled back.

Snuggles dodged my outstretched fingers and thundered toward Minnie. Undeterred by her menacing gestures, he zipped between her legs and hopped into the shelter of my open backpack, where he hunkered down. Strange how cats loved small, enclosed spaces. I'd read somewhere that a confined space provides felines with a measure of security, both physically and psychologically.

"Okay, out you come," I said, breathing hard while shaking the bag of cat treats I kept handy for kitty emergencies. He didn't budge. Testing my growing rapport with Snuggles, I bent down to remove him. A hiss and lightning-swift slash of claws made me re-think my position on stowaways. "Fine. Stay where you are."

"Please tell me you're not taking Snuggles with us," Minnie said.

"We're running late, he's happy where he is, so yeah, he's coming. We have to rescue Eleanor as quickly as possible. She shouldn't be up at the mine by herself. There were bear sightings near there. And if she tries walking back, she could do permanent damage to her ankle." Acting quickly, I placed the cat treat bag in an outside pocket of the backpack where Snuggles couldn't reach it. Leaving the opening untied so he could peek out if he wanted, I slipped my arms into the straps and hoisted it onto my back.

"I hope you're not planning to reward him."

"No. But if he escapes, a treat might be the only way to coax him to return."

Once everything was stashed, laced, and buckled, Minnie said, "Let's go. We can't make Eleanor wait too long. She's hurt and probably scared and thirsty."

I wrapped my cousin in a warm hug. "You're the best," I said, meaning it from the bottom of my heart. "Eleanor's lucky to count you as a friend."

With the cat's cute little head poking out the backpack's opening, we set off.

We were in for a rough drive, so I selected the same pickup truck we'd taken to Calgary. With Minnie in the passenger seat and Snuggles tucked away in my backpack and plotting either his escape or, more likely, his revenge, I drove in silence. It occurred to me I should have told Hawk I loved him with all my heart. If he left today, I'd never get another chance to tell him how I felt.

I'd used Google Maps to find the mine, and assumed the faint, white line leading to it indicated the old unpaved road. The mine wasn't far from Grizzly Gulch as the crow flies, only a twenty minute walk at a brisk pace, but it took a good half hour on back roads. Turning onto a dirt track, I hoped this was the right place. We bumped along, avoiding potholes and the occasional boulder. Scrubby brush and trees edged the rutted trail and clawed at the pickup.

"Are you sure this road goes to the mine?" Minnie asked.

"Pretty sure. They don't post signposts to abandoned mines."

At last, the road petered out, ending in a rolling meadow dotted with boulders and hardy wildflowers. The open area spread out in front of us, ending abruptly at the foot of a granite cliff. I stared in silence at what was surely the mine entrance. A sturdy wooden frame, crisscrossed by boards, was attached to the cliff wall. Between gaps, I could discern a gaping black hole.

I gestured to the entrance. "Welcome to the Rushing Waters Mine."

Minnie said, "Let's drive as close and possible. These backpacks are heavy."

I shook my head. "We're walking in from here. We can't afford a new pickup." I squinted at the distant mine entrance. "I wonder where Eleanor is."

"She didn't say. I assumed she was somewhere near the mine entrance." Minnie scanned the vicinity. "I don't see her."

The hair on the back of my neck prickled, as if someone might be watching us. I texted our location to Abby and hopped out. Mewing his approval, Snuggles scrambled from the backpack, leaped outside, and streaked away. No problem. A shake of kitty treats would lure him back. We disembarked and hefted our backpacks onto the ground.

"Let's go," Minnie said. "The sooner we find Eleanor, the better."

"Hang on," I said, gripping my phone. "I'm turning off my ringer and setting my phone to *Audio Record*."

"Why?"

"Call it insurance. I intend to capture every second of this rescue on my cell phone—just in case there's something fishy going on."

"Like what?"

I couldn't think of anything. "I don't know. It doesn't feel right. Call me paranoid."

If this was truly our insurance, I needed a better hiding place than a pocket. My gaze landed on the resealable bag of cat treats in my backpack. I inserted my cell phone in the treat bag, covering it with liver crunchies. As an afterthought, I tossed in my Swiss army knife as well, zipped the bag shut, and tossed it on top. There was no way Snuggles would allow anyone but me to mess with his treats.

"Now that's what I call a brilliant hiding spot," Minnie commented.

After helping one another into our backpacks, the full weight of the October sunlight slapped us in the face. We headed for a jumble of large boulders near the entrance. Snuggles scampered along beside us, taking the occasional detour to investigate interesting burrows.

Along the way, we called Eleanor's name to let her know help was on the way.

"Maybe she passed out," Minnie murmured.

On reaching our destination, I set my backpack down on a flat rock and scanned the area for Eleanor. There was no sign of her, so I bent over to rummage for tensor bandages, the icepack, and a water bottle, fussing with the opening and making sure to leave the pack open and the kitty treats easily accessible.

While I was busy, Minnie dumped her backpack on the ground beside us. Breathing hard, she sat on a rock. "That walk across rough ground was a killer."

"Truer words were never spoken."

I straightened. A greasy chill slithered down my spine. Phyllis, dressed in her usual beige-and-gray getup, a nice camouflage among rocks, had soundlessly slipped a wiry arm around Minnie's waist from behind. A knife at her throat glinted in the bright sunlight. Minnie's eyes telegraphed terror. No wonder she hadn't uttered a sound.

I strove for calm. "Phyllis! Where's Eleanor? Put that knife down."

"You two certainly took your sweet time getting here," Phyllis said.

A bright trickle of red told me she'd sliced the tender skin of Minnie's throat.

"Eleanor told Minnie she'd sprained her ankle," I said, my brain struggling to reconcile what was happening. "She didn't mention you."

"I needed to get both of you here. I knew Minnie would tell her people-pleaser cousin about Eleanor's nasty little accident."

"You released the goats," I said. "At yoga, you heard me mention how Dodie had let the goats escape, and it took an entire afternoon to round them up."

Phyllis threw her head back and laughed. "Bingo. You have no one to blame but yourself. I had to make sure no one else rescued me."

"That was very clever of you," I said, playing to Phyllis' ego. "I'm guessing you stole Eleanor's phone."

Phyllis released a carefree little giggle that caused my skin to crawl. "It was too easy. When the tour coach for Kananaskis arrived, I guess Grizzly Gulch was the first pickup stop because it was empty. The driver went inside to notify the front desk he was there. While he was inside, Eleanor climbed on board, left her purse on the best pair of seats, and went inside, presumably to get Wayne. Remembering I had some unfinished business, I took it as a sign and hopped on board, removed the phone from her purse, and left before anyone saw me. It couldn't have been easier."

"What do you want from us?"

"I need you to pry off those wooden boards blocking the entrance. Don't try any funny stuff or Minnie will suffer."

Keeping the knife at Minnie's throat, Phyllis dug into a pocket with her other hand and tossed something onto the ground before resuming her grip around Minnie's waist. "Those things are zip ties. I want you to use one to secure her hands. One false move, I'll cut deeper. You don't want that, so walk over here. Slowly."

"I d-don't think she's kidding," Minnie croaked.

Hopefully, my cell phone was recording every word. Even if it didn't save us, at least it would incriminate Phyllis.

Phyllis said, "Minnie, place your hands together in front of you like a good girl."

Minnie didn't argue.

As I slipped the zip tie around Minnie's wrists and tightened the loop with shaking fingers, I whispered, "Snuggles?"

"Behind you."

"Tighter," Phyllis ordered with a giggle. "We can't have those hands slipping out, can we? By the end of the afternoon, you two will be at the bottom of the chasm and I'll be calling Charles to invite him out for dinner once we're both back at Lifestyle Manor."

"Charles? What does Charles have to do with anything?" Minnie asked in a choked voice.

I held my breath, waiting for the answer.

"Don't pretend you don't know. I invited you to visit Lifestyle Manor to see if you would enjoy living there. I thought you were my friend. I never dreamed you would move in and steal another man I loved."

"Charles?"

"Yes, Charles. You're stringing him along, aren't you? Just like you did Jimmy, leading him on, then dumping him as soon as he marries you. Charles is so busy drooling over you, he doesn't see that I'm perfect for him. But once you're gone, he'll notice me. I'll make sure of it."

"I bet you will." Minnie's voice was steady. "Look, you don't have a quarrel with Clara. Let her go."

"Sorry. No can do. I can't leave a witness alive." Phyllis nudged me with her foot. Hard. "Tighten that zip tie or I'll get rid of you first."

I did what Phyllis ordered, tightening the zip tie enough notches to make it seem realistic without cutting off circulation.

"Better." Holding the knife to Minnie's neck, Phyllis told me, "Now toss out your bear spray. I know you have one. You won't be needing it where you're going."

I tossed the canister to the ground. Ignoring the roaring in my ears, I managed to keep my voice calm. "Why not kill us here and now? It would be much easier."

"But less fun, and so much messier. There would be forensic evidence. No, you two will jump into the chasm, I'll nail the boards back in place, and no one will think to hunt for you inside the mine." She threw her head back with a hysterical laugh, jerking the knife against Minnie's neck. "This would have been so much easier if Minnie'd had the good grace to drown when I pushed her into the river."

"So it *was* you," Minnie whispered.

"Of course."

Phyllis glared and bared her teeth. "Minnie was supposed to drown when I pushed her into the river." Her mouth twisted in a snarl. "I already knew someone else was trying to kill her. I figured if I pushed her in, either the other person would be blamed or everyone would think the drowning was a tragic accident. Either way, she would be out of my hair."

"How did you know someone was trying to kill Minnie," I asked. "We never mentioned that little detail."

"Don't you remember I was in your apartment right after the gunshot? You really should keep your door locked. I'd heard enough to figure out someone had tried to shoot Minnie before you hustled me out of there."

"You haven't killed anyone yet, Phyllis. Release us, and nothing will happen."

"In your dreams." Phyllis pressed the knife to Minnie's throat again. "Now, sit on this boulder and behave."

Again, Minnie didn't argue.

"You're next," she told me. "But first, sit beside Minnie, pick up a zip tie, and fasten it around her feet."

My throat tightened, but I obeyed.

"Good. I'll do a pat-down first, then I want you to dump out your backpack and the same with Minnie's." She waved her knife under my nose. "Don't try anything fancy or your cousin dies."

The pat-downs yielded the knife Minnie had stuffed down her sock. Our last chance rested on a bag of cat treats and Snuggles.

"Now the backpacks. Dump Minnie's first."

I emptied the contents of Minnie's backpack. Phyllis sifted through the items and determined there was nothing dangerous.

"Now your backpack," she said, her voice cold.

Minnie and I exchanged a glance before I scattered the contents of my backpack on the ground. With any luck, Phyllis wouldn't think of the pockets. One thing was guaranteed. No matter what Phyllis said or did, I would never jump into a cold, dark abyss, at least not voluntarily.

Using a toe, Phyllis separated the items. Stooping, she picked up the hatchet and stuck it in her belt. "Now open up the pockets."

I obeyed her, locating the cat treats and crumpling the bag with a loud scrunching sound.

"Drop that thing."

I gave the bag a good shake and tossed it to the ground.

She picked up the resealable bag. "What's this?" she asked, shaking the bag. The rattle was surprisingly loud.

On cue, Snuggles, his whiskers twitching, emerged slowly from behind a boulder. With his belly scraping the ground, he crept forward, his eyes glowing hot with hatred, and fixed on the enemy messing with his treats.

"A pack of cat treats," I answered, hoping to draw Phyllis' attention away from the cat. "Hungry?"

She shook the bag again. "It's awfully heavy for cat treats."

"They're homemade. I give Snuggles nothing but the best."

Snuggles glided closer to his prey, step by silent step. Crouched low to the ground, every muscle of the cat's body quivered. I sensed what was coming next, and held my breath.

"Perhaps I should open the bag to see what's inside. What do you think?"

Snuggles knew what *he* thought. His leap took him onto Phyllis' head. His claws gripped her scalp while she launched into an awkward dance, circling with much arm waving, and springing higher than any of the goats. Her prolonged and high-pitched shriek echoed off the cliff and seemed to repeat forever. Every bird in the vicinity exploded from cover and flapped away.

With blood trickling down her face, she scrabbled her fingers, trying to extricate a furious cat from her hair. Her knife bounced off a boulder and the bag of cat treats landed near my feet.

I swooped in to scoop up her knife and grabbed the hatchet from her belt. For lack of anywhere better to put them, I stuck both weapons in my belt. With Snuggles' tail obscuring Phyllis' vision, I wrestled her hands together, secured them with a zip tie, and stepped nimbly out of kicking range.

Although Phyllis still careened around, screeching, cursing, and generally being a huge pain in the ass, I didn't let hard feelings prevent me from being charitable. To distract Snuggles, I picked up the bag of cat treats and opened it, extracting my Swiss army knife.

The cat leaped down to scamper to my side. "Who's a good boy?" I tossed him a treat.

Next, I tackled Phyllis to the ground and went to work on those thrashing feet. After thwarting her gyrations and attempted mule kicks, I secured her feet and removed her neckerchief, which I used to staunch the trickle of blood on her forehead before rolling her onto her back. She hurled more insults.

"Shut up, Phyllis," I said, "or I'll gag you with your own neckerchief."

Phyllis glared up at me, her hands and feet trussed like a Thanksgiving turkey's. At least she was silent now.

In a flash, I was beside Minnie and severing the zip ties with my Swiss army knife, first hands, then feet. Minnie massaged her wrists while I rescued my phone. Snuggles pounced on a liver-flavored nugget and crunched down. After finishing every bite, he wound around my legs. His purring resembled a little sewing machine.

"Mew," he said.

Giddy and downright euphoric, I reached down and scratched his head. As expected, he closed his eyes in ecstasy. "I'm going to find a way to keep you, Snuggles. There's no way I'm giving you up. You are officially my cat from now on."

Minnie, in the meantime, poked Phyllis none-too-gently with her boot. "How do you propose we get this one back to the truck? I don't recommend undoing her feet."

I shrugged while pocketing my phone and pepper spray. "She's fairly small. Let's try dragging her."

"Too difficult. You could call Hawk."

"Not happening." I gripped Phyllis' feet and hauled.

"There's an easier solution."

I ignored Minnie and struggled along, letting Phyllis' head thump over the rough terrain. My strength faded after a short distance. I dropped her feet, enjoying the heavy thud, although it triggered a string of muffled curses. As an afterthought, I gave her a thorough pat down and confiscated Eleanor's cellphone. Leaving Phyllis lying there, I wandered away, needing to escape her toxic presence.

Minnie followed me. "Or you could call your sisters. One of them might be available."

"Better."

We plopped down on the grass. Snuggles must have been stalking us because he hopped onto my lap and curled into a tight, furry ball. Minnie didn't complain or flee, signifying she was as drained as I was.

At the sight of movement on the road, I froze. Two ATVs roared into sight. One of the drivers' was Zeke, The other's ramrod posture looked suspiciously like Hawk's.

Minnie shaded her eyes and laughed. "I do believe your knight on a white charger—excuse me, I mean black and white ATV—has arrived."

I squinted at the ATVs drawing closer. Yeah, Zeke and Hawk.

I uttered a low moan. My afternoon activities, not the least of which included our reckless rescue attempt and subsequent capture and near-murder, would no doubt cement Hawk's low opinion of me.

Chapter 26: The Long Road Home

Minnie and I remained flopped down against a rock, too drained to move. Even Snuggles appeared content to remain curled up on my lap next to Minnie. Across the meadow, the distant figures of Hawk and Zeke roared toward the mine entrance. Without dismounting, Hawk tugged on the boards nailed to the frame, presumably wondering if we'd entered—or been forced to enter—the mine. Perhaps it was my imagination, but when the boards didn't budge, his shoulders seemed to relax a teeny-tiny bit.

The sun glinted off the lenses of his binoculars as he scanned the meadow until they finally pointed straight at us. After gesturing to Zeke, Hawk gunned the motor and aimed his ATV in our direction.

Minnie nudged me. "Here comes Hawk, aiming for you like a homing pigeon. Poor Zeke must have drawn the short straw because he's headed for Phyllis."

I dragged my gaze away from Hawk. Sure enough, Zeke was driving to the spot where I'd parked Phyllis, who was nicely secured with zip ties.

Minnie released a loud cackle. "Watch. The closer Zeke gets to Phyllis, the slower he drives. Can't say I blame him."

I focused all my attention on Hawk. My hands buzzed with adrenaline. Under different circumstances, the speed of his approach would have been flattering. But I didn't try to kid myself. Today's rescue attempt would undoubtedly count as an avoidable risk and drive him away. I swallowed against the dryness in my throat and straightened my spine. No matter how angry he was, no matter what he said, I refused to grovel.

I was officially no longer a people-pleaser.

When Hawk reached our rock, he halted and in a single vault, leaped off the ATV and raced to my side. Ignoring Minnie's presence, he dropped to his knees and gripped my hand so hard, his knuckles whitened. "I came back looking for you. When I realized you'd disappeared, I turned Grizzly Gulch upside down hunting for you," he said softly. "Minnie and Snuggles were missing too. I didn't know what to think until Abby told me … never mind. You're alive."

Unless I was mistaken, he sounded more than a little choked up. With some difficulty, I extricated my hand and flexed my fingers to restore blood circulation. "Alive and very happy to see you. Can we talk?"

Duh! Way to scare him off, and what was I thinking? He'd made it clear he had nothing more to say.

Snuggles jumped off my lap to investigate my backpack, no doubt hoping to find a loose kitty treat.

Hawk ducked my question. "Are you hurt?"

"No." Hey, if he wanted nothing more to do with me, I refused to grovel. I countered with another question. "Why were you hunting for me?"

"Because I needed—need—to talk to you …" He broke off and swung his gaze toward Minnie, who'd propped herself up on one elbow, and was avidly listening. "Uh, in private."

"Pretend I'm invisible."

"Sorry, Minnie. I need a moment alone with Clara. Would you mind giving us some space?"

"This had better be good," Minnie grumbled, scrambling to her feet. "I'll keep Zeke company in case Phyllis convinces him to remove her zip ties. You two lovebirds take your time, eh?" She walked away leaving me alone with Hawk.

I stiffened my spine. There was time enough to fall to pieces later. "What did you need to talk to me about? No, forget it. Not important. I don't want to know. You made it clear you never wanted to see me again."

Hawk sat cross-legged facing me and took my hand and ran a gentle finger across my palm. "I needed to tell you I was an idiot to break up with you." His eyes betrayed his anguish. "I refused to listen when you tried to make things right. I'm in love with you, Clara. I can't imagine my life without you in it."

All the air whooshed from my lungs. This was the last thing I'd expected to hear from the man who'd dumped me for snooping in Gabby's cabin. I struggled to stay calm. "Even though I didn't break a promise, technically speaking, you'll want to dump me all over again once you hear what I did this afternoon. Well, here's a newsflash. I got your message the first time, loud and clear. There's no need to revisit the pain."

He studied my face. "Nothing you said or did today will change how I feel."

I edged away from his big, warm body, which stirred up too many emotions. "Time will tell. How did you find us?"

"While I was hunting for you, the rest of the staff finally corralled the goats. That's when Abby checked her messages and filled me in—Eleanor's phone call about hurting herself at the mine, then you and Minnie racing to the rescue. I'd already chatted with Eleanor and Wayne as they got on the tour coach, so I figured you must be in big trouble."

"And you brought ATVs. We were wondering how to get Phyllis back. I was about to phone Abby or Dodie for help."

"Why not call me?" He sounded hurt.

"Seriously? After you made it clear you never wanted to hear from me again? I paused, then said, "Fine. Let's get this over with. I suppose you should hear what happened today." I fiddled with my phone.

"Are you planning to tell me, or should I guess?"

"Neither. I set my cell phone to Audio Record. All the proof you'll need to get Phyllis arrested is here on my phone. It recorded everything, including a confession that she pushed Minnie into the river." I punched a button.

For the next ten minutes, we listened to the recording. Once it was over, I held my breath.

Hawk let several beats of silence pass. "Surely, you knew I would be back. You should have waited for me."

I blew out a shaky breath and stared up at him. His face gave away no indication of his thoughts. It was not encouraging.

I cleared my throat. "For all I knew, you'd decided to move out. Okay, I admit it was a foolhardy plan, but I had no choice. Eleanor was a guest, everyone else was unavailable, and I couldn't stand the thought of her lying there alone and in pain. She'd never make it back without help."

"Sweet baby Jesus."

"How could I let her stay here alone? I wouldn't have been able to live with myself. Minnie insisted on helping, so we took precautions. She hid a knife down her sock, and I had my bear spray, a hatchet, and a Swiss army knife."

Hawk released a heartfelt sigh. "Don't forget your secret weapon—Snuggles."

My jaw must have dropped, because he said, "It's all right. I don't like it that you walked into another potentially dangerous situation, I never will, but I do understand why you felt compelled to go."

"You do?" I was certain my eyes were bugging out of my head. "Why the sudden change of heart?"

"I've done some soul-searching. I guess it's time to tell you why I overreacted."

Although I had a weird urge to do a happy dance, I sat in silence, my heart thundering in my chest.

At last, he sucked in a deep, shuddering breath. "This may sound strange, but I've always been surrounded by strong-willed, intelligent women who refused to listen to my excellent advice." He stopped talking.

I held my breath and willed myself not to make any movement that might distract him.

When he spoke again, his voice, although still calm, had taken on an edge. "So I lectured my kids for years about driving our snowmobile on the frozen lake. Each year, too many knuckleheads went through the ice and drowned. When my daughter turned sixteen, she beseeched us to let her drive our snowmobile, promised she'd never take it onto the lake. I finally gave in. It was mid-January, but it had thawed. I made her promise to stay on the trail. But teenagers have hormones instead of brains. What does she do? She follows a pack of boys onto the lake and crashes through the ice. Miraculously, a cottager heard the shouting and rescued my daughter.

"A year later, I told my sister not to get behind the wheel after she'd had a few too many and that I would come and pick her up. She promised she'd wait, but got impatient. She was lucky to come out alive after driving into the path of a pickup. I was first at the scene of the accident. Luckily no one died that time either."

I picked up on the words *that time*. On a sudden flash of intuition, I raised my gaze to meet his. "There's more, isn't there?"

"Yeah." He let out a short breath, rising to his feet to pace. Three steps one way, three the other. At last, he said, "My wife, Kimi, well she wasn't so lucky. On the night of the worst snowstorm in years, I convinced her to stay at a hotel near her office. She promised she wouldn't drive in the blizzard. I'll never know what made Kimi change her mind, but she never made it home. Her car slid off the road into a ravine." He stopped pacing. "They told me she died instantly."

"Oh, Hawk. I am so, so sorry. I had no idea."

He hunkered down beside me again. "How could you? I've never told anyone the whole story. I don't like to think about it, never mind re-live it."

"My actions caused you to re-live the worst moments of your life. I made promises intended to keep me out of danger, then found a way to circumvent them. Bottom line is, either Gabby or Phyllis might have killed me. You may not believe me, but I'm not normally a risk-taker. Just the opposite."

"I was afraid I would arrive too late."

"Now it's my turn to explain." I took his hand and stared into his eyes. "After my husband died, I convinced myself I didn't need a man to make me happy. Time after time, I'd twisted myself inside-out trying to morph into someone I barely recognized, all to please a man—first, my daddy, then my husband. I had no idea who I was. In fact, I'd lost myself. My solution was to bubble-wrap myself by avoiding every possible risk, and by risk, I mean both physical and emotional. I craved safety."

He threw back his head and laughed. "It seems in the space of two short days, you've tackled physical risk with a vengeance."

"There were compelling reasons both times—saving Minnie's life. Mine too, this time."

"I know. I hope you can find equally compelling reasons to take the emotional leap." He pressed a kiss to my hand and helped me to my feet. "I don't know what I would do without you."

Every cell in my body released some lingering tension. "Hawk." His name came out in a whisper. "I'm willing to try if you are."

He brushed his lips against mine while his fingers went to my hair. Head reeling, I wrapped my arms around his neck and surrendered to the heat, dizzy with the taste of him, the feel of him, the freedom to be myself.

Minnie was the one to break the spell. "You planning to jump one another's bones right here, right now?"

We sprang apart. "Don't be ridiculous." I ran a hand over my hair in a futile attempt to smooth it down. "It's getting late and I'm hungry."

Hawk laughed, removed a Snickers bar from his shirt pocket, and tossed it to me. "You two can share this. I'd best take Phyllis in the truck. You can have the ATVs. One of you gets Zeke."

We exchanged keys.

Minnie and I waited until Hawk loaded Phyllis into the open truck bed and ordered her to sit. Using the duct tape he found in the truck, he attached her zip-tied wrists to a convenient metal hoop welded to the floor.

Phyllis glared up at us and bared her teeth. "It wasn't supposed to end like this.

"Time to leave," Hawk said. "I'll let Abby know we're on our way."

The trip home took half an hour with the truck leading the way. On the off chance Phyllis might find a way to escape, the two ATVs followed close behind,.

I hoped Hawk had the radio maxed up to drown out her yelling. Who knew Phyllis had a champion pottymouth?

Our return was memorable in more ways than one. Although we'd taken a back road to avoid unwanted attention, a welcoming committee consisting of sixty or so guests, most of the staff, and two Mounties, summoned by Abby to apprehend Phyllis, greeted us. Word of our capture and escape had spread throughout Grizzly Gulch.

While Phyllis snarled and struggled like a caged wolverine, the pair of Mounties hauled her off the truck bed, replaced the zip ties with handcuffs, and crammed her into a police vehicle while a local journalist captured it all on video. Due to multiple requests, Minnie, Hawk, Zeke, and I, with Snuggles in my arms, posed for a photo shoot. Minnie and I were celebrated as the courageous heroines who, with some feline assistance, took down a dangerous felon. Snuggles, in particular, received much applause as the fiercest, cutest, and most unlikely furry hero ever.

Although Hawk and Zeke were permitted in the photos, they received somewhat less fanfare for their minor role in the rescue, something that no doubt rankled, seeing as how they were both alpha males.

After the excitement faded and everyone dispersed, Hawk and I managed a private afternoon celebration of our own, slipping away quietly to his place with a couple of bottles of Dom Perignon. Our bedroom rodeo was so outstanding we never did make it downstairs for dinner. To mix my metaphors, we achieved several spectacular home runs.

By midnight, I was so worn out I could hardly walk. Seeing my dilemma, Hawk scooped me into his arms. "It's best nobody sees your walk of shame, so I'm taking you home now."

Ever-so-quietly, he carried me into my apartment and deposited me on my bed. After kissing me tenderly, he disappeared back to his borrowed unit.

How romantic, thoughtful, and tactful was that? Good grief. I must be falling hard.

I was so worn out with all the excitement, not to mention a champagne-fueled sexual marathon on top of a kidnapping and near-death at the hands of a seriously deranged woman, I immediately fell asleep, secure in the knowledge I'd faced down the worst imaginable situation and come away stronger than ever.

It had to be an omen. Nothing could stop me now. Against all odds, I would create a winning Thanksgiving celebration, one that our guests would never forget.

Chapter 27: Medical Crisis Resolved

I WAS SOUND ASLEEP IN MY own bed when frantic hammering on my door jolted me from the most erotic dream I'd ever experienced. A moment later, Abby's muffled words accompanied the hammering. "Clara. Get your ass out of bed. Now."

"Don't get your knickers in a twist," I mumbled, pushing myself upright. I squinted at my bedside clock. 5:00 a.m. on Thanksgiving morning. I'd only been asleep for one hour, two max.

I was tempted to roll over for an extra hour of sleep, but swung my feet to the floor. Disoriented and a still little dizzy from the wine I'd consumed, I wobbled down the hall into my foyer. Flinging the front door open I found myself face-to-face with Abby.

"This had better be good," I mumbled under my breath.

She stomped past me, slamming the door shut behind her.

"Do come in," I muttered. "Make yourself at home."

She took my arm and tugged me into the living room. "I think you should sit down to hear this news." Collapsing onto the sofa, she yanked me down beside her, more to prevent my escape, I suspected, than for emotional support.

"Hey," I protested. "I haven't had coffee yet."

"Forget coffee. We have a problem. Our staff held a midnight party down by the pond to celebrate your safe return."

"That's the big news? They're young and hardy. They'll survive. I, on the other hand, may not. I need my beauty sleep."

She hesitated a long beat, then said, "All our wranglers plus most of the kitchen, housekeeping, and hospitality staff have food poisoning."

"Huh? How? Why?" I shook my head to clear it. "Come again."

"You heard me. They're deathly ill. Zeke was so worried he hauled me out of bed at 2:00 a.m. I called the doctor, then woke Dodie up.

"You should have woken me. I would have helped."

"And interrupt your chance to get lucky? I'm not that cruel."

Not only was Abby too perceptive, she undoubtedly believed she'd done me a huge favor. To be fair, she had—in a way. But on the flip side, she'd treated me the way she usually did, like her fragile baby sister who would freak out in the middle of a staff emergency. And as usual, I swallowed my indignation.

I must have fooled her because she continued, "The vomiting and diarrhea was so bad, Dodie insisted on remaining in the staff quarters, where she's mopping foreheads and holding back women's hair while they vomit."

"What does Doc Sutherland think caused the illness?"

"That their late-night fun was fueled by poutine from a local takeout dive washed down by gallons of Alberta beer. She's pretty sure the culprit was the poutine gravy. She collected gravy samples for testing, and also pumped antibiotics into over two dozen butts right away. Everyone is supposed to drink plenty of sports drinks to replace lost electrolytes and eat only bananas, rice, apples, and toast, maybe oatmeal or fat-free yogurt. Nothing else."

"Will the staff be okay."

"Eventually. But you haven't heard the worst. Doctor's orders are that everyone experiencing symptoms of food poisoning must avoid contact with the guests' food for the next couple of days. If one of the guests falls ill because someone ignores the order, Grizzly Gulch would be legally liable."

I stared at Abby blankly. My mouth opened and closed, opened and closed. "But the Thanksgiving celebration is today." I shot to my feet and hollered, "Noooooooo! This can't be happening."

Abby sat there quietly and watched me sink to the sofa to hide my face in my hands. Once I got my act together, I raised my head. "We need a solution or we'll lose the contest."

"I'm well aware of the ramifications. I've had most of the night to think about it. Believe me, there's no magic solution to replacing the missing staff. We might as well prepare for foreclosure."

"In other words, you think we're screwed."

"I do."

Minnie chose that moment to join us. "What's all the racket out here? How are you guys screwed—other than the fun way, of course?" She winked at me.

And here I thought Hawk and I had been discreet.

Abby described the disaster to Minnie, who took a moment to absorb the bad news before rendering her verdict. "You're right. You are *so* screwed."

I willed my brain to function. "No we're not. Not yet at any rate. Between the three of us, surely we can find a solution." I considered our options. "Although most of our employees live in staff accommodations, a few, like Chef Armand, live in their own houses and likely didn't attend the party. Also, our Boomers' Thanksgiving Fling ends tomorrow. Our guests leave after breakfast. That's only four meals. The two breakfast meals and today's lunch shouldn't pose a problem, assuming we serve them buffet-style. It's tonight's dinner we have to worry about."

Minnie clapped. "We'll all pitch in."

Abby closed her eyes briefly, as if in pain. "Have you forgotten we committed to delivering a Thanksgiving feast with all the bells and whistles?"

"Of course I didn't forget." I tried to keep the testiness out of my reply. "Let's try to think outside the box. Be proactive."

"Got any more clichés?" Abby asked. "I don't see any way out."

Nice little sisters didn't punch out a big sister during times of stress. Abby was lucky I attributed her condescension, not to mention negative attitude, to exhaustion and stress. So instead of showing my anger, I folded, my habitual reaction when confronting an older sibling.

Minnie had no such qualms. "What about serving Thanksgiving pizza? Some take-out joints are open on Thanksgiving."

While I appreciated Minnie's effort to help, I flinched. Pizza, although tasty, did not factor into a memorable Thanksgiving dinner. Shocked into action, my cerebral cortex stirred, yawned, and sparked to life. Neurons fired, hummed, pulsed, and established connections, giving birth to a strategy for turning the most recent disaster into a triumph.

Once Minnie paused for breath, I blurted, "We can do better than take-out."

Abby shook her head. "I don't have a better answer. Do you?" Without giving me a chance to reply, she rattled on, "We have no other choice."

"I have an idea that might work," I said.

"I very much doubt that."

"Shouldn't we hear Clara's idea?" Minnie wrinkled her forehead, her confusion evident.

Abby shook her head sorrowfully and said, "When times get tough, my little sister is prone to flights of fancy."

"Hey, I'm right here," I said.

Abby whirled to face me. "Magical thinking never worked when you were a child, and sadly, it won't work now."

Okay, so Abby remembered how I'd lived in a fantasy world during Daddy's frequent alcoholic binges. In her mind, the baby of the family couldn't possibly function under pressure. Not until now did I realize how desperately I yearned for her respect. Dodie's too. "Cut me some slack," I said. "I haven't been a child for five decades. I've learned a few things since then. Furthermore, there's nothing wrong with optimism."

Abby's eyes filled with pity. "I hate to rain on your parade, hon, but all the optimism in the world won't help us create a major feast without any staff, especially during a power outage. Like you, I doubt Thanksgiving take-out will win us the hospitality contest, but I don't see any other solution. We need to wrap our minds around the idea of foreclosure."

The slap of Abby's words left me reeling. She hadn't asked about my idea. She didn't believe her space cadet of a baby sister could possibly formulate a decent idea, never mind a brilliant one based on an understanding of human nature, an idea that would give us a fighting chance to win the contest thus avoiding financial disaster.

"You're wrong," I said. "Believe it or not, I have a better approach that will solve our problems."

"Is that a fact?" Abby replied. "Do tell."

I broad-beamed what I hoped was a confident smile. "My idea is based on the knowledge that elderly people, myself included, reach a phase of life where the desire to help others intensifies. In spite of our wrinkles, a few memory lapses, muscle twinges, and other ailments, we're still above ground, active, and eager to contribute to society. In short, we have a universal need to feel relevant."

"I love it," Minnie stated at the same time as Abby said, "How does that help solve the problem?"

I took a deep breath. "I intend to ask all our guests to pitch in and help with the meals." Joy of joys, I'd articulated my idea quickly, concisely, and best of all, calmly.

After a long silence, Abby said, "No way. We can't ask them to work."

"Sorry, Abs. Like it or not, this special Thanksgiving week is my show, my monkey. We'll do it my way. I'll break the ice by admitting the truth to our guests right away, preferably before breakfast is served."

"And apologize. Groveling is always good," Minnie added.

"Right. Groveling is one of my greatest gifts. Did you or did you not meet our daddy? And please don't get me started on my apology to Phyllis."

Abby flicked a glance at me and sighed. "I don't know. It's a huge risk. There's a Canmore take-out joint was featured in *Diners, Drive-Ins and Dives*. They'll deliver a festive array of Thanksgiving pizzas, shawarmas, and subs. If we ask, I'm certain they'll stay open especially for us."

I could read her mind. She thought I couldn't handle the situation. Strangely enough, I remained calm, in control, and able to contradict my big sister.

"I appreciate your suggestion, Abs, but I can make it work. Trust me on this." I knew how to solve our staffing problem, and solve it I would.

After a long pause, Abby said, "I do trust you. It'll be perfect." I could swear I caught a glint of respect in her eyes.

Confidence surged through me. "We need a management meeting in the main kitchen. Chef Armand always arrives early. You invite Zeke and Dodie, I'll take care of Hawk.

"I thought you already did that." Minnie's cackle made me blush.

One short hour later, we'd finished a kitchen de-brief to update Chef Armand, listened to his initial squawks about his lack of staff, and settled him down with my solution. I would ask the guests to help with the meals. Then we all got busy. Abby and Dodie helped prepare breakfast for sixty guests, while Minnie and I set tables and arranged the condiments, dozens of domed food containers and serving implements for the buffet. Hawk assisted anywhere he was needed, mainly as a runner between the kitchen and outdoor cooking stations. Zeke, who, like Abby, was operating on zero sleep, headed for the stables to attend to the animals. Once he was finished, he returned and set up the microphone and podium I'd requested for my announcement.

Two hours later, everything was ready.

Hawk and I stood on the front porch, a good vantage point in front of the dining hall to await the guests. A light breeze wafted the sweet, clean fragrance of grass, undercut by the smell of bacon, toward us. Once Chef Armand gave the signal, the oversized brass bell for the ten-minute warning would ring. The next half hour would determine Grizzly Gulch's ultimate fate and, possibly, my relationship with my sisters.

As if sensing my uneasiness, Hawk snugged his arm around my waist and drew me close. "You're awfully quiet," he said, his voice low and rough with worry. "Are you having second thoughts about last night?"

I stroked his cheek. "Of course not. I can't wait to do it again. Right now, though, I'm nervous. What if the guests don't respond the way I hope."

Hawk lifted his hand and let it linger on my hair. "You impress me beyond anything I could have imagined. Your idea is brilliant. I can't believe I'm fortunate enough to share this special day with you." His fingers traced the curve of my neck.

I'd responded with a soft sigh and a grateful murmur when Minnie appeared in the doorway. "All right, boys and girls. It's game time."

With the sun warm on my shoulders, my pulse raced with anticipation. I gripped the bell with both hands and rang it exactly ten times.

Hungry guests swarmed past us into the dining room. Little did they know what lay in store for them—assuming everything went the way I anticipated.

Once the last straggler entered, Hawk gave me an arm-squeeze and sat with Wayne and Eleanor. I, on the other hand, walked to the front of the room and climbed onto the low dais where Zeke had set up a pedestal and microphone. I waited until I got my nerves under control. With luck, no one would notice my trembling hands. The next few minutes would make it or break it for the future of Grizzly Gulch. I hoped Abby would forgive me if I failed.

I switched on the mic. "If I could get your attention, please."

The hubbub died away with remarkable speed, leaving the air electric with anticipation. The guests seemed to sense something important was going down.

I took a deep breath. "Thank you and good morning all."

A chorus of, "Good morning, Clara," was music to my ears. One jokester parroted his favorite expressions during last week's charades, "Are we having fun yet?"

Laughing, I replied, "If I were having any more fun, I'd have to be twins." Yeah, this was a friendly crowd. In spite of spending much of my time with the Lifestyle Manor group, I'd bonded with many of our other guests over tournaments and activities during the last few days. The recent takedown of Lizzie's murderer and Minnie's attacker would only help my cause. I had a feeling everything would work out the way I anticipated.

I gripped the podium for support. "I have a couple of important announcements to make before this morning's buffet-style breakfast." I paused, gathering my thoughts, then launched into it. "Last night, our staff held a party down by the pond. This morning, some of you may have noticed there aren't many staff members around to help you. It's my unhappy task to inform you that over 90 percent of Grizzly Gulch's staff fell victim to food poisoning from the tainted poutine gravy they consumed during the party."

The room exploded into a barrage of concerned comments.

"*That's terrible! … I'm so sorry. … Will they be okay?*"

I saw no point in holding back. The more the guests knew, the more they would identify with our predicament. Once I got going, the words spilled out. I explained everything I'd learned about last night's events—the sudden and cruel onset of illness, the mass antibiotic jabs, and, the most important point of all, a medical directive that all afflicted staff members were forbidden to handle the guests' food, including food preparation and serving.

I ended my explanation on a note of genuine sorrow. "Due to this illness, I regret to inform you we have a sudden staff shortage." I clutched the podium for support. "My sisters and I offer our deepest apologies for the disappointment."

Simply saying the words aloud caused my worries—and those worries were many and varied—to expand until they coalesced into a writhing, toxic ball of emotion in my chest. Our troubles, from our staff members' health, to my relationship with my sisters, to the fate of Grizzly Gulch, to ensuring our elderly guests' enjoyment, it all threatened to overwhelm me.

To my horror, a sob gathered my chest, preventing me from proposing my solution. The harder I tried to suppress my feelings, the more the pressure accumulated, filling my chest, demanding release, until finally, the urgency grew too strong to hold inside.

I let 'er rip.

Our ultra-sensitive mic amplified my sobs, filling the Hoodoo Dining Room with the penetrating wails, snorts and roars of a howler monkey on steroids. Simultaneously, a deluge of tears flowed down my cheeks to accompany the mucus exploding from my nostrils—twin gushes of utter humiliation, which seemed to last forever.

Angel of Death, please take me now.

Upturned faces swam into my tear-blurred field of vision. At the shocked expressions, I ruthlessly wrestled my emotions under control, swallowing another impending volley of sobs.

Hiding the lower part of my face with one hand to conceal oozing fluids, I spoke into the mic, which, to my astonishment, my other hand still clutched in a death grip. "Sorry about this, folks." Although my nose was blocked tighter than a submarine's airlock, I soldiered on. "Some speakers experience wardrobe malfunctions, let's call this an emotional malfunction. I hope you can forgive me."

Flo darted up to the podium, pressed a linen napkin into my hand, and whispered, "Blow your nose, dearie." She scooted away to her seat beside Lois.

I'd been going for vulnerability, but utter humiliation was another story. Any sane person would have dashed away to nurse their mortification in private, but not me. Nope. I hadn't finished what I needed to say. I held up one warning finger and turned my back on the audience to perform mop-up activities. I blew, I snorted, and I wiped, a combo of activities that is surprisingly mortifying when conducted in public.

Once I was finished, I faced the audience. "I believe I have hit on a solution, but that depends on you." I waited on a response, but encountered only blank stares. Digging deep, I flung my arms in the air, and shouted, "Who in this room—besides me, that is—is willing to help with the dinner?"

Two quavering words rang out to fill the silence. "I will."

I slowly scanned the crowd until I found the speaker. Edna McGillicuddy was an avid gambler who'd spent every morning engaged in a lively penny-a-point bridge game on our back deck. I wanted nothing more than to throw my arms around her in a fervent bear hug, but that might snap several elderly bones. "Thank you, Edna. I'm grateful for your support."

The next thing I knew, Gladys Kandinsky, a retired schoolteacher, who'd added a purple streak to her white hair to match a purple velour tracksuit, shot up her hand. "I will too."

Fighting a triumphant grin, I acknowledged her support.

One hand shot up, then another, and another. "*Of course I'll help … It'll be a hoot" … I wouldn't miss it for the world … Wait until my grandkids hear about this! …*" A woman yelled, "*I'll make stuffing,*" preceded a chorus of, "*The salads are all mine … I'm a lousy cook but a great potato peeler … They call me 'Barbecue King' for a reason … I have a way with Brussel's sprouts … Tell me what you need and consider it done …*"

In response to our guests' generosity of spirit, my heart swelled to the point where I imagined it would explode with sheer joy. From the Dodie and Abby's expressions, they felt identical emotions.

Eventually, the room grew quiet enough for me to be heard. "I'm sure I speak for Abby and Dodie as well when I say we are profoundly humbled and grateful to all of you. With your help, we will create more than a feast. We will create beautiful memories." I beckoned to Chef Armand, who'd emerged from the kitchen area. "Chef, would you please join me up here and refresh my memory about tonight's Thanksgiving feast.

Chef Armand's response was instantaneous. "*Mais oui.*" Never a man to avoid the limelight, he moved at top speed, squeezing his bulk between tables to join me on the dais. "Some of you may have observed our staff digging a large pit yesterday, yes?"

"Yeah," Roland yelled. "We were hoping it wasn't a grave."

A roar of laughter greeted this response. There was nothing like morbid humor to elicit laughter from a group of retirees.

Chef Armand curled his lip at Roland's comment. "*Mais non.* This is the fire pit. *La pièce de résistance* of dinner will be the turkeys, baked for the entire day in the fire pit."

Wayne spoke up. "I love the idea. I can help you there. During my misspent youth, I attended a Hawaiian luau in Maui. Although I was barely twenty, I still remember how delicious that pork meat was. It fell off the bone."

Eleanor slipped a possessive hand around Wayne's arm. "I imagine you have happy memories of more than one pig at that luau, and I'm not talking about the roasted one." Her comment elicited a loud burst of laughter. I surmised most of the guests had noticed Eleanor's jealous streak.

Once everyone settled down, Chef Armand intoned, "In addition to the turkeys, there will be the cornbread stuffing, accompanied by Brussels sprouts with bacon and maple syrup, mashed potatoes and gravy, and for dessert, two types of pie and *la crème glacée* from our barn manager's freezer. We will gather long sticks to use during a barbaric custom so popular in this country—toasting marshmallows for, how do you call it?"

"S'mores," the guests chorused.

"Yes, those. Since the weather is favorable, the meal will be outside. I will supervise the cooking efforts, while our Clara will soothe the ruffled feathers, and Abby will be the boss of setup and cleanup."

"Didn't you forget someone?" Dodie asked with an exaggerated pout.

"It goes without saying you will provide entertainment during the cooking extravaganza whenever not otherwise engaged."

Someone in the crowd chanted, "*Tur-key! Turkey!*" Soon everyone in the room joined in the chant.

Yeah, it promised to be an outstanding Thanksgiving extravaganza.

Chapter 28: Thanksgiving Extravaganza

WITH EVERY ABLE PERSON'S HELP, the Thanksgiving feast was a triumph. Music, laughter, and the heady aroma of roasting meat drifted through the air. Friendships were struck, rivalries abandoned, and quarrels resolved.

I spent much of the afternoon and evening circulating among the guests praising their efforts, thanking them, and helping anywhere I was needed, while always reminding them to post five-star reviews. I'd learned to ask directly for what I wanted.

Minnie headed up the barbecue station, where she supervised helpers, basted meats, turned spits, and generally ensured everything was cooked to perfection.

Predictably, Dodie, wearing her turkey costume, was a huge hit.

Abby had possibly the most difficult job of all. She remained in the kitchen with Chef Armand, where she managed several teams of guests and administered small amounts of alcohol to the temperamental chef whenever required, which was often, thereby ensuring he remained relatively unruffled, yet not too inebriated to lead the cooking effort.

Later, guests told us they were happier than they'd been for years because they felt useful and needed, something that had been lacking in their lives. They had no idea helping out could be so enjoyable. Many were all fired up to do volunteer work once they returned to their residences or retirement homes. Sitting around the campfire, they tossed around areas of service. Ideas included helping at homeless shelters, reading to shut-ins, and offering computer assistance to residents in senior care homes.

Once the cleanup was completed and everything put away except some plates and cutlery destined for Zeke's dishwasher, Hawk and I led a sing-song around a campfire, selecting well-known songs from the 50s, 60s, and 70s. The singing was so much fun, most guests were willing to forego their usual 10:00 bedtime. They used cell phones instead of lighters to show their approval while belting out everything from folk songs like *Five Hundred Miles* and *Lemon Tree*, to ballads like *Sounds of Silence*, *Sweet Caroline*, and *Margaritaville*, ending with a duo of *Good Night Irene* and *Show Me the Way to Go Home*.

At midnight, replete with delicious food and mellowed out with goodwill, possibly the result of several joints being passed around, the last of our fun-seekers called it a night and rolled off to their cabins. At the same time a gentleman named Melvin, swaying while a couple of his buddies propped him upright, proclaimed to the night sky that the Boomers' Thanksgiving Fling was the best week he could remember, and he was posting a five-star review.

Alone in the shadows, I did a happy dance before heading directly to the picnic table where I'd left a stack of review forms for the Hospitality Contest. They were all gone. My pulse leaped with excitement. If every guest left a decent review, Grizzly Gulch stood a chance of winning first prize.

"There you are, Clara." Dodie's words emerged from the shadows. "If you're looking for the forms, Abby and I handed one to each guest. Abby told them that if they needed help using the contest's online system, or if they needed to borrow a laptop, a staff member would be in the lobby bright and early to help." Her teeth flashed white. "Employees who feel better can still provide technology instructions."

"It sounds as if you guys thought of everything." A pang of guilt hit me. "I should have been here instead of at the campfire."

"Don't be silly." Dodie drew closer. At some point, she'd changed out of her turkey outfit and into jeans, turtleneck, and hoodie. "You and Hawk were the big attraction around the campfire. We didn't want the party to break up."

I covered my surprise at the compliment with a gracious nod. My sisters valued my contribution. "You think Hawk and I were the drawing cards?"

"You should sing more often. You have such a lovely voice." Looping her arm in mine Dodie forced me toward the fire. A shower of sparks arose as someone tossed on a log, revealing the faces of Abby, Zeke, Hawk, and Minnie. They beckoned us over.

On our arrival, Hawk stood and gestured to a chair beside Minnie. "This seat's for you. Your sisters have a little something for you both."

I rested my gaze first on Abby, then studied Dodie's face. Hoping no one noticed the apprehension filling every cell of my body, I said, "What?"

"You'll see."

Dodie gripped my shoulders and exerted downward pressure, forcing me to either sit or create a scene. I sat. Some things never change.

Abby stooped and picked up what appeared to be two posters. Rising, she positioned herself beside Dodie, meaning both sisters towered over me.

Feeling squirmy, I said, "What's that you're holding?" I tried to whisk the poster out of Abby's grasp, but she knew me well enough to back away. Resigned to my fate, I remained seated beside Minnie and wracked my brain. This little chat was surely about my emotional meltdown during the announcement. What if Abby and Dodie had interpreted my distress as more baby sister dramatics? Primed to defend myself, I swallowed the lump in my throat and gazed at Abby. "Fine. It's been a long day. I thought the dinner went extraordinarily well, so if you're unhappy about something—"

Abby grimaced. "I am unhappy. With myself. Minnie tells me I screwed up with you this morning. She's right, and I want to apologize."

I nearly fell off my chair. "No need."

"Oh, but there is." She cleared her throat. "I want you to know how sorry I am for blowing you off. I've been stressing so much about the prospect of bank foreclosure that the food poisoning pushed me over the edge. That's when I lost all hope. There was no doubt in my mind we were going to lose the ranch."

Something deep inside me loosened. "Why didn't you explain?"

She shrugged. "This may not make any sense to you, but I guess I was trying to protect my baby sister from disappointment. By doing so, I was underestimating you, and for that, I am so, so sorry."

Abby handed the two pieces of Bristol board to Dodie and knelt in front of my chair. Gleaming in the firelight, tears welled in her eyes. She gripped my hands. "I think you're the most courageous of the three of us, and of course, I trust you. I would trust you with my life."

Everyone around the bonfire had stopped talking to listen.

Dodie sniffled through a smile. "I feel the same way. Clara, you're my hero."

I glanced over at Hawk to find him gesturing to the pieces of Bristol board Dodie held. "You going to do anything with those?"

"Of course. We got sidetracked." Abby took one and stood in front of me, while Dodie took the other and stood in front of Minnie.

In unison, they said, "We are honored to present these posters commemorating the remarkable courage of two exceptional women." Abby handed me one while Dodie handed the other to Minnie.

"These were the staff's idea," Abby explained. "They insisted on making these posters to show you both how much they love and respect you."

Each poster contained four remarkably lifelike cartoons, one in each corner, leaving the middle open for every staff member to scrawl a personal message. There were so many messages, there wasn't a square centimeter of unused space.

On my poster, one cartoon portrayed me as a sleuth toting a huge magnifying glass while entering a guest cabin. The next one showed the same sleuth hauling on a rope connected to two people about to be swept over a waterfall. In another, the sleuth disarmed a small woman bearing an uncanny resemblance to Phyllis. An angry cat clung to her head. The last drawing portrayed the sleuth in a torrid embrace with a Mountie, legs wrapped around his waist. Thankfully, darkness concealed my hot blush. How did anyone know?

On Minnie's poster, the first cartoon depicted her yelling and waving her arms while bobbing down a raging river. Another depicted her as a yogini sitting cross-legged in front of a giant gong while surrounded by goats, one with a paper bag dangling from its mouth. The third illustration showed Minnie riding a ferocious Bucking Bully, while the fourth was of Minnie peeling endless potatoes, two bushel baskets beside her.

Simultaneously, we said, "I'm getting this framed." We both rose to our feet. Immediately, Dodie and Abby swept us into a warm circle-hug. The men gave us several minutes of girl-time before joining us.

Never had I felt more accepted or more loved. I sensed I had won the respect of both my sisters, the man I loved, and perhaps the entire Grizzly Gulch staff. No matter what else happened, no matter if we won the contest, I felt valued. And that was enough for me.

Chapter 29: The Moment of Truth

TWO WEEKS AFTER THE LAST Thanksgiving guest had departed, I found myself sitting behind the reception desk. I'd volunteered to replace the afternoon receptionist, who had a dental appointment in Calgary.

Since the holiday, I'd focused on practicing the Law of Attraction, which stated that whatever consumed your thoughts is what you would manifest in life. Several times a day, I closed my eyes and visualized how great I would feel when Grizzly Gulch won the contest. Abby would call it magical thinking, but hey, it beat pessimism hands down.

Today, the day the contest results would be announced, I did extra visualization.

Snuggles wandered over, leaped up onto my desk, and sat on my keyboard, as if to offer encouragement. Ever since the incident at the mine, he'd calmed down so much, I felt comfortable letting him wander around. No one had claimed him, so I figured he was mine.

One, by one, Abby, Dodie, and Minnie, who I'd invited to stay with me until we'd received the contest results, trailed into the lobby, ostensibly to keep me company, but I suspected they wanted to be with me on the front line in case Grizzly Gulch lost.

We were rehashing the week when my phone's ringtone, *Satisfaction* by The Rolling Stones, blasted into the reception area. Snuggles leaped from the desk and darted away. My hands trembled so violently I fumbled when I tried to answer.

Frustrated by my futile attempts to answer the call, Dodie lunged for the phone. I held it out of reach.

"Who is it?" Abby asked.

"Um … caller id says 'Global Destinations.' "

Abby, who seldom lost her cool, snapped, "We ain't gonna get no satisfaction if you ignore it. Answer it, why don't you?"

"But if I answer and find out we've lost, all hope is gone. If I don't answer, we can hang onto hope a little longer."

The phone continued to belt out *Satisfaction.*

Dodie scowled at me. "Ignoring it won't help. The judges have made their decision."

We all looked up when Hawk walked into the lobby and headed for the reception desk. "What's up?" he asked.

Abby indicated the phone I clutched as it blasted out another stanza of *Satisfaction.* "It's Global Destinations with the contest results. Clara's afraid to answer it."

Hawk pried the phone from my hand. "Grizzly Gulch Guest Ranch, Clara Foster's office. How may I help you?"

He remained silent while listening to someone talk at the other end. After glancing at his avid audience, he picked up a pen from my desk and jotted something down in a notepad. "Yes, I understand ... Okay ... You have the email address? … Yes. I'll be sure to give her the message. Thank you." He ended the call.

"Tell us," I demanded.

He let us wait several heart-pumping seconds, then yelled, "Grizzly Gulch won first prize by a landslide." He gave a loud whoop accompanied by a fist-pump.

"We didn't!"

"Yep." Hawk consulted his notes. "The judges are notifying the three top winners today. An official letter has also gone out to all contestants. Your acceptance speech will be broadcast throughout global mass media. Best of all, Global Destinations will run a full spread on Grizzly Gulch as well as articles and full-page ads every month for an entire year. The head office is interested in the huge surge of reviews you received recently and has asked you to call, preferably today, to set up interviews. I wrote down the name and number."

Laughing and crying at the same time. Abby, Dodie, and I wrapped our arms around one another and did a wild celebration dance.

Minnie said, “I’m so happy for you. Why don’t you draw straws to decide who makes the final acceptance speech?”

“No straws,” Abby said. “If anyone deserves the honor, it’s Clara.” She wrapped her arms around me. “The win was all your doing. You saved Grizzly Gulch, so you get to deliver our acceptance speech.”

I laughed aloud and looked around at all the people I loved. “I guess this truly is a day for being thankful.”

Other Books by Maureen Fisher

Horsing Around with Murder (A Senior Sleuth Cozy Mystery - Book 1) When three retired sisters inherit a dude ranch in the Alberta Foothills, the last things they need are one seriously amorous gelding (yes, it happens), a runaway stud, dwarf goats, a spitting llama, and an uncooperative stallion. Oh, yeah. And the mysterious death of the horse trainer. Will they finger the killer or will one of them become another victim?

"An exciting novel that left me doubled over in laughter"
"a wonderful hilarious comedy … a warm and enjoyable read"

Cold Feet Fever (The Fever Series, Book 2) 'One for the Money' with steamy romance meets 'The Sopranos'. A bad boy gambler and a mortician-turned-event-planner find romance while overcoming obstacles such as a goofy dog, ruthless thugs, exploding trucks, an eccentric granddaddy, disappearing corpses, an unfortunate synchronized swimming episode, and the threat of live cremation.

"An exciting novel that left me doubled over in laughter"
"a wonderful hilarious comedy … a warm and enjoyable read"

Fur Ball Fever (The Fever Series, Book 1) This romantic crime mystery features romance (sizzling hot), a second chance at love (hope and heart), crime (dastardly), an aging aunt (bawdy), dogs with personality (many), and humor (may cause mascara to run).

"It entertains, it heals, it delivers a message."
"… hilarious, moving, and sexy."

The Jaguar Legacy Romance, suspense, and adventure explode in the steamy Mexican jungle. A secretive archaeologist guards his discovery, the ruins of a hidden Olmec city, while a journalist on the trail of an ancient Olmec curse experiences flashbacks to her past life where shapeshifting is a reality.

"...magnificent characters and scenarios."
"An intricately woven tale of mystery, romance
and occult. Definitely a keeper."

Thanks from Maureen

I would like to offer my sincerest thanks for reading Deadly Thanksgiving. If you have a moment, I would be grateful if you would leave an honest review online at your retailer of choice. Reviews are crucial for authors. Even a line or two, nothing fancy, can make a huge difference. I appreciate your time and support.

Many thanks!
Maureen

About Maureen Fisher

After eons in the I.T. consulting world, I live with my husband in Ottawa, Canada's beautiful capital city, where I write fresh and funny novels featuring romance, mystery, suspense, and always an animal or two. I'm also a besotted grandma, a voracious reader, an avid bridge player, yoga enthusiast, seeker of personal and spiritual growth, pickleball player, and infrequent but avid gourmet cook. My husband and I love to hike, bicycle, and travel. I've swum with sharks in the Galapagos, walked with Bushmen in the Serengeti, sampled lamb criadillas (don't ask!!!) in Iguazu Falls, snorkeled on the Great Barrier Reef, ridden an elephant in Thailand, watched the sun rise over Machu Picchu, and bounced from Johannesburg to Cape Town on a bus named Marula.

Please feel free to keep in touch with me using the following links:

Website: http://booksbymaureen.com
Twitter: https://twitter.com/AuthorMaureen
Facebook: https://www.facebook.com/MaureenFisherAuthor
Goodreads: https://www.goodreads.com/author/show/845094.Maureen_Fisher

Made in the USA
Columbia, SC
30 October 2022